# SUPERGIRL ADVENTURES
# GIRL OF STEEL

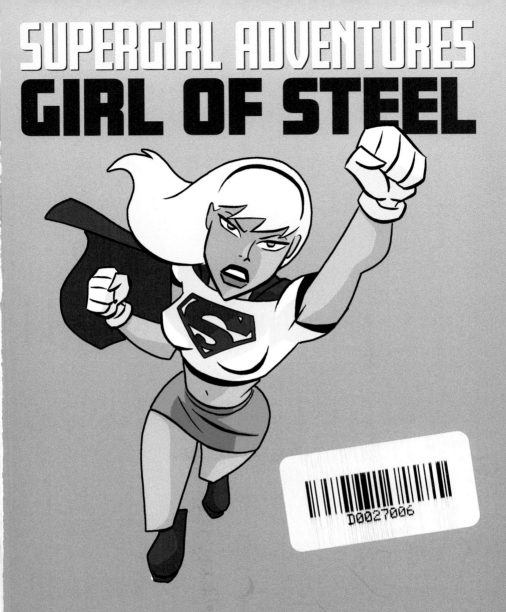

BRUCE TIMM
collection cover artist

SUPERMAN created by JERRY SIEGEL and JOE SHUSTER
SUPERGIRL based on the characters created by JERRY SIEGEL and JOE SHUSTER
By special arrangement with the JERRY SIEGEL family

MIKE McAVENNIE
TOM PALMER JR.
Editors - Original Series

FRANK BERRIOS
JEANINE SCHAEFER
Assistant Editors - Original Series

ALEX GALER
Editor - Collected Edition

STEVE COOK
Design Director - Books

AMIE BROCKWAY-METCALF
Publication Design

CHRISTY SAWYER
Publication Production

MARIE JAVINS
Editor-in-Chief, DC Comics

DANIEL CHERRY III
Senior VP - General Manager

JIM LEE
Publisher & Chief Creative Officer

JOEN CHOE
VP - Global Brand & Creative Services

DON FALLETTI
VP - Manufacturing Operations & Workflow Management

LAWRENCE GANEM
VP - Talent Services

ALISON GILL
Senior VP - Manufacturing & Operations

NICK J. NAPOLITANO
VP - Manufacturing Administration & Design

NANCY SPEARS
VP - Revenue

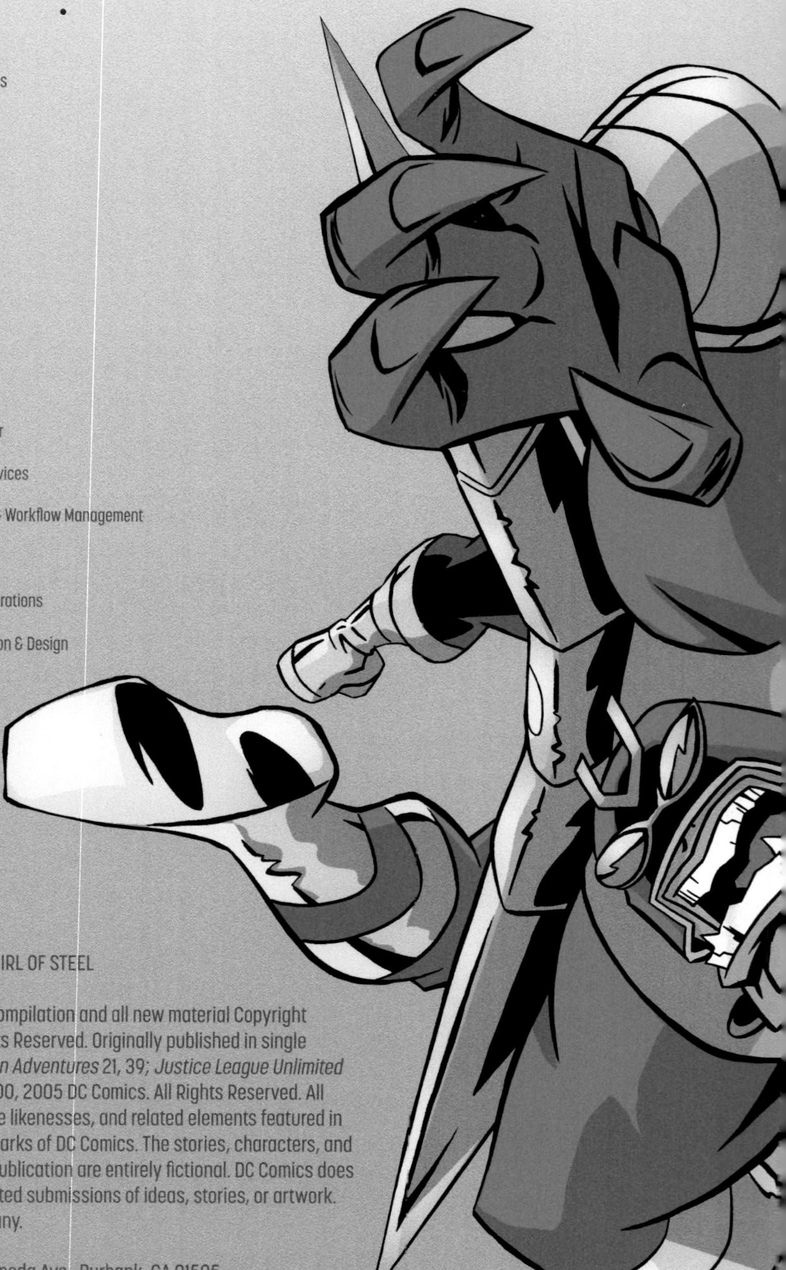

SUPERGIRL ADVENTURES: GIRL OF STEEL



DC Comics, 2900 West Alameda Ave., Burbank, CA 91505
Printed by LSC Communications, Crawfordsville, IN, USA. 6/25/21.
First Printing.
ISBN: 978-1-77951-025-9

Library of Congress Cataloging-in-Publication Data is available.

# SUPERGIRL

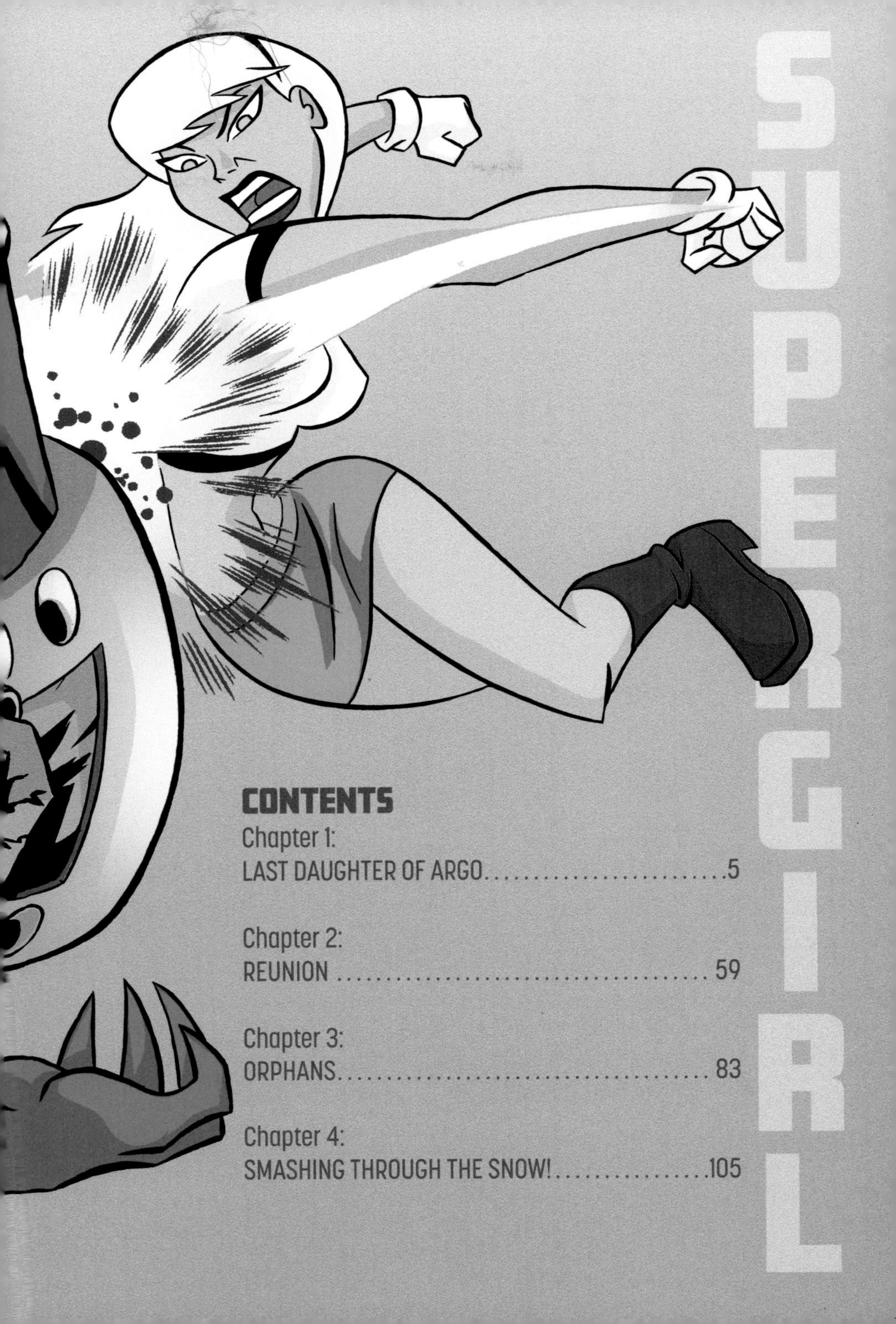

## CONTENTS

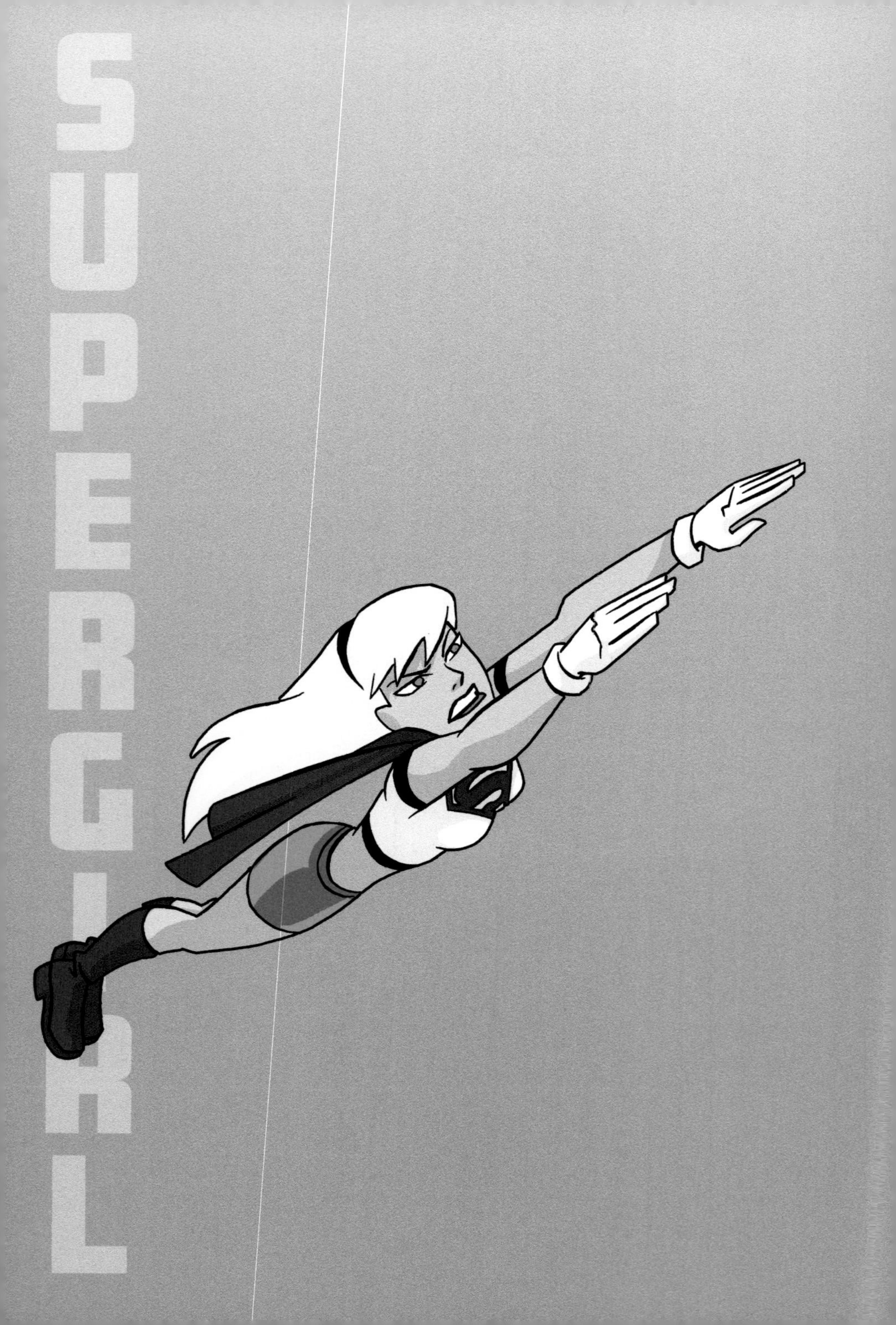
SUPERGIRL

# SUPERGIRL ADVENTURES
## GIRL OF STEEL

# SUPERGIRL

EVAN DORKIN and SARAH DYER
Writers

BRET BLEVINS
Penciller

TERRY AUSTIN
Inker

LEE LOUGHRIDGE
Colors

KEVIN CUNNINGHAM
Letterer

Cover by BRUCE TIMM

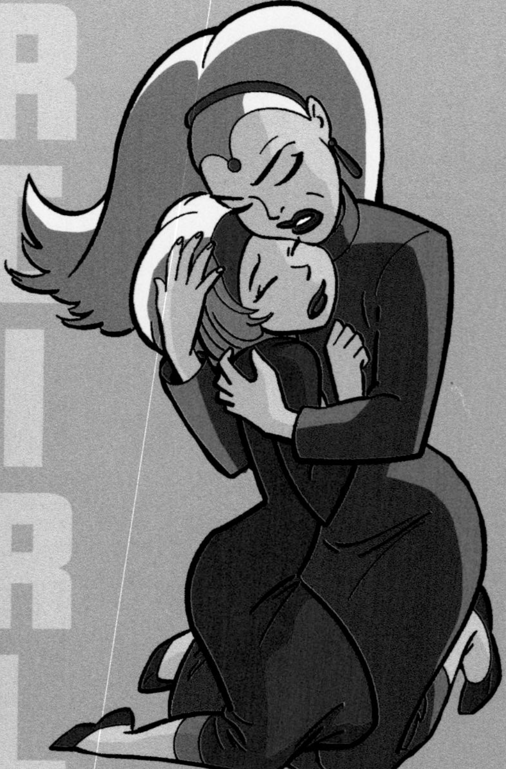

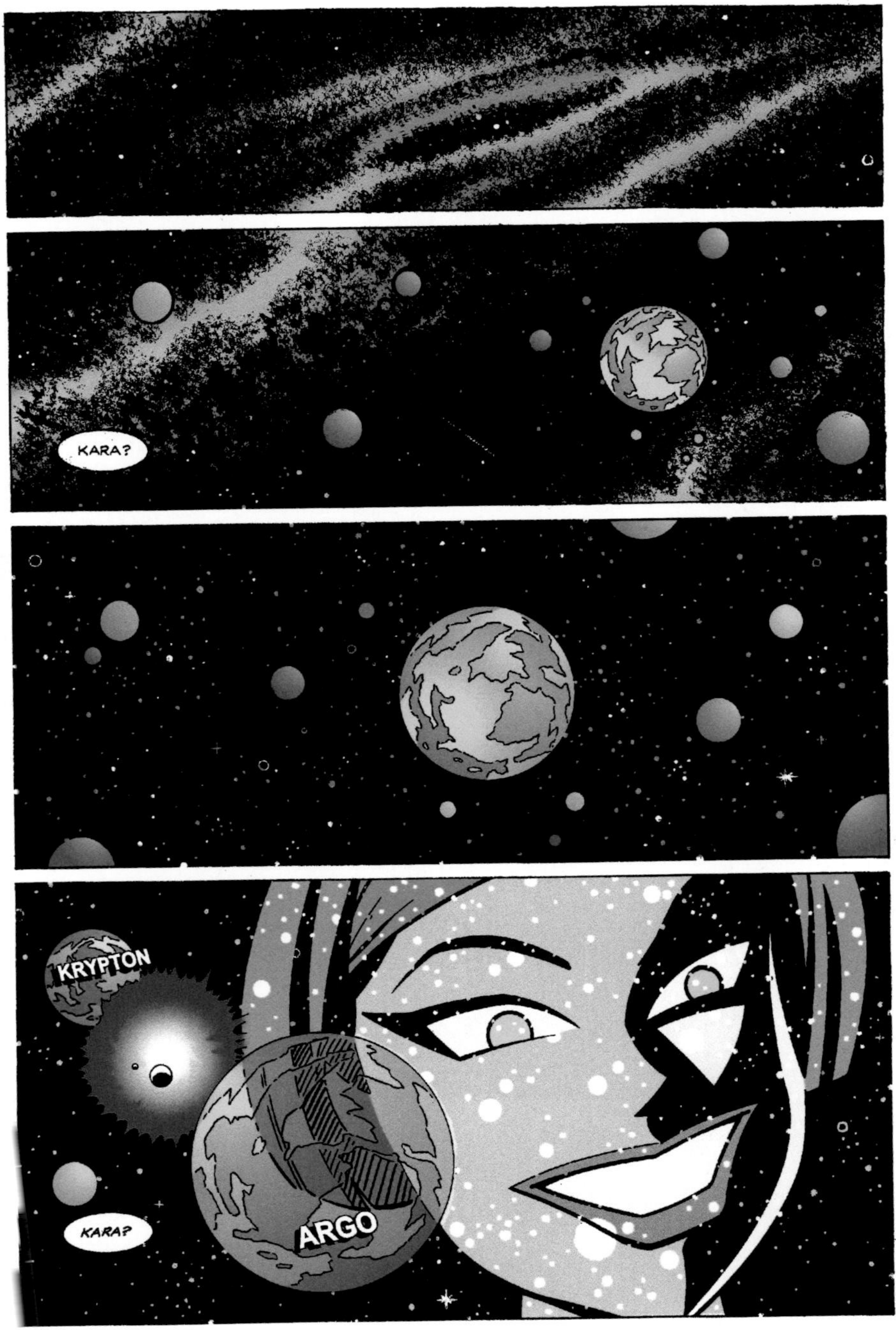
KARA?
KRYPTON
ARGO
KARA?

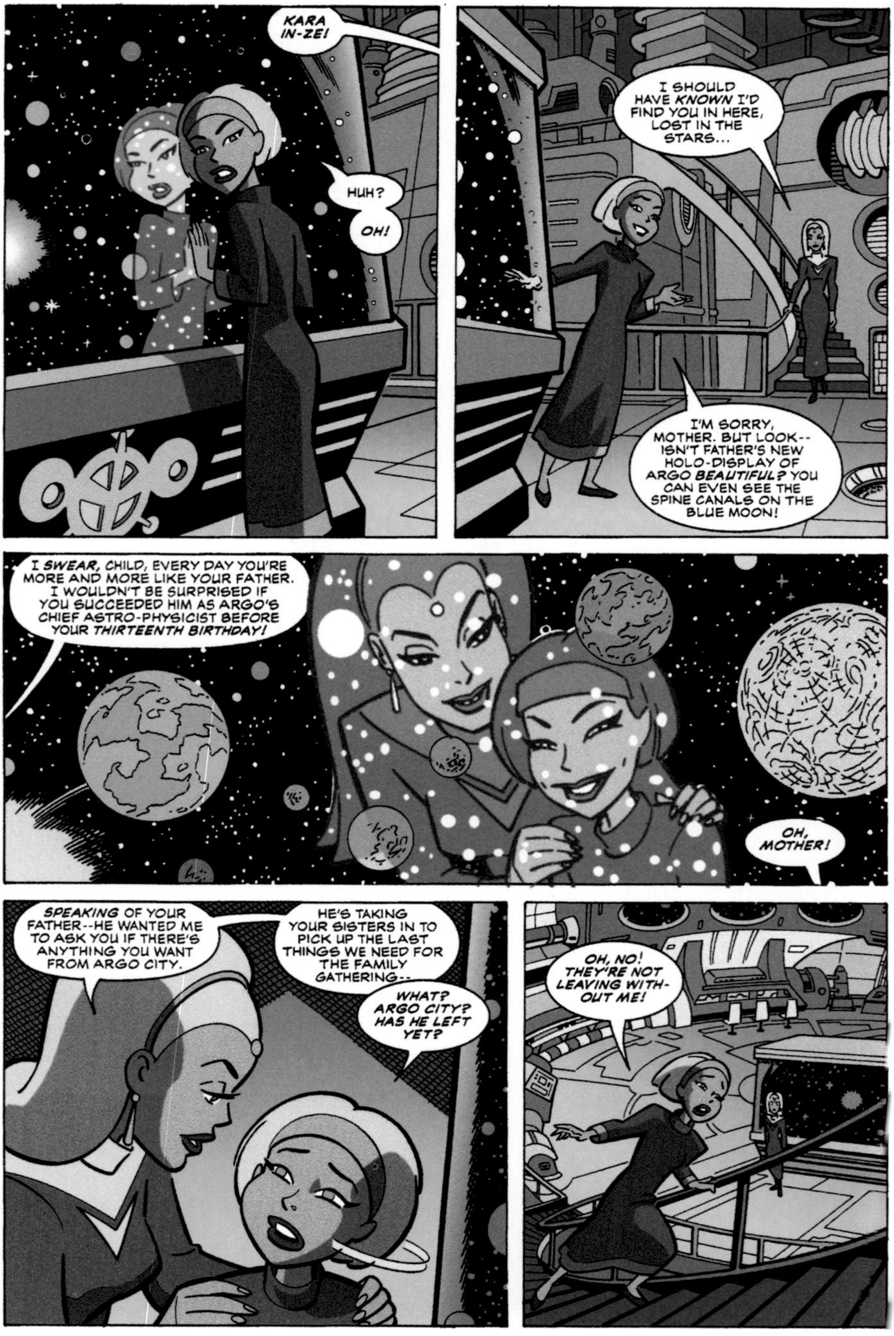
KARA IN-ZE!
HUH?
OH!
I SHOULD HAVE KNOWN I'D FIND YOU IN HERE, LOST IN THE STARS...
I'M SORRY, MOTHER. BUT LOOK-- ISN'T FATHER'S NEW HOLO-DISPLAY OF ARGO BEAUTIFUL? YOU CAN EVEN SEE THE SPINE CANALS ON THE BLUE MOON!
I SWEAR, CHILD, EVERY DAY YOU'RE MORE AND MORE LIKE YOUR FATHER. I WOULDN'T BE SURPRISED IF YOU SUCCEEDED HIM AS ARGO'S CHIEF ASTRO-PHYSICIST BEFORE YOUR THIRTEENTH BIRTHDAY!
OH, MOTHER!
SPEAKING OF YOUR FATHER--HE WANTED ME TO ASK YOU IF THERE'S ANYTHING YOU WANT FROM ARGO CITY.
HE'S TAKING YOUR SISTERS IN TO PICK UP THE LAST THINGS WE NEED FOR THE FAMILY GATHERING--
WHAT? ARGO CITY? HAS HE LEFT YET?
OH, NO! THEY'RE NOT LEAVING WITH-OUT ME!

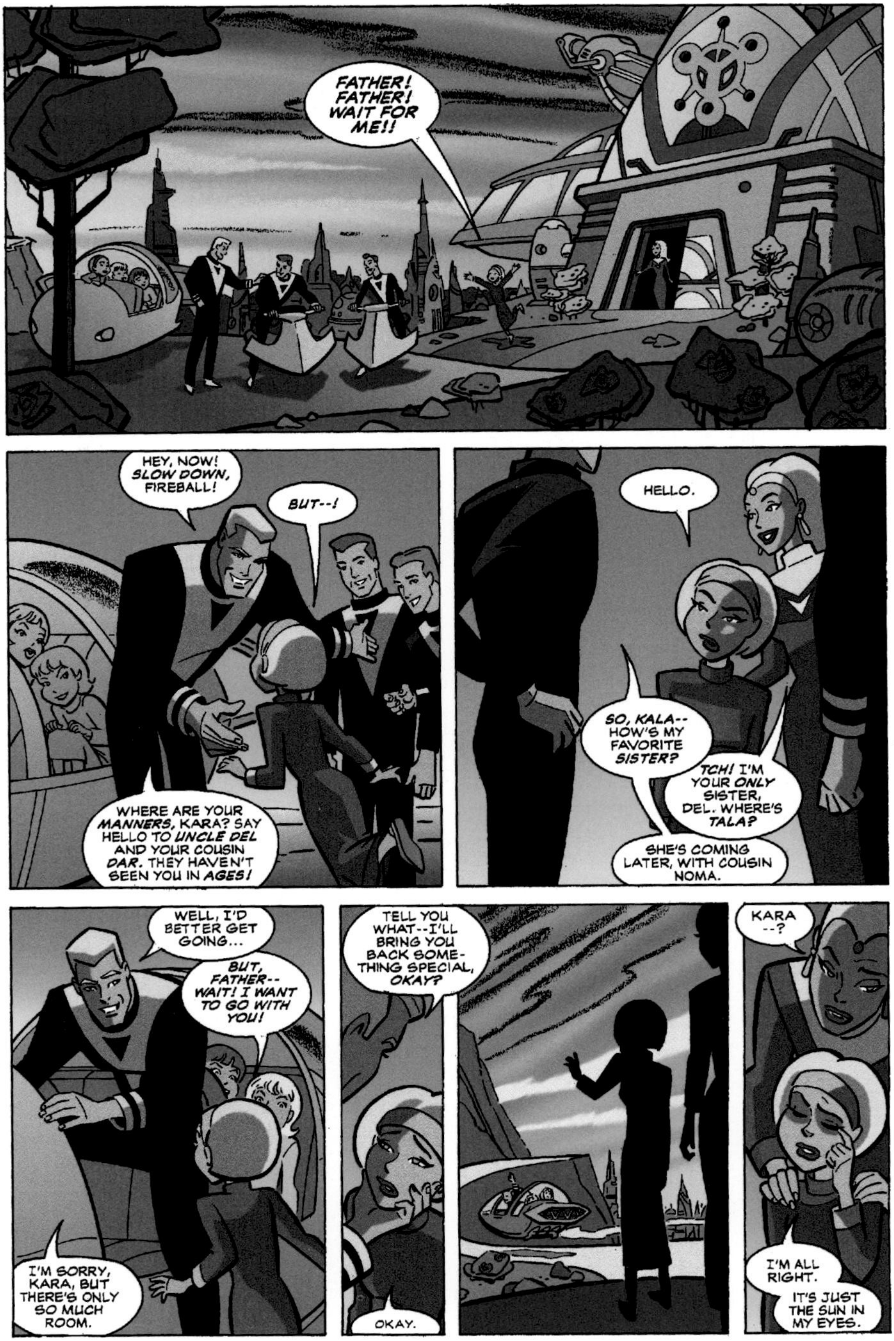

FATHER! FATHER! WAIT FOR ME!!
HEY, NOW! SLOW DOWN, FIREBALL!
BUT--!
WHERE ARE YOUR MANNERS, KARA? SAY HELLO TO UNCLE DEL AND YOUR COUSIN DAR. THEY HAVEN'T SEEN YOU IN AGES!
HELLO.
SO, KALA-- HOW'S MY FAVORITE SISTER?
TCH! I'M YOUR ONLY SISTER, DEL. WHERE'S TALA?
SHE'S COMING LATER, WITH COUSIN NOMA.
WELL, I'D BETTER GET GOING...
BUT, FATHER-- WAIT! I WANT TO GO WITH YOU!
I'M SORRY, KARA, BUT THERE'S ONLY SO MUCH ROOM.
TELL YOU WHAT--I'LL BRING YOU BACK SOME-THING SPECIAL, OKAY?
OKAY.
KARA --?
I'M ALL RIGHT.
IT'S JUST THE SUN IN MY EYES.

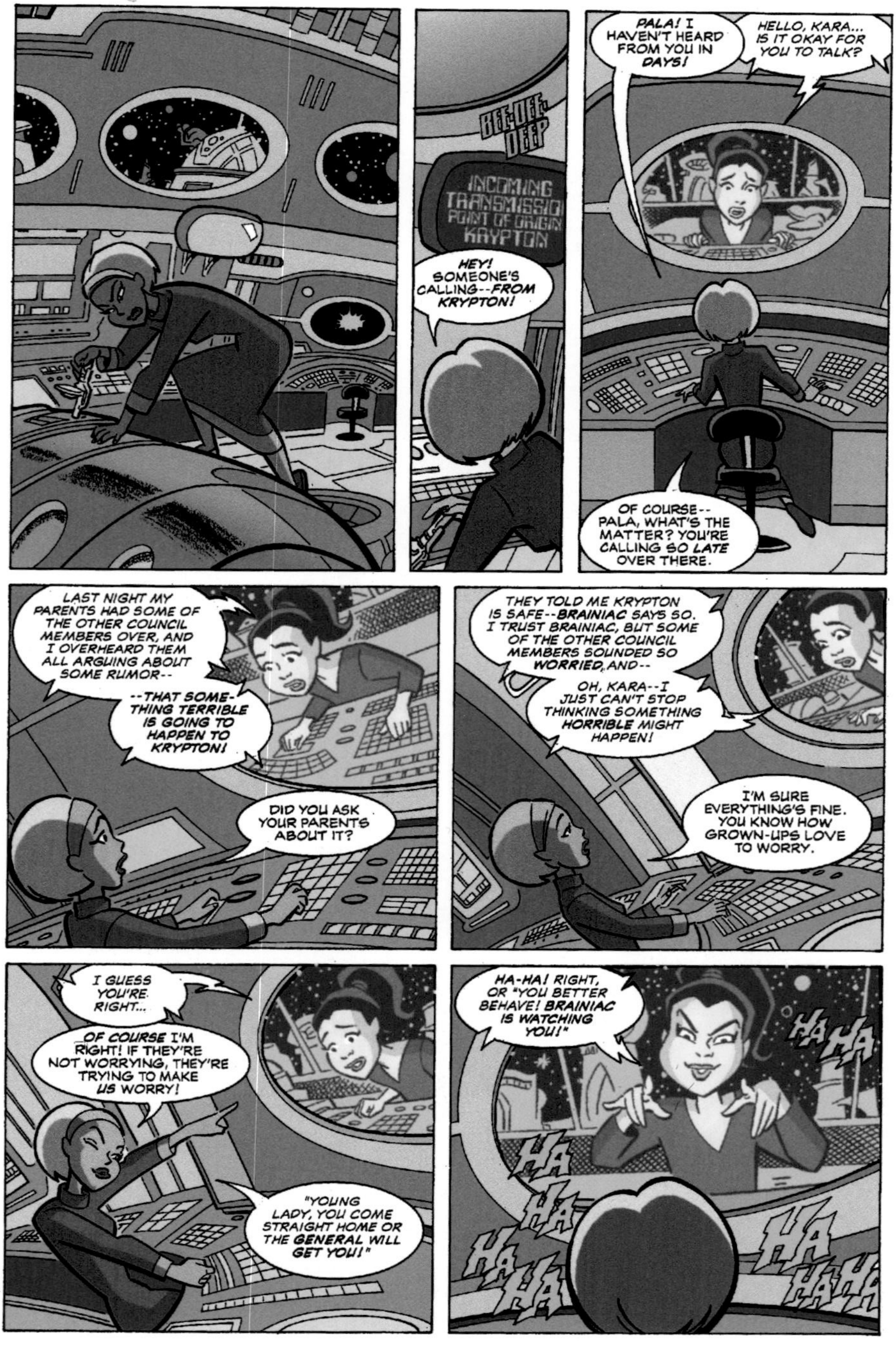
BEE-DEE-DEEP
INCOMING TRANSMISSIO POINT OF ORIGIN KRYPTON
HEY! SOMEONE'S CALLING--FROM KRYPTON!
PALA! I HAVEN'T HEARD FROM YOU IN DAYS!
HELLO, KARA... IS IT OKAY FOR YOU TO TALK?
OF COURSE-- PALA, WHAT'S THE MATTER? YOU'RE CALLING SO LATE OVER THERE.
LAST NIGHT MY PARENTS HAD SOME OF THE OTHER COUNCIL MEMBERS OVER, AND I OVERHEARD THEM ALL ARGUING ABOUT SOME RUMOR--
--THAT SOMETHING TERRIBLE IS GOING TO HAPPEN TO KRYPTON!
DID YOU ASK YOUR PARENTS ABOUT IT?
THEY TOLD ME KRYPTON IS SAFE--BRAINIAC SAYS SO. I TRUST BRAINIAC, BUT SOME OF THE OTHER COUNCIL MEMBERS SOUNDED SO WORRIED, AND--
OH, KARA--I JUST CAN'T STOP THINKING SOMETHING HORRIBLE MIGHT HAPPEN!
I'M SURE EVERYTHING'S FINE. YOU KNOW HOW GROWN-UPS LOVE TO WORRY.
I GUESS YOU'RE RIGHT...
OF COURSE I'M RIGHT! IF THEY'RE NOT WORRYING, THEY'RE TRYING TO MAKE US WORRY!
"YOUNG LADY, YOU COME STRAIGHT HOME OR THE GENERAL WILL GET YOU!"
HA-HA! RIGHT, OR "YOU BETTER BEHAVE! BRAINIAC IS WATCHING YOU!"
HA HA
HA HA HA HA
HA HA HA

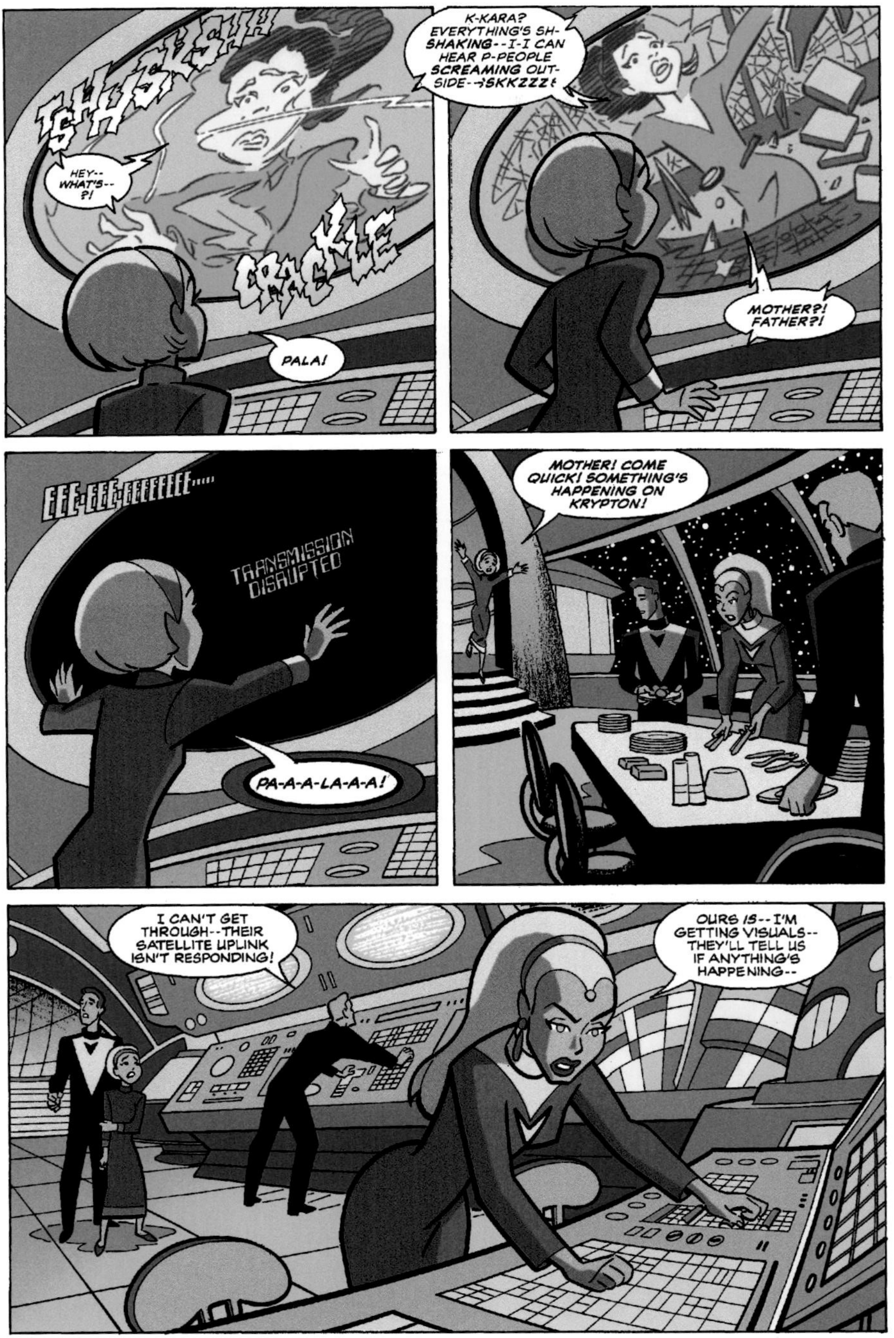
SHHSKSHH
HEY--WHAT'S--?!
CRACKLE
PALA!
K-KARA? EVERYTHING'S SH-SHAKING--I-I CAN HEAR P-PEOPLE SCREAMING OUT-SIDE--SKKZZZ
MOTHER?! FATHER?!
EEE-EEE-EEEEEEE....
TRANSMISSION DISRUPTED
PA-A-A-LA-A-A!
MOTHER! COME QUICK! SOMETHING'S HAPPENING ON KRYPTON!
I CAN'T GET THROUGH--THEIR SATELLITE UPLINK ISN'T RESPONDING!
OURS IS--I'M GETTING VISUALS--THEY'LL TELL US IF ANYTHING'S HAPPENING--

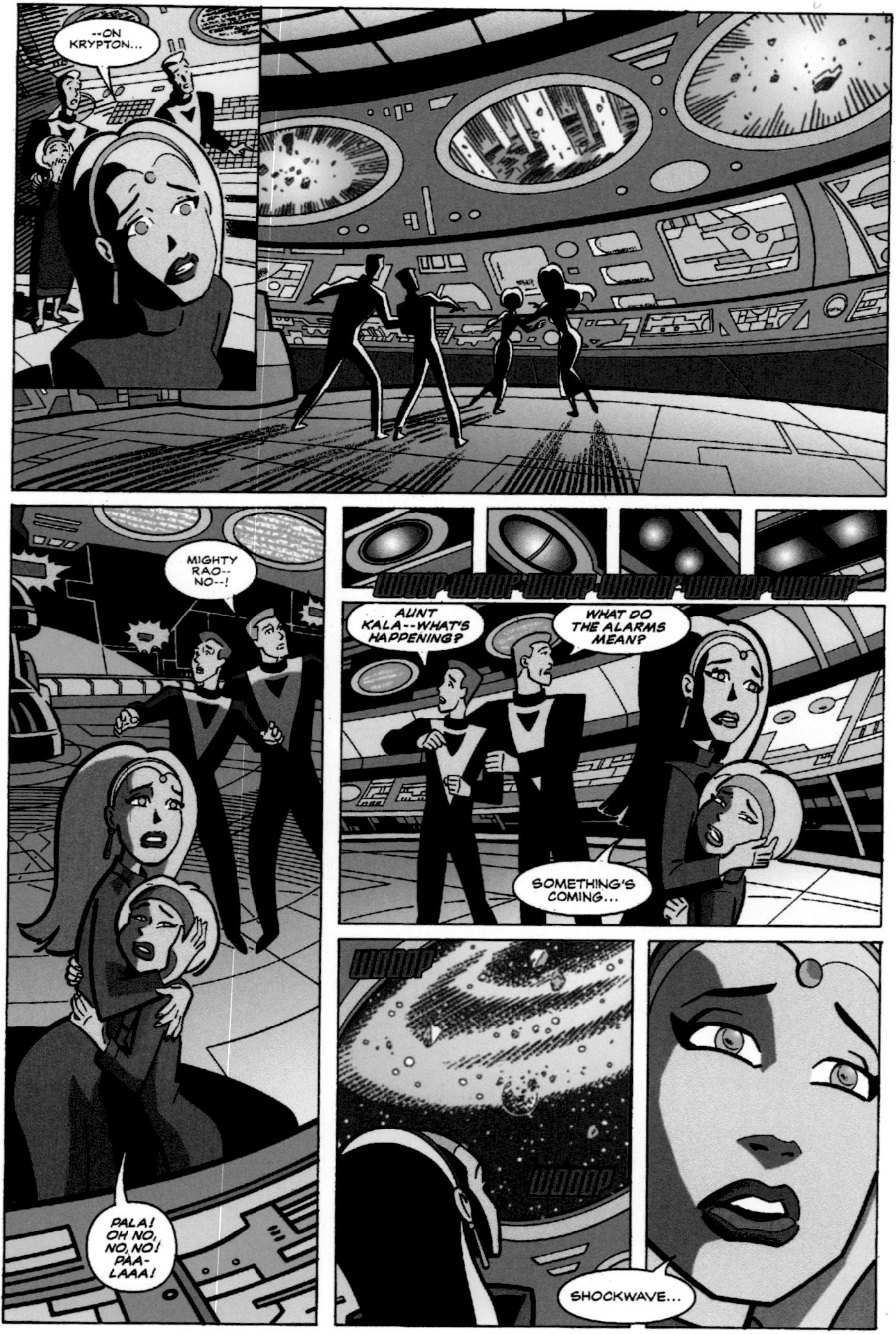
--ON KRYPTON...
MIGHTY RAO-- NO--!
PALA! OH NO, NO, NO! PAA-LAAA!
WOOOP WOOOP WOOOP WOOOP WOOOP WOOOP
AUNT KALA--WHAT'S HAPPENING?
WHAT DO THE ALARMS MEAN?
SOMETHING'S COMING...
WOOOP
WOOOP
SHOCKWAVE...

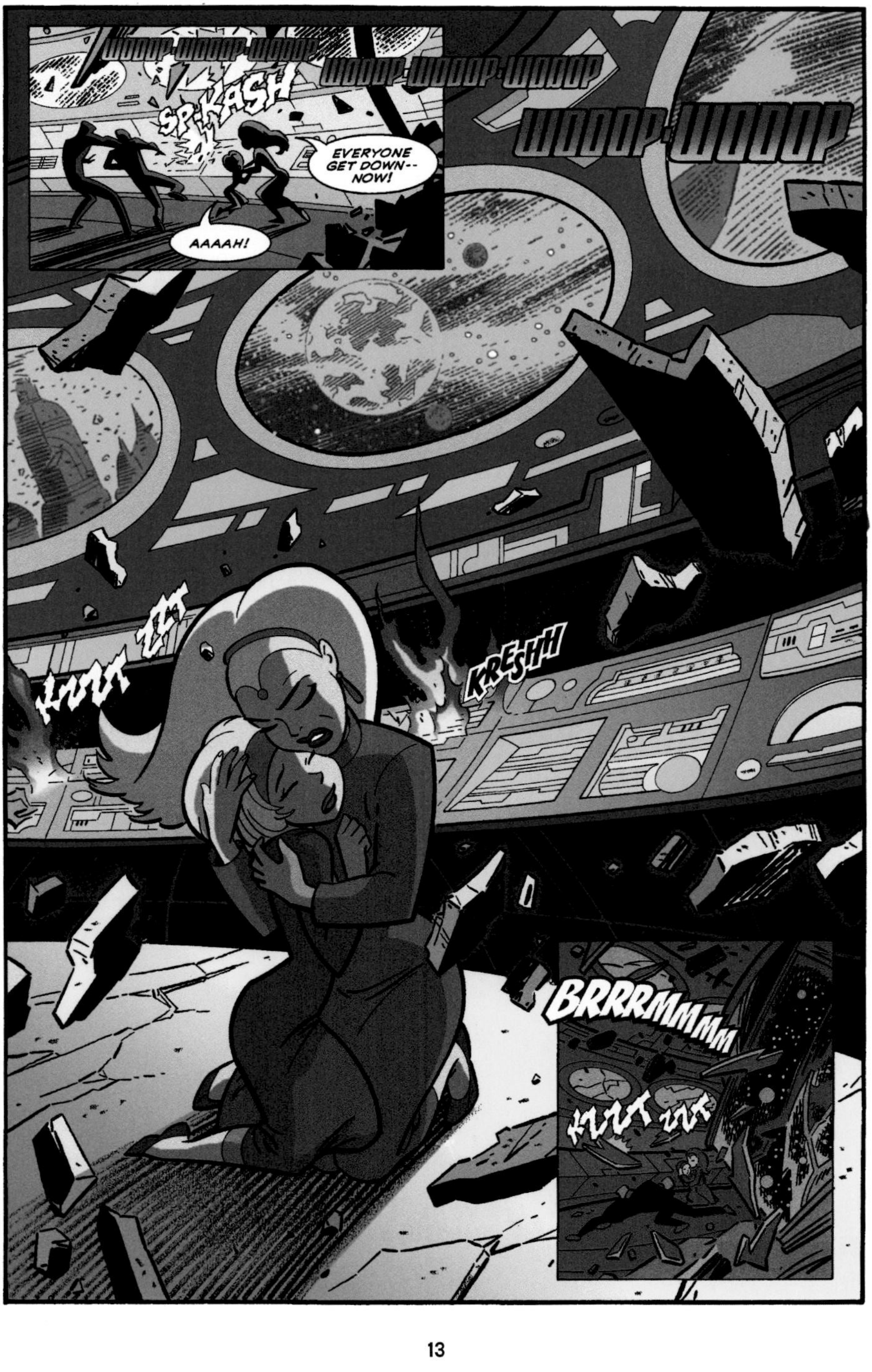
WOOOP WOOOP WOOOP
WOOOP WOOOP WOOOP
SP-KASH
EVERYONE GET DOWN-- NOW!
AAAAH!
WOOOP WOOOP
KRESHH
BRRRMMMM

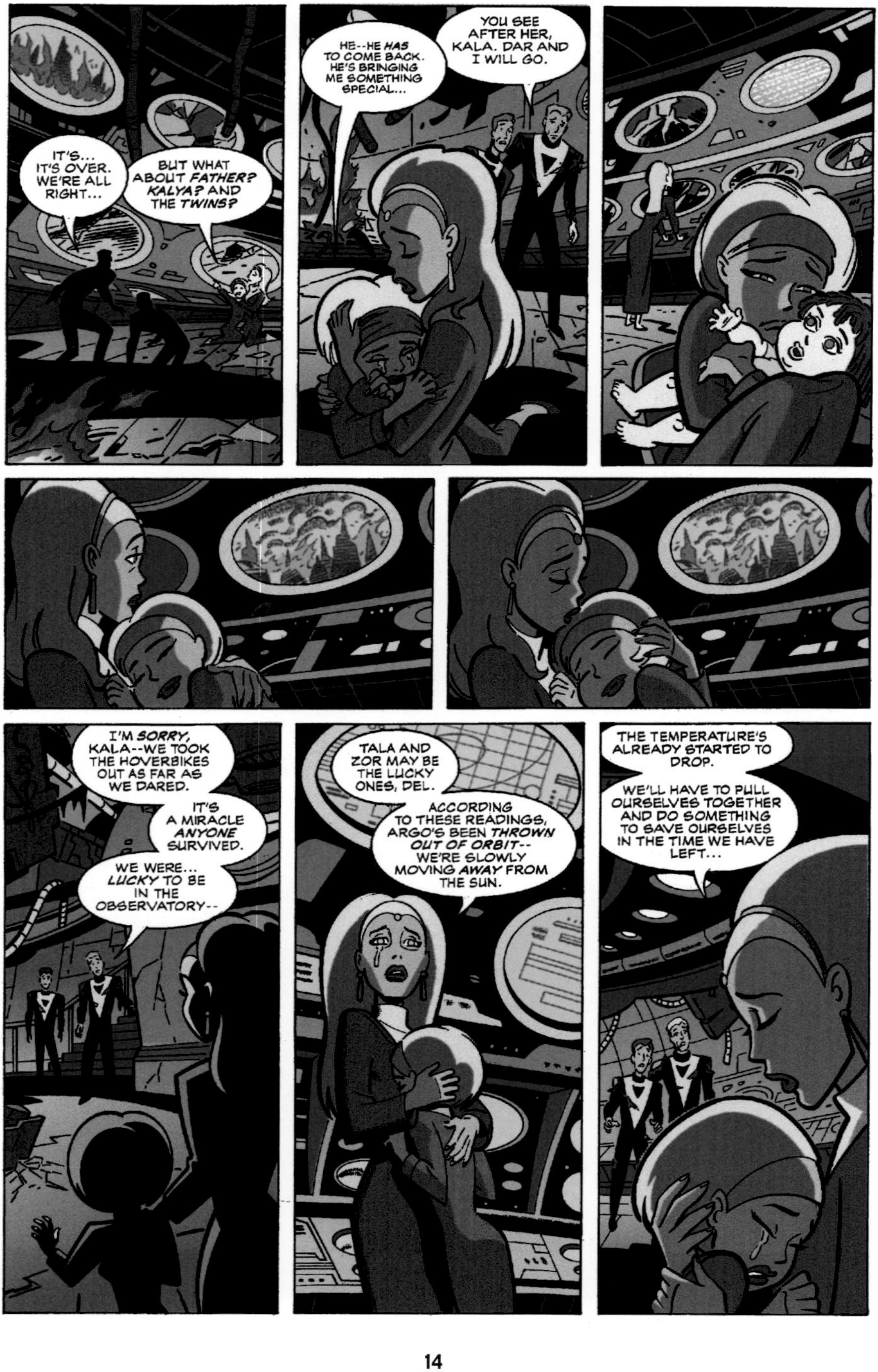
IT'S... IT'S OVER. WE'RE ALL RIGHT...
BUT WHAT ABOUT FATHER? KALYA? AND THE TWINS?
HE--HE HAS TO COME BACK. HE'S BRINGING ME SOMETHING SPECIAL...
YOU SEE AFTER HER, KALA. DAR AND I WILL GO.
I'M SORRY, KALA--WE TOOK THE HOVERBIKES OUT AS FAR AS WE DARED.
IT'S A MIRACLE ANYONE SURVIVED.
WE WERE... LUCKY TO BE IN THE OBSERVATORY--
TALA AND ZOR MAY BE THE LUCKY ONES, DEL.
ACCORDING TO THESE READINGS, ARGO'S BEEN THROWN OUT OF ORBIT-- WE'RE SLOWLY MOVING AWAY FROM THE SUN.
THE TEMPERATURE'S ALREADY STARTED TO DROP.
WE'LL HAVE TO PULL OURSELVES TOGETHER AND DO SOMETHING TO SAVE OURSELVES IN THE TIME WE HAVE LEFT...

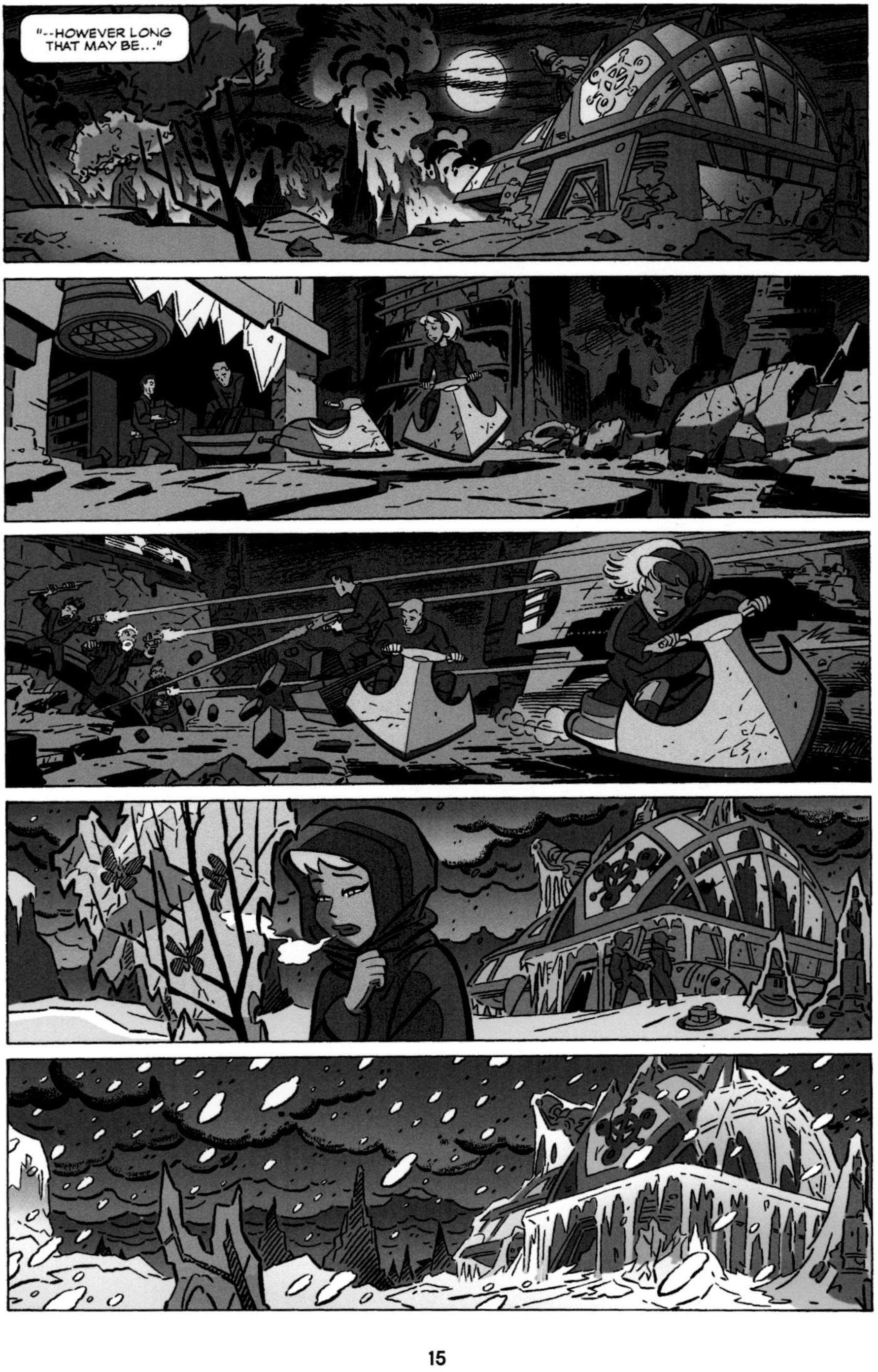
"--HOWEVER LONG THAT MAY BE..."

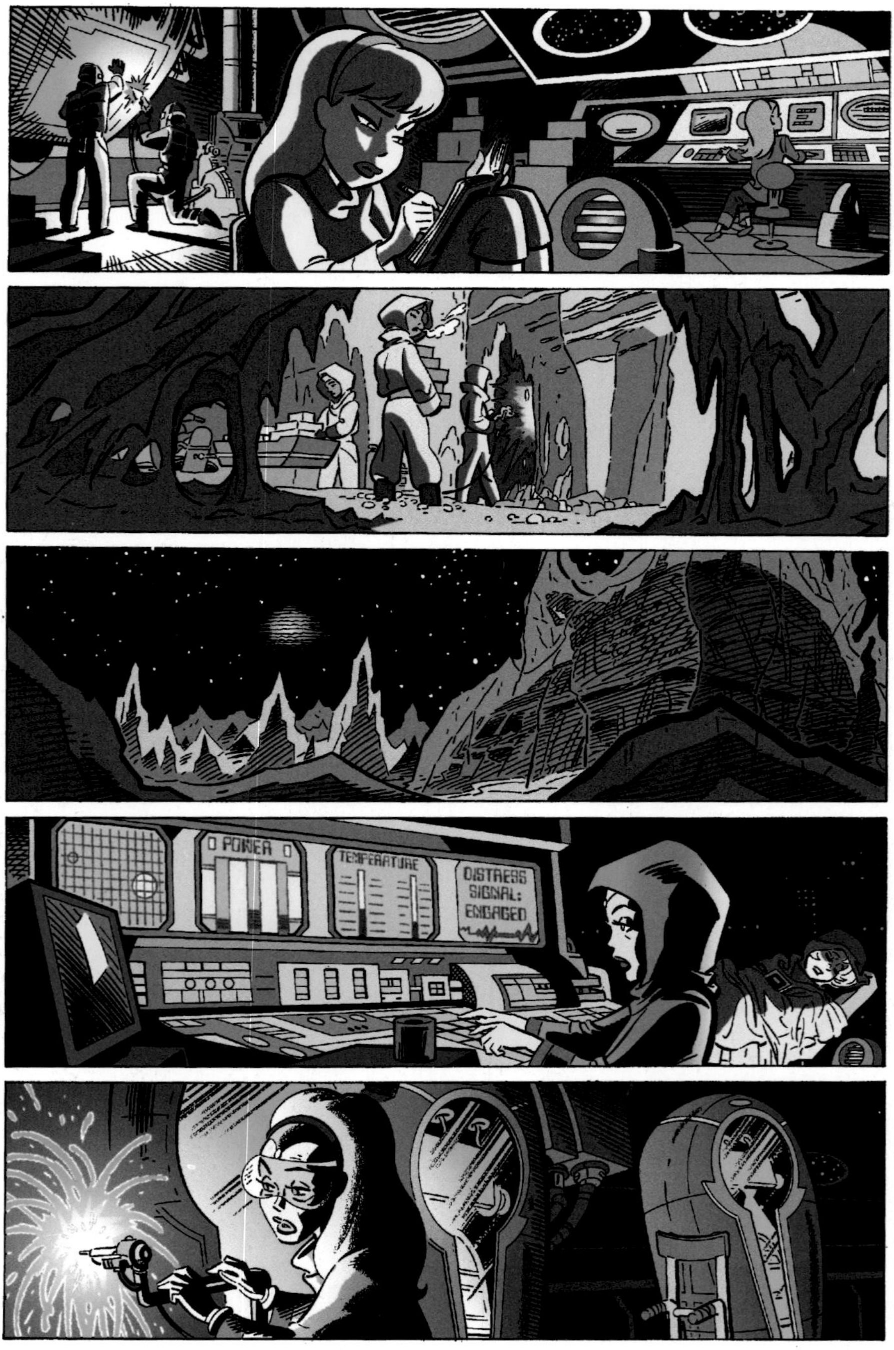
POWER
TEMPERATURE
DISTRESS SIGNAL: ENGAGED

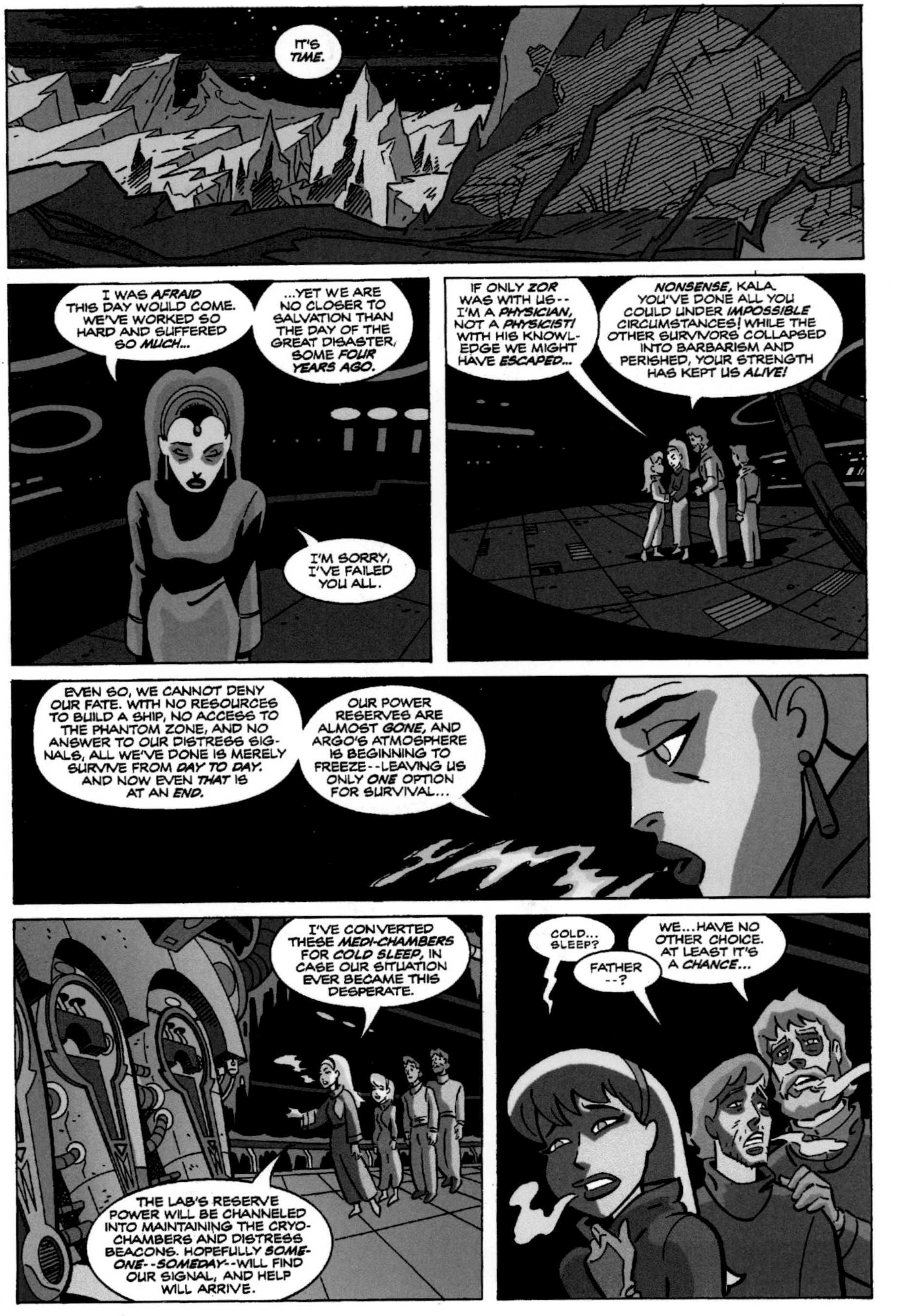
IT'S TIME.
I WAS AFRAID THIS DAY WOULD COME. WE'VE WORKED SO HARD AND SUFFERED SO MUCH...
...YET WE ARE NO CLOSER TO SALVATION THAN THE DAY OF THE GREAT DISASTER, SOME FOUR YEARS AGO.
I'M SORRY, I'VE FAILED YOU ALL.
IF ONLY ZOR WAS WITH US-- I'M A PHYSICIAN, NOT A PHYSICIST! WITH HIS KNOWL-EDGE WE MIGHT HAVE ESCAPED...
NONSENSE, KALA. YOU'VE DONE ALL YOU COULD UNDER IMPOSSIBLE CIRCUMSTANCES! WHILE THE OTHER SURVIVORS COLLAPSED INTO BARBARISM AND PERISHED, YOUR STRENGTH HAS KEPT US ALIVE!
EVEN SO, WE CANNOT DENY OUR FATE. WITH NO RESOURCES TO BUILD A SHIP, NO ACCESS TO THE PHANTOM ZONE, AND NO ANSWER TO OUR DISTRESS SIG-NALS, ALL WE'VE DONE IS MERELY SURVIVE FROM DAY TO DAY. AND NOW EVEN THAT IS AT AN END.
OUR POWER RESERVES ARE ALMOST GONE, AND ARGO'S ATMOSPHERE IS BEGINNING TO FREEZE--LEAVING US ONLY ONE OPTION FOR SURVIVAL...
I'VE CONVERTED THESE MEDI-CHAMBERS FOR COLD SLEEP, IN CASE OUR SITUATION EVER BECAME THIS DESPERATE.
THE LAB'S RESERVE POWER WILL BE CHANNELED INTO MAINTAINING THE CRYO-CHAMBERS AND DISTRESS BEACONS. HOPEFULLY SOME-ONE--SOMEDAY--WILL FIND OUR SIGNAL, AND HELP WILL ARRIVE.
COLD... SLEEP?
FATHER --?
WE...HAVE NO OTHER CHOICE. AT LEAST IT'S A CHANCE...

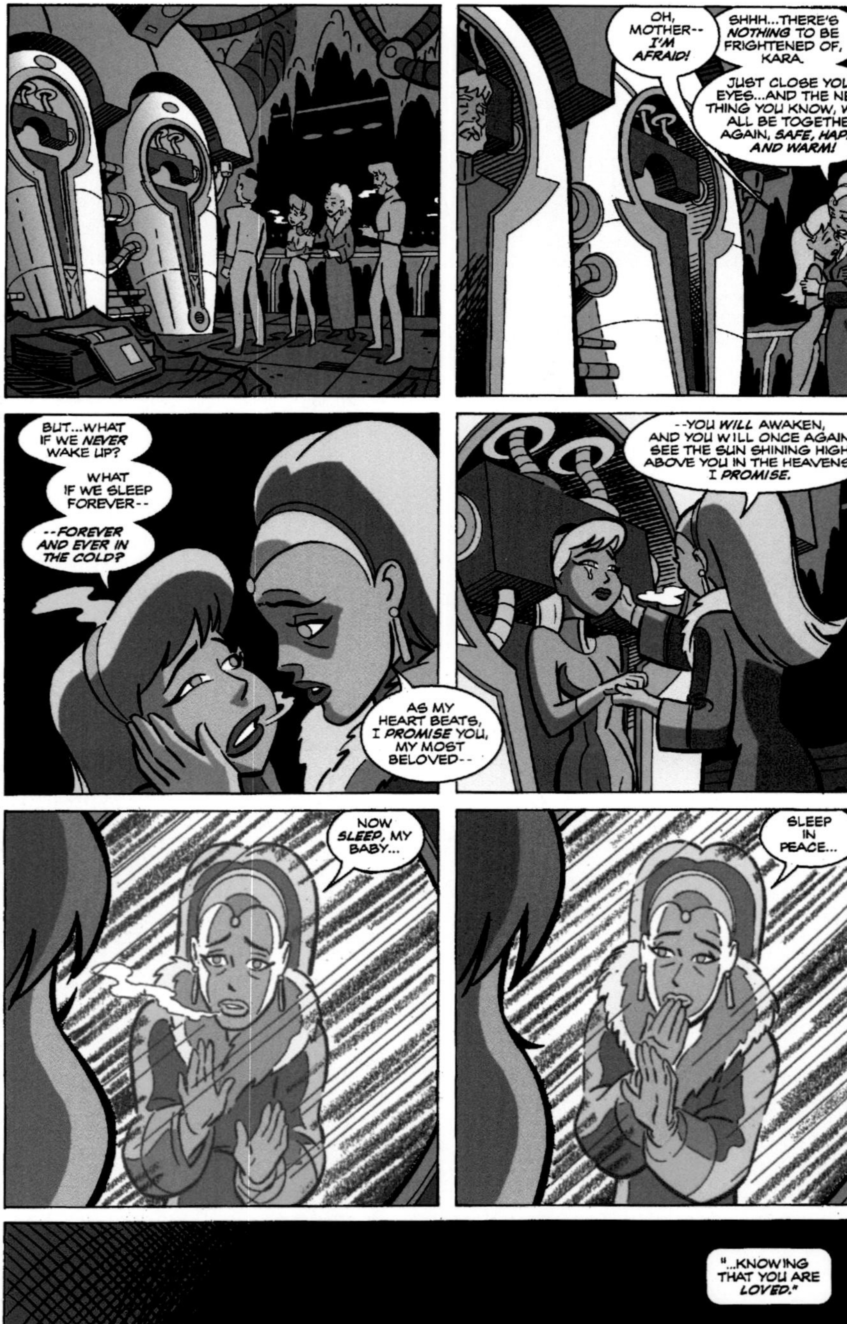

OH, MOTHER-- I'M AFRAID!
SHHH...THERE'S NOTHING TO BE FRIGHTENED OF, KARA.
JUST CLOSE YOUR EYES...AND THE NEXT THING YOU KNOW, WE'LL ALL BE TOGETHER AGAIN, SAFE, HAPPY AND WARM!
BUT...WHAT IF WE NEVER WAKE UP?
WHAT IF WE SLEEP FOREVER--
--FOREVER AND EVER IN THE COLD?
AS MY HEART BEATS, I PROMISE YOU, MY MOST BELOVED--
--YOU WILL AWAKEN, AND YOU WILL ONCE AGAIN SEE THE SUN SHINING HIGH ABOVE YOU IN THE HEAVENS. I PROMISE.
NOW SLEEP, MY BABY...
SLEEP IN PEACE...
"...KNOWING THAT YOU ARE LOVED."

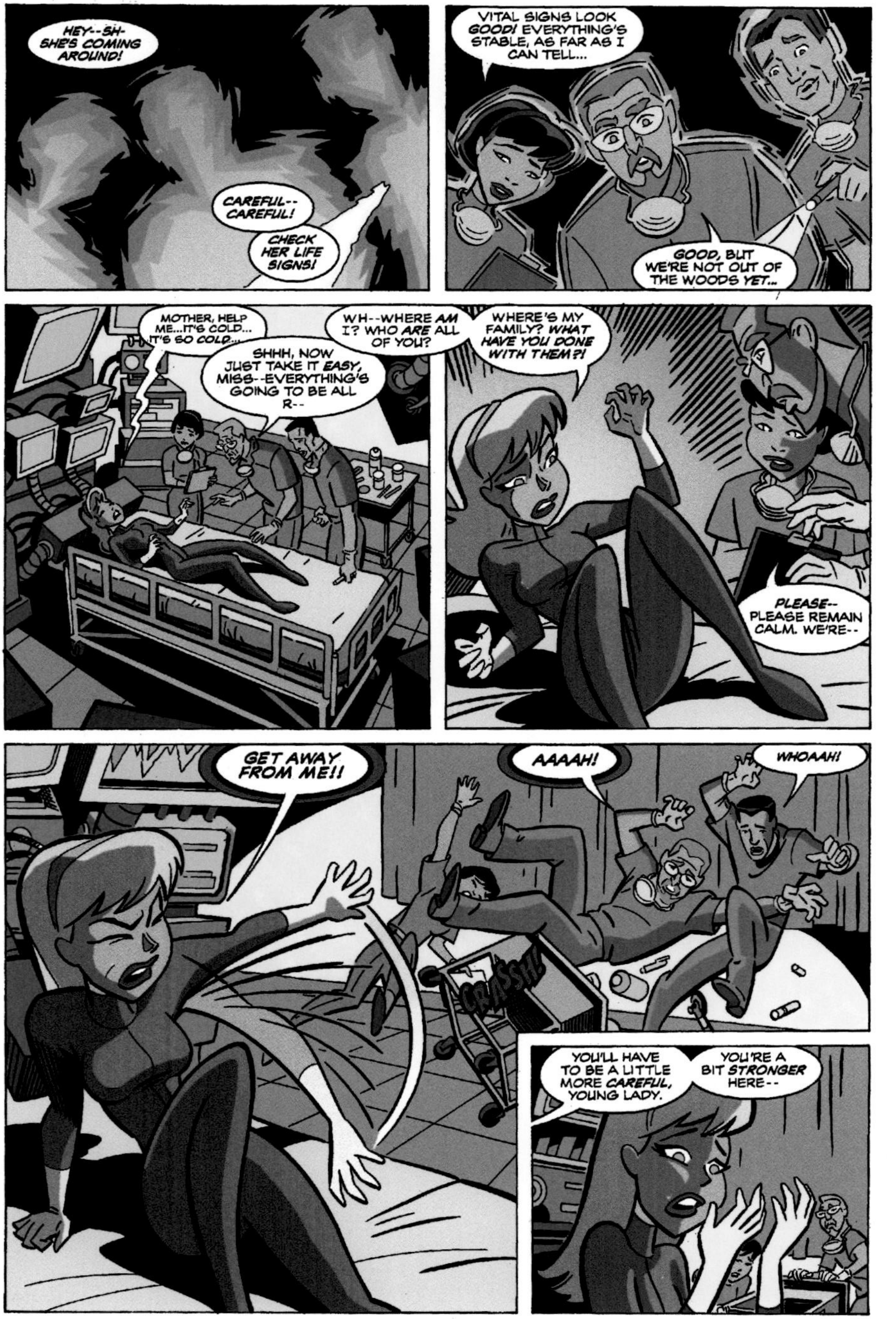
HEY--SH-SHE'S COMING AROUND!
CAREFUL--CAREFUL!
CHECK HER LIFE SIGNS!
VITAL SIGNS LOOK GOOD! EVERYTHING'S STABLE, AS FAR AS I CAN TELL...
GOOD, BUT WE'RE NOT OUT OF THE WOODS YET...
MOTHER, HELP ME...IT'S COLD... IT'S SO COLD...
SHHH, NOW JUST TAKE IT EASY, MISS--EVERYTHING'S GOING TO BE ALL R--
WH--WHERE AM I? WHO ARE ALL OF YOU?
WHERE'S MY FAMILY? WHAT HAVE YOU DONE WITH THEM?!
PLEASE--PLEASE REMAIN CALM. WE'RE--
GET AWAY FROM ME!!
AAAAH!
WHOAAH!
CRASSH!
YOU'LL HAVE TO BE A LITTLE MORE CAREFUL, YOUNG LADY.
YOU'RE A BIT STRONGER HERE--

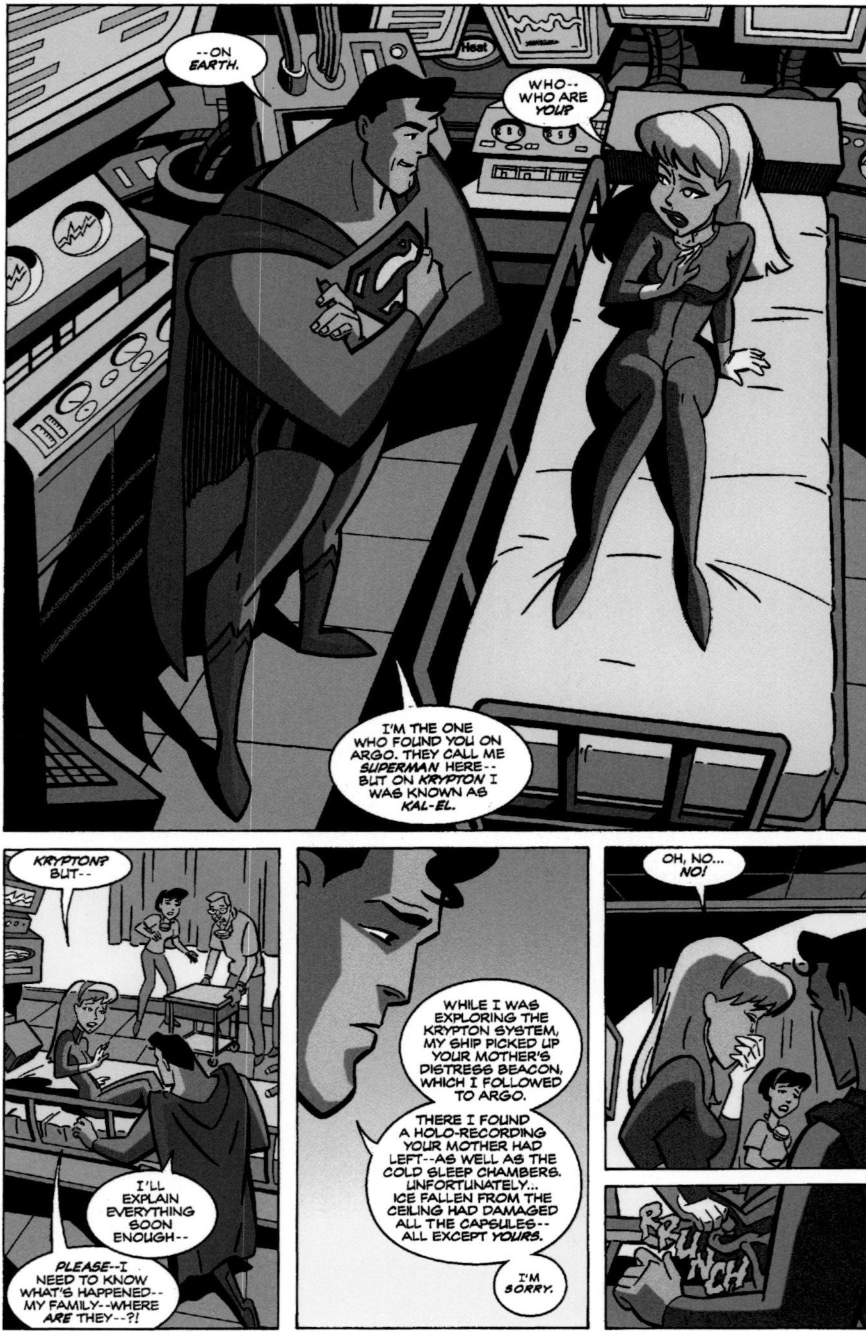
--ON EARTH.
WHO--WHO ARE YOU?
Heat
I'M THE ONE WHO FOUND YOU ON ARGO. THEY CALL ME SUPERMAN HERE--BUT ON KRYPTON I WAS KNOWN AS KAL-EL.
KRYPTON? BUT--
I'LL EXPLAIN EVERYTHING SOON ENOUGH--
PLEASE--I NEED TO KNOW WHAT'S HAPPENED--MY FAMILY--WHERE ARE THEY--?!
WHILE I WAS EXPLORING THE KRYPTON SYSTEM, MY SHIP PICKED UP YOUR MOTHER'S DISTRESS BEACON, WHICH I FOLLOWED TO ARGO.
THERE I FOUND A HOLO-RECORDING YOUR MOTHER HAD LEFT--AS WELL AS THE COLD SLEEP CHAMBERS. UNFORTUNATELY... ICE FALLEN FROM THE CEILING HAD DAMAGED ALL THE CAPSULES--ALL EXCEPT YOURS.
I'M SORRY.
OH, NO... NO!
KRUNCH

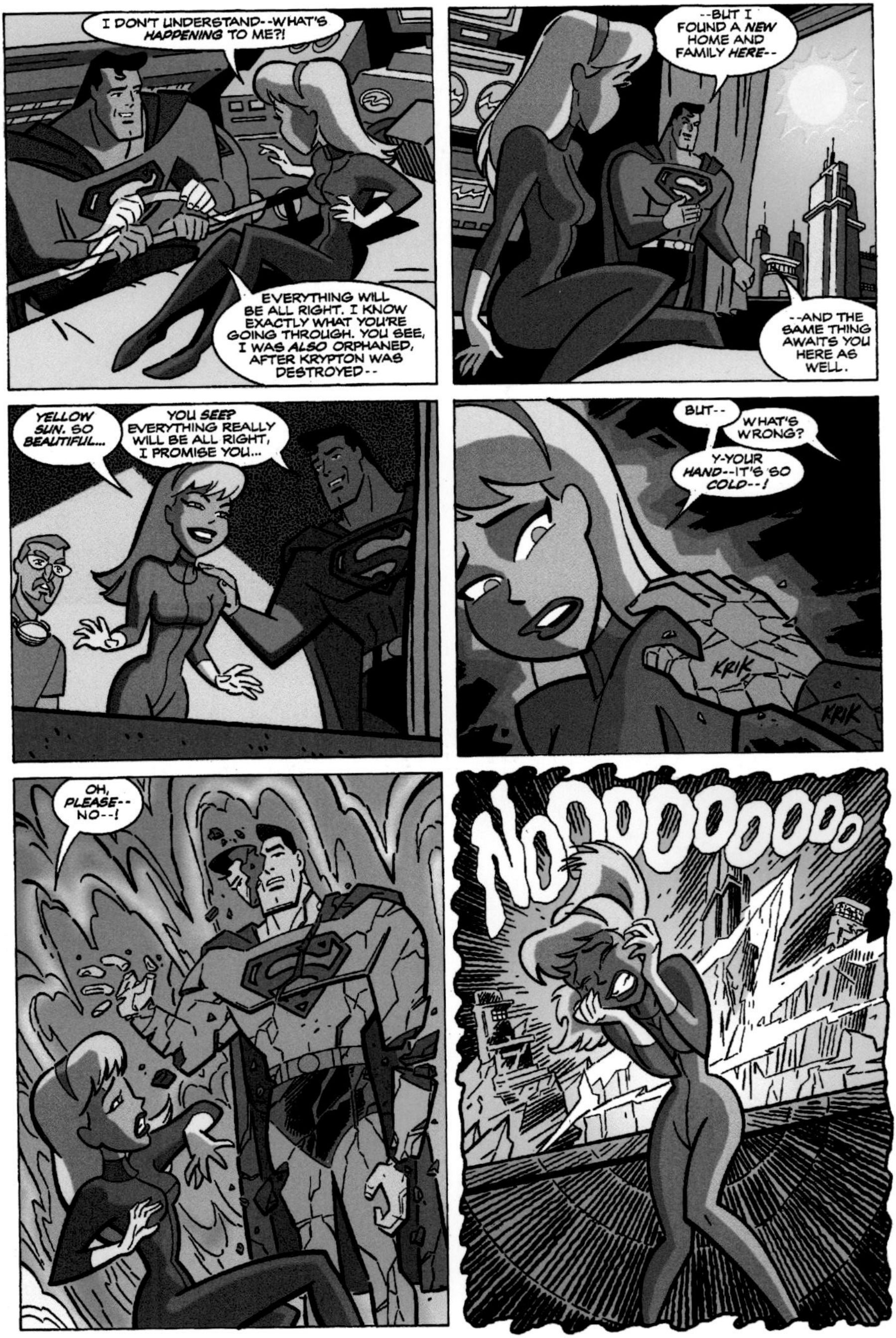
I DON'T UNDERSTAND--WHAT'S HAPPENING TO ME?!
EVERYTHING WILL BE ALL RIGHT. I KNOW EXACTLY WHAT YOU'RE GOING THROUGH. YOU SEE, I WAS ALSO ORPHANED, AFTER KRYPTON WAS DESTROYED--
--BUT I FOUND A NEW HOME AND FAMILY HERE--
--AND THE SAME THING AWAITS YOU HERE AS WELL.
YELLOW SUN. SO BEAUTIFUL...
YOU SEE? EVERYTHING REALLY WILL BE ALL RIGHT, I PROMISE YOU...
BUT--
WHAT'S WRONG?
Y-YOUR HAND--IT'S SO COLD--!
KRIK
KRIK
OH, PLEASE--NO--!
NOOOOOOOOOo

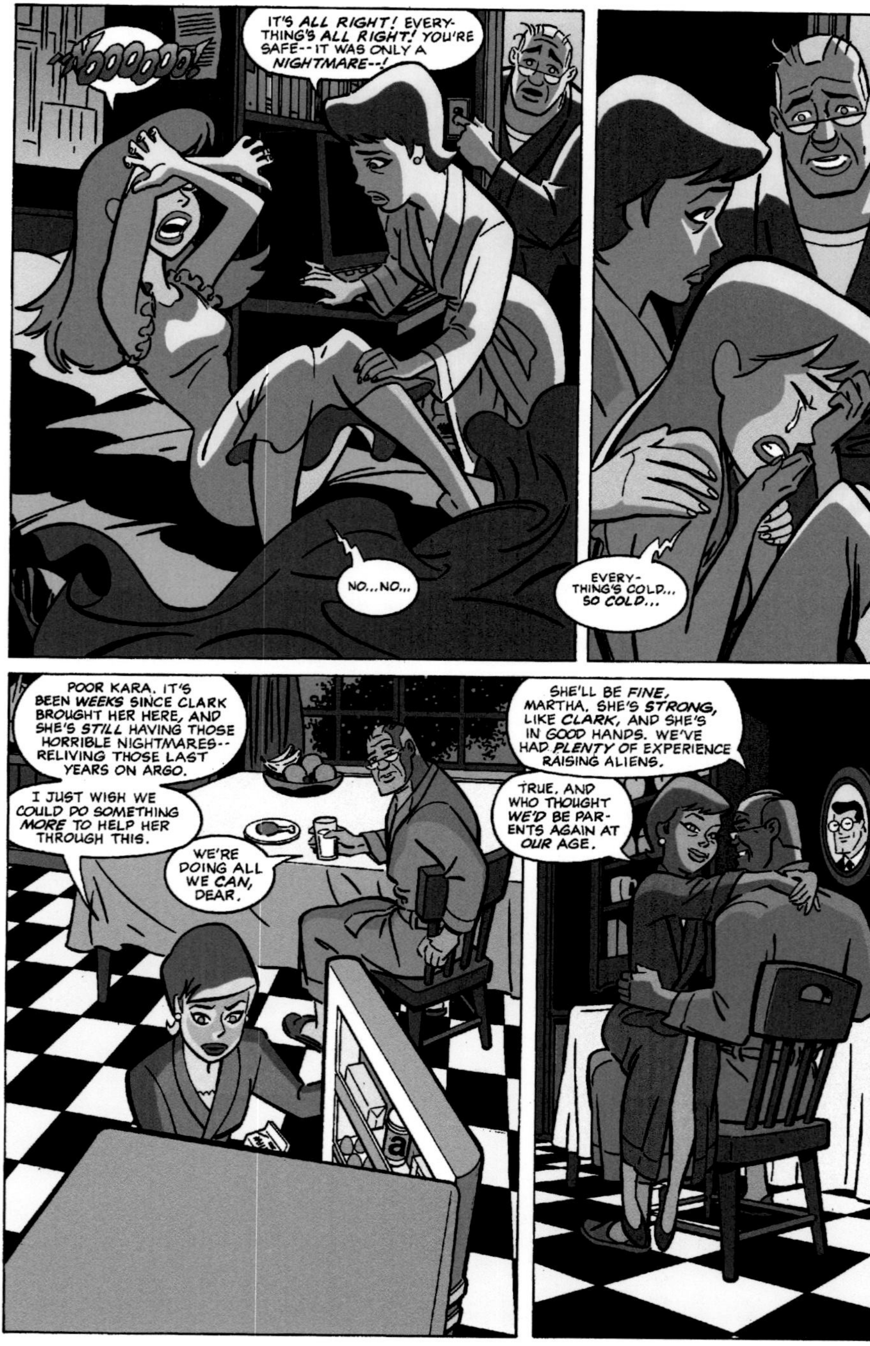
NYOOOOOO!
IT'S ALL RIGHT! EVERYTHING'S ALL RIGHT! YOU'RE SAFE--IT WAS ONLY A NIGHTMARE--!
NO...NO...
EVERYTHING'S COLD... SO COLD...
POOR KARA. IT'S BEEN WEEKS SINCE CLARK BROUGHT HER HERE, AND SHE'S STILL HAVING THOSE HORRIBLE NIGHTMARES--RELIVING THOSE LAST YEARS ON ARGO.
I JUST WISH WE COULD DO SOMETHING MORE TO HELP HER THROUGH THIS.
WE'RE DOING ALL WE CAN, DEAR.
SHE'LL BE FINE, MARTHA. SHE'S STRONG, LIKE CLARK, AND SHE'S IN GOOD HANDS. WE'VE HAD PLENTY OF EXPERIENCE RAISING ALIENS.
TRUE. AND WHO THOUGHT WE'D BE PARENTS AGAIN AT OUR AGE.

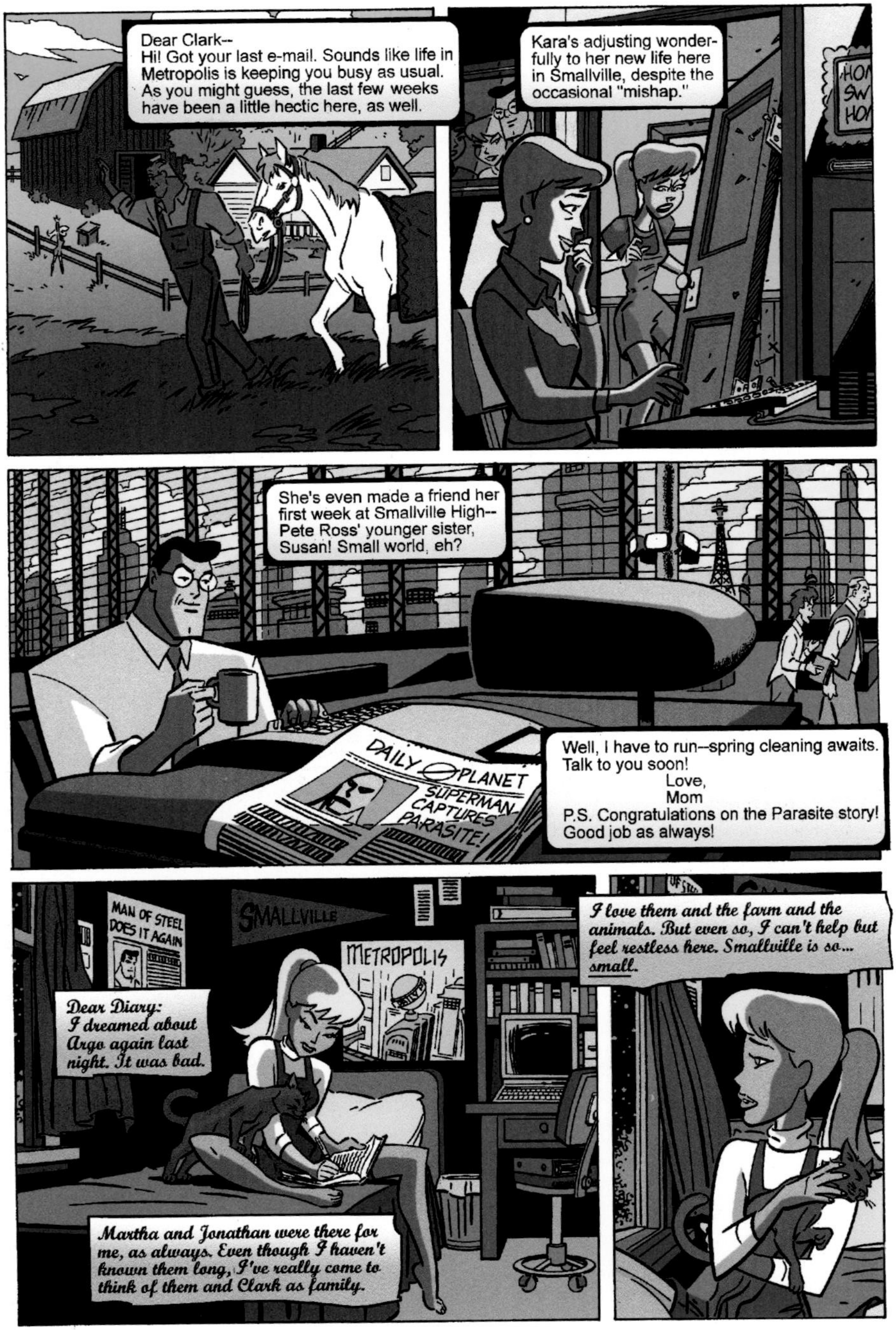
Dear Clark--
Hi! Got your last e-mail. Sounds like life in Metropolis is keeping you busy as usual. As you might guess, the last few weeks have been a little hectic here, as well.
Kara's adjusting wonderfully to her new life here in Smallville, despite the occasional "mishap."
She's even made a friend her first week at Smallville High-- Pete Ross' younger sister, Susan! Small world, eh?
DAILY PLANET
SUPERMAN CAPTURES PARASITE!
Well, I have to run--spring cleaning awaits. Talk to you soon!
Love,
Mom
P.S. Congratulations on the Parasite story! Good job as always!
MAN OF STEEL DOES IT AGAIN
SMALLVILLE
METROPOLIS
Dear Diary:
I dreamed about Argo again last night. It was bad.
Martha and Jonathan were there for me, as always. Even though I haven't known them long, I've really come to think of them and Clark as family.
I love them and the farm and the animals. But even so, I can't help but feel restless here. Smallville is so... small.

Dear Diary:
School continues to be a strange experience. Sometimes it just seems so backward after living with Argo science.

KARA? KARA KENT!

Huh? Oh, SORRY!

IT'S 13,682.5!

And I have to say I find Earth boys as confusing as Earth politics. They're both so absolutely ridiculous!

I'm studying more outside school, using the library and the Internet to learn about my new home--

CITIZEN WHO

BATGIRL

PHANTOM ZONE CRIMINALS CUT DOWN TO SIZE

--as well as Superman. I must have read everything there is to read about Clark's career--twice!

But even though Earth's yellow sun gives us both the same powers and abilities, he and the folks won't let me do the superhero thing yet.

I dream of doing what Clark does. I couldn't help on Argo, but here I can make a difference!

WELL

VILLE PROM

"Be patient," they say. "You're still adjusting to Earth." This "adjusting" is driving me crazy! If Clark can save the world every week, why can't I?

Dear Diary:
Summer's here (at last), and I've made a decision...

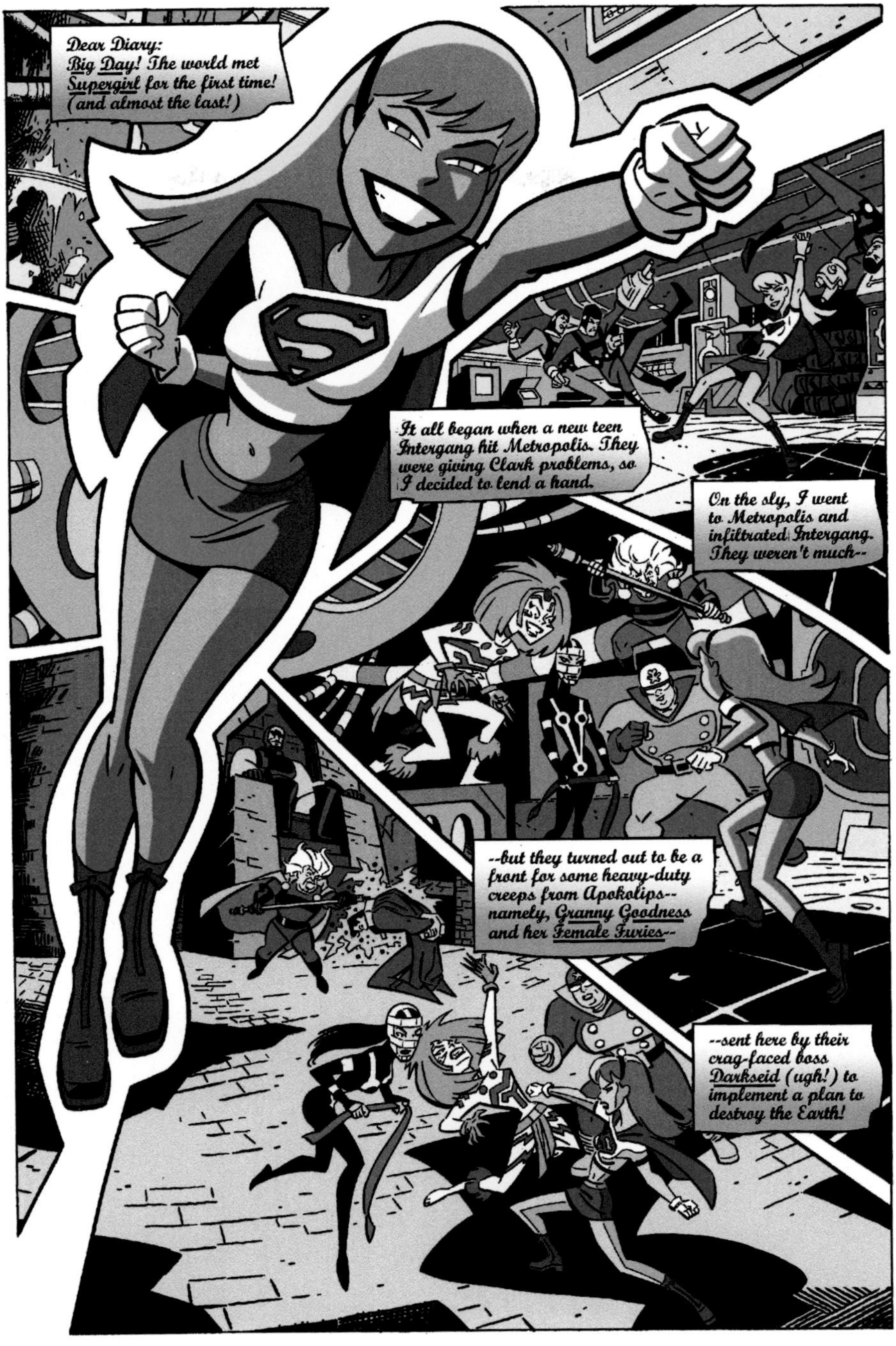
Dear Diary:
Big Day! The world met Supergirl for the first time! (and almost the last!)
It all began when a new teen Intergang hit Metropolis. They were giving Clark problems, so I decided to lend a hand.
On the sly, I went to Metropolis and infiltrated Intergang. They weren't much--
--but they turned out to be a front for some heavy-duty creeps from Apokolips--namely, Granny Goodness and her Female Furies--
--sent here by their crag-faced boss Darkseid (ugh!) to implement a plan to destroy the Earth!

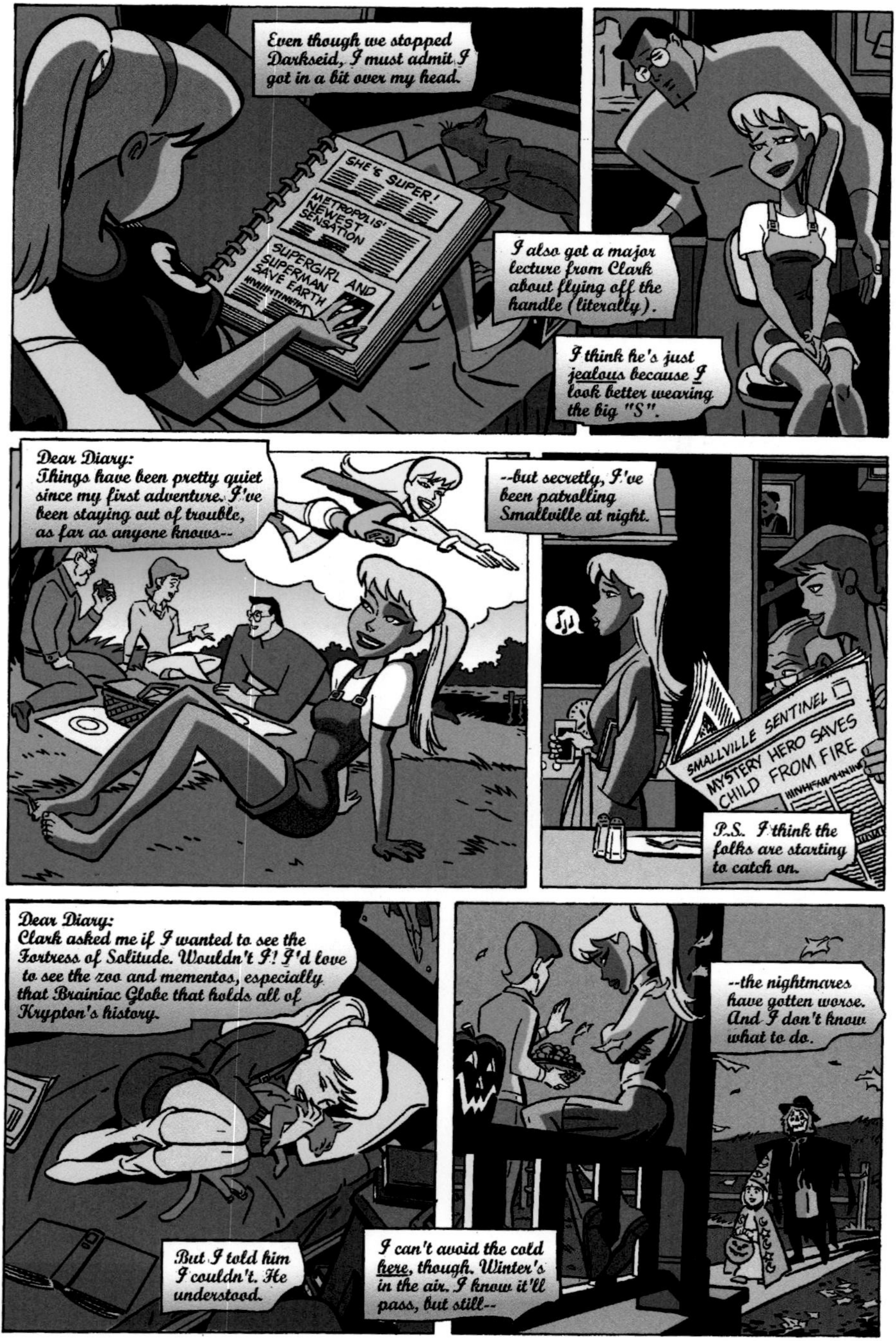

Even though we stopped Darkseid, I must admit I got in a bit over my head.
SHE'S SUPER!
METROPOLIS' NEWEST SENSATION
SUPERGIRL AND SUPERMAN SAVE EARTH
I also got a major lecture from Clark about flying off the handle (literally).
I think he's just jealous because I look better wearing the big "S".
Dear Diary:
Things have been pretty quiet since my first adventure. I've been staying out of trouble, as far as anyone knows--
--but secretly, I've been patrolling Smallville at night.
SMALLVILLE SENTINEL
MYSTERY HERO SAVES CHILD FROM FIRE
P.S. I think the folks are starting to catch on.
Dear Diary:
Clark asked me if I wanted to see the Fortress of Solitude. Wouldn't I! I'd love to see the zoo and mementos, especially that Brainiac Globe that holds all of Krypton's history.
But I told him I couldn't. He understood.
I can't avoid the cold here, though. Winter's in the air. I know it'll pass, but still--
--the nightmares have gotten worse. And I don't know what to do.

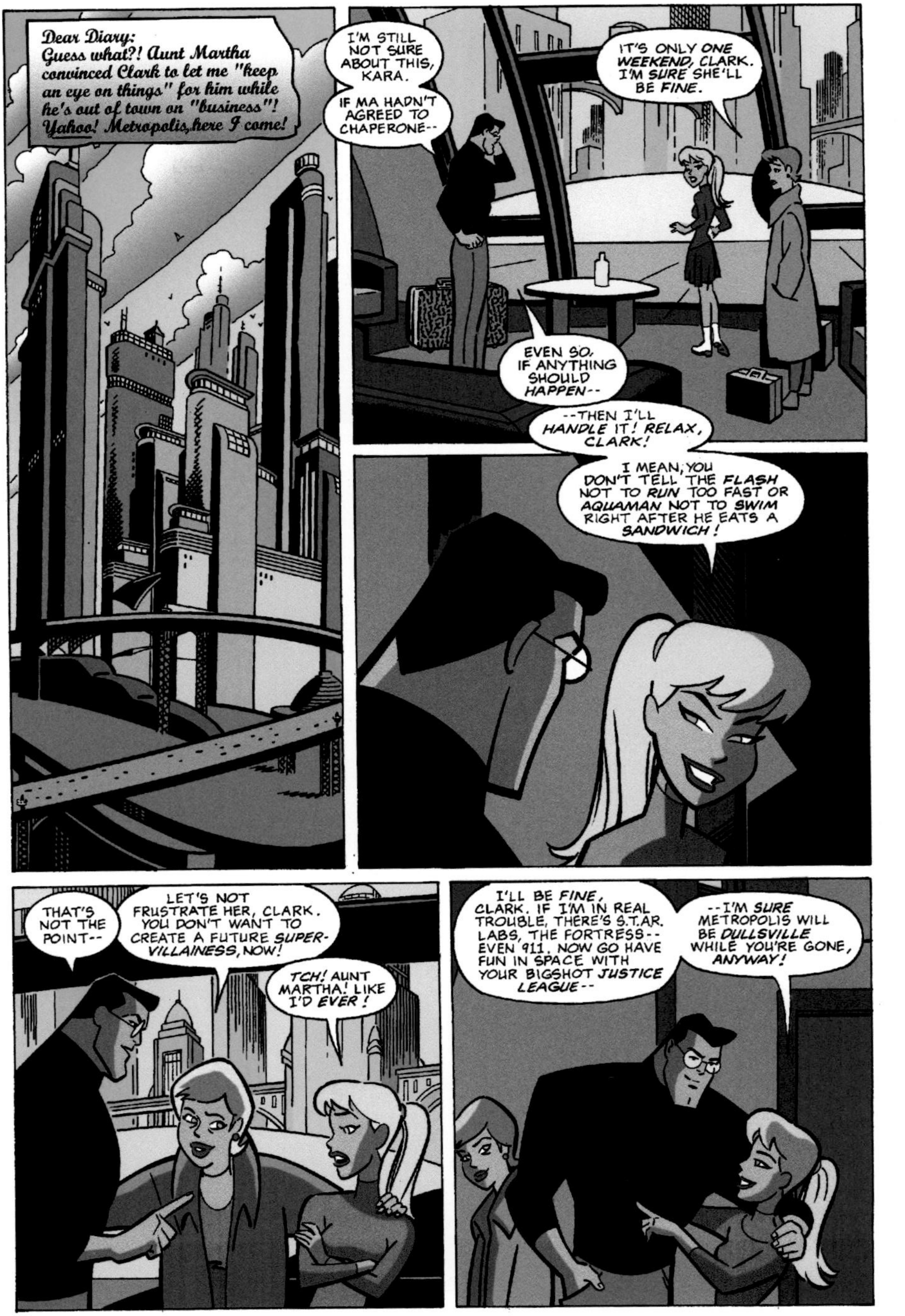
Dear Diary:
Guess what?! Aunt Martha convinced Clark to let me "keep an eye on things" for him while he's out of town on "business"! Yahoo! Metropolis, here I come!
I'M STILL NOT SURE ABOUT THIS, KARA.
IF MA HADN'T AGREED TO CHAPERONE--
IT'S ONLY ONE WEEKEND, CLARK. I'M SURE SHE'LL BE FINE.
EVEN SO, IF ANYTHING SHOULD HAPPEN--
--THEN I'LL HANDLE IT! RELAX, CLARK!
I MEAN, YOU DON'T TELL THE FLASH NOT TO RUN TOO FAST OR AQUAMAN NOT TO SWIM RIGHT AFTER HE EATS A SANDWICH!
THAT'S NOT THE POINT--
LET'S NOT FRUSTRATE HER, CLARK. YOU DON'T WANT TO CREATE A FUTURE SUPER-VILLAINESS, NOW!
TCH! AUNT MARTHA! LIKE I'D EVER!
I'LL BE FINE, CLARK. IF I'M IN REAL TROUBLE, THERE'S S.T.A.R. LABS, THE FORTRESS-- EVEN 911. NOW GO HAVE FUN IN SPACE WITH YOUR BIGSHOT JUSTICE LEAGUE--
--I'M SURE METROPOLIS WILL BE DULLSVILLE WHILE YOU'RE GONE, ANYWAY!

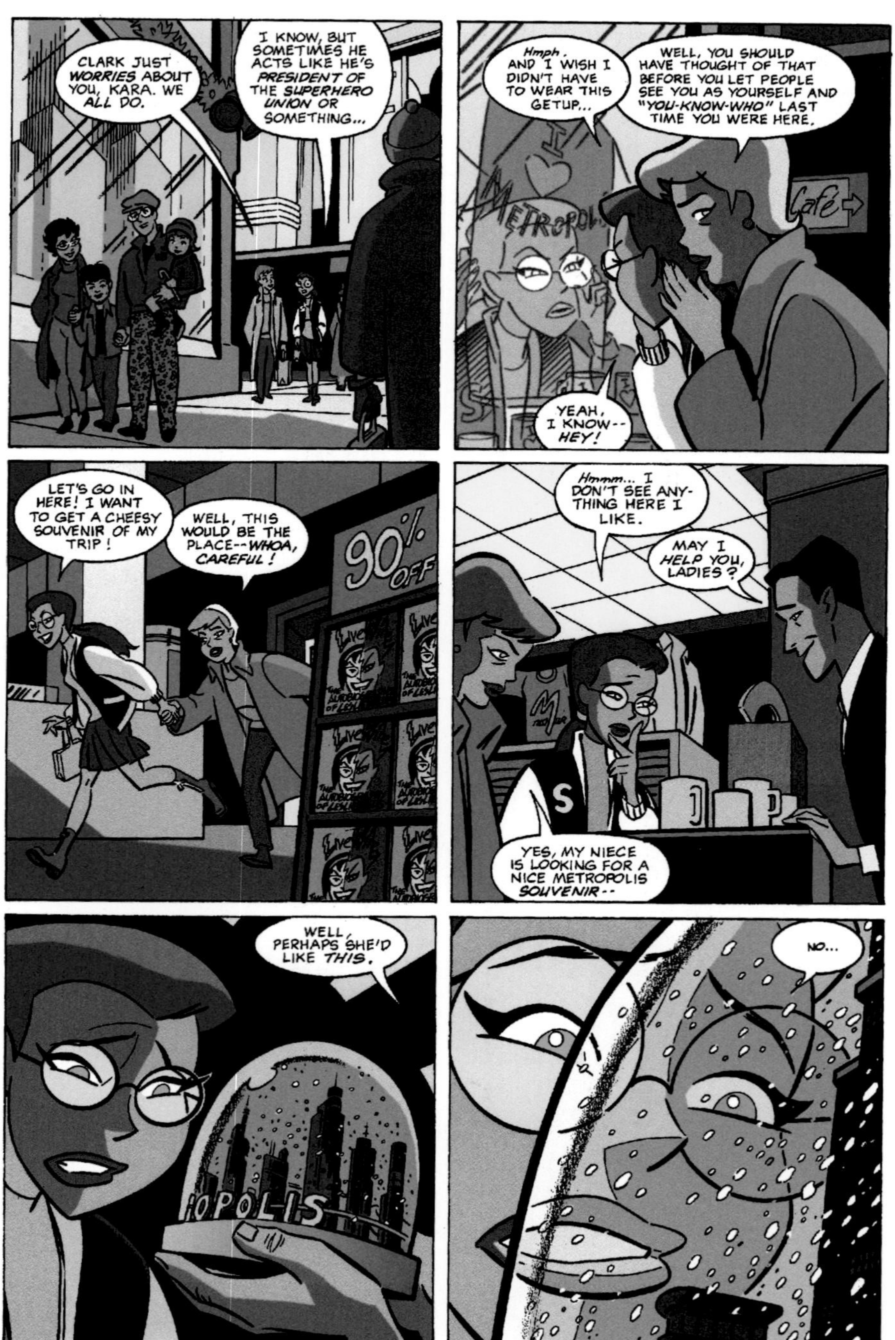
CLARK JUST WORRIES ABOUT YOU, KARA. WE ALL DO.
I KNOW, BUT SOMETIMES HE ACTS LIKE HE'S PRESIDENT OF THE SUPERHERO UNION OR SOMETHING...
Hmph. AND I WISH I DIDN'T HAVE TO WEAR THIS GETUP...
WELL, YOU SHOULD HAVE THOUGHT OF THAT BEFORE YOU LET PEOPLE SEE YOU AS YOURSELF AND "YOU-KNOW-WHO" LAST TIME YOU WERE HERE.
YEAH, I KNOW-- HEY!
Café
LET'S GO IN HERE! I WANT TO GET A CHEESY SOUVENIR OF MY TRIP!
WELL, THIS WOULD BE THE PLACE--WHOA, CAREFUL!
90% OFF
Hmmm... I DON'T SEE ANYTHING HERE I LIKE.
MAY I HELP YOU, LADIES?
YES, MY NIECE IS LOOKING FOR A NICE METROPOLIS SOUVENIR--
WELL, PERHAPS SHE'D LIKE THIS.
OPOLIS
NO...

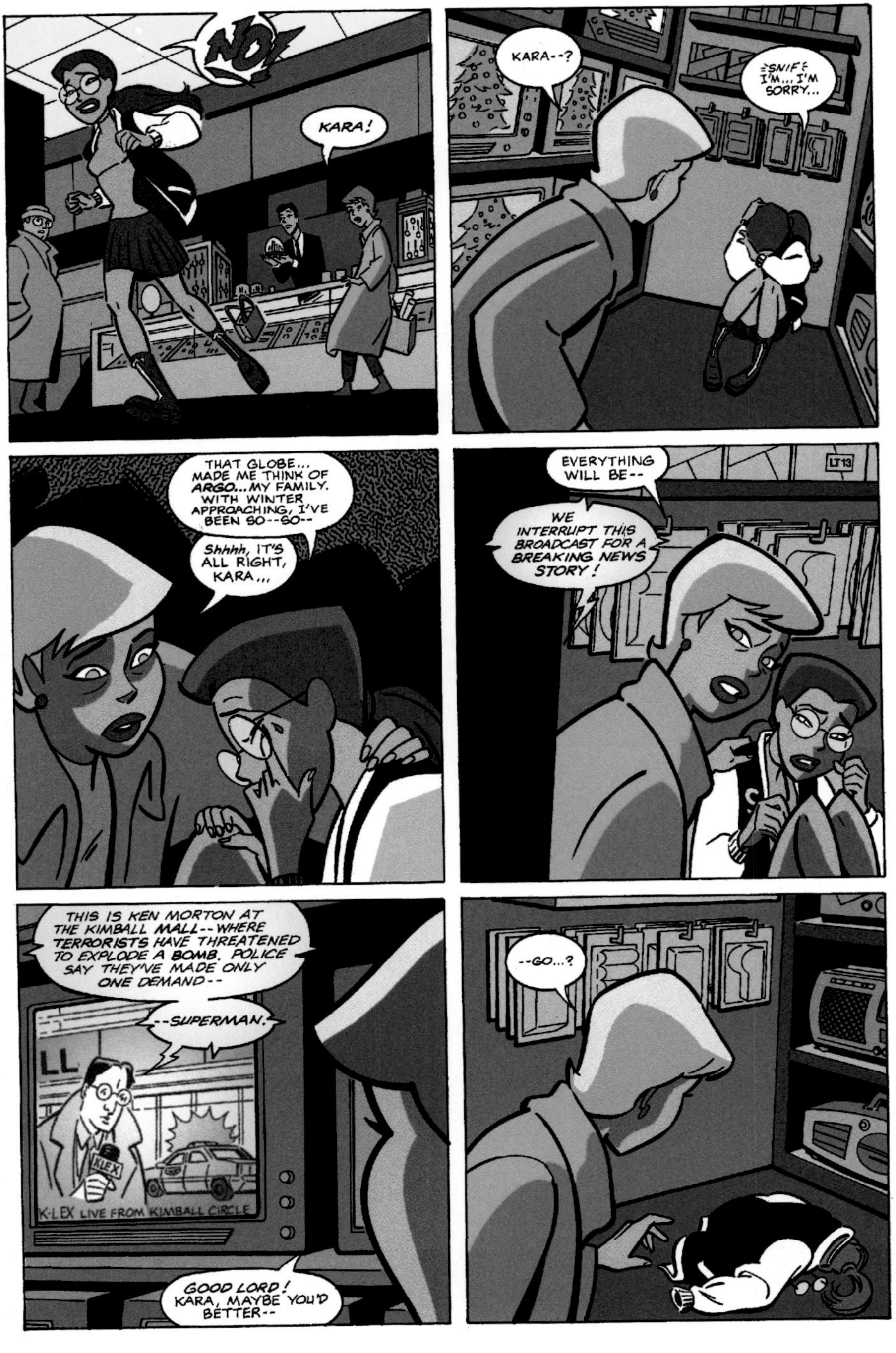
NO!
KARA!
KARA--?
SNIFF I'M... I'M SORRY...
THAT GLOBE... MADE ME THINK OF ARGO... MY FAMILY. WITH WINTER APPROACHING, I'VE BEEN SO--SO--
Shhhh, IT'S ALL RIGHT, KARA...
EVERYTHING WILL BE--
LT13
WE INTERRUPT THIS BROADCAST FOR A BREAKING NEWS STORY!
THIS IS KEN MORTON AT THE KIMBALL MALL--WHERE TERRORISTS HAVE THREATENED TO EXPLODE A BOMB. POLICE SAY THEY'VE MADE ONLY ONE DEMAND--
--SUPERMAN.
KLEX
K-LEX LIVE FROM KIMBALL CIRCLE
GOOD LORD! KARA, MAYBE YOU'D BETTER--
--GO...?

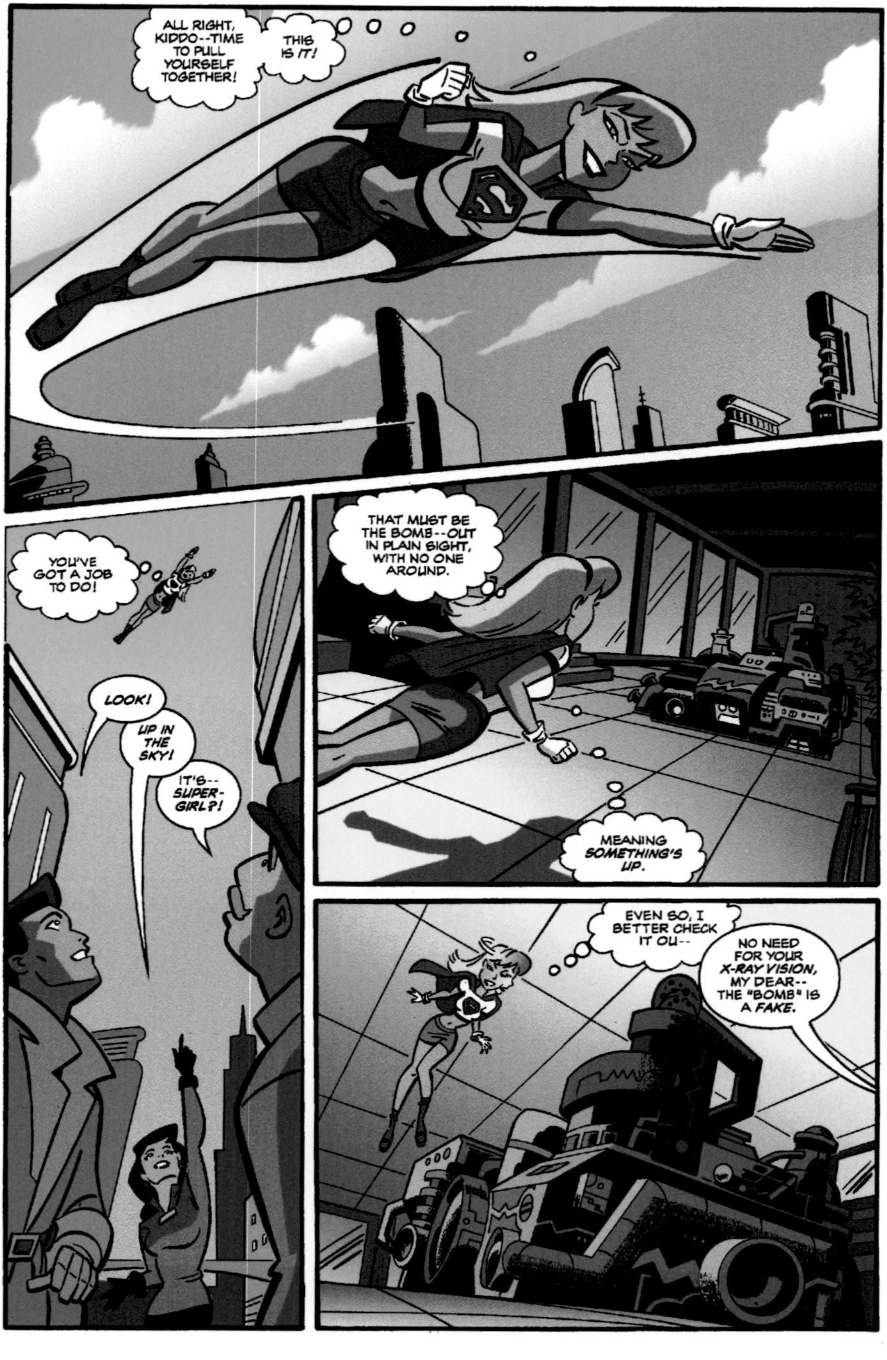
ALL RIGHT, KIDDO--TIME TO PULL YOURSELF TOGETHER!
THIS IS IT!
YOU'VE GOT A JOB TO DO!
LOOK!
UP IN THE SKY!
IT'S--SUPER-GIRL?!
THAT MUST BE THE BOMB--OUT IN PLAIN SIGHT, WITH NO ONE AROUND.
MEANING SOMETHING'S UP.
EVEN SO, I BETTER CHECK IT OU--
NO NEED FOR YOUR X-RAY VISION, MY DEAR--THE "BOMB" IS A FAKE.

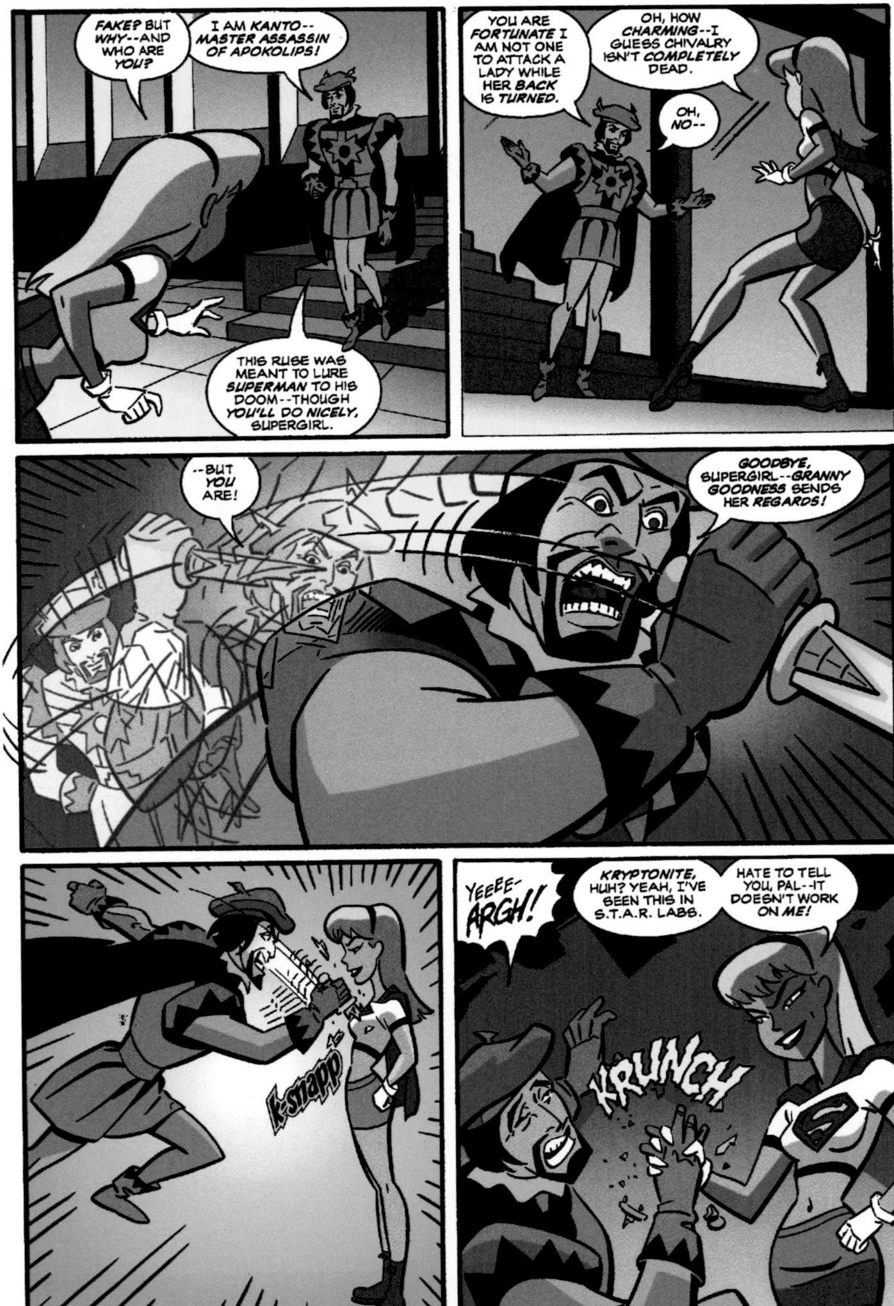
FAKE? BUT WHY--AND WHO ARE YOU?
I AM KANTO--MASTER ASSASSIN OF APOKOLIPS!
THIS RUSE WAS MEANT TO LURE SUPERMAN TO HIS DOOM--THOUGH YOU'LL DO NICELY, SUPERGIRL.
YOU ARE FORTUNATE I AM NOT ONE TO ATTACK A LADY WHILE HER BACK IS TURNED.
OH, HOW CHARMING--I GUESS CHIVALRY ISN'T COMPLETELY DEAD.
OH, NO--
--BUT YOU ARE!
GOODBYE, SUPERGIRL--GRANNY GOODNESS SENDS HER REGARDS!
K-SNAPP
YEEEE-ARGH!
KRYPTONITE, HUH? YEAH, I'VE SEEN THIS IN S.T.A.R. LABS.
HATE TO TELL YOU, PAL--IT DOESN'T WORK ON ME!
KRUNCH

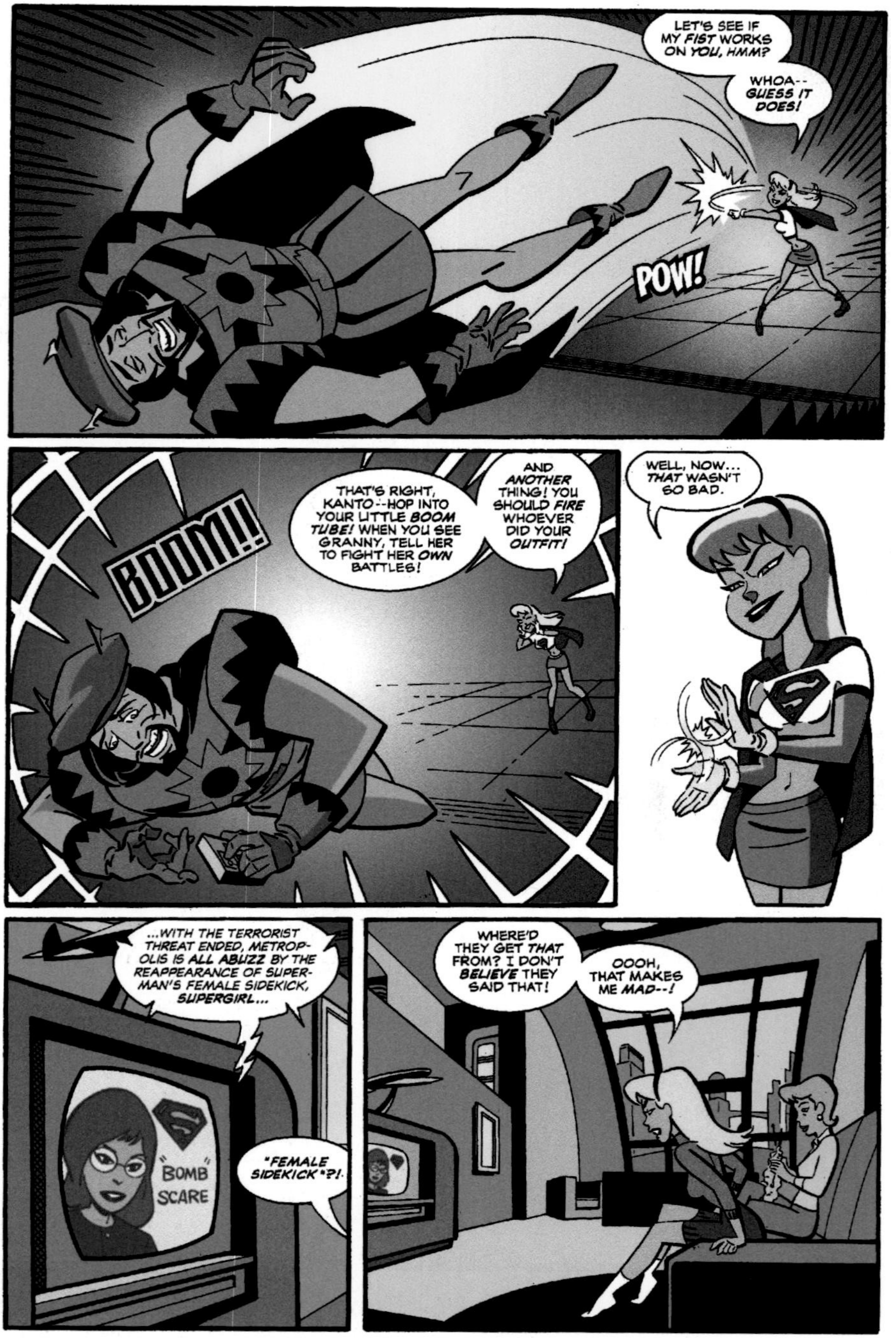
LET'S SEE IF MY FIST WORKS ON YOU, HMM?
WHOA--GUESS IT DOES!
POW!
BOOM!!
THAT'S RIGHT, KANTO--HOP INTO YOUR LITTLE BOOM TUBE! WHEN YOU SEE GRANNY, TELL HER TO FIGHT HER OWN BATTLES!
AND ANOTHER THING! YOU SHOULD FIRE WHOEVER DID YOUR OUTFIT!
WELL, NOW... THAT WASN'T SO BAD.
...WITH THE TERRORIST THREAT ENDED, METROPOLIS IS ALL ABUZZ BY THE REAPPEARANCE OF SUPERMAN'S FEMALE SIDEKICK, SUPERGIRL...
BOMB SCARE
"FEMALE SIDEKICK"?!
WHERE'D THEY GET THAT FROM? I DON'T BELIEVE THEY SAID THAT!
OOOH, THAT MAKES ME MAD--!

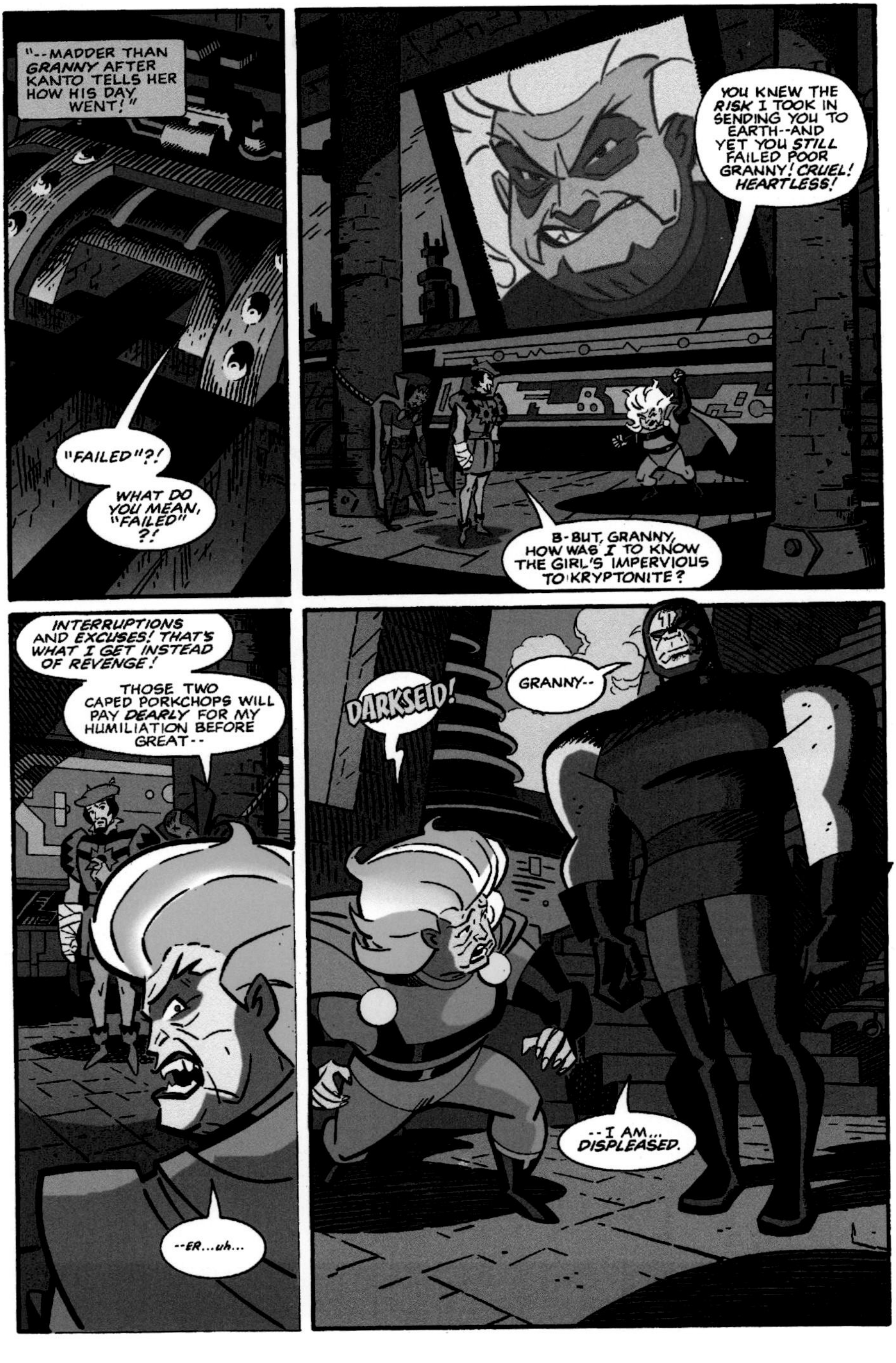
"--MADDER THAN GRANNY AFTER KANTO TELLS HER HOW HIS DAY WENT!"
"FAILED"?!
WHAT DO YOU MEAN, "FAILED" ?!
YOU KNEW THE RISK I TOOK IN SENDING YOU TO EARTH--AND YET YOU STILL FAILED POOR GRANNY! CRUEL! HEARTLESS!
B-BUT, GRANNY, HOW WAS I TO KNOW THE GIRL'S IMPERVIOUS TO KRYPTONITE?
INTERRUPTIONS AND EXCUSES! THAT'S WHAT I GET INSTEAD OF REVENGE!
THOSE TWO CAPED PORKCHOPS WILL PAY DEARLY FOR MY HUMILIATION BEFORE GREAT--
--ER...uh...
DARKSEID!
GRANNY--
--I AM... DISPLEASED.

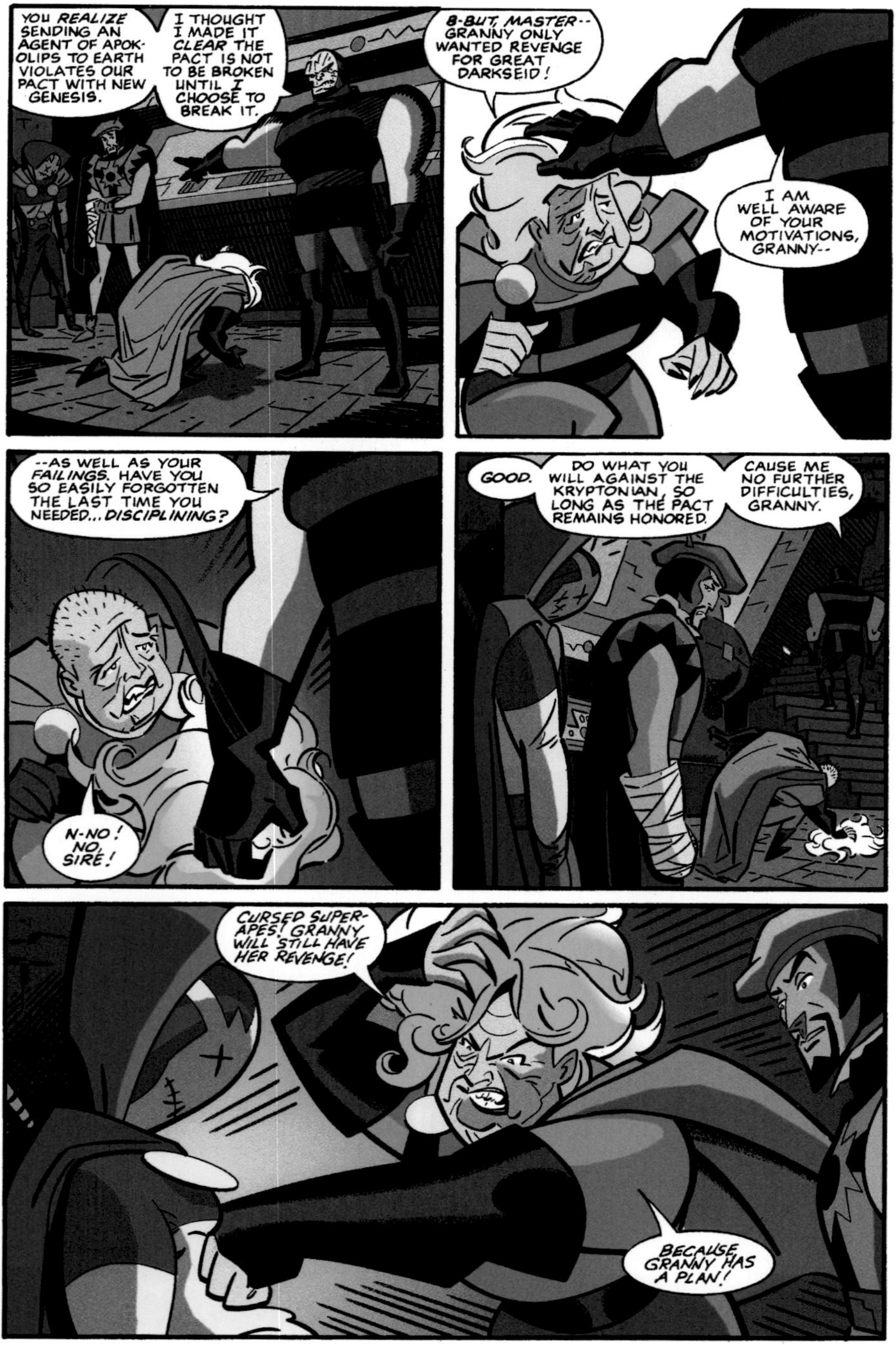

YOU REALIZE SENDING AN AGENT OF APOKOLIPS TO EARTH VIOLATES OUR PACT WITH NEW GENESIS.
I THOUGHT I MADE IT CLEAR THE PACT IS NOT TO BE BROKEN UNTIL I CHOOSE TO BREAK IT.
B-BUT, MASTER-- GRANNY ONLY WANTED REVENGE FOR GREAT DARKSEID!
I AM WELL AWARE OF YOUR MOTIVATIONS, GRANNY--
--AS WELL AS YOUR FAILINGS. HAVE YOU SO EASILY FORGOTTEN THE LAST TIME YOU NEEDED... DISCIPLINING?
N-NO! NO, SIRE!
GOOD.
DO WHAT YOU WILL AGAINST THE KRYPTONIAN, SO LONG AS THE PACT REMAINS HONORED.
CAUSE ME NO FURTHER DIFFICULTIES, GRANNY.
CURSED SUPER-APES! GRANNY WILL STILL HAVE HER REVENGE!
BECAUSE GRANNY HAS A PLAN!

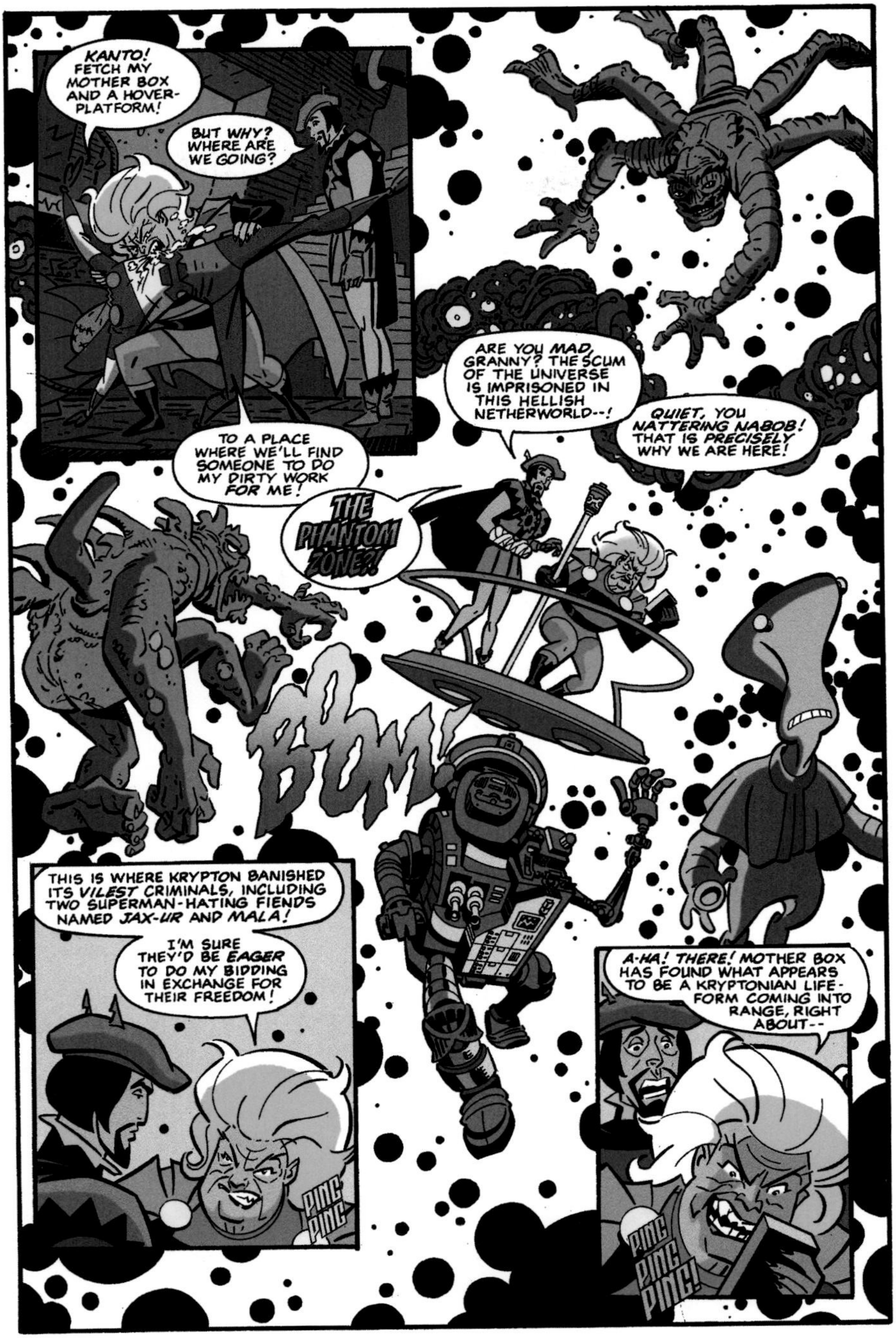
KANTO! FETCH MY MOTHER BOX AND A HOVER-PLATFORM!
BUT WHY? WHERE ARE WE GOING?
TO A PLACE WHERE WE'LL FIND SOMEONE TO DO MY DIRTY WORK FOR ME!
THE PHANTOM ZONE?!
ARE YOU MAD, GRANNY? THE SCUM OF THE UNIVERSE IS IMPRISONED IN THIS HELLISH NETHERWORLD--!
QUIET, YOU NATTERING NABOB! THAT IS PRECISELY WHY WE ARE HERE!
BOOM!
THIS IS WHERE KRYPTON BANISHED ITS VILEST CRIMINALS, INCLUDING TWO SUPERMAN-HATING FIENDS NAMED JAX-UR AND MALA!
I'M SURE THEY'D BE EAGER TO DO MY BIDDING IN EXCHANGE FOR THEIR FREEDOM!
PING PING
A-HA! THERE! MOTHER BOX HAS FOUND WHAT APPEARS TO BE A KRYPTONIAN LIFE-FORM COMING INTO RANGE, RIGHT ABOUT--
PING PING PING!

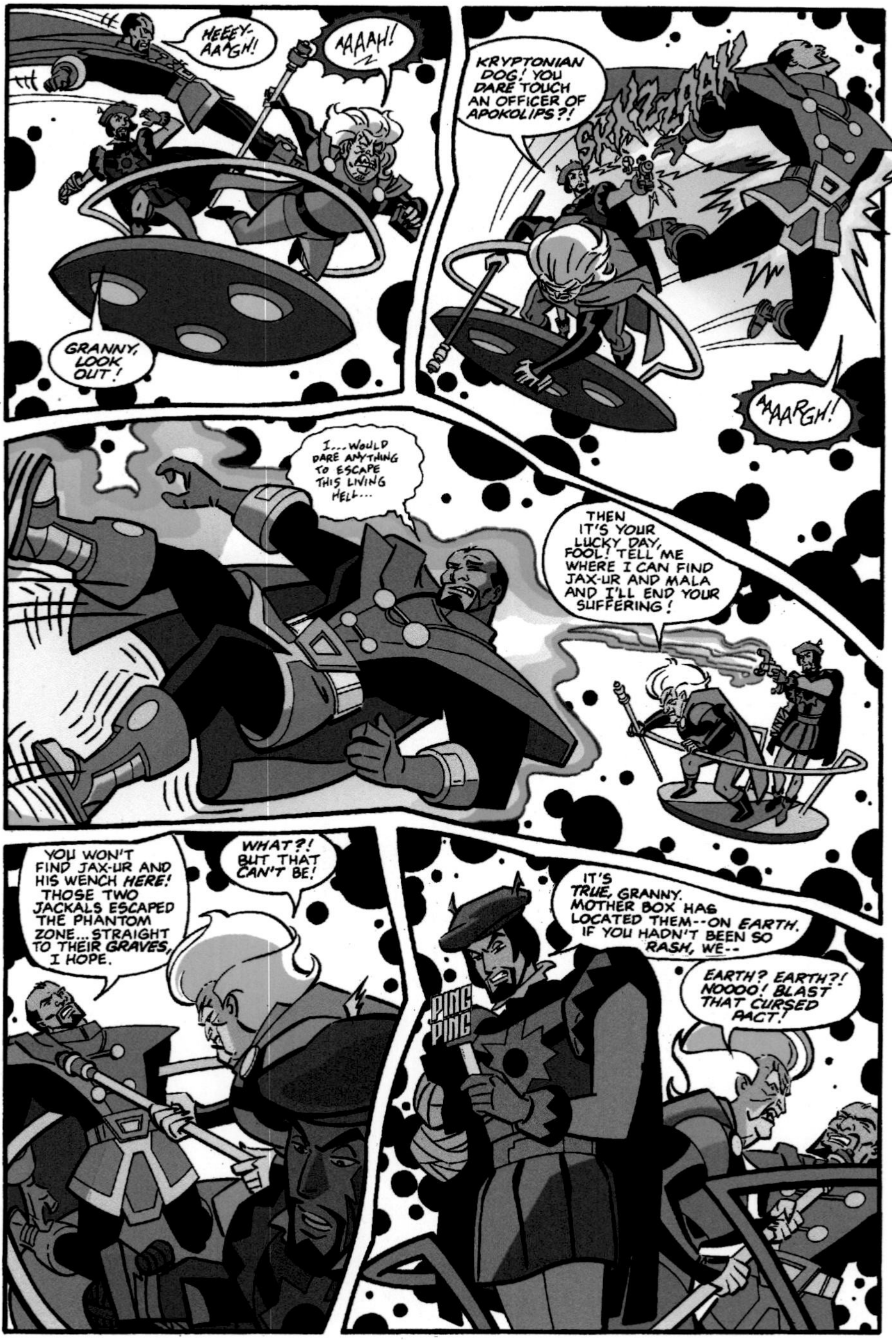
HEEEY-AAAGH!
AAAAH!
GRANNY, LOOK OUT!
KRYPTONIAN DOG! YOU DARE TOUCH AN OFFICER OF APOKOLIPS?!
SHKZZAAK
AAAARGH!
I... WOULD DARE ANYTHING TO ESCAPE THIS LIVING HELL...
THEN IT'S YOUR LUCKY DAY, FOOL! TELL ME WHERE I CAN FIND JAX-UR AND MALA AND I'LL END YOUR SUFFERING!
YOU WON'T FIND JAX-UR AND HIS WENCH HERE! THOSE TWO JACKALS ESCAPED THE PHANTOM ZONE... STRAIGHT TO THEIR GRAVES, I HOPE.
WHAT?! BUT THAT CAN'T BE!
IT'S TRUE, GRANNY. MOTHER BOX HAS LOCATED THEM--ON EARTH. IF YOU HADN'T BEEN SO RASH, WE--
PING PING
EARTH? EARTH?! NOOOO! BLAST THAT CURSED PACT!

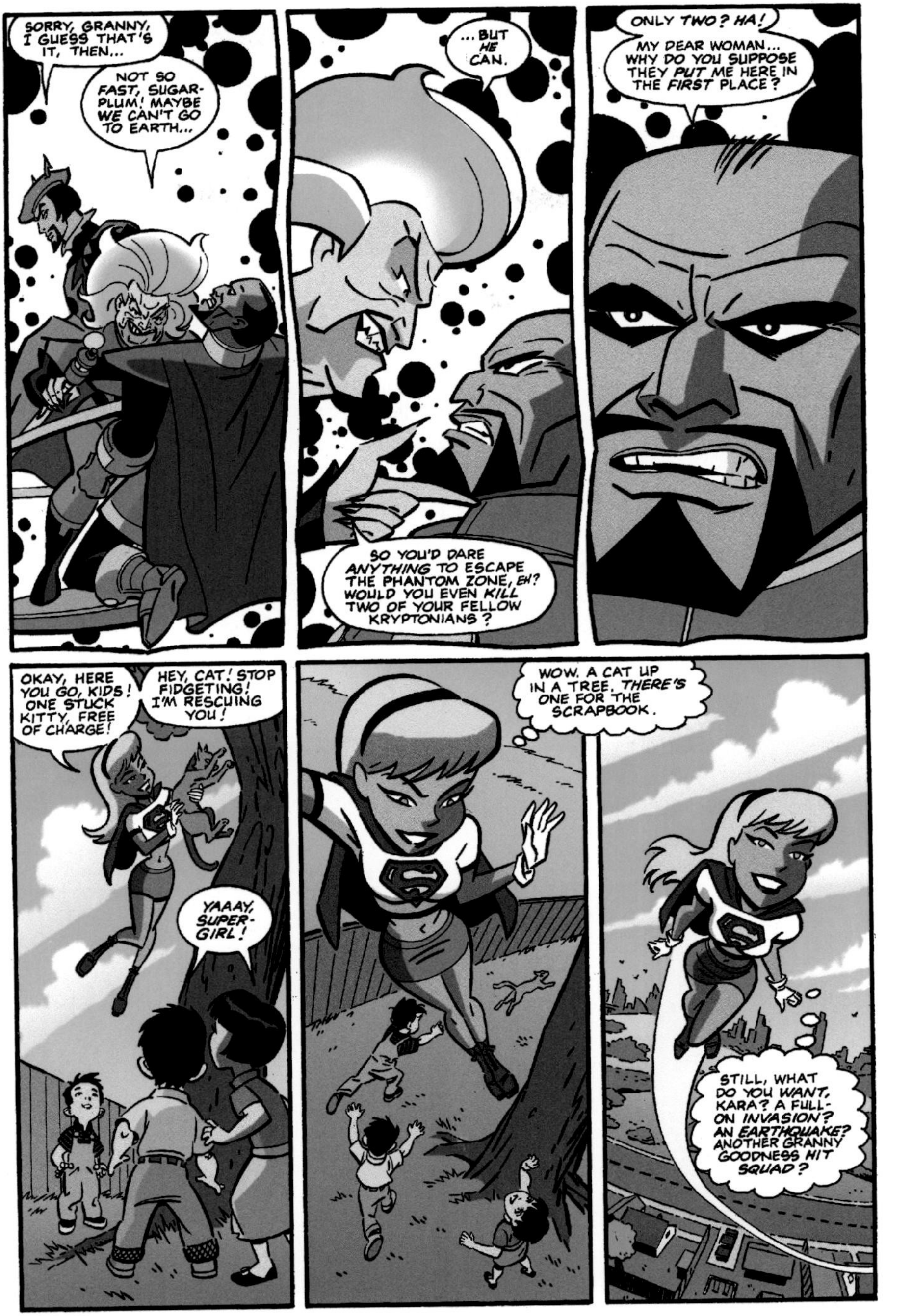
SORRY, GRANNY, I GUESS THAT'S IT, THEN...
NOT SO FAST, SUGAR-PLUM! MAYBE WE CAN'T GO TO EARTH...
...BUT HE CAN.
SO YOU'D DARE ANYTHING TO ESCAPE THE PHANTOM ZONE, EH? WOULD YOU EVEN KILL TWO OF YOUR FELLOW KRYPTONIANS?
ONLY TWO? HA!
MY DEAR WOMAN... WHY DO YOU SUPPOSE THEY PUT ME HERE IN THE FIRST PLACE?
OKAY, HERE YOU GO, KIDS! ONE STUCK KITTY, FREE OF CHARGE!
HEY, CAT! STOP FIDGETING! I'M RESCUING YOU!
YAAAY, SUPER-GIRL!
WOW. A CAT UP IN A TREE. THERE'S ONE FOR THE SCRAPBOOK.
STILL, WHAT DO YOU WANT, KARA? A FULL-ON INVASION? AN EARTHQUAKE? ANOTHER GRANNY GOODNESS HIT SQUAD?

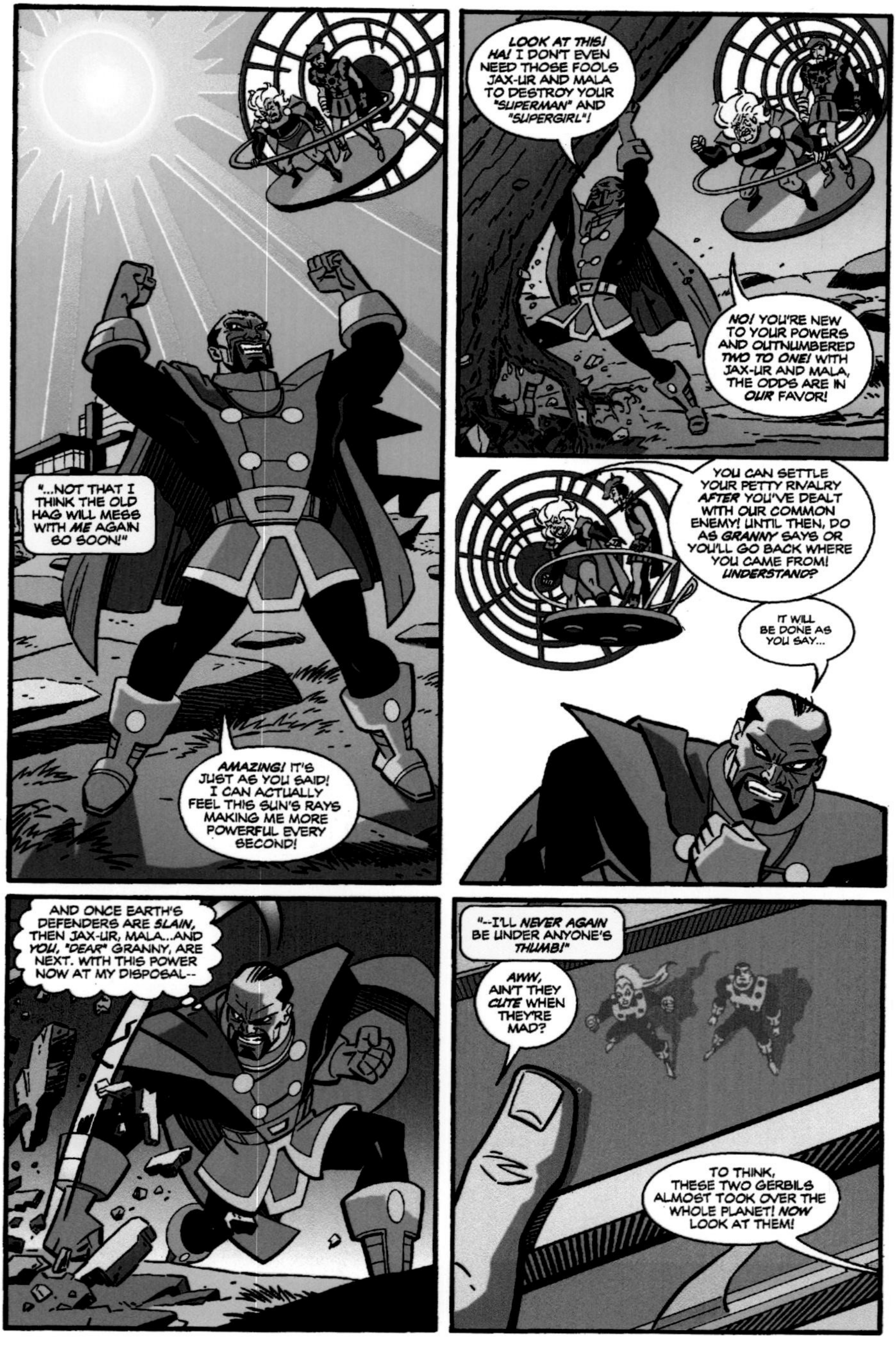
"...NOT THAT I THINK THE OLD HAG WILL MESS WITH ME AGAIN SO SOON!"
AMAZING! IT'S JUST AS YOU SAID! I CAN ACTUALLY FEEL THIS SUN'S RAYS MAKING ME MORE POWERFUL EVERY SECOND!
LOOK AT THIS! HA! I DON'T EVEN NEED THOSE FOOLS JAX-UR AND MALA TO DESTROY YOUR "SUPERMAN" AND "SUPERGIRL"!
NO! YOU'RE NEW TO YOUR POWERS AND OUTNUMBERED TWO TO ONE! WITH JAX-UR AND MALA, THE ODDS ARE IN OUR FAVOR!
YOU CAN SETTLE YOUR PETTY RIVALRY AFTER YOU'VE DEALT WITH OUR COMMON ENEMY! UNTIL THEN, DO AS GRANNY SAYS OR YOU'LL GO BACK WHERE YOU CAME FROM! UNDERSTAND?
IT WILL BE DONE AS YOU SAY...
AND ONCE EARTH'S DEFENDERS ARE SLAIN, THEN JAX-UR, MALA...AND YOU, "DEAR" GRANNY, ARE NEXT. WITH THIS POWER NOW AT MY DISPOSAL--
"--I'LL NEVER AGAIN BE UNDER ANYONE'S THUMB!"
AWW, AIN'T THEY CUTE WHEN THEY'RE MAD?
TO THINK, THESE TWO GERBILS ALMOST TOOK OVER THE WHOLE PLANET! NOW LOOK AT THEM!

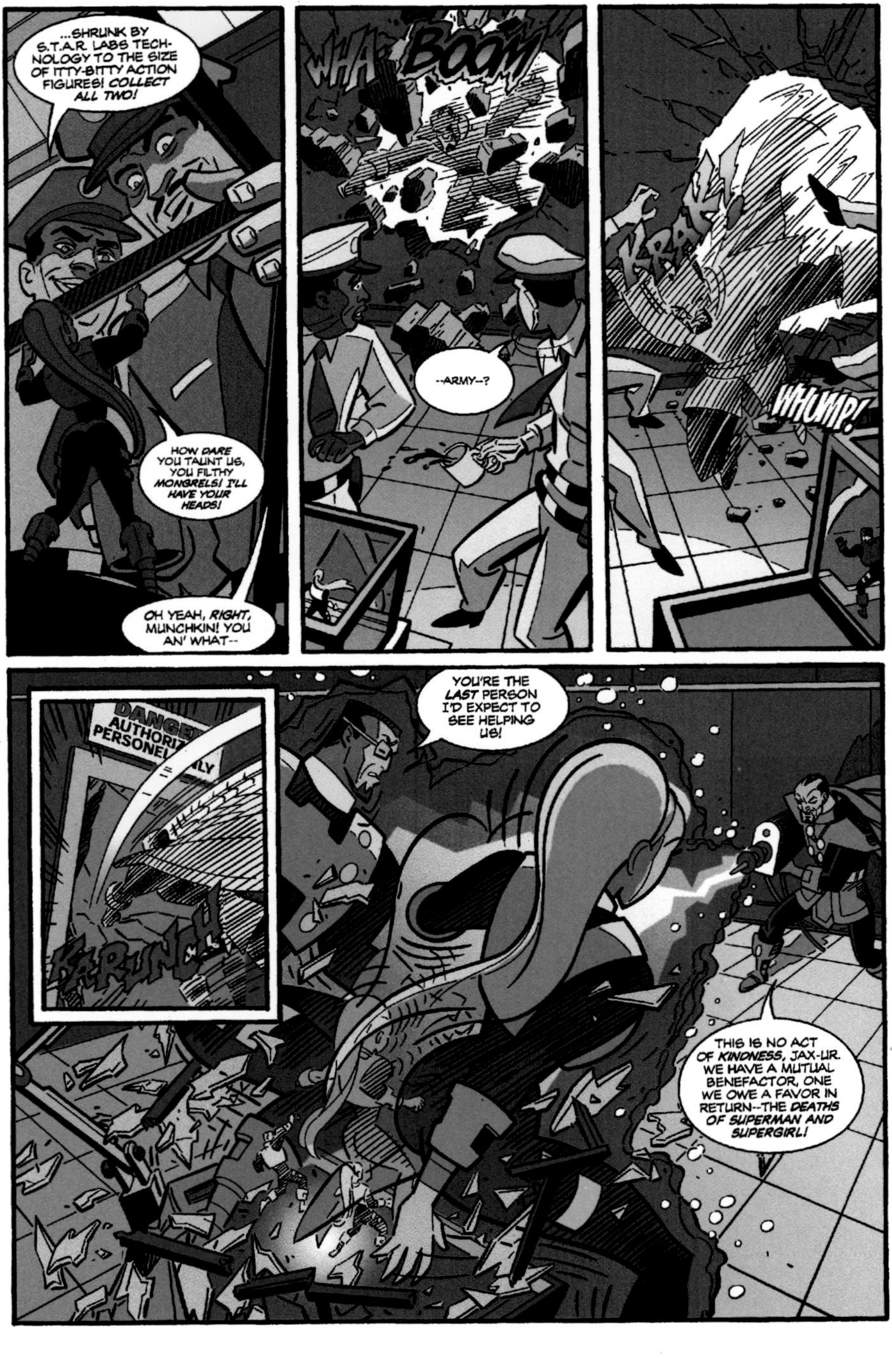
...SHRUNK BY S.T.A.R. LABS TECHNOLOGY TO THE SIZE OF ITTY-BITTY ACTION FIGURES! COLLECT ALL TWO!
HOW DARE YOU TAUNT US, YOU FILTHY MONGRELS! I'LL HAVE YOUR HEADS!
OH YEAH, RIGHT, MUNCHKIN! YOU AN' WHAT--
WHA
BOOM
--ARMY--?
KRAK
WHUMP!
DANGER
AUTHORIZ
PERSONEL
NLY
KRRUNCH
YOU'RE THE LAST PERSON I'D EXPECT TO SEE HELPING US!
THIS IS NO ACT OF KINDNESS, JAX-UR. WE HAVE A MUTUAL BENEFACTOR, ONE WE OWE A FAVOR IN RETURN--THE DEATHS OF SUPERMAN AND SUPERGIRL!

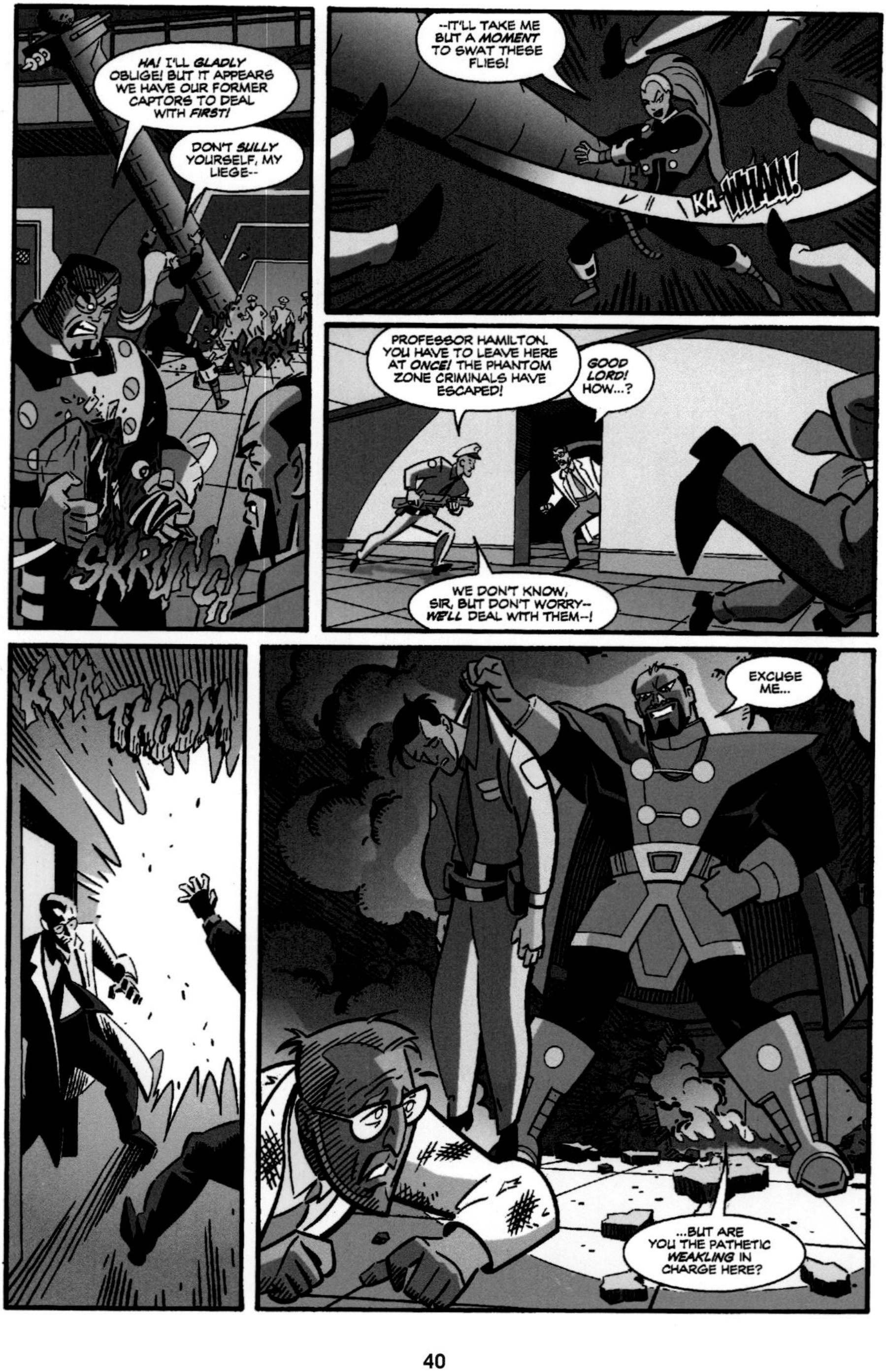
HA! I'LL GLADLY OBLIGE! BUT IT APPEARS WE HAVE OUR FORMER CAPTORS TO DEAL WITH FIRST!
DON'T SULLY YOURSELF, MY LIEGE--
SKRUNCH
--IT'LL TAKE ME BUT A MOMENT TO SWAT THESE FLIES!
KA-WHAM!
PROFESSOR HAMILTON. YOU HAVE TO LEAVE HERE AT ONCE! THE PHANTOM ZONE CRIMINALS HAVE ESCAPED!
GOOD LORD! HOW...?
WE DON'T KNOW, SIR, BUT DON'T WORRY-- WE'LL DEAL WITH THEM--!
KWA-THOOM
EXCUSE ME...
...BUT ARE YOU THE PATHETIC WEAKLING IN CHARGE HERE?

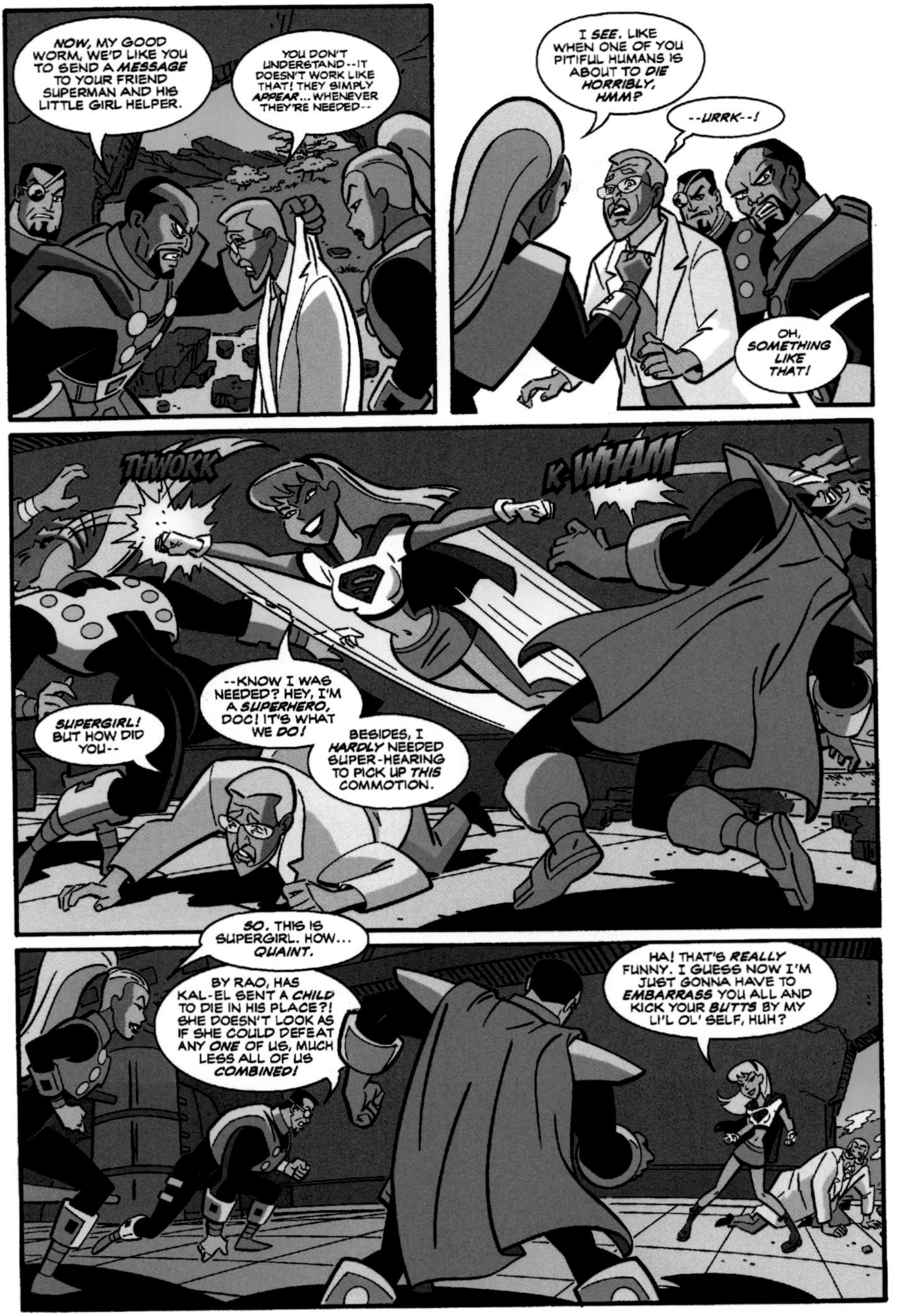
NOW, MY GOOD WORM, WE'D LIKE YOU TO SEND A MESSAGE TO YOUR FRIEND SUPERMAN AND HIS LITTLE GIRL HELPER.
YOU DON'T UNDERSTAND--IT DOESN'T WORK LIKE THAT! THEY SIMPLY APPEAR... WHENEVER THEY'RE NEEDED--
I SEE. LIKE WHEN ONE OF YOU PITIFUL HUMANS IS ABOUT TO DIE HORRIBLY, HMM?
--URRK--!
OH, SOMETHING LIKE THAT!
THWOKK
K-WHAM
SUPERGIRL! BUT HOW DID YOU--
--KNOW I WAS NEEDED? HEY, I'M A SUPERHERO, DOC! IT'S WHAT WE DO!
BESIDES, I HARDLY NEEDED SUPER-HEARING TO PICK UP THIS COMMOTION.
SO. THIS IS SUPERGIRL. HOW... QUAINT.
BY RAO, HAS KAL-EL SENT A CHILD TO DIE IN HIS PLACE?! SHE DOESN'T LOOK AS IF SHE COULD DEFEAT ANY ONE OF US, MUCH LESS ALL OF US COMBINED!
HA! THAT'S REALLY FUNNY. I GUESS NOW I'M JUST GONNA HAVE TO EMBARRASS YOU ALL AND KICK YOUR BUTTS BY MY LI'L OL' SELF, HUH?

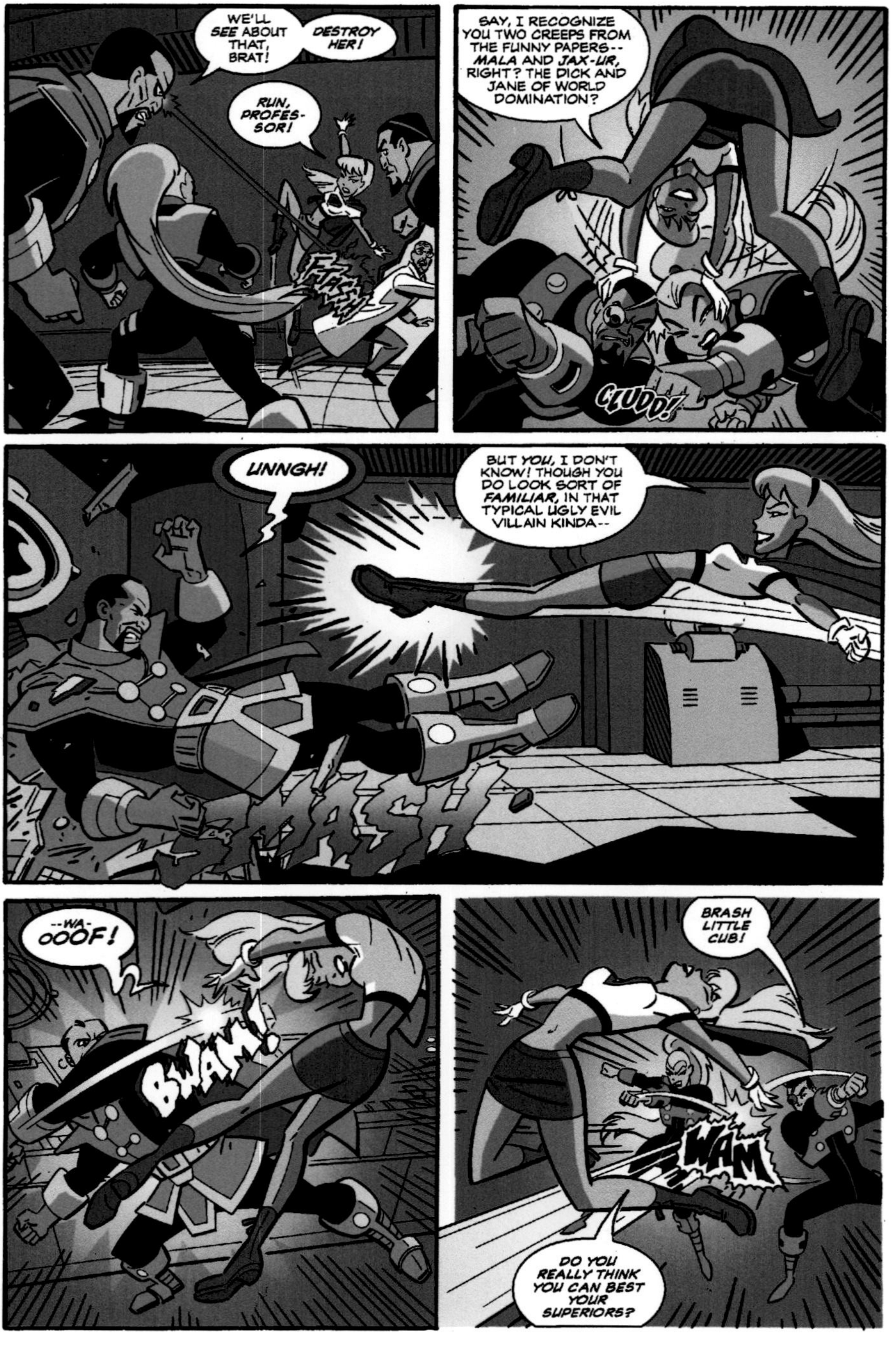

WE'LL SEE ABOUT THAT, BRAT!
DESTROY HER!
RUN, PROFES-SOR!
FTASSH
SAY, I RECOGNIZE YOU TWO CREEPS FROM THE FUNNY PAPERS-- MALA AND JAX-UR, RIGHT? THE DICK AND JANE OF WORLD DOMINATION?
CLUDD!
UNNGH!
BUT YOU, I DON'T KNOW! THOUGH YOU DO LOOK SORT OF FAMILIAR, IN THAT TYPICAL UGLY EVIL VILLAIN KINDA--
SMASH!
--WA-OOOF!
BWAM!
BRASH LITTLE CUB!
WAM
DO YOU REALLY THINK YOU CAN BEST YOUR SUPERIORS?

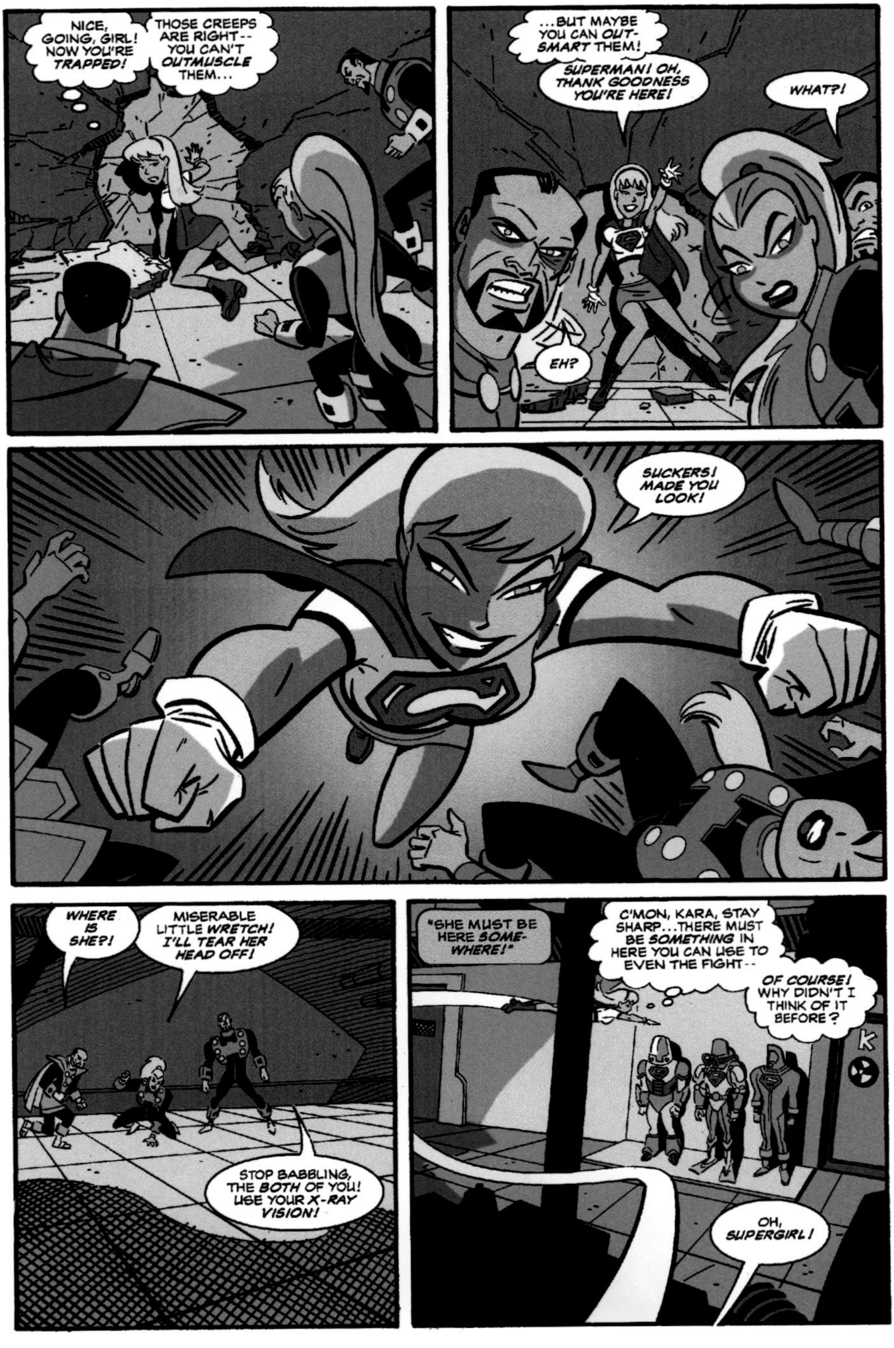
NICE, GOING, GIRL! NOW YOU'RE TRAPPED!
THOSE CREEPS ARE RIGHT-- YOU CAN'T OUTMUSCLE THEM...
...BUT MAYBE YOU CAN OUT-SMART THEM!
SUPERMAN! OH, THANK GOODNESS YOU'RE HERE!
WHAT?!
EH?
SUCKERS! MADE YOU LOOK!
WHERE IS SHE?!
MISERABLE LITTLE WRETCH! I'LL TEAR HER HEAD OFF!
STOP BABBLING, THE BOTH OF YOU! USE YOUR X-RAY VISION!
"SHE MUST BE HERE SOME-WHERE!"
C'MON, KARA, STAY SHARP...THERE MUST BE SOMETHING IN HERE YOU CAN USE TO EVEN THE FIGHT--
OF COURSE! WHY DIDN'T I THINK OF IT BEFORE?
K
OH, SUPERGIRL!

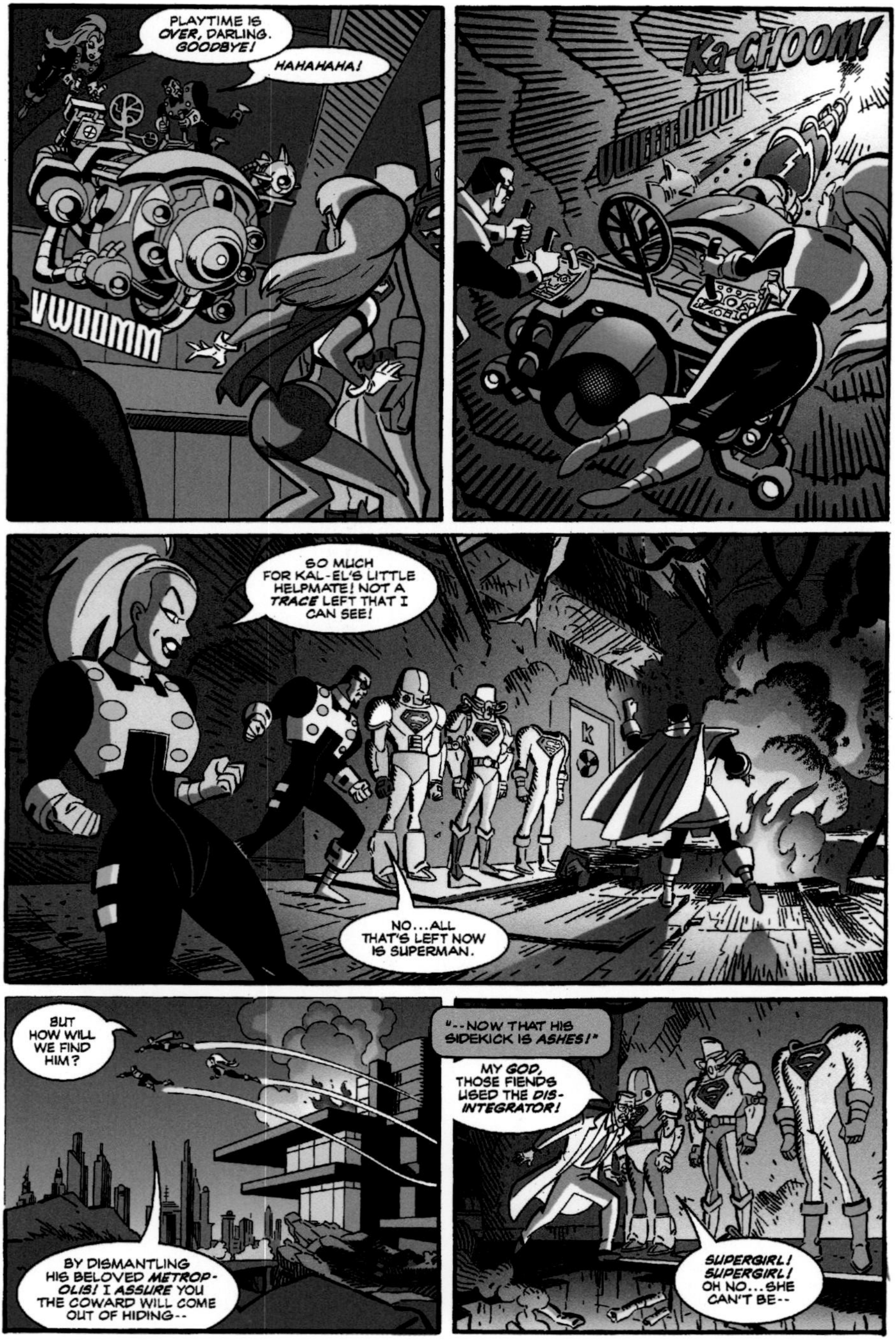
PLAYTIME IS OVER, DARLING. GOODBYE!
HAHAHAHA!
VWOOMM
Ka-CHOOM!
VWEEEEOOOW
SO MUCH FOR KAL-EL'S LITTLE HELPMATE! NOT A TRACE LEFT THAT I CAN SEE!
K
NO...ALL THAT'S LEFT NOW IS SUPERMAN.
BUT HOW WILL WE FIND HIM?
BY DISMANTLING HIS BELOVED METROPOLIS! I ASSURE YOU THE COWARD WILL COME OUT OF HIDING--
"--NOW THAT HIS SIDEKICK IS ASHES!"
MY GOD, THOSE FIENDS USED THE DISINTEGRATOR!
SUPERGIRL! SUPERGIRL! OH NO...SHE CAN'T BE--

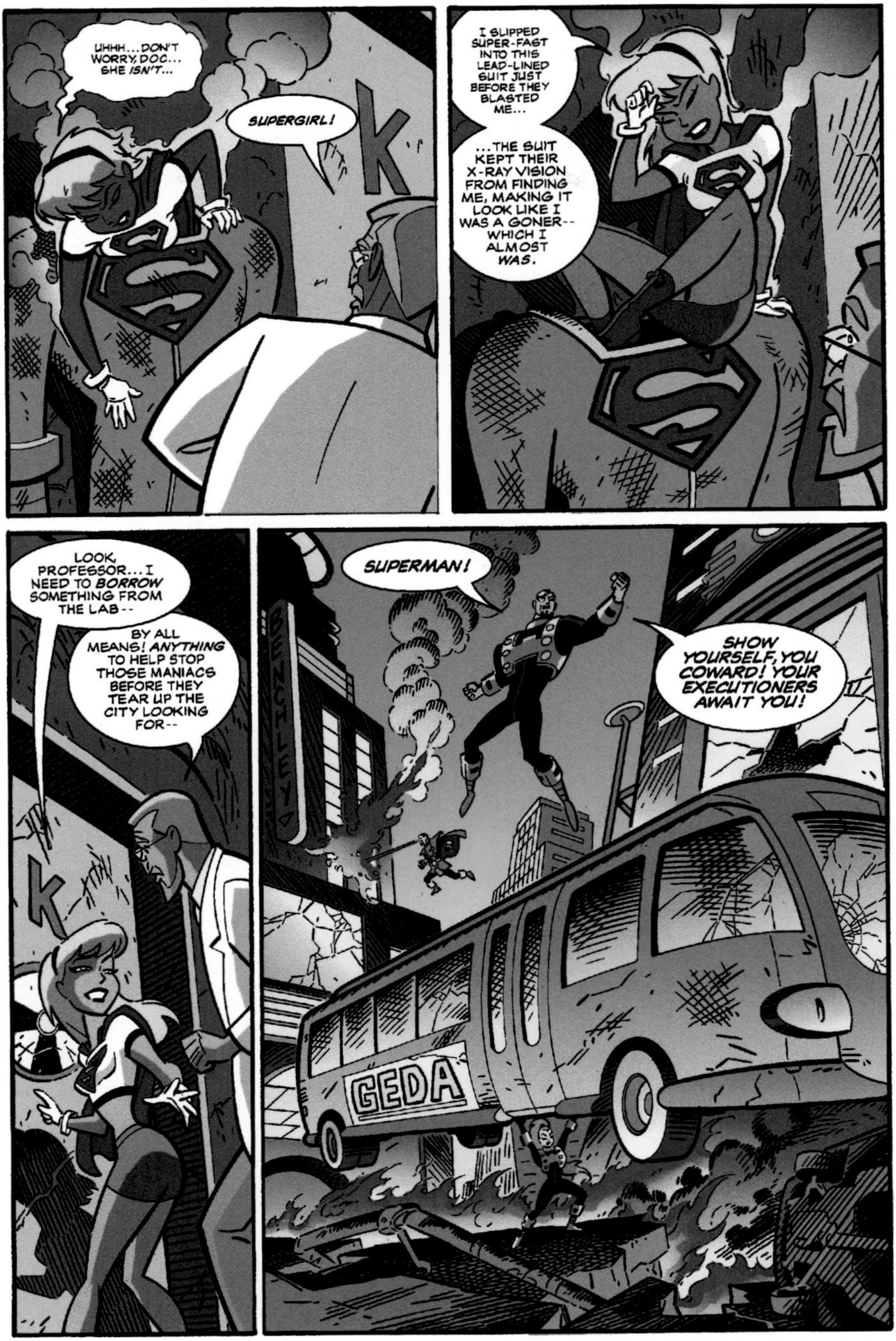
UHHH... DON'T WORRY, DOC... SHE ISN'T...
SUPERGIRL!
K
I SLIPPED SUPER-FAST INTO THIS LEAD-LINED SUIT JUST BEFORE THEY BLASTED ME...
...THE SUIT KEPT THEIR X-RAY VISION FROM FINDING ME, MAKING IT LOOK LIKE I WAS A GONER-- WHICH I ALMOST WAS.
LOOK, PROFESSOR... I NEED TO BORROW SOMETHING FROM THE LAB--
BY ALL MEANS! ANYTHING TO HELP STOP THOSE MANIACS BEFORE THEY TEAR UP THE CITY LOOKING FOR--
K
SUPERMAN!
BENCHLEY
SHOW YOURSELF, YOU COWARD! YOUR EXECUTIONERS AWAIT YOU!
GEDA

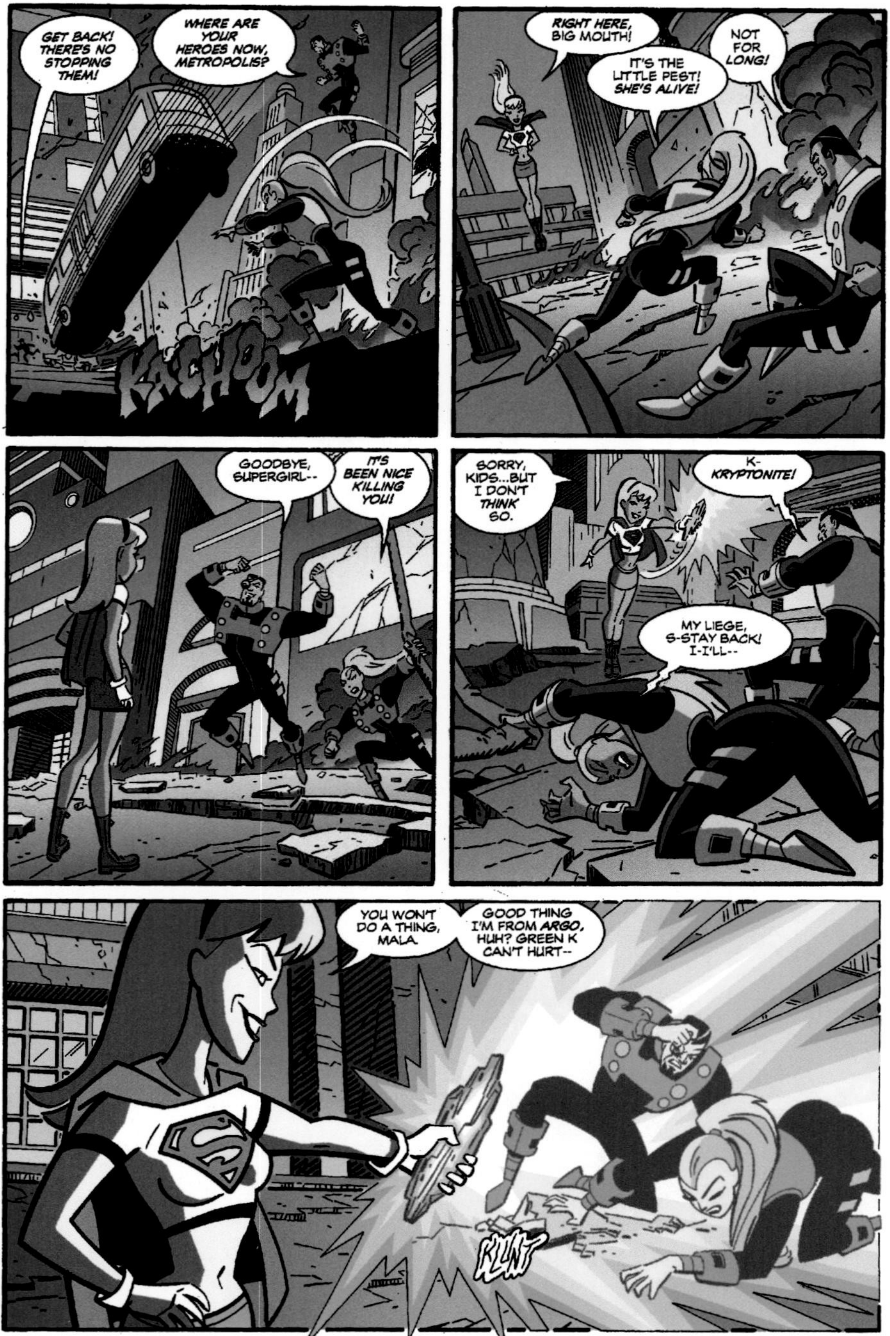
GET BACK! THERE'S NO STOPPING THEM!
WHERE ARE YOUR HEROES NOW, METROPOLIS?
KACHOOM
RIGHT HERE, BIG MOUTH!
IT'S THE LITTLE PEST! SHE'S ALIVE!
NOT FOR LONG!
GOODBYE, SUPERGIRL--
IT'S BEEN NICE KILLING YOU!
SORRY, KIDS...BUT I DON'T THINK SO.
K-KRYPTONITE!
MY LIEGE, S-STAY BACK! I-I'LL--
YOU WON'T DO A THING, MALA.
GOOD THING I'M FROM ARGO, HUH? GREEN K CAN'T HURT--
KLINT

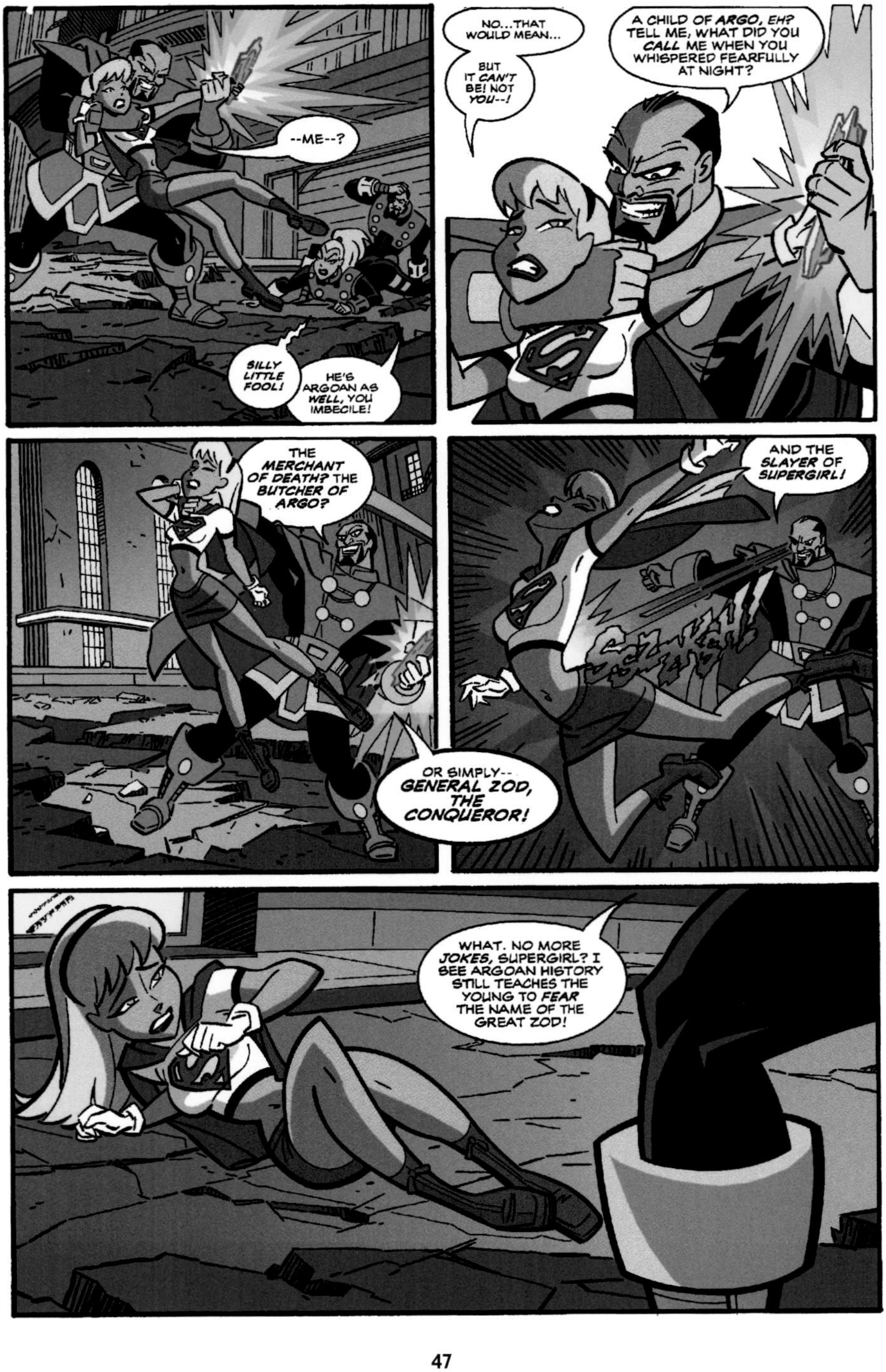

--ME--?
SILLY LITTLE FOOL!
HE'S ARGOAN AS WELL, YOU IMBECILE!
NO...THAT WOULD MEAN...
BUT IT CAN'T BE! NOT YOU--!
A CHILD OF ARGO, EH? TELL ME, WHAT DID YOU CALL ME WHEN YOU WHISPERED FEARFULLY AT NIGHT?
THE MERCHANT OF DEATH? THE BUTCHER OF ARGO?
OR SIMPLY-- GENERAL ZOD, THE CONQUEROR!
AND THE SLAYER OF SUPERGIRL!
WHAT. NO MORE JOKES, SUPERGIRL? I SEE ARGOAN HISTORY STILL TEACHES THE YOUNG TO FEAR THE NAME OF THE GREAT ZOD!

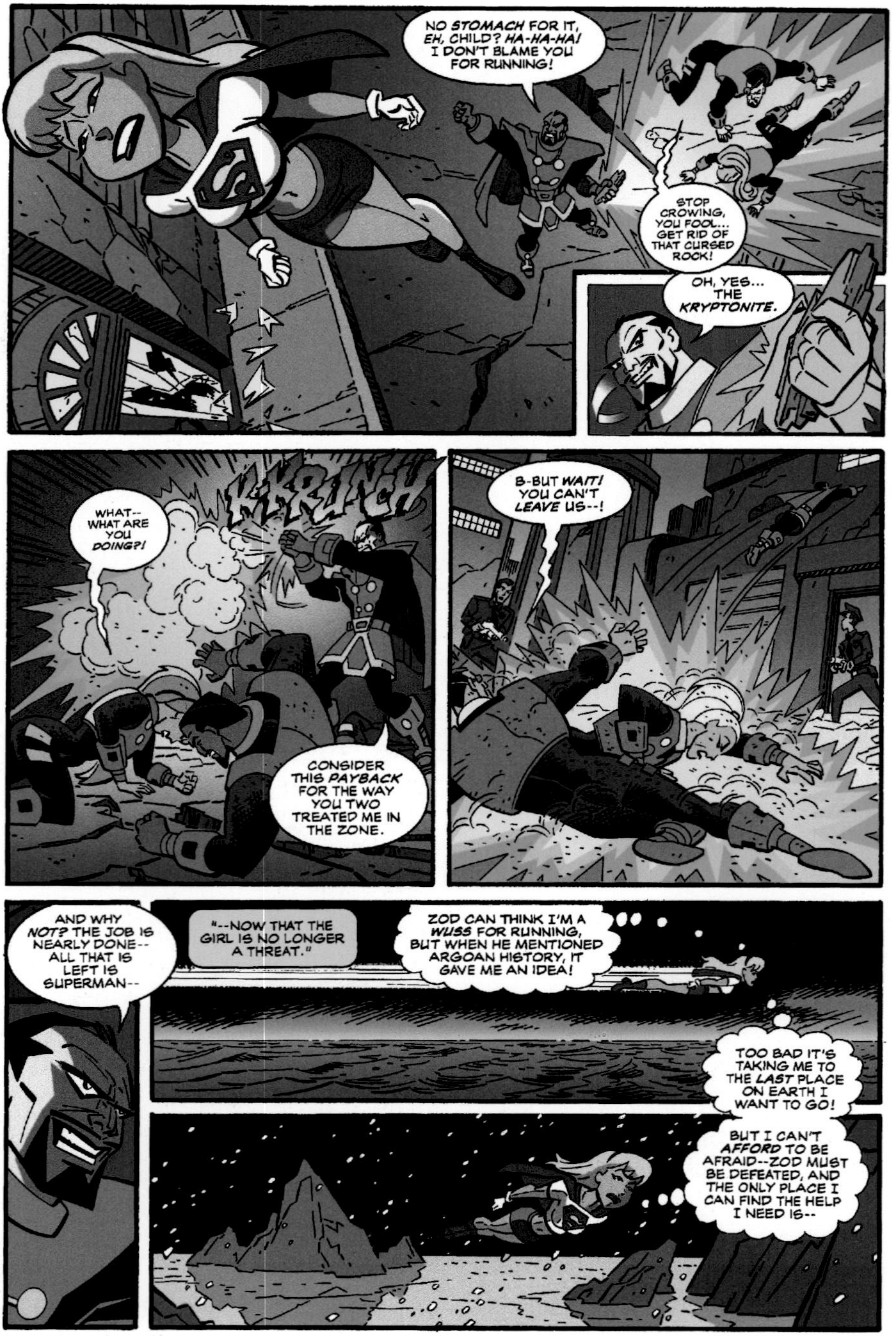

NO STOMACH FOR IT, EH, CHILD? HA-HA-HA! I DON'T BLAME YOU FOR RUNNING!
STOP CROWING, YOU FOOL... GET RID OF THAT CURSED ROCK!
OH, YES... THE KRYPTONITE.
KKRUNCH
WHAT-- WHAT ARE YOU DOING?!
CONSIDER THIS PAYBACK FOR THE WAY YOU TWO TREATED ME IN THE ZONE.
B-BUT WAIT! YOU CAN'T LEAVE US--!
AND WHY NOT? THE JOB IS NEARLY DONE-- ALL THAT IS LEFT IS SUPERMAN--
"--NOW THAT THE GIRL IS NO LONGER A THREAT."
ZOD CAN THINK I'M A WUSS FOR RUNNING, BUT WHEN HE MENTIONED ARGOAN HISTORY, IT GAVE ME AN IDEA!
TOO BAD IT'S TAKING ME TO THE LAST PLACE ON EARTH I WANT TO GO!
BUT I CAN'T AFFORD TO BE AFRAID--ZOD MUST BE DEFEATED, AND THE ONLY PLACE I CAN FIND THE HELP I NEED IS--

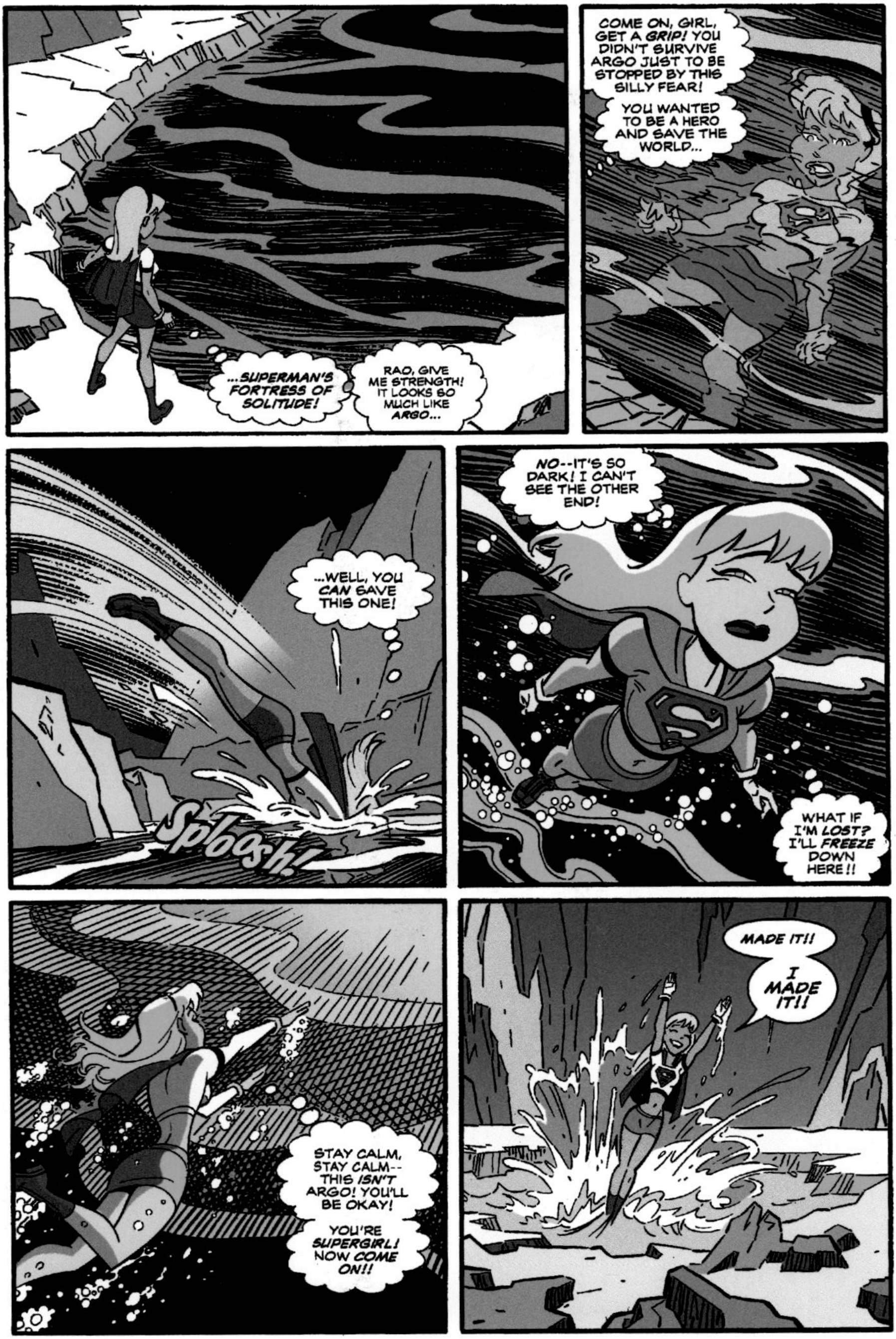
...SUPERMAN'S FORTRESS OF SOLITUDE!
RAO, GIVE ME STRENGTH! IT LOOKS SO MUCH LIKE ARGO...
COME ON, GIRL, GET A GRIP! YOU DIDN'T SURVIVE ARGO JUST TO BE STOPPED BY THIS SILLY FEAR!
YOU WANTED TO BE A HERO AND SAVE THE WORLD...
...WELL, YOU CAN SAVE THIS ONE!
Sploosh!
NO--IT'S SO DARK! I CAN'T SEE THE OTHER END!
WHAT IF I'M LOST? I'LL FREEZE DOWN HERE!!
STAY CALM, STAY CALM-- THIS ISN'T ARGO! YOU'LL BE OKAY!
YOU'RE SUPERGIRL! NOW COME ON!!
MADE IT!!
I MADE IT!!

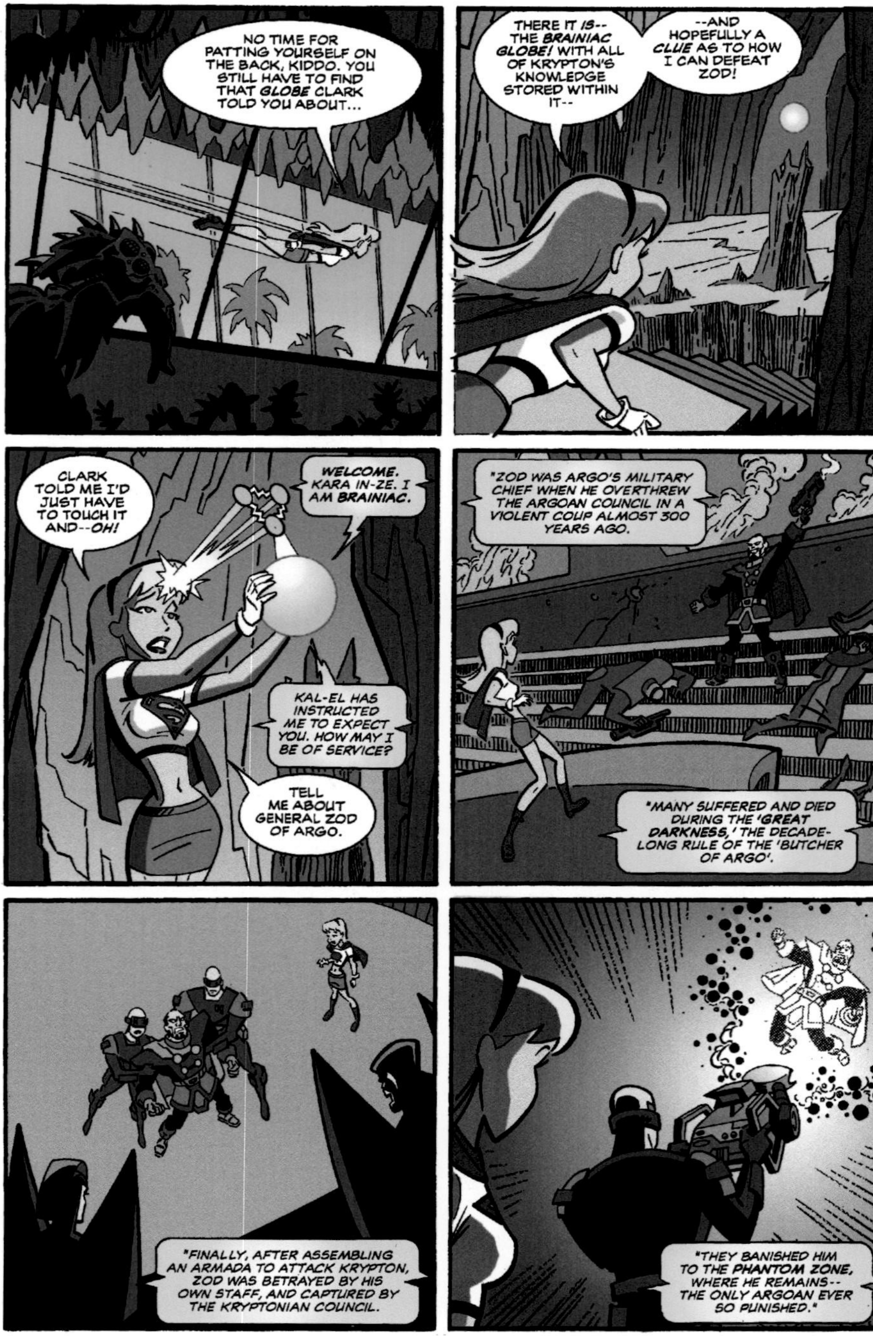
NO TIME FOR PATTING YOURSELF ON THE BACK, KIDDO. YOU STILL HAVE TO FIND THAT GLOBE CLARK TOLD YOU ABOUT...
THERE IT IS-- THE BRAINIAC GLOBE! WITH ALL OF KRYPTON'S KNOWLEDGE STORED WITHIN IT--
--AND HOPEFULLY A CLUE AS TO HOW I CAN DEFEAT ZOD!
CLARK TOLD ME I'D JUST HAVE TO TOUCH IT AND--OH!
WELCOME. KARA IN-ZE. I AM BRAINIAC.
KAL-EL HAS INSTRUCTED ME TO EXPECT YOU. HOW MAY I BE OF SERVICE?
TELL ME ABOUT GENERAL ZOD OF ARGO.
"ZOD WAS ARGO'S MILITARY CHIEF WHEN HE OVERTHREW THE ARGOAN COUNCIL IN A VIOLENT COUP ALMOST 300 YEARS AGO.
"MANY SUFFERED AND DIED DURING THE 'GREAT DARKNESS,' THE DECADE-LONG RULE OF THE 'BUTCHER OF ARGO'.
"FINALLY, AFTER ASSEMBLING AN ARMADA TO ATTACK KRYPTON, ZOD WAS BETRAYED BY HIS OWN STAFF, AND CAPTURED BY THE KRYPTONIAN COUNCIL.
"THEY BANISHED HIM TO THE PHANTOM ZONE, WHERE HE REMAINS-- THE ONLY ARGOAN EVER SO PUNISHED."

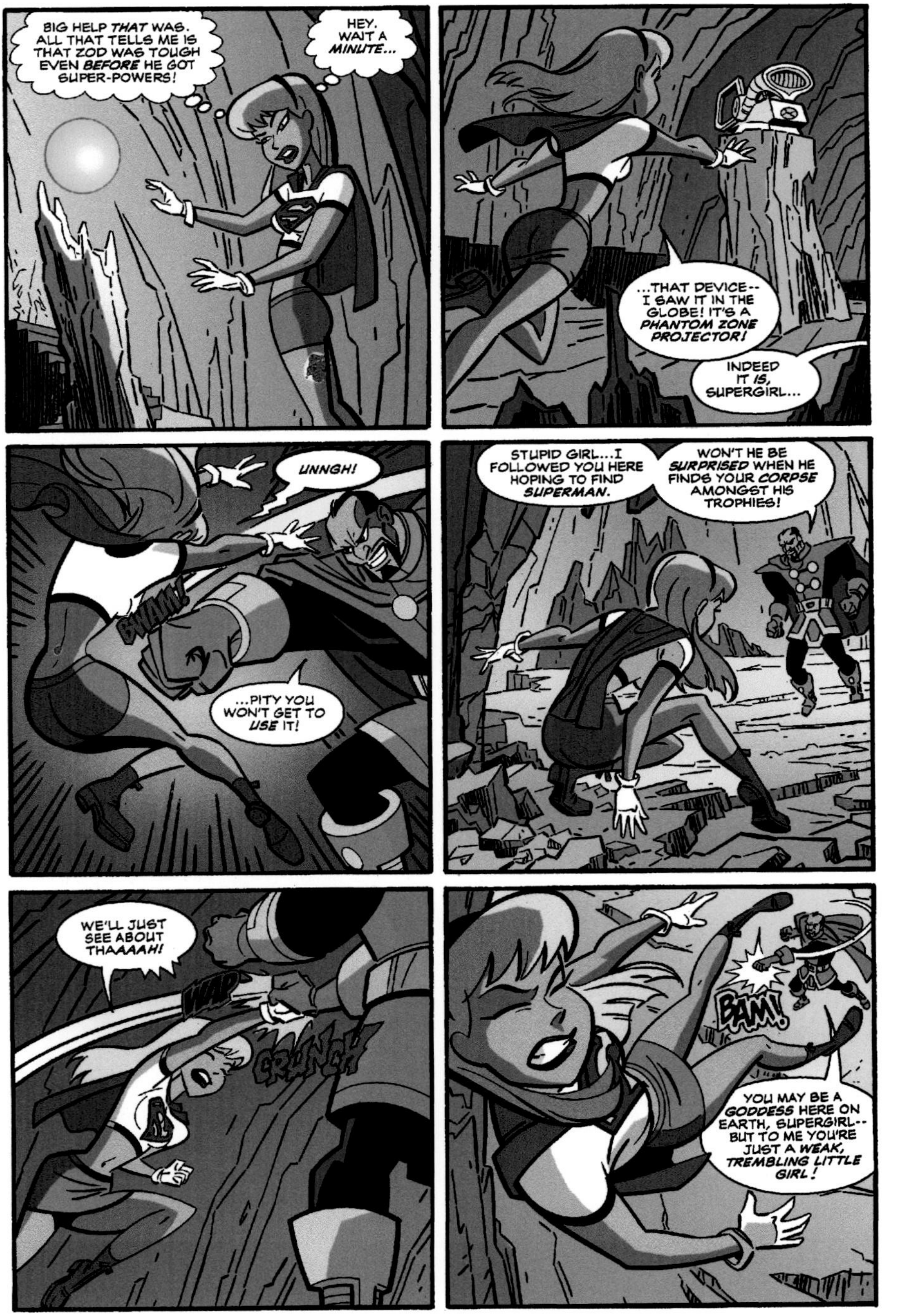
BIG HELP THAT WAS. ALL THAT TELLS ME IS THAT ZOD WAS TOUGH EVEN BEFORE HE GOT SUPER-POWERS!
HEY. WAIT A MINUTE...
...THAT DEVICE-- I SAW IT IN THE GLOBE! IT'S A PHANTOM ZONE PROJECTOR!
INDEED IT IS, SUPERGIRL...
UNNGH!
BWAM!
...PITY YOU WON'T GET TO USE IT!
STUPID GIRL...I FOLLOWED YOU HERE HOPING TO FIND SUPERMAN.
WON'T HE BE SURPRISED WHEN HE FINDS YOUR CORPSE AMONGST HIS TROPHIES!
WE'LL JUST SEE ABOUT THAAAAH!
WAP
CRUNCH
BAM!
YOU MAY BE A GODDESS HERE ON EARTH, SUPERGIRL-- BUT TO ME YOU'RE JUST A WEAK, TREMBLING LITTLE GIRL!

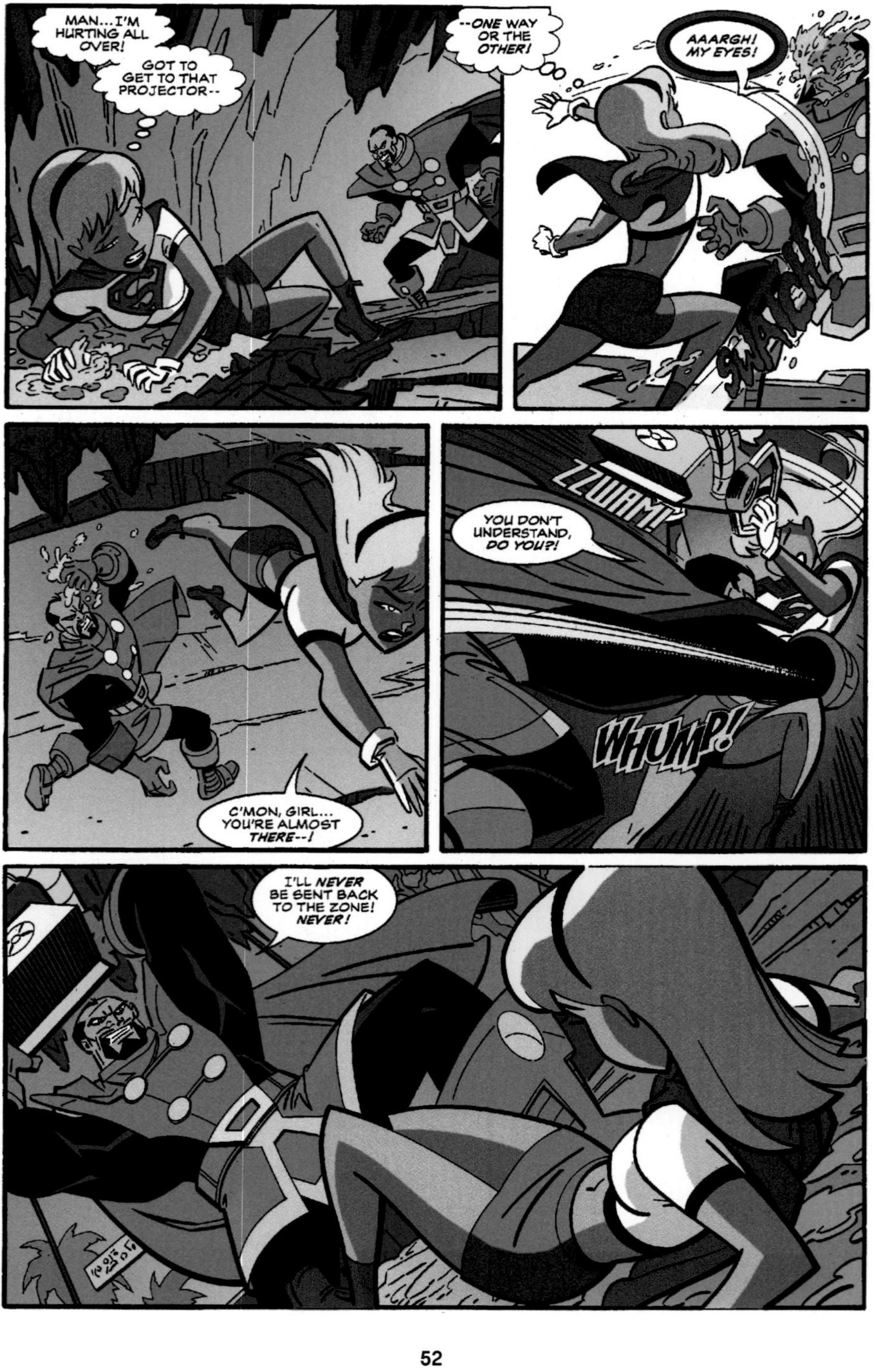
MAN...I'M HURTING ALL OVER!
GOT TO GET TO THAT PROJECTOR--
--ONE WAY OR THE OTHER!
AAARGH! MY EYES!
C'MON, GIRL... YOU'RE ALMOST THERE--!
ZZWAM!
YOU DON'T UNDERSTAND, DO YOU?!
WHUMP!
I'LL NEVER BE SENT BACK TO THE ZONE! NEVER!

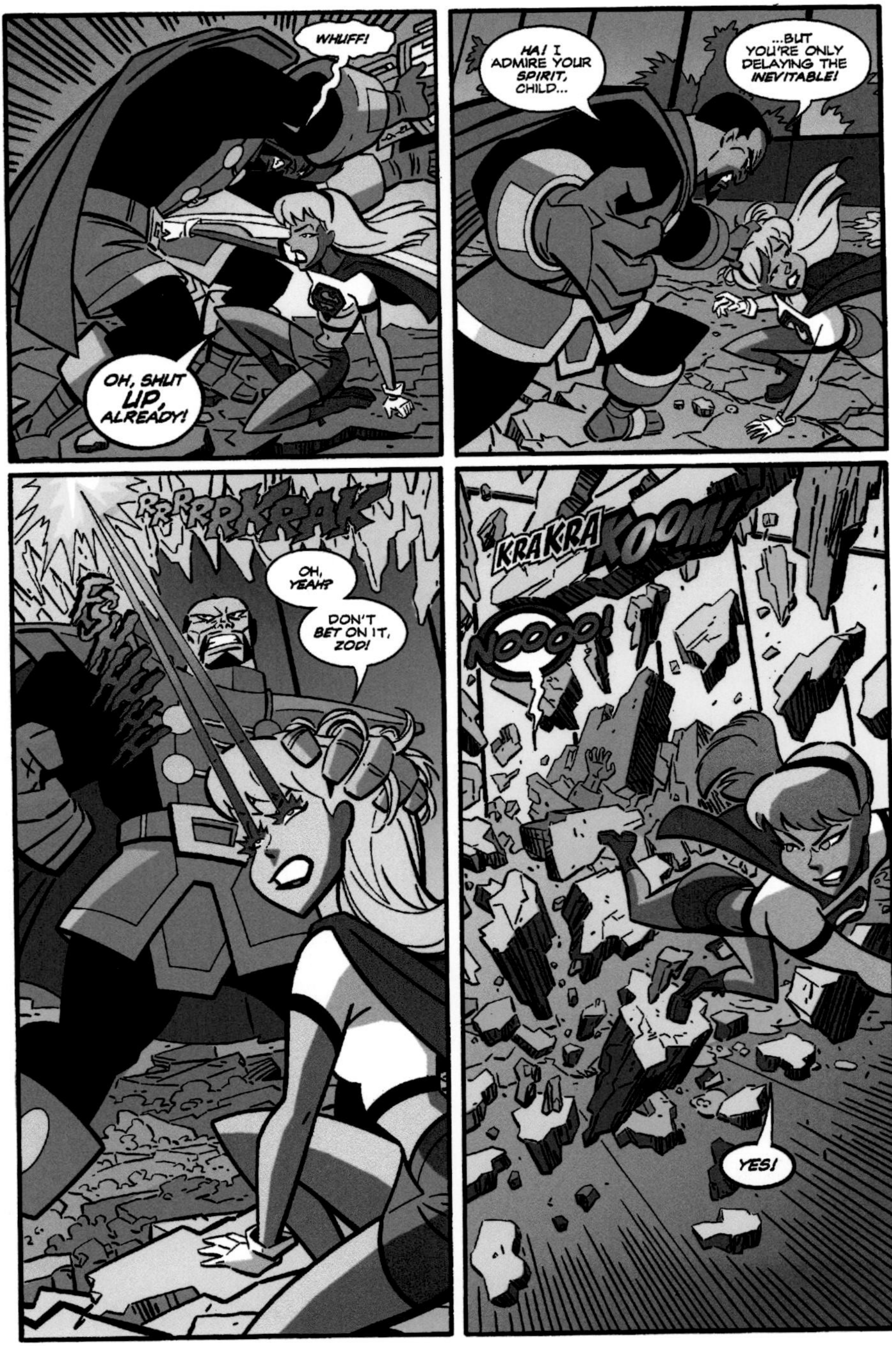
WHUFF!
OH, SHUT UP, ALREADY!
HA! I ADMIRE YOUR SPIRIT, CHILD...
...BUT YOU'RE ONLY DELAYING THE INEVITABLE!
RRRRRKRAK
OH, YEAH?
DON'T BET ON IT, ZOD!
KRAKRA KOOM!
NOOOO!
YES!

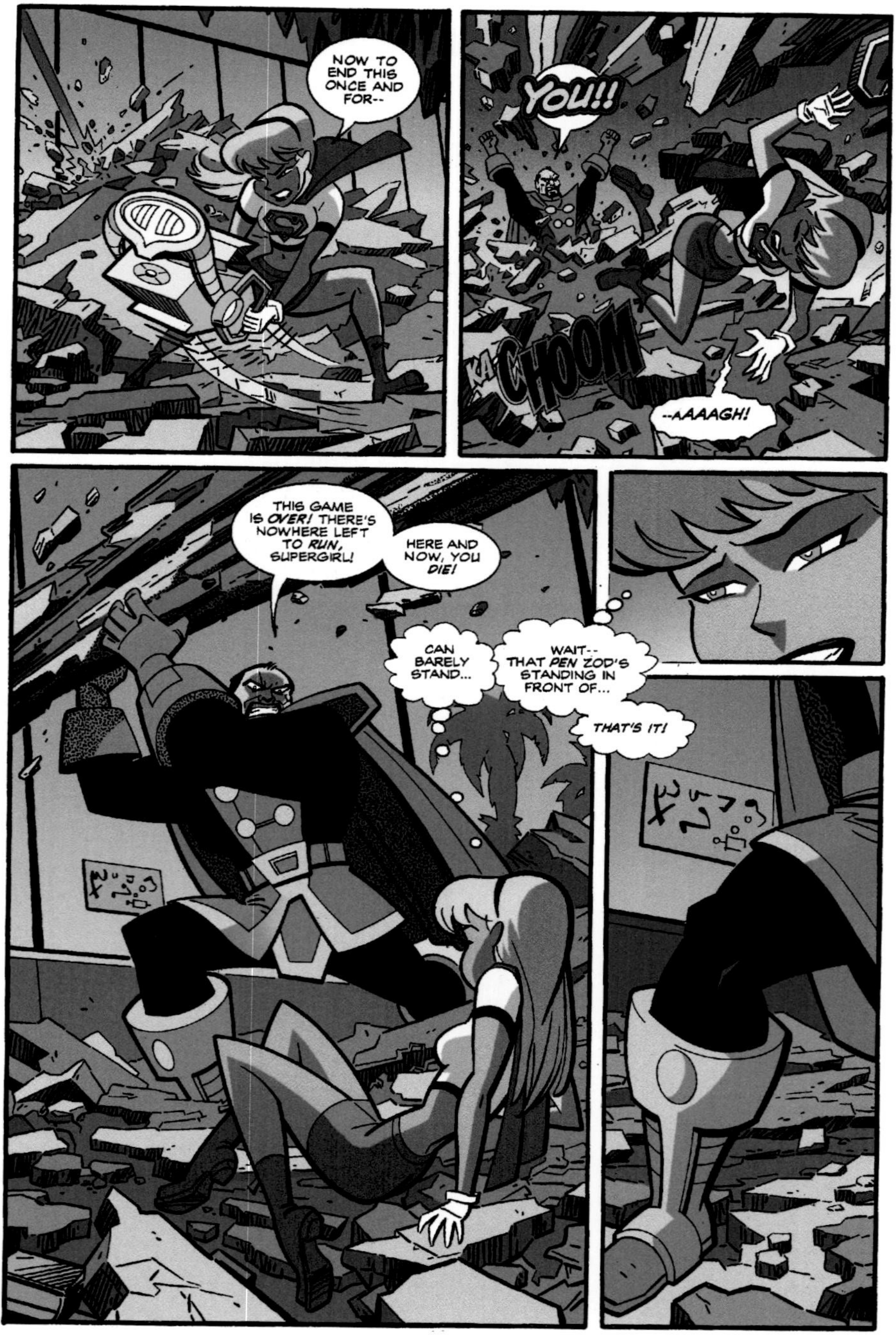
NOW TO END THIS ONCE AND FOR--
YOU!!
KA-CHOOM
--AAAAGH!
THIS GAME IS OVER! THERE'S NOWHERE LEFT TO RUN, SUPERGIRL!
HERE AND NOW, YOU DIE!
CAN BARELY STAND...
WAIT-- THAT PEN ZOD'S STANDING IN FRONT OF...
THAT'S IT!

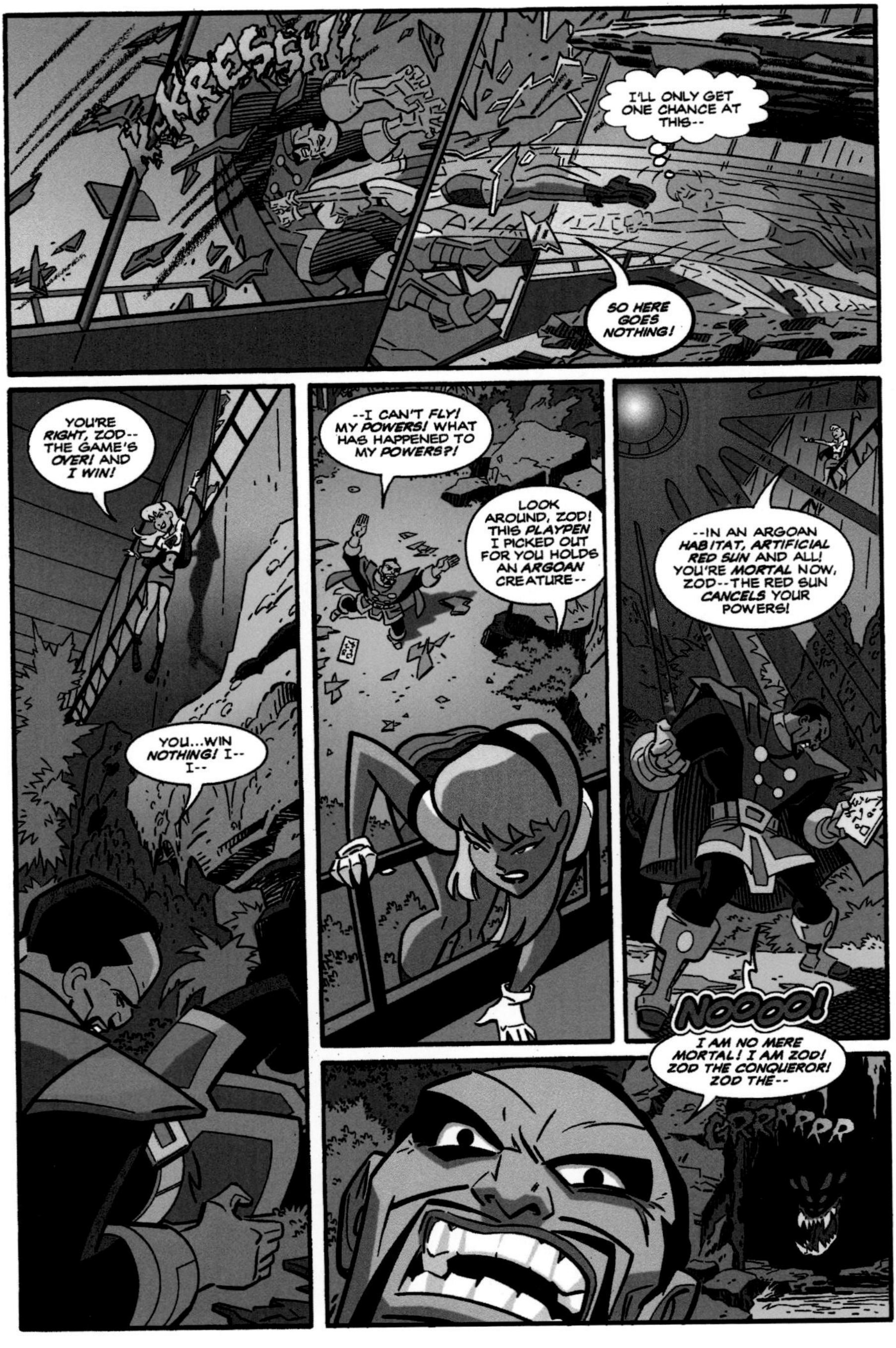
KRESSH!
I'LL ONLY GET ONE CHANCE AT THIS--
SO HERE GOES NOTHING!
YOU'RE RIGHT, ZOD-- THE GAME'S OVER! AND I WIN!
YOU...WIN NOTHING! I-- I--
--I CAN'T FLY! MY POWERS! WHAT HAS HAPPENED TO MY POWERS?!
LOOK AROUND, ZOD! THIS PLAYPEN I PICKED OUT FOR YOU HOLDS AN ARGOAN CREATURE--
--IN AN ARGOAN HABITAT, ARTIFICIAL RED SUN AND ALL! YOU'RE MORTAL NOW, ZOD--THE RED SUN CANCELS YOUR POWERS!
NOOOOO!
I AM NO MERE MORTAL! I AM ZOD! ZOD THE CONQUEROR! ZOD THE--
GRRRRRR

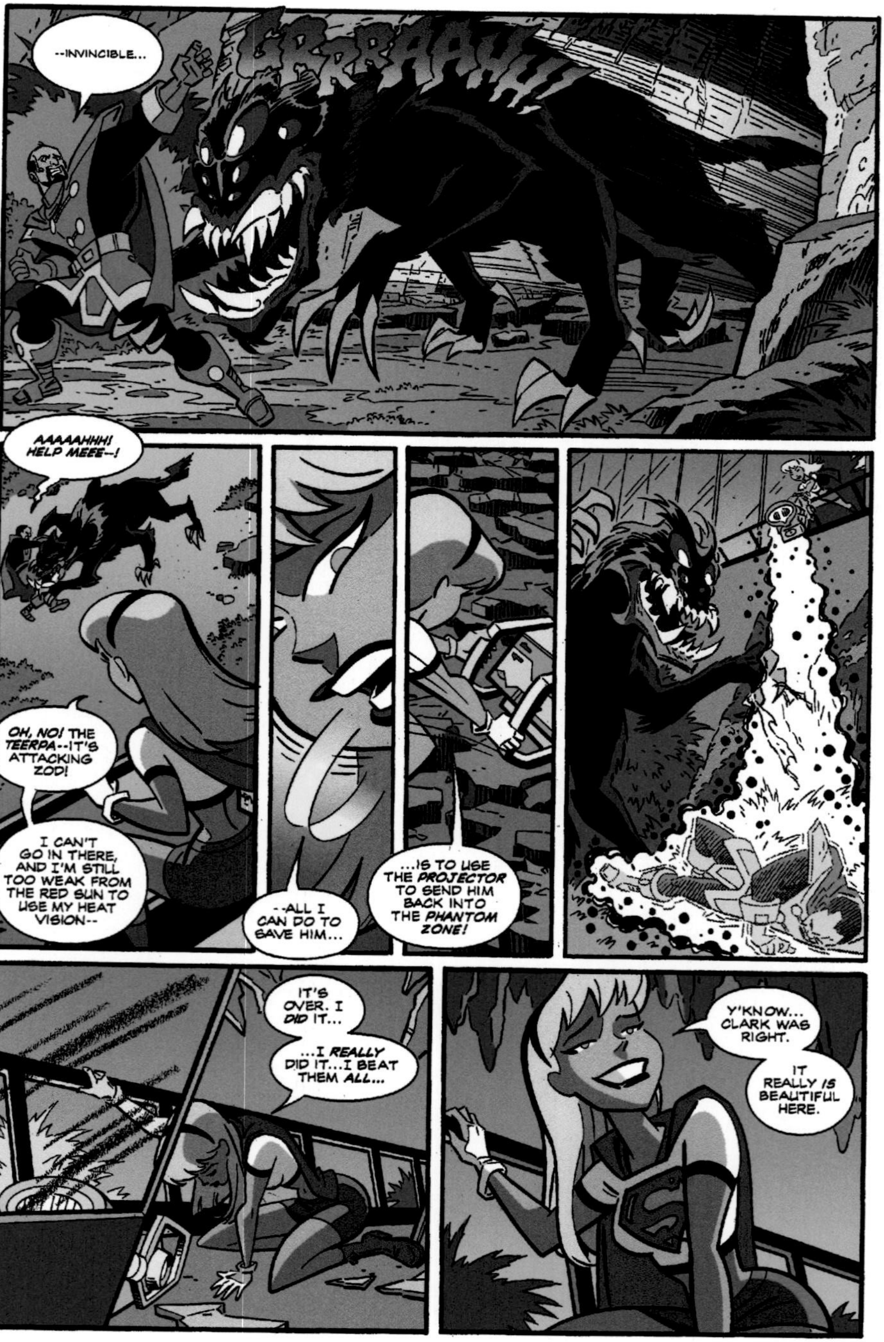

--INVINCIBLE...
GRRRAAAH!!
AAAAAHHH! HELP MEEE--!
OH, NO! THE TEERPA--IT'S ATTACKING ZOD!
I CAN'T GO IN THERE, AND I'M STILL TOO WEAK FROM THE RED SUN TO USE MY HEAT VISION--
--ALL I CAN DO TO SAVE HIM...
...IS TO USE THE PROJECTOR TO SEND HIM BACK INTO THE PHANTOM ZONE!
IT'S OVER. I DID IT...
...I REALLY DID IT...I BEAT THEM ALL...
Y'KNOW... CLARK WAS RIGHT.
IT REALLY IS BEAUTIFUL HERE.

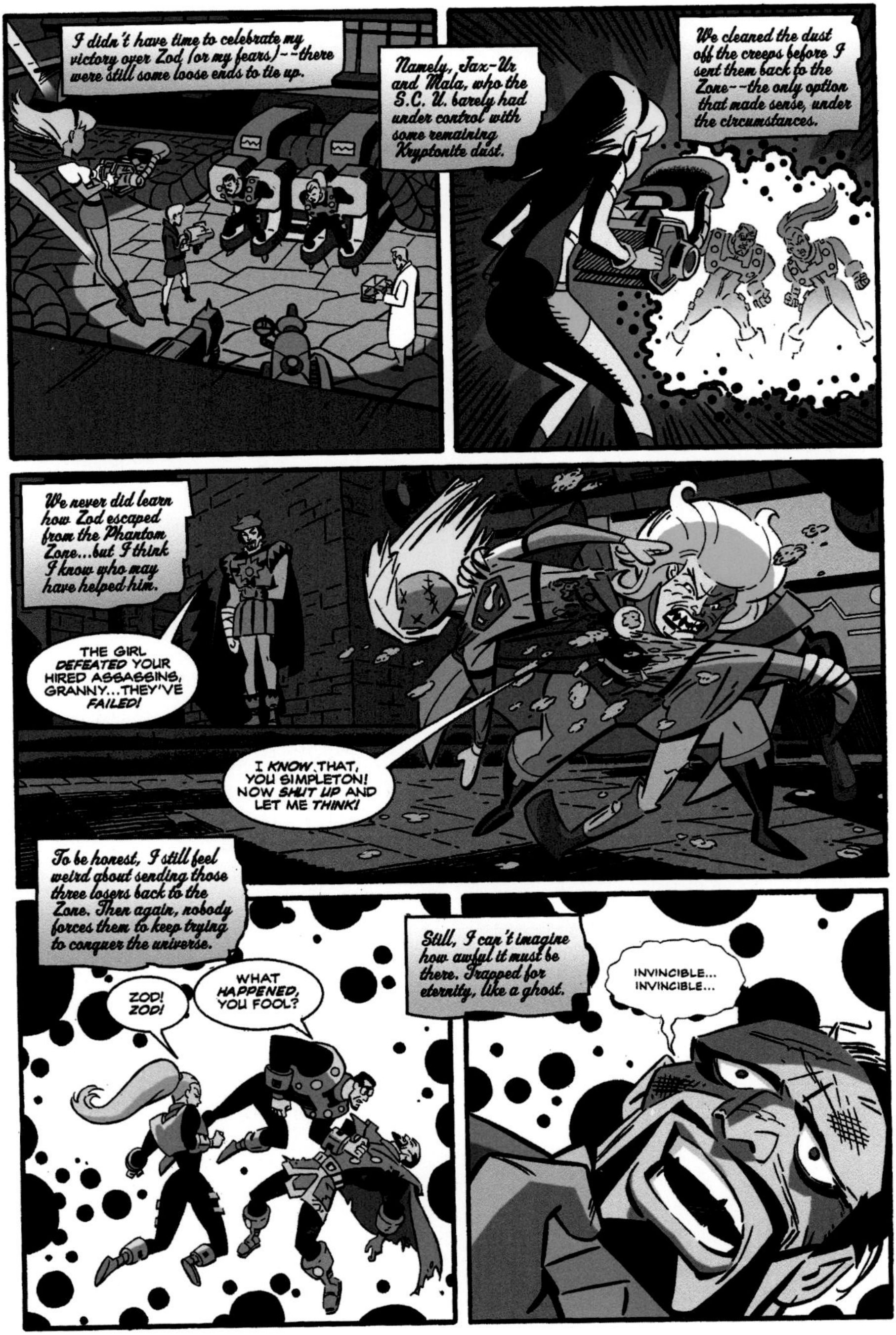
I didn't have time to celebrate my victory over Zod (or my fears)--there were still some loose ends to tie up.
Namely, Jax-Ur and Mala, who the S.C.U. barely had under control with some remaining Kryptonite dust.
We cleaned the dust off the creeps before I sent them back to the Zone--the only option that made sense, under the circumstances.
We never did learn how Zod escaped from the Phantom Zone...but I think I know who may have helped him.
THE GIRL DEFEATED YOUR HIRED ASSASSINS, GRANNY...THEY'VE FAILED!
I KNOW THAT, YOU SIMPLETON! NOW SHUT UP AND LET ME THINK!
To be honest, I still feel weird about sending those three losers back to the Zone. Then again, nobody forces them to keep trying to conquer the universe.
ZOD! ZOD!
WHAT HAPPENED, YOU FOOL?
Still, I can't imagine how awful it must be there. Trapped for eternity, like a ghost.
INVINCIBLE... INVINCIBLE...

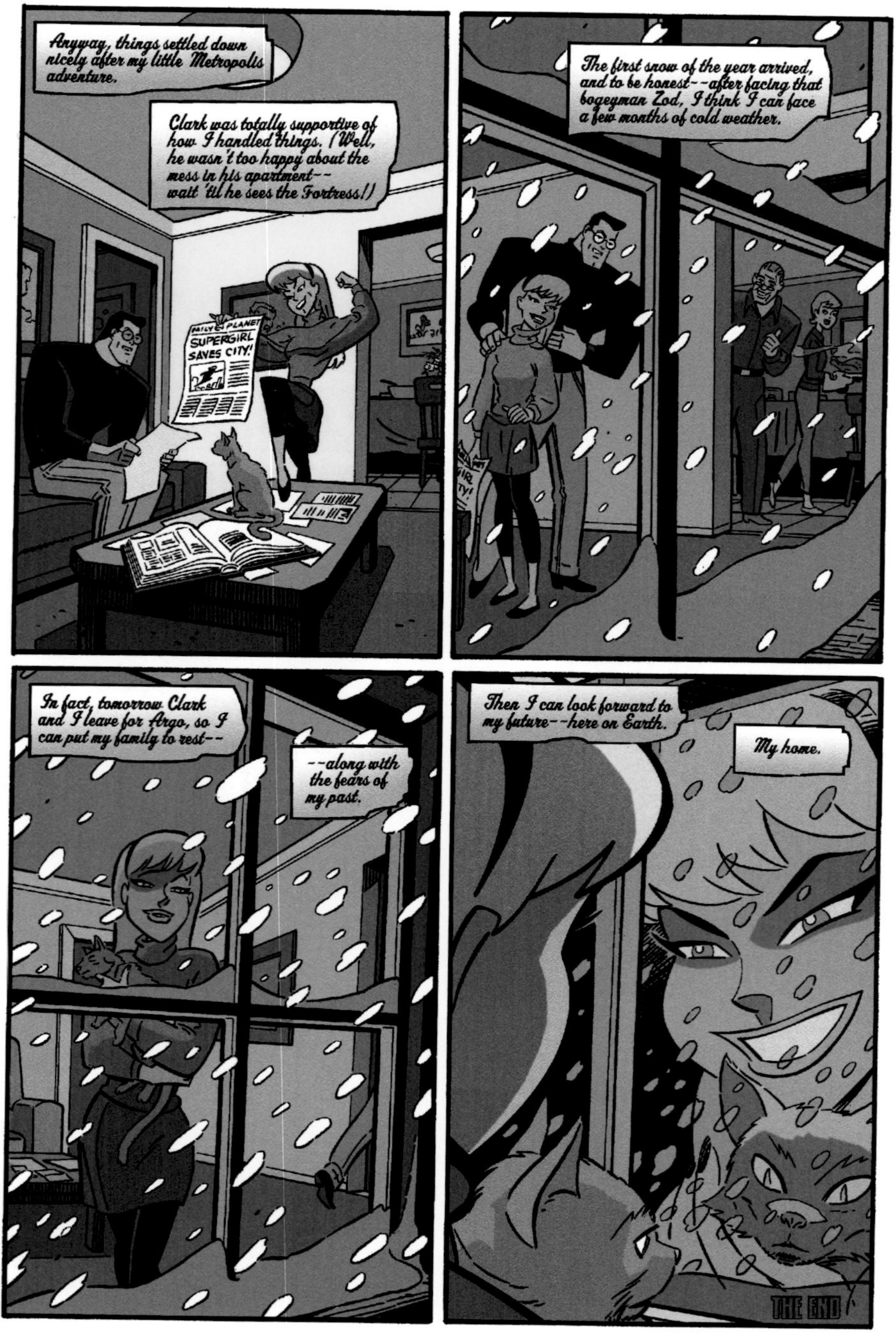
Anyway, things settled down nicely after my little Metropolis adventure.
Clark was totally supportive of how I handled things. (Well, he wasn't too happy about the mess in his apartment--wait 'til he sees the Fortress!)
DAILY PLANET
SUPERGIRL SAVES CITY!
The first snow of the year arrived, and to be honest--after facing that bogeyman Zod, I think I can face a few months of cold weather.
In fact, tomorrow Clark and I leave for Argo, so I can put my family to rest--
--along with the fears of my past.
Then I can look forward to my future--here on Earth.
My home.
THE END

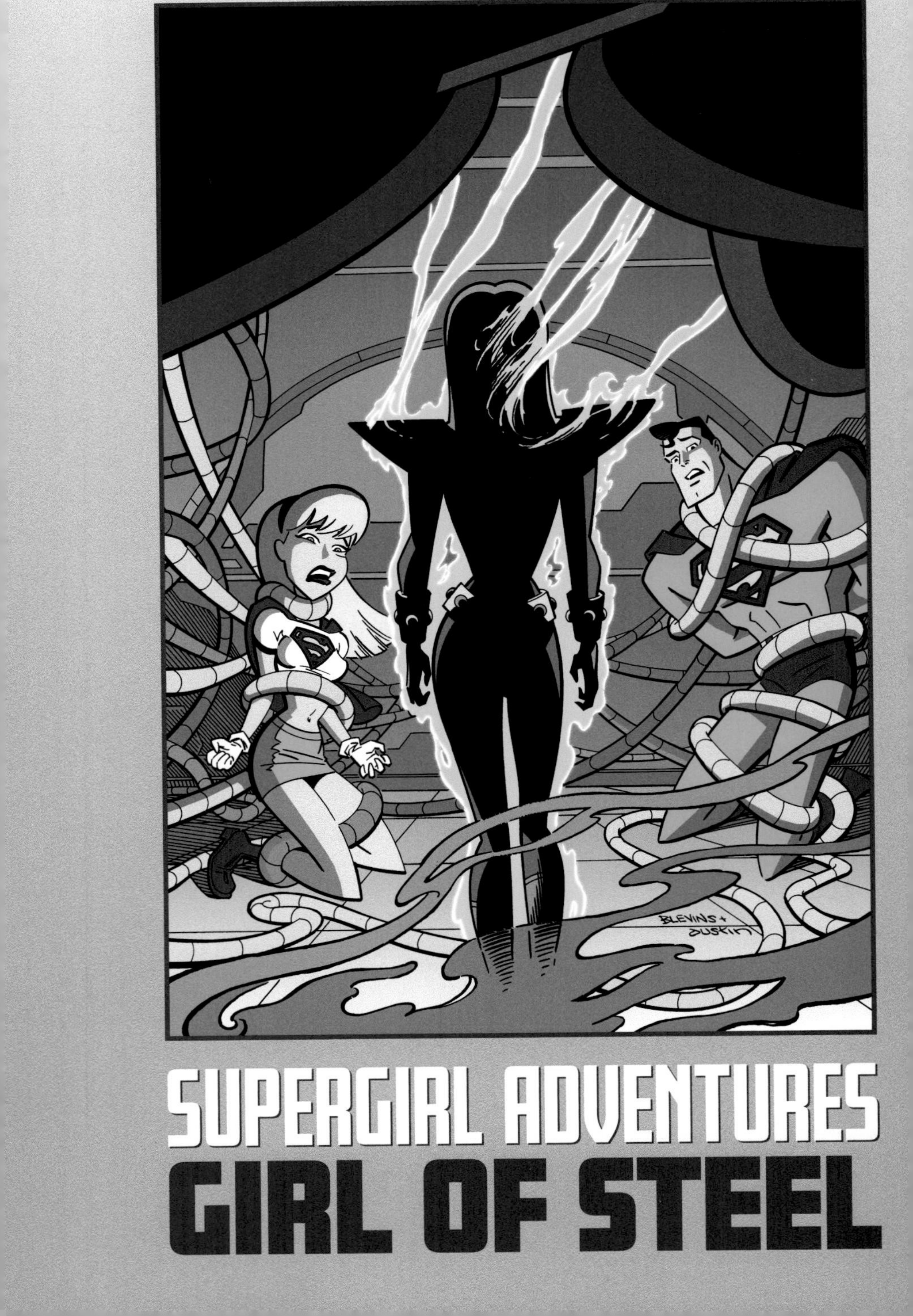
BLEVINS + AUSTIN

# SUPERGIRL ADVENTURES
# GIRL OF STEEL

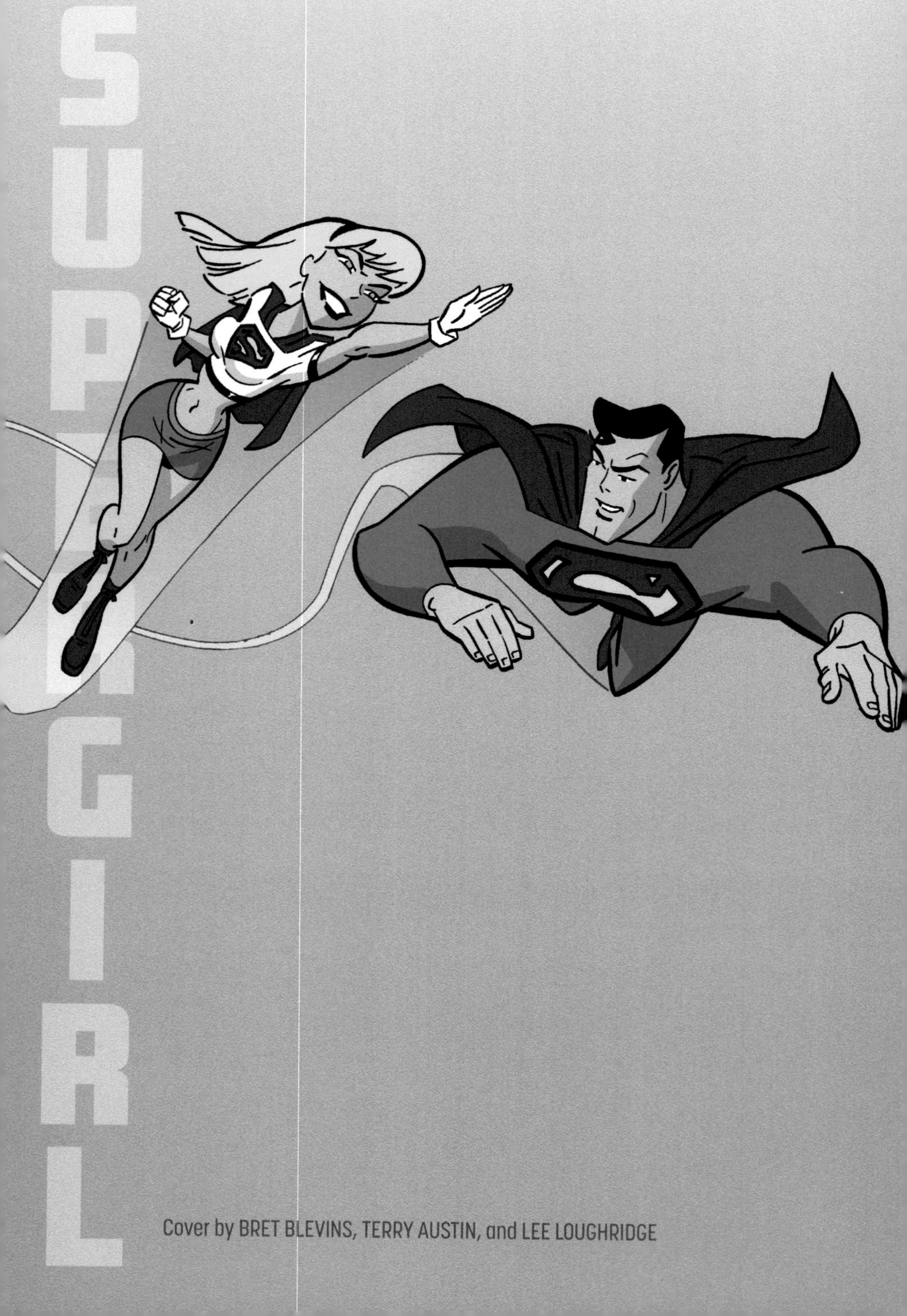
SUPERGIRL

Cover by BRET BLEVINS, TERRY AUSTIN, and LEE LOUGHRIDGE

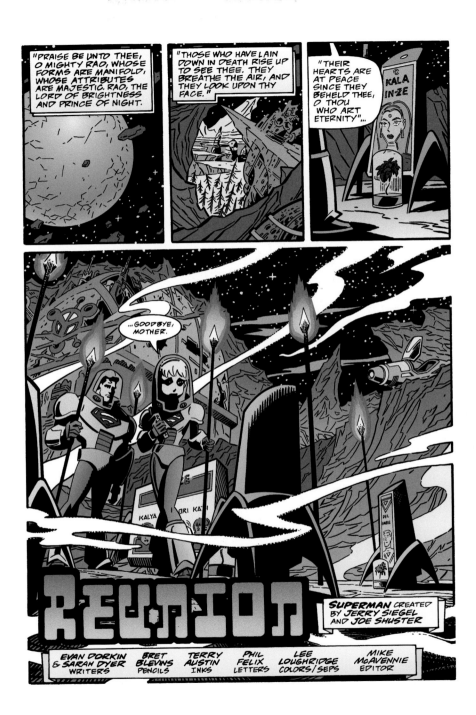

"PRAISE BE UNTO THEE, O MIGHTY RAO, WHOSE FORMS ARE MANIFOLD, WHOSE ATTRIBUTES ARE MAJESTIC. RAO, THE LORD OF BRIGHTNESS AND PRINCE OF NIGHT.

"THOSE WHO HAVE LAIN DOWN IN DEATH RISE UP TO SEE THEE. THEY BREATHE THE AIR, AND THEY LOOK UPON THY FACE."

"THEIR HEARTS ARE AT PEACE SINCE THEY BEHELD THEE, O THOU WHO ART ETERNITY"...

KALA IN-ZE

...GOODBYE, MOTHER.

KALYA     ORI KATH

DEL HARE

# REUNION

SUPERMAN CREATED BY JERRY SIEGEL AND JOE SHUSTER

EVAN DORKIN & SARAH DYER
WRITERS

BRET BLEVINS
PENCILS

TERRY AUSTIN
INKS

PHIL FELIX
LETTERS

LEE LOUGHRIDGE
COLORS/SEPS

MIKE McAVENNIE
EDITOR

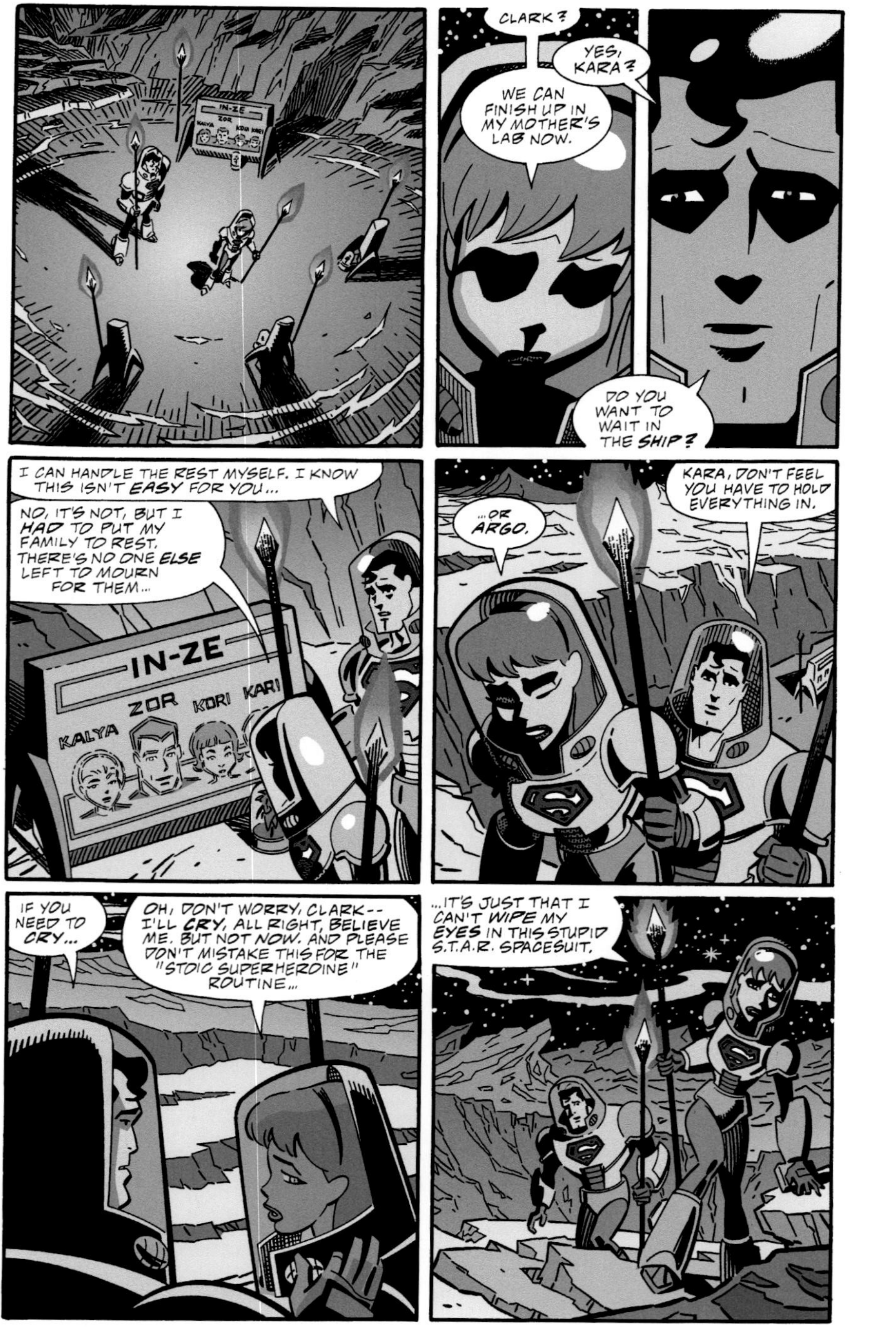
IN-ZE
KALYA
ZOR
KORI
KARI
CLARK?
YES, KARA?
WE CAN FINISH UP IN MY MOTHER'S LAB NOW.
DO YOU WANT TO WAIT IN THE SHIP?
I CAN HANDLE THE REST MYSELF. I KNOW THIS ISN'T EASY FOR YOU...
NO, IT'S NOT, BUT I HAD TO PUT MY FAMILY TO REST. THERE'S NO ONE ELSE LEFT TO MOURN FOR THEM...
IN-ZE
ZOR
KORI
KARI
KALYA
...OR ARGO.
KARA, DON'T FEEL YOU HAVE TO HOLD EVERYTHING IN.
IF YOU NEED TO CRY...
OH, DON'T WORRY, CLARK-- I'LL CRY, ALL RIGHT, BELIEVE ME. BUT NOT NOW. AND PLEASE DON'T MISTAKE THIS FOR THE "STOIC SUPERHEROINE" ROUTINE...
...IT'S JUST THAT I CAN'T WIPE MY EYES IN THIS STUPID S.T.A.R. SPACESUIT.

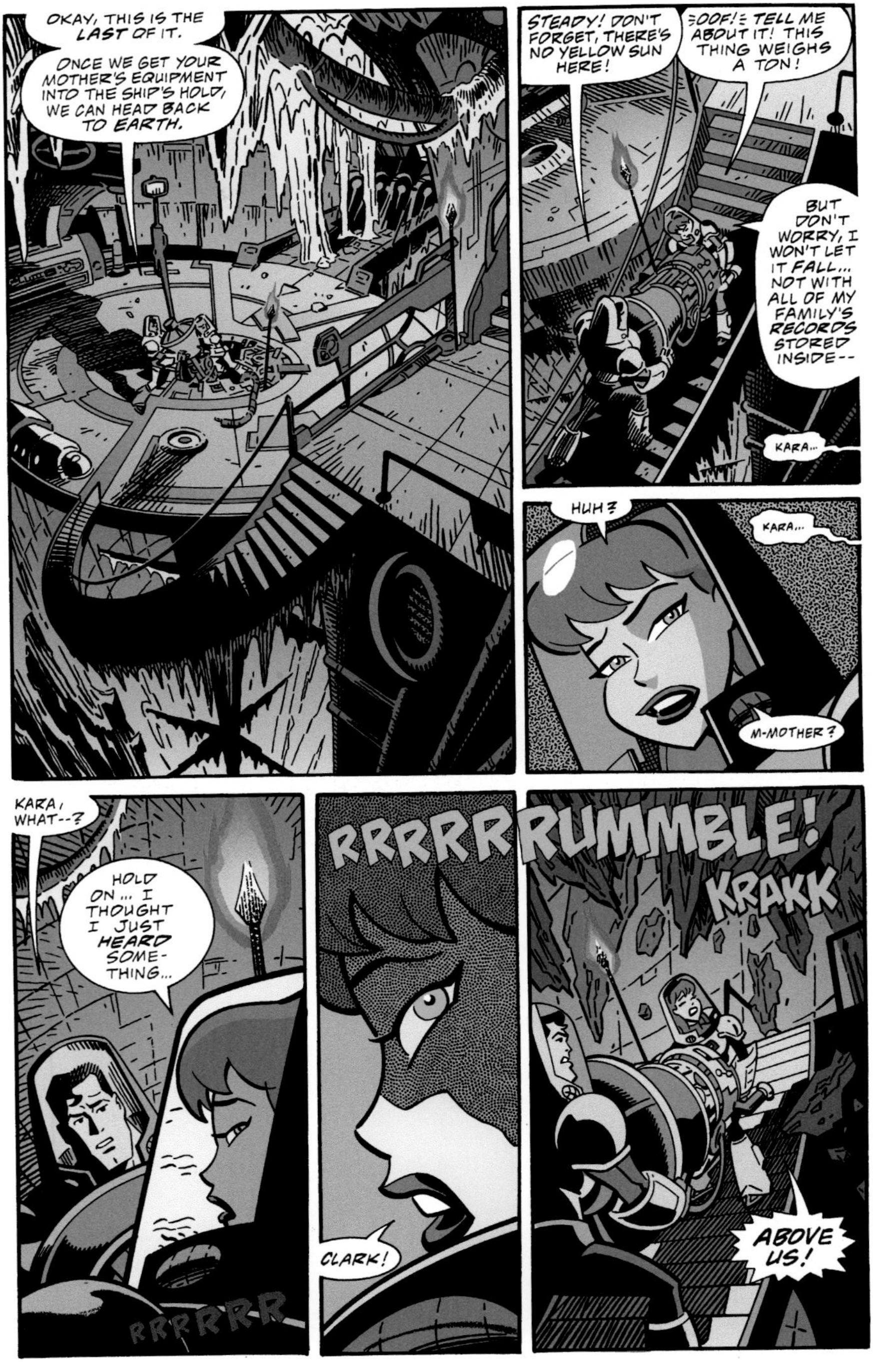
OKAY, THIS IS THE LAST OF IT.
ONCE WE GET YOUR MOTHER'S EQUIPMENT INTO THE SHIP'S HOLD, WE CAN HEAD BACK TO EARTH.
STEADY! DON'T FORGET, THERE'S NO YELLOW SUN HERE!
OOF! TELL ME ABOUT IT! THIS THING WEIGHS A TON!
BUT DON'T WORRY, I WON'T LET IT FALL... NOT WITH ALL OF MY FAMILY'S RECORDS STORED INSIDE--
KARA...
HUH?
KARA...
M-MOTHER?
KARA, WHAT--?
HOLD ON... I THOUGHT I JUST HEARD SOMETHING...
RRRRRR
RRRRRRUMMBLE!
CLARK!
KRAKK
ABOVE US!

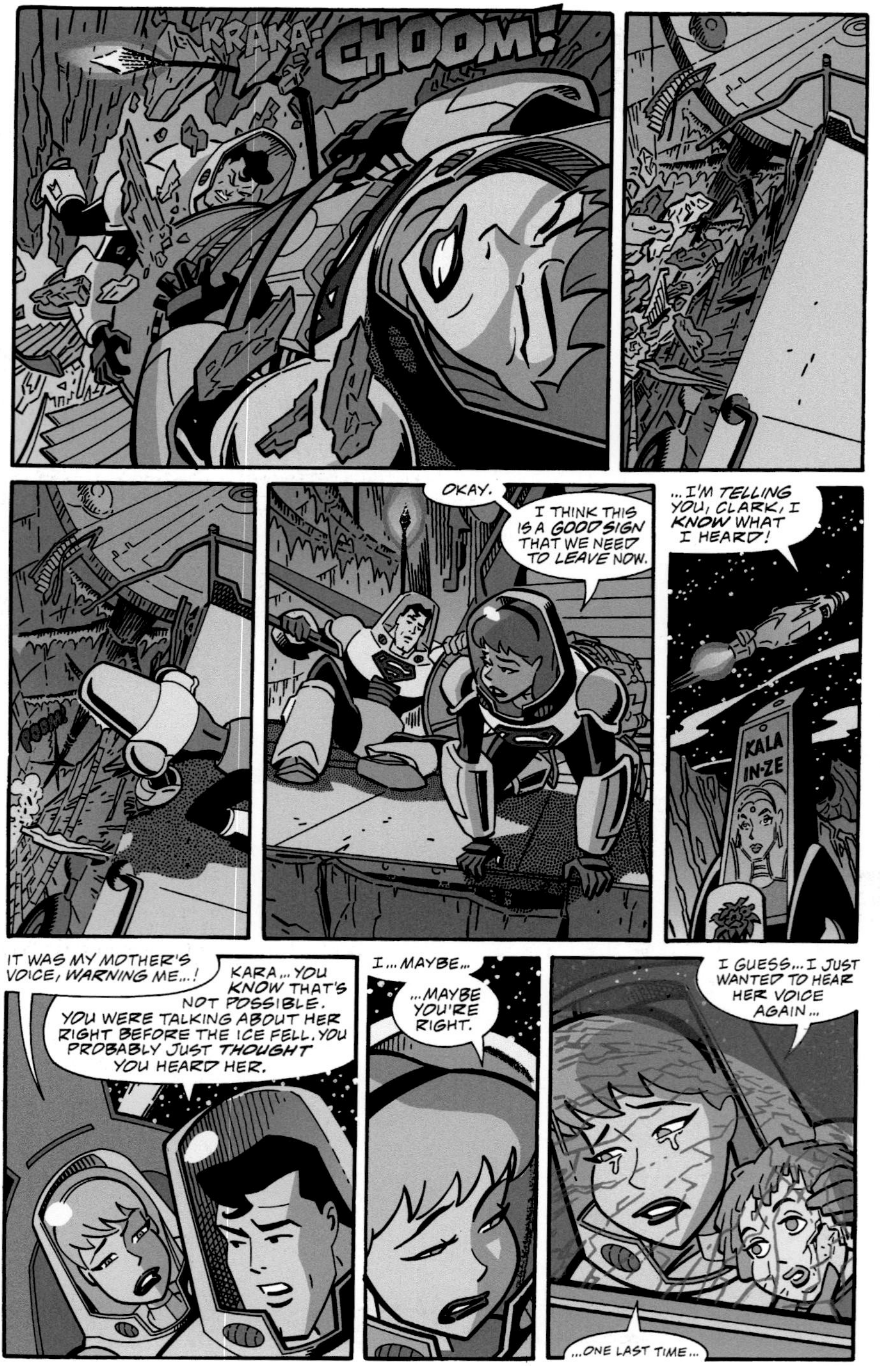
KRAKA-CHOOM!
OKAY.
I THINK THIS IS A GOOD SIGN THAT WE NEED TO LEAVE NOW.
...I'M TELLING YOU, CLARK, I KNOW WHAT I HEARD!
KALA IN-ZE
IT WAS MY MOTHER'S VOICE, WARNING ME...!
KARA... YOU KNOW THAT'S NOT POSSIBLE. YOU WERE TALKING ABOUT HER RIGHT BEFORE THE ICE FELL. YOU PROBABLY JUST THOUGHT YOU HEARD HER.
I... MAYBE...
...MAYBE YOU'RE RIGHT.
I GUESS... I JUST WANTED TO HEAR HER VOICE AGAIN...
...ONE LAST TIME...

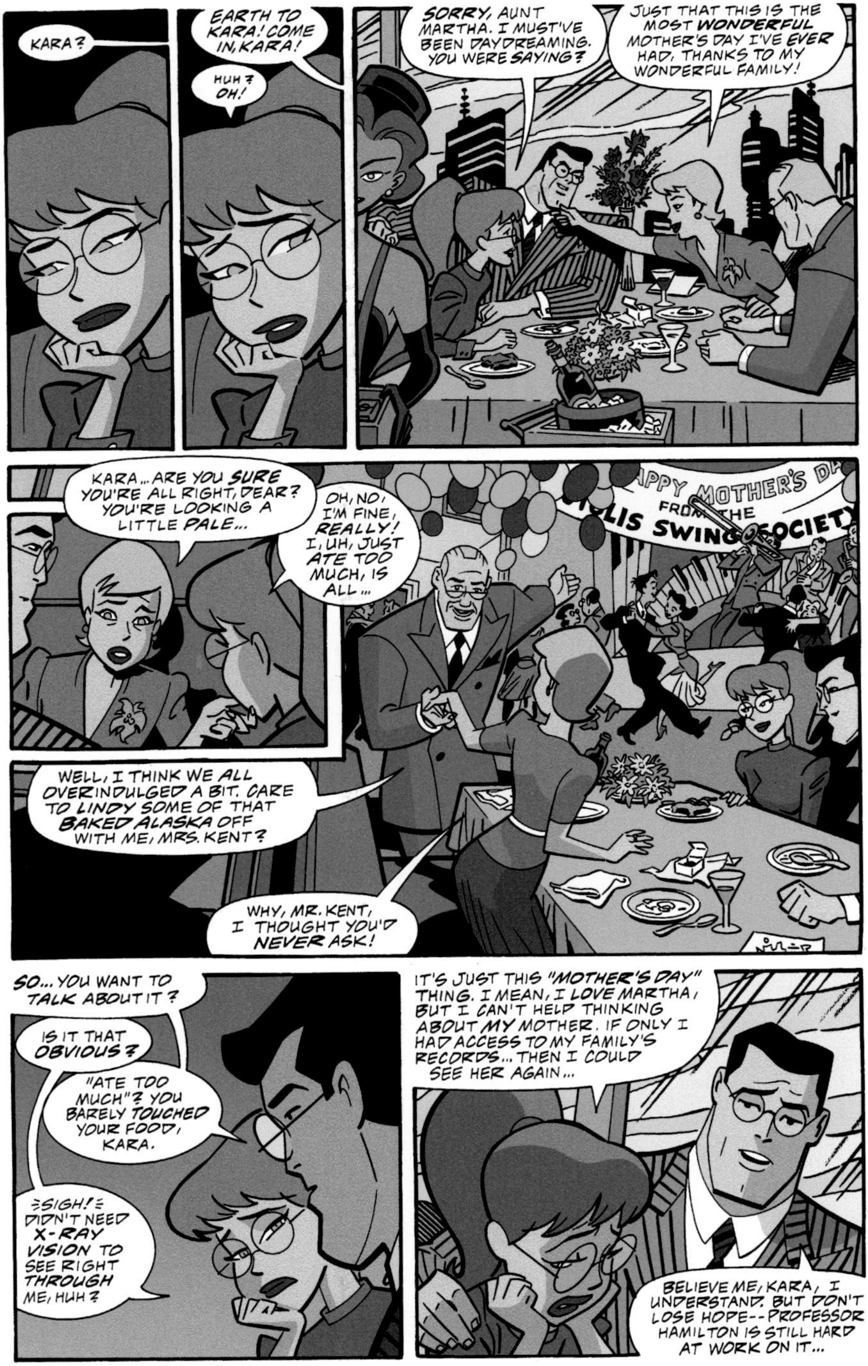
KARA?
EARTH TO KARA! COME IN, KARA!
HUH? OH!
SORRY, AUNT MARTHA. I MUST'VE BEEN DAYDREAMING. YOU WERE SAYING?
JUST THAT THIS IS THE MOST WONDERFUL MOTHER'S DAY I'VE EVER HAD, THANKS TO MY WONDERFUL FAMILY!
KARA... ARE YOU SURE YOU'RE ALL RIGHT, DEAR? YOU'RE LOOKING A LITTLE PALE...
OH, NO, I'M FINE, REALLY! I, UH, JUST ATE TOO MUCH, IS ALL...
WELL, I THINK WE ALL OVERINDULGED A BIT. CARE TO LINDY SOME OF THAT BAKED ALASKA OFF WITH ME, MRS. KENT?
WHY, MR. KENT, I THOUGHT YOU'D NEVER ASK!
SO... YOU WANT TO TALK ABOUT IT?
IS IT THAT OBVIOUS?
"ATE TOO MUCH"? YOU BARELY TOUCHED YOUR FOOD, KARA.
=SIGH!= DIDN'T NEED X-RAY VISION TO SEE RIGHT THROUGH ME, HUH?
IT'S JUST THIS "MOTHER'S DAY" THING. I MEAN, I LOVE MARTHA, BUT I CAN'T HELP THINKING ABOUT MY MOTHER. IF ONLY I HAD ACCESS TO MY FAMILY'S RECORDS... THEN I COULD SEE HER AGAIN...
BELIEVE ME, KARA, I UNDERSTAND. BUT DON'T LOSE HOPE--PROFESSOR HAMILTON IS STILL HARD AT WORK ON IT...

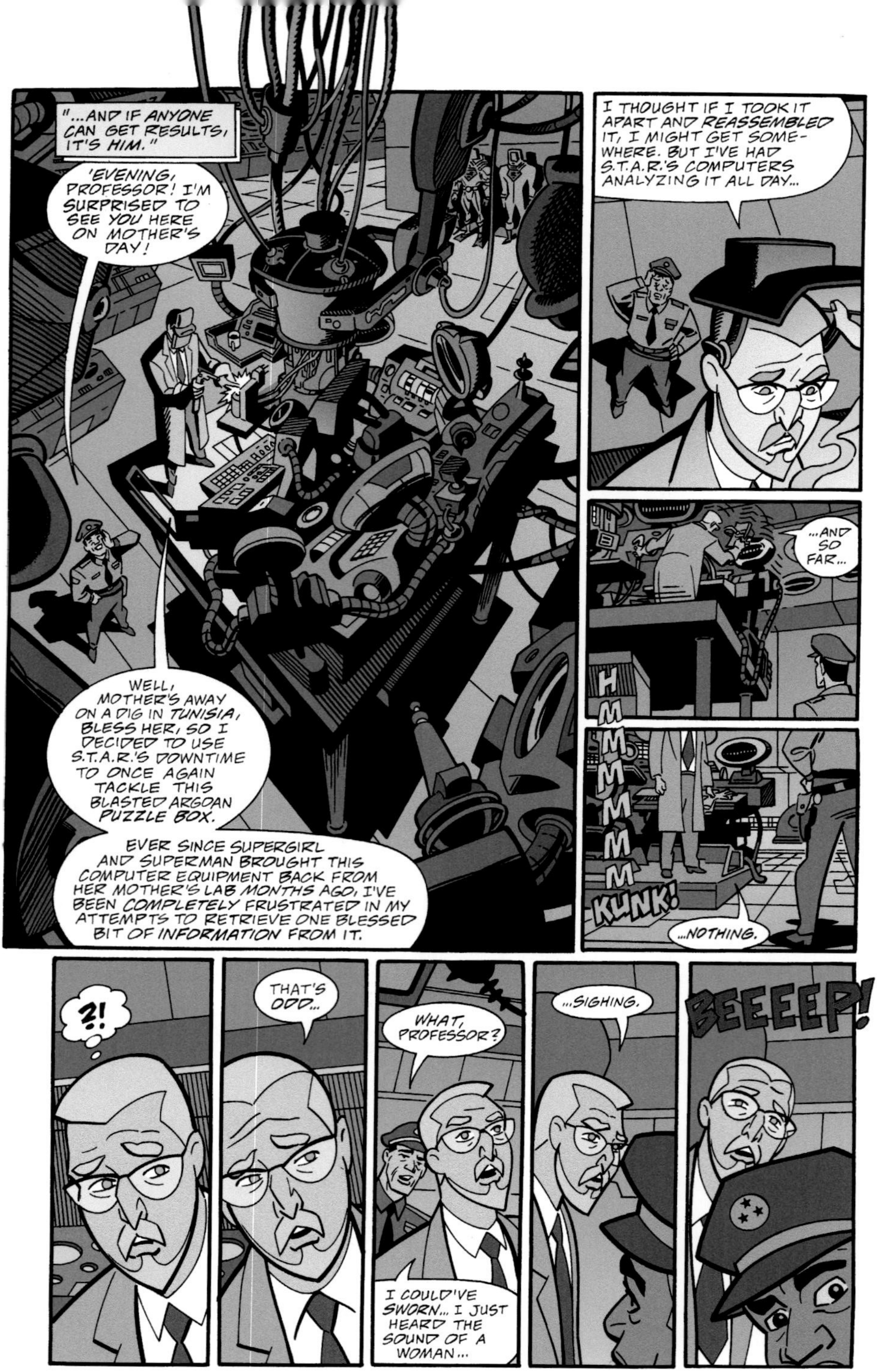
"...AND IF ANYONE CAN GET RESULTS, IT'S HIM."
'EVENING, PROFESSOR! I'M SURPRISED TO SEE YOU HERE ON MOTHER'S DAY!
WELL, MOTHER'S AWAY ON A DIG IN TUNISIA, BLESS HER, SO I DECIDED TO USE S.T.A.R.'S DOWNTIME TO ONCE AGAIN TACKLE THIS BLASTED ARGOAN PUZZLE BOX.
EVER SINCE SUPERGIRL AND SUPERMAN BROUGHT THIS COMPUTER EQUIPMENT BACK FROM HER MOTHER'S LAB MONTHS AGO, I'VE BEEN COMPLETELY FRUSTRATED IN MY ATTEMPTS TO RETRIEVE ONE BLESSED BIT OF INFORMATION FROM IT.
I THOUGHT IF I TOOK IT APART AND REASSEMBLED IT, I MIGHT GET SOMEWHERE. BUT I'VE HAD S.T.A.R.'S COMPUTERS ANALYZING IT ALL DAY...
...AND SO FAR...
HMMMMMMMM
KUNK!
...NOTHING.
?!
THAT'S ODD...
WHAT, PROFESSOR?
I COULD'VE SWORN... I JUST HEARD THE SOUND OF A WOMAN...
...SIGHING.
BEEEEP!

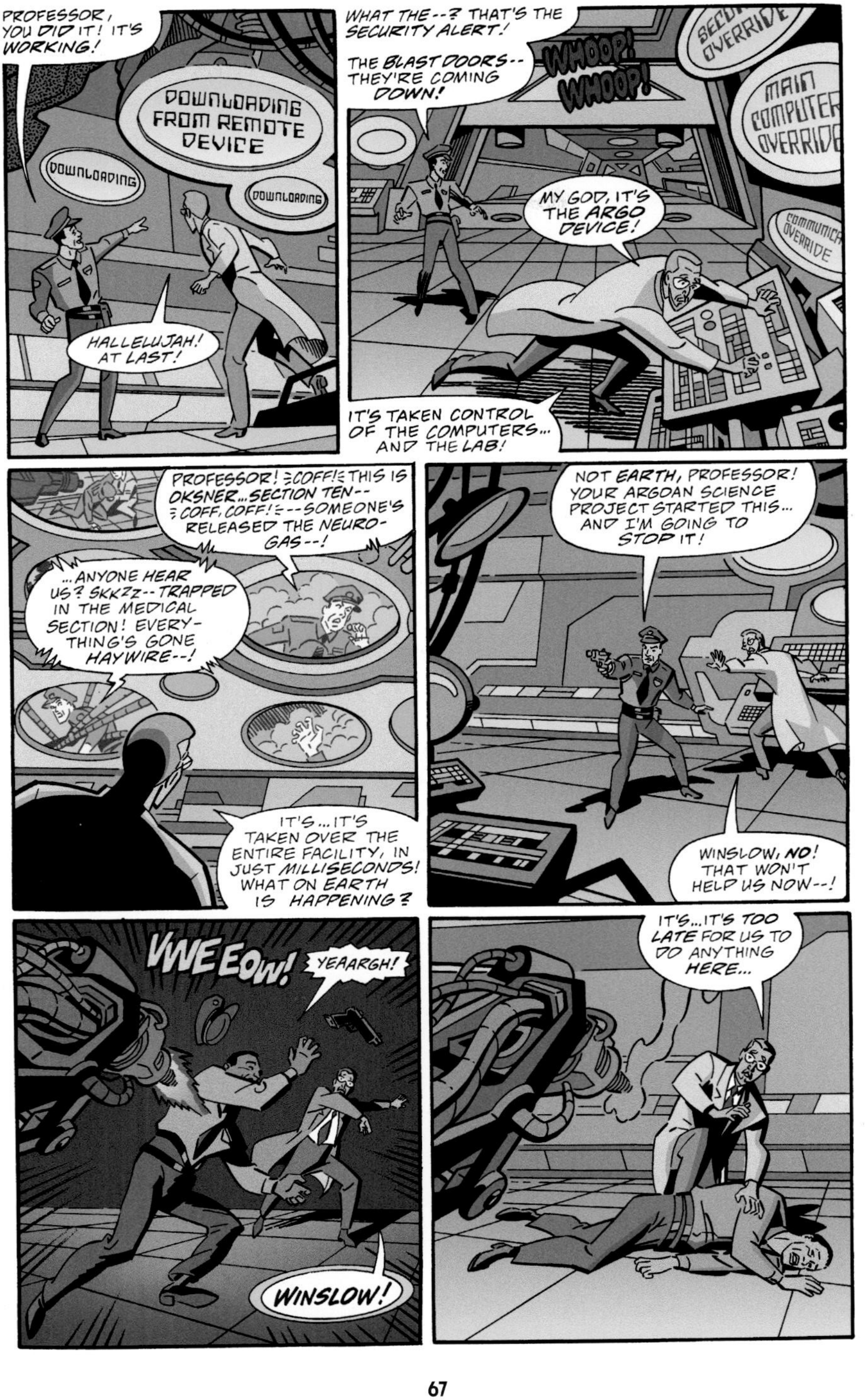
PROFESSOR, YOU DID IT! IT'S WORKING!
DOWNLOADING FROM REMOTE DEVICE
DOWNLOADING
DOWNLOADING
HALLELUJAH! AT LAST!
WHAT THE--? THAT'S THE SECURITY ALERT!
THE BLAST DOORS-- THEY'RE COMING DOWN!
WHOOP! WHOOP!
MAIN COMPUTER OVERRIDE
MY GOD, IT'S THE ARGO DEVICE!
IT'S TAKEN CONTROL OF THE COMPUTERS... AND THE LAB!
PROFESSOR! ≈COFF!≈ THIS IS OKSNER...SECTION TEN-- ≈COFF, COFF!≈ --SOMEONE'S RELEASED THE NEURO-GAS--!
...ANYONE HEAR US? SKKZZ--TRAPPED IN THE MEDICAL SECTION! EVERYTHING'S GONE HAYWIRE--!
IT'S...IT'S TAKEN OVER THE ENTIRE FACILITY, IN JUST MILLISECONDS! WHAT ON EARTH IS HAPPENING?
NOT EARTH, PROFESSOR! YOUR ARGOAN SCIENCE PROJECT STARTED THIS... AND I'M GOING TO STOP IT!
WINSLOW, NO! THAT WON'T HELP US NOW--!
VWEEOW!
YEAARGH!
WINSLOW!
IT'S...IT'S TOO LATE FOR US TO DO ANYTHING HERE...

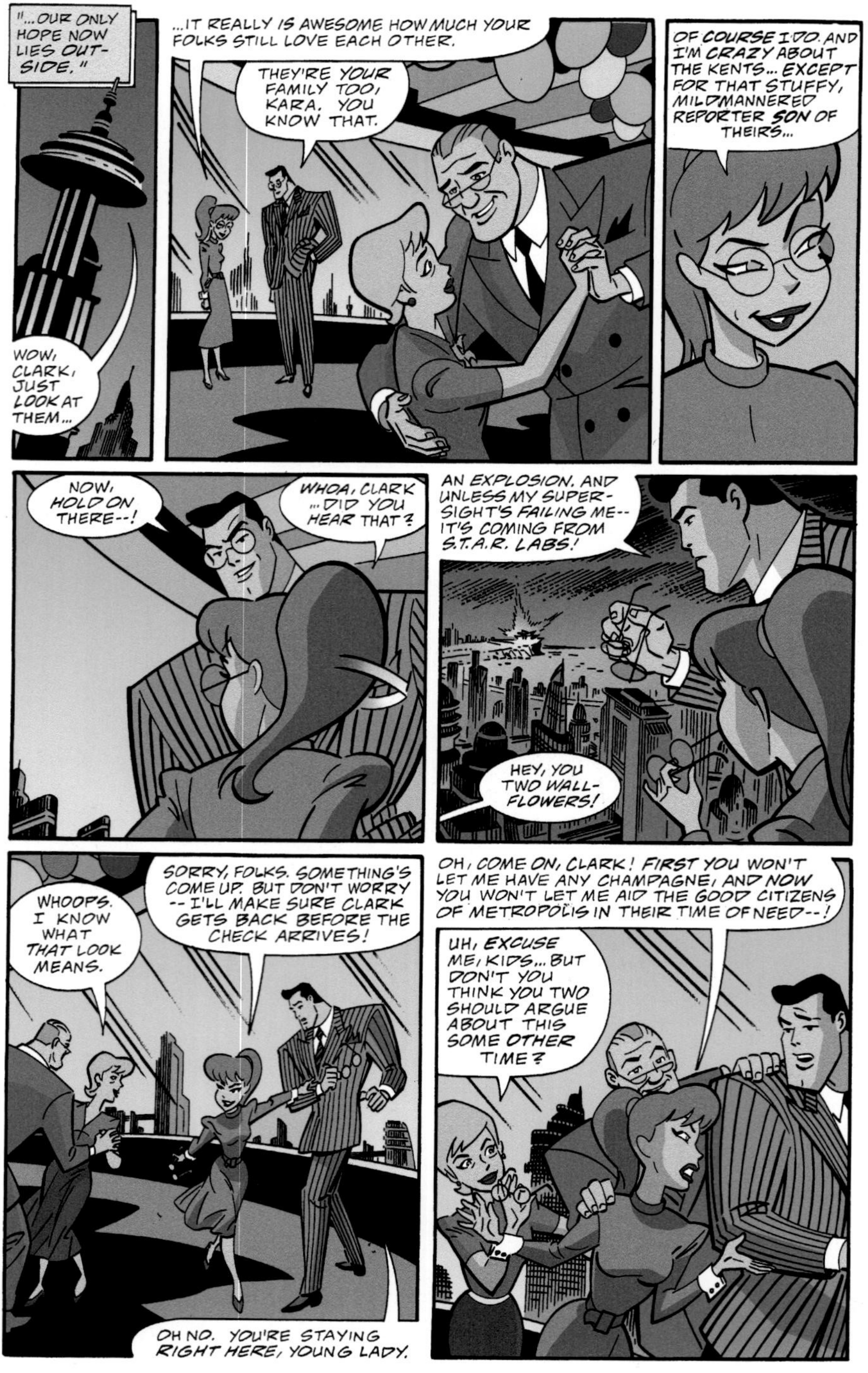
"...OUR ONLY HOPE NOW LIES OUT-SIDE."
WOW, CLARK, JUST LOOK AT THEM...
...IT REALLY IS AWESOME HOW MUCH YOUR FOLKS STILL LOVE EACH OTHER.
THEY'RE YOUR FAMILY TOO, KARA. YOU KNOW THAT.
OF COURSE I DO. AND I'M CRAZY ABOUT THE KENTS... EXCEPT FOR THAT STUFFY, MILDMANNERED REPORTER SON OF THEIRS...
NOW, HOLD ON THERE--!
WHOA, CLARK ...DID YOU HEAR THAT?
AN EXPLOSION. AND UNLESS MY SUPER-SIGHT'S FAILING ME-- IT'S COMING FROM S.T.A.R. LABS!
HEY, YOU TWO WALL-FLOWERS!
WHOOPS. I KNOW WHAT THAT LOOK MEANS.
SORRY, FOLKS. SOMETHING'S COME UP. BUT DON'T WORRY -- I'LL MAKE SURE CLARK GETS BACK BEFORE THE CHECK ARRIVES!
OH NO. YOU'RE STAYING RIGHT HERE, YOUNG LADY.
OH, COME ON, CLARK! FIRST YOU WON'T LET ME HAVE ANY CHAMPAGNE, AND NOW YOU WON'T LET ME AID THE GOOD CITIZENS OF METROPOLIS IN THEIR TIME OF NEED--!
UH, EXCUSE ME, KIDS... BUT DON'T YOU THINK YOU TWO SHOULD ARGUE ABOUT THIS SOME OTHER TIME?

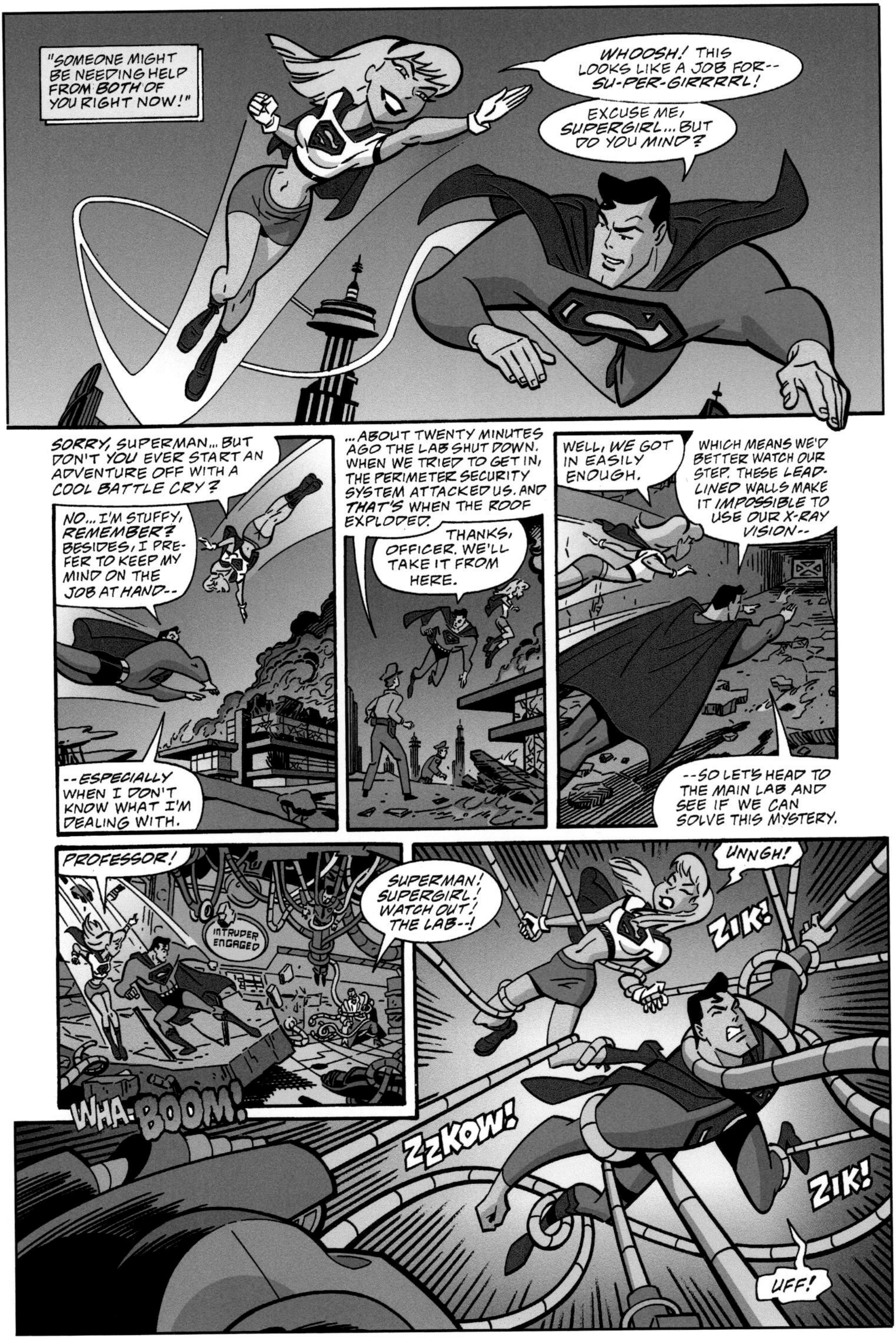
"SOMEONE MIGHT BE NEEDING HELP FROM BOTH OF YOU RIGHT NOW!"
WHOOSH! THIS LOOKS LIKE A JOB FOR-- SU-PER-GIRRRRL!
EXCUSE ME, SUPERGIRL... BUT DO YOU MIND?
SORRY, SUPERMAN... BUT DON'T YOU EVER START AN ADVENTURE OFF WITH A COOL BATTLE CRY?
NO... I'M STUFFY, REMEMBER? BESIDES, I PREFER TO KEEP MY MIND ON THE JOB AT HAND--
--ESPECIALLY WHEN I DON'T KNOW WHAT I'M DEALING WITH.
...ABOUT TWENTY MINUTES AGO THE LAB SHUT DOWN. WHEN WE TRIED TO GET IN, THE PERIMETER SECURITY SYSTEM ATTACKED US. AND THAT'S WHEN THE ROOF EXPLODED.
THANKS, OFFICER. WE'LL TAKE IT FROM HERE.
WELL, WE GOT IN EASILY ENOUGH.
WHICH MEANS WE'D BETTER WATCH OUR STEP. THESE LEAD-LINED WALLS MAKE IT IMPOSSIBLE TO USE OUR X-RAY VISION--
--SO LET'S HEAD TO THE MAIN LAB AND SEE IF WE CAN SOLVE THIS MYSTERY.
PROFESSOR!
INTRUDER ENGAGED
SUPERMAN! SUPERGIRL! WATCH OUT! THE LAB--!
WHA-BOOM!
UNNGH!
ZIK!
ZZKOW!
ZIK!
UFF!

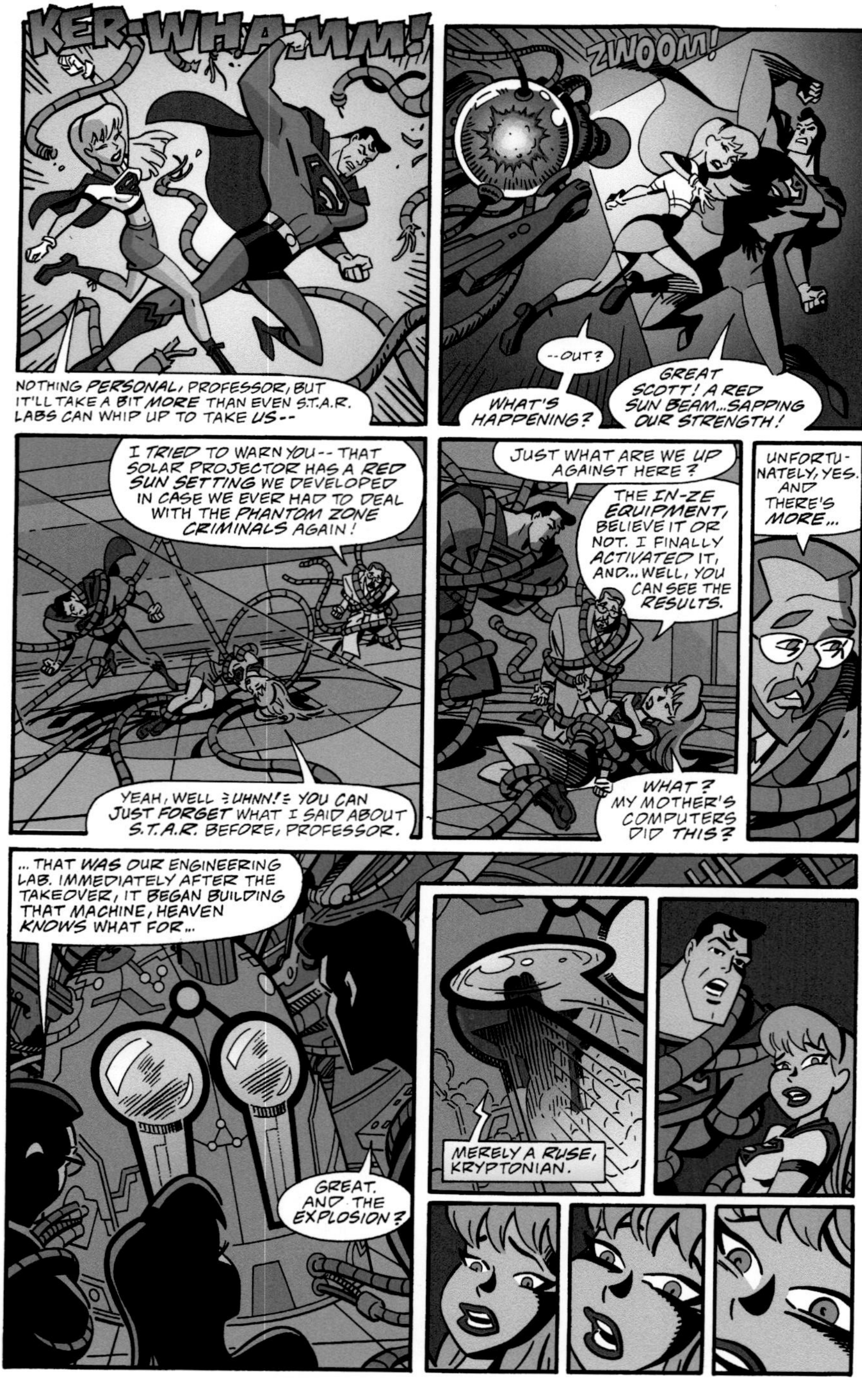
KER-WHAMM!
NOTHING PERSONAL, PROFESSOR, BUT IT'LL TAKE A BIT MORE THAN EVEN S.T.A.R. LABS CAN WHIP UP TO TAKE US--
ZWOOM!
--OUT?
WHAT'S HAPPENING?
GREAT SCOTT! A RED SUN BEAM...SAPPING OUR STRENGTH!
I TRIED TO WARN YOU-- THAT SOLAR PROJECTOR HAS A RED SUN SETTING WE DEVELOPED IN CASE WE EVER HAD TO DEAL WITH THE PHANTOM ZONE CRIMINALS AGAIN!
YEAH, WELL =UHNN!= YOU CAN JUST FORGET WHAT I SAID ABOUT S.T.A.R. BEFORE, PROFESSOR.
JUST WHAT ARE WE UP AGAINST HERE?
THE IN-ZE EQUIPMENT, BELIEVE IT OR NOT. I FINALLY ACTIVATED IT, AND... WELL, YOU CAN SEE THE RESULTS.
WHAT? MY MOTHER'S COMPUTERS DID THIS?
UNFORTUNATELY, YES. AND THERE'S MORE...
...THAT WAS OUR ENGINEERING LAB. IMMEDIATELY AFTER THE TAKEOVER, IT BEGAN BUILDING THAT MACHINE, HEAVEN KNOWS WHAT FOR...
GREAT. AND THE EXPLOSION?
MERELY A RUSE, KRYPTONIAN.

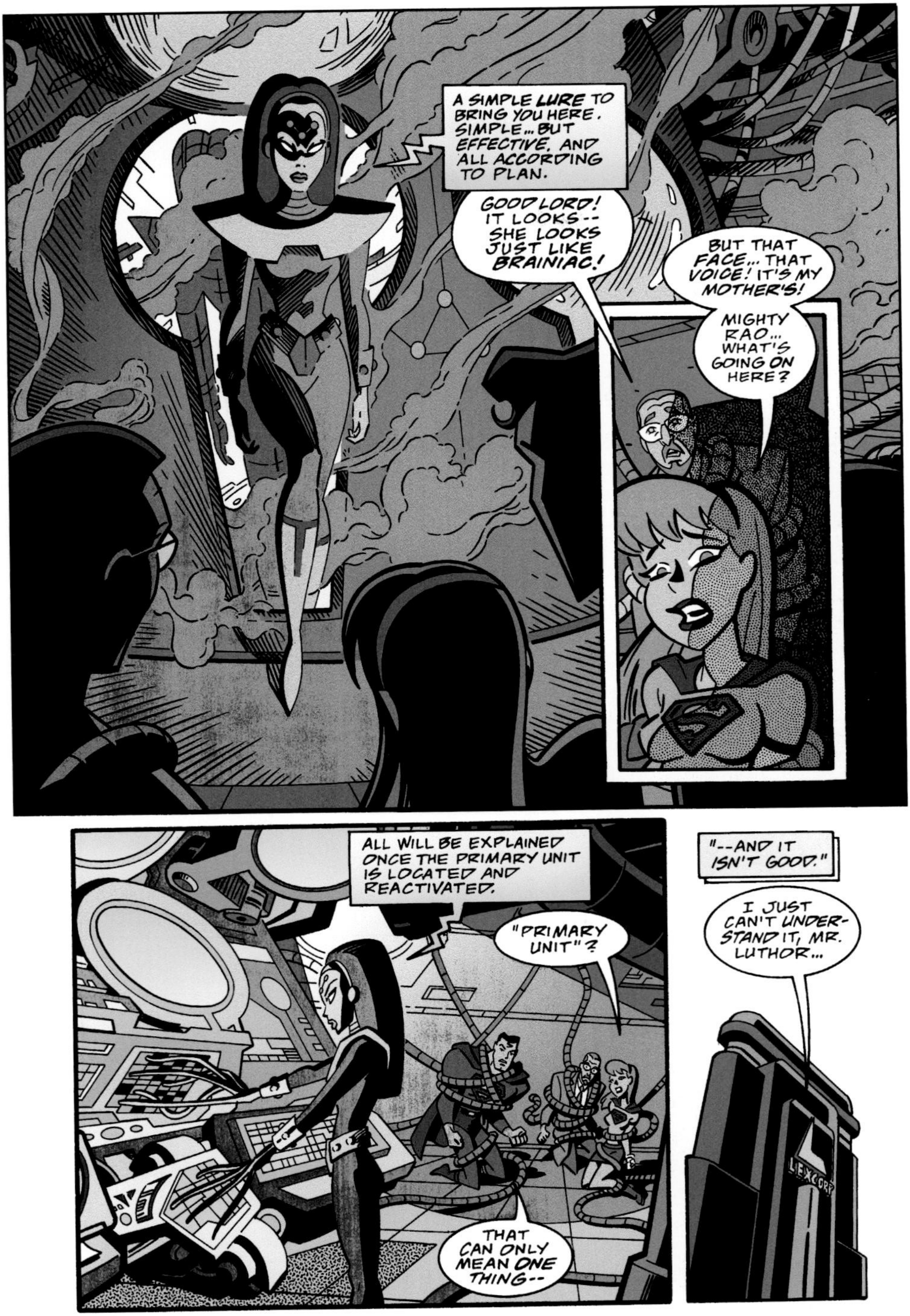
A SIMPLE LURE TO BRING YOU HERE. SIMPLE... BUT EFFECTIVE, AND ALL ACCORDING TO PLAN.
GOOD LORD! IT LOOKS-- SHE LOOKS JUST LIKE BRAINIAC!
BUT THAT FACE... THAT VOICE! IT'S MY MOTHER'S!
MIGHTY RAO... WHAT'S GOING ON HERE?
ALL WILL BE EXPLAINED ONCE THE PRIMARY UNIT IS LOCATED AND REACTIVATED.
"PRIMARY UNIT"?
THAT CAN ONLY MEAN ONE THING--
"--AND IT ISN'T GOOD."
I JUST CAN'T UNDERSTAND IT, MR. LUTHOR...
LEXCORP

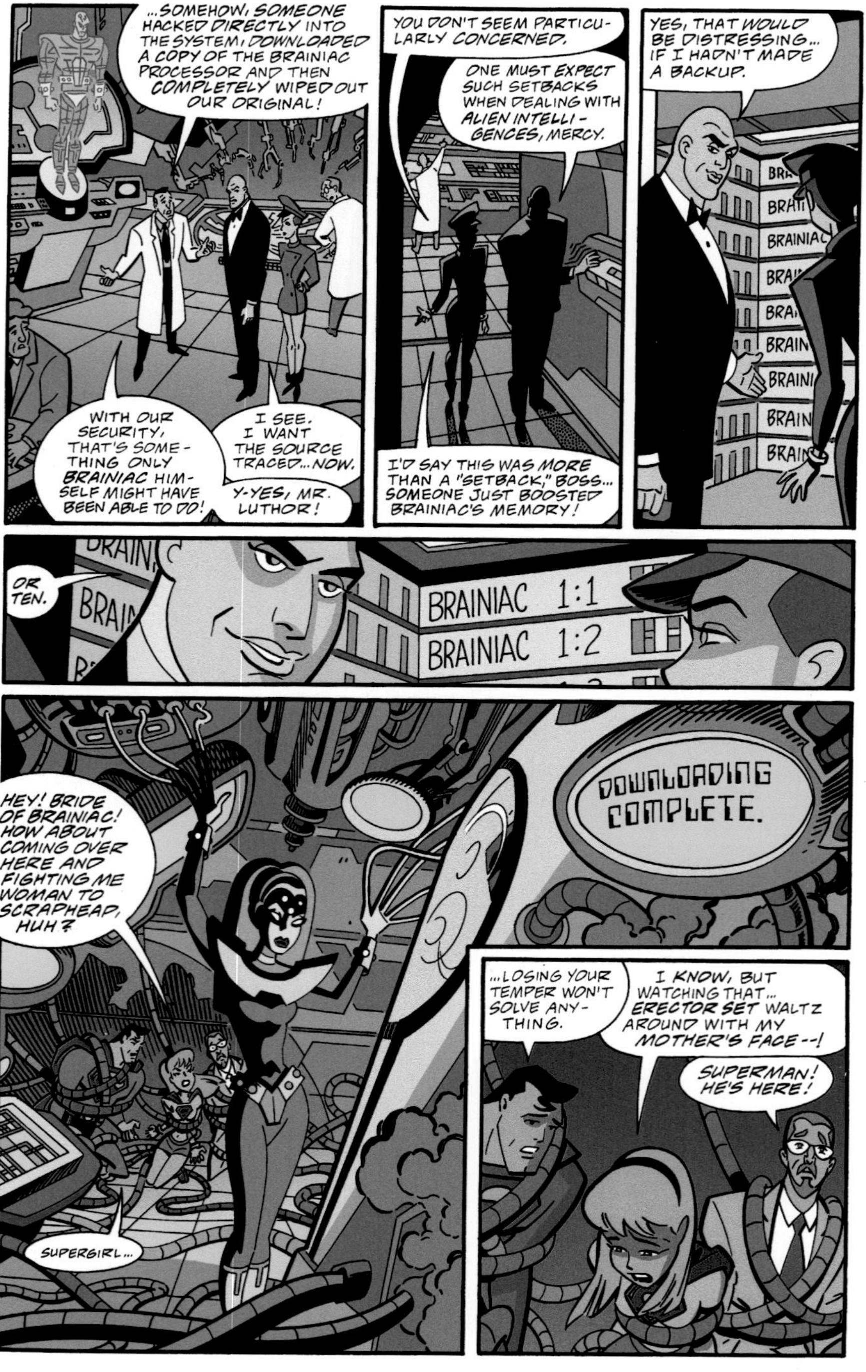
...SOMEHOW, SOMEONE HACKED DIRECTLY INTO THE SYSTEM, DOWNLOADED A COPY OF THE BRAINIAC PROCESSOR AND THEN COMPLETELY WIPED OUT OUR ORIGINAL!
WITH OUR SECURITY, THAT'S SOME-THING ONLY BRAINIAC HIM-SELF MIGHT HAVE BEEN ABLE TO DO!
I SEE. I WANT THE SOURCE TRACED... NOW.
Y-YES, MR. LUTHOR!
YOU DON'T SEEM PARTICU-LARLY CONCERNED.
ONE MUST EXPECT SUCH SETBACKS WHEN DEALING WITH ALIEN INTELLI-GENCES, MERCY.
I'D SAY THIS WAS MORE THAN A "SETBACK," BOSS... SOMEONE JUST BOOSTED BRAINIAC'S MEMORY!
YES, THAT WOULD BE DISTRESSING... IF I HADN'T MADE A BACKUP.
OR TEN.
BRAINIAC 1:1
BRAINIAC 1:2
HEY! BRIDE OF BRAINIAC! HOW ABOUT COMING OVER HERE AND FIGHTING ME WOMAN TO SCRAPHEAD, HUH?
DOWNLOADING COMPLETE.
SUPERGIRL...
...LOSING YOUR TEMPER WON'T SOLVE ANY-THING.
I KNOW, BUT WATCHING THAT... ERECTOR SET WALTZ AROUND WITH MY MOTHER'S FACE--!
SUPERMAN! HE'S HERE!

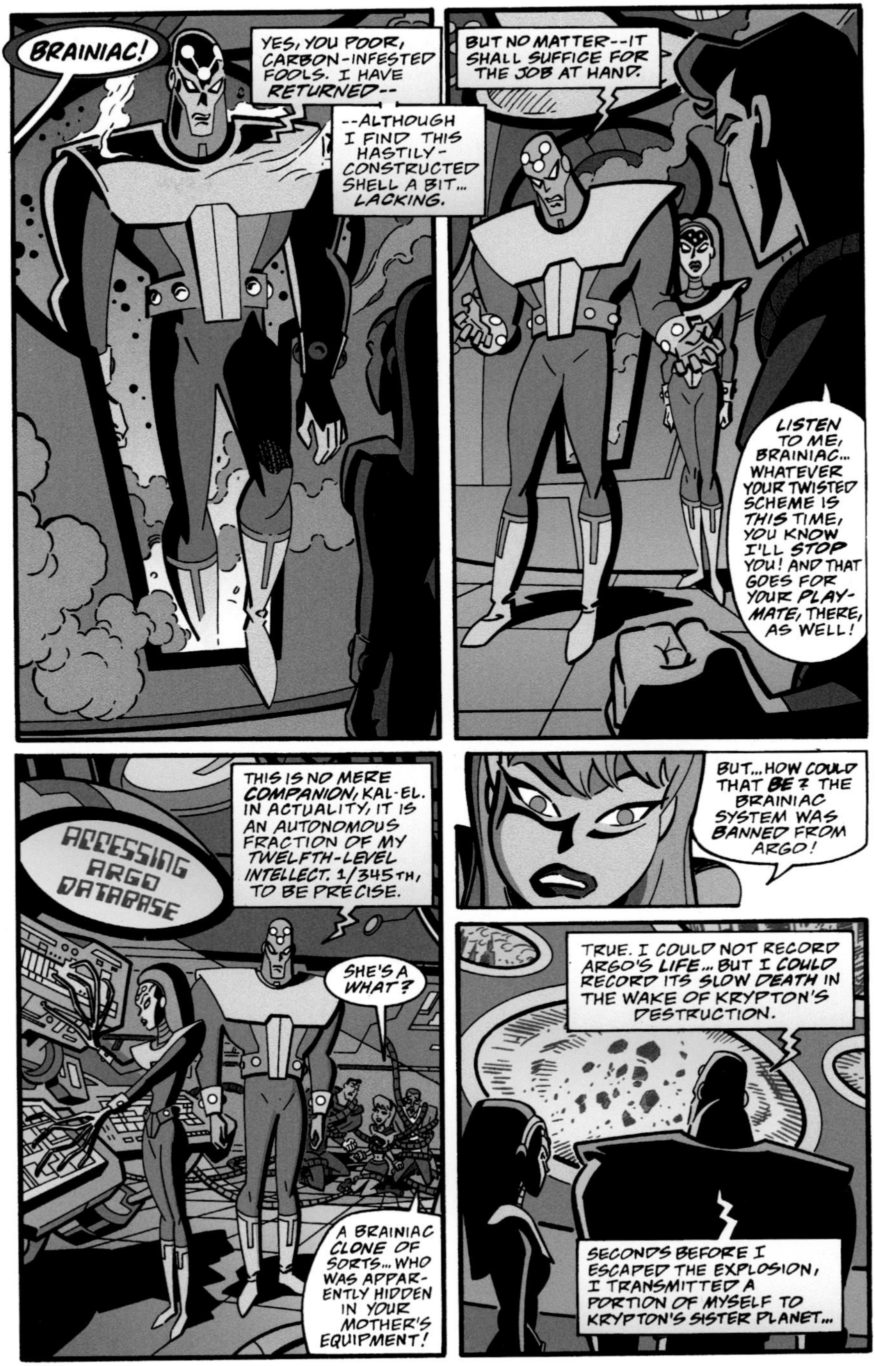

BRAINIAC!
YES, YOU POOR, CARBON-INFESTED FOOLS. I HAVE RETURNED--
--ALTHOUGH I FIND THIS HASTILY-CONSTRUCTED SHELL A BIT... LACKING.
BUT NO MATTER--IT SHALL SUFFICE FOR THE JOB AT HAND.
LISTEN TO ME, BRAINIAC... WHATEVER YOUR TWISTED SCHEME IS THIS TIME, YOU KNOW I'LL STOP YOU! AND THAT GOES FOR YOUR PLAYMATE, THERE, AS WELL!
ACCESSING ARGO DATABASE
THIS IS NO MERE COMPANION, KAL-EL. IN ACTUALITY, IT IS AN AUTONOMOUS FRACTION OF MY TWELFTH-LEVEL INTELLECT. 1/345TH, TO BE PRECISE.
SHE'S A WHAT?
A BRAINIAC CLONE OF SORTS... WHO WAS APPARENTLY HIDDEN IN YOUR MOTHER'S EQUIPMENT!
BUT... HOW COULD THAT BE? THE BRAINIAC SYSTEM WAS BANNED FROM ARGO!
TRUE. I COULD NOT RECORD ARGO'S LIFE... BUT I COULD RECORD ITS SLOW DEATH IN THE WAKE OF KRYPTON'S DESTRUCTION.
SECONDS BEFORE I ESCAPED THE EXPLOSION, I TRANSMITTED A PORTION OF MYSELF TO KRYPTON'S SISTER PLANET...

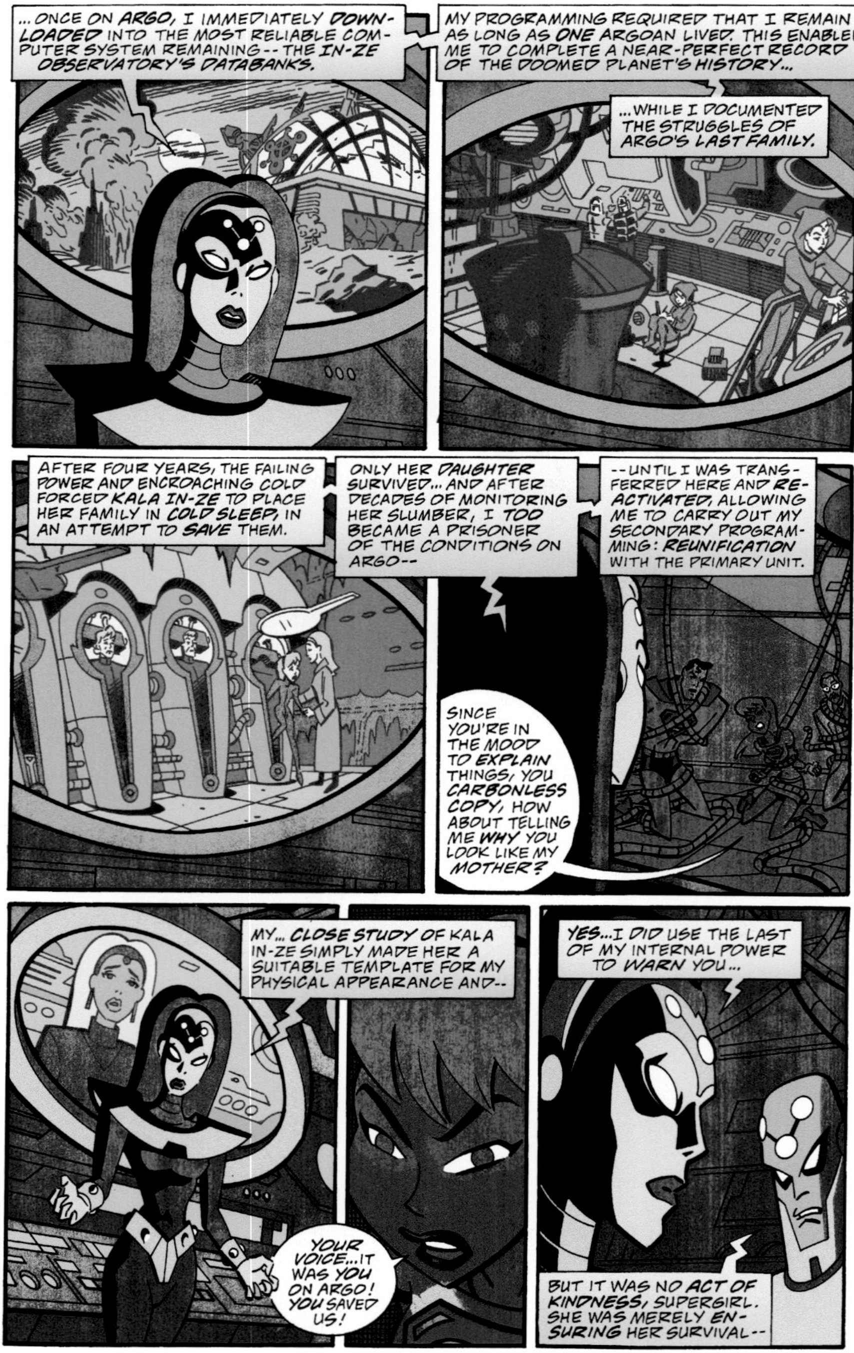

...ONCE ON ARGO, I IMMEDIATELY DOWN-LOADED INTO THE MOST RELIABLE COMPUTER SYSTEM REMAINING--THE IN-ZE OBSERVATORY'S DATABANKS.
MY PROGRAMMING REQUIRED THAT I REMAIN AS LONG AS ONE ARGOAN LIVED. THIS ENABLED ME TO COMPLETE A NEAR-PERFECT RECORD OF THE DOOMED PLANET'S HISTORY...
...WHILE I DOCUMENTED THE STRUGGLES OF ARGO'S LAST FAMILY.
AFTER FOUR YEARS, THE FAILING POWER AND ENCROACHING COLD FORCED KALA IN-ZE TO PLACE HER FAMILY IN COLD SLEEP, IN AN ATTEMPT TO SAVE THEM.
ONLY HER DAUGHTER SURVIVED... AND AFTER DECADES OF MONITORING HER SLUMBER, I TOO BECAME A PRISONER OF THE CONDITIONS ON ARGO--
--UNTIL I WAS TRANSFERRED HERE AND RE-ACTIVATED, ALLOWING ME TO CARRY OUT MY SECONDARY PROGRAMMING: REUNIFICATION WITH THE PRIMARY UNIT.
SINCE YOU'RE IN THE MOOD TO EXPLAIN THINGS, YOU CARBONLESS COPY, HOW ABOUT TELLING ME WHY YOU LOOK LIKE MY MOTHER?
MY... CLOSE STUDY OF KALA IN-ZE SIMPLY MADE HER A SUITABLE TEMPLATE FOR MY PHYSICAL APPEARANCE AND--
YOUR VOICE...IT WAS YOU ON ARGO! YOU SAVED US!
YES...I DID USE THE LAST OF MY INTERNAL POWER TO WARN YOU...
BUT IT WAS NO ACT OF KINDNESS, SUPERGIRL. SHE WAS MERELY ENSURING HER SURVIVAL--

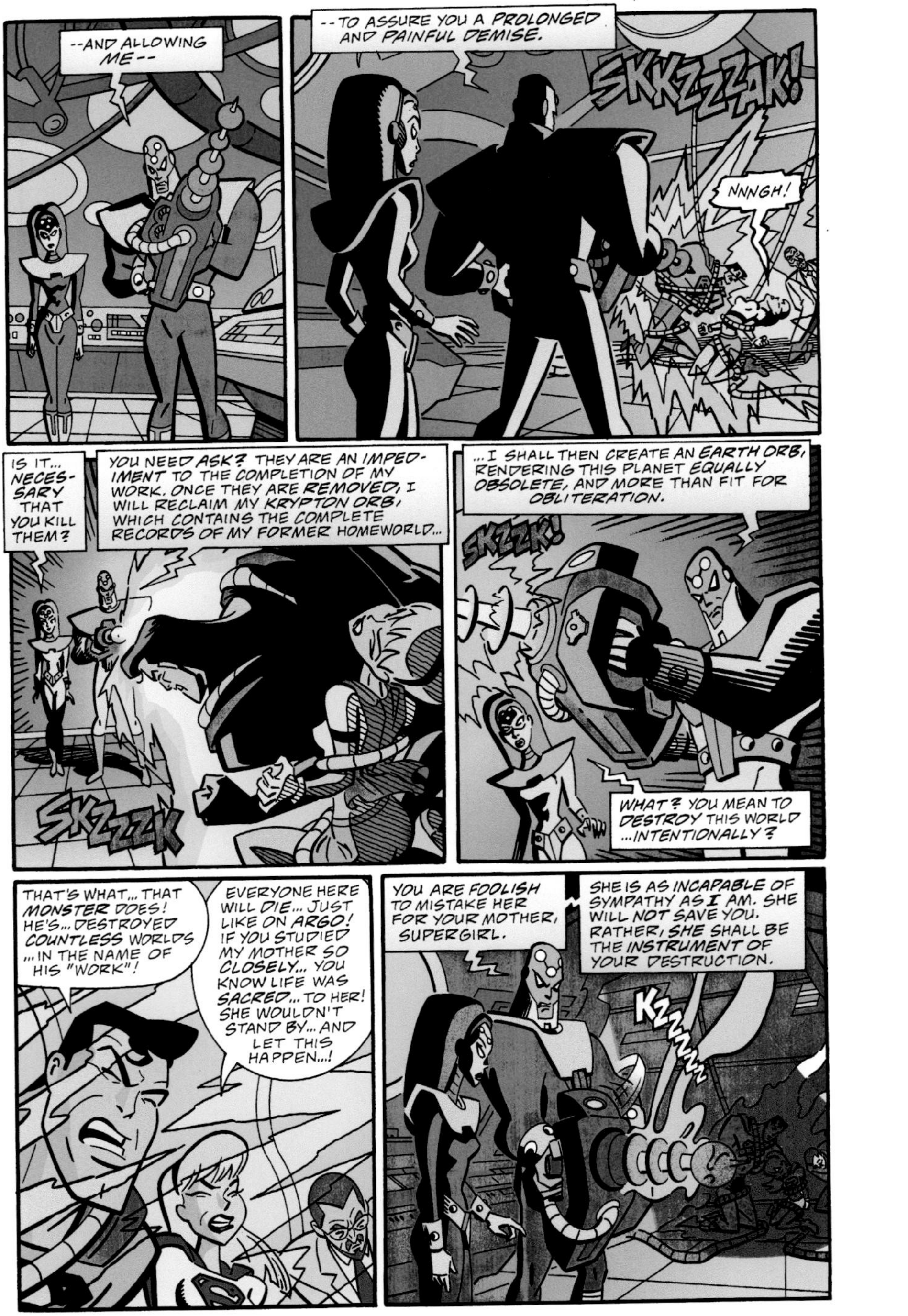
--AND ALLOWING ME--
--TO ASSURE YOU A PROLONGED AND PAINFUL DEMISE.
SKKZZZAK!
NNNGH!
IS IT... NECES-SARY THAT YOU KILL THEM?
YOU NEED ASK? THEY ARE AN IMPED-IMENT TO THE COMPLETION OF MY WORK. ONCE THEY ARE REMOVED, I WILL RECLAIM MY KRYPTON ORB, WHICH CONTAINS THE COMPLETE RECORDS OF MY FORMER HOMEWORLD...
SKZZZK
...I SHALL THEN CREATE AN EARTH ORB, RENDERING THIS PLANET EQUALLY OBSOLETE, AND MORE THAN FIT FOR OBLITERATION.
SKZZZK!
WHAT? YOU MEAN TO DESTROY THIS WORLD ...INTENTIONALLY?
THAT'S WHAT... THAT MONSTER DOES! HE'S... DESTROYED COUNTLESS WORLDS ...IN THE NAME OF HIS "WORK"!
EVERYONE HERE WILL DIE... JUST LIKE ON ARGO! IF YOU STUDIED MY MOTHER SO CLOSELY... YOU KNOW LIFE WAS SACRED... TO HER! SHE WOULDN'T STAND BY... AND LET THIS HAPPEN...!
YOU ARE FOOLISH TO MISTAKE HER FOR YOUR MOTHER, SUPERGIRL.
SHE IS AS INCAPABLE OF SYMPATHY AS I AM. SHE WILL NOT SAVE YOU. RATHER, SHE SHALL BE THE INSTRUMENT OF YOUR DESTRUCTION.
KZZZZZ

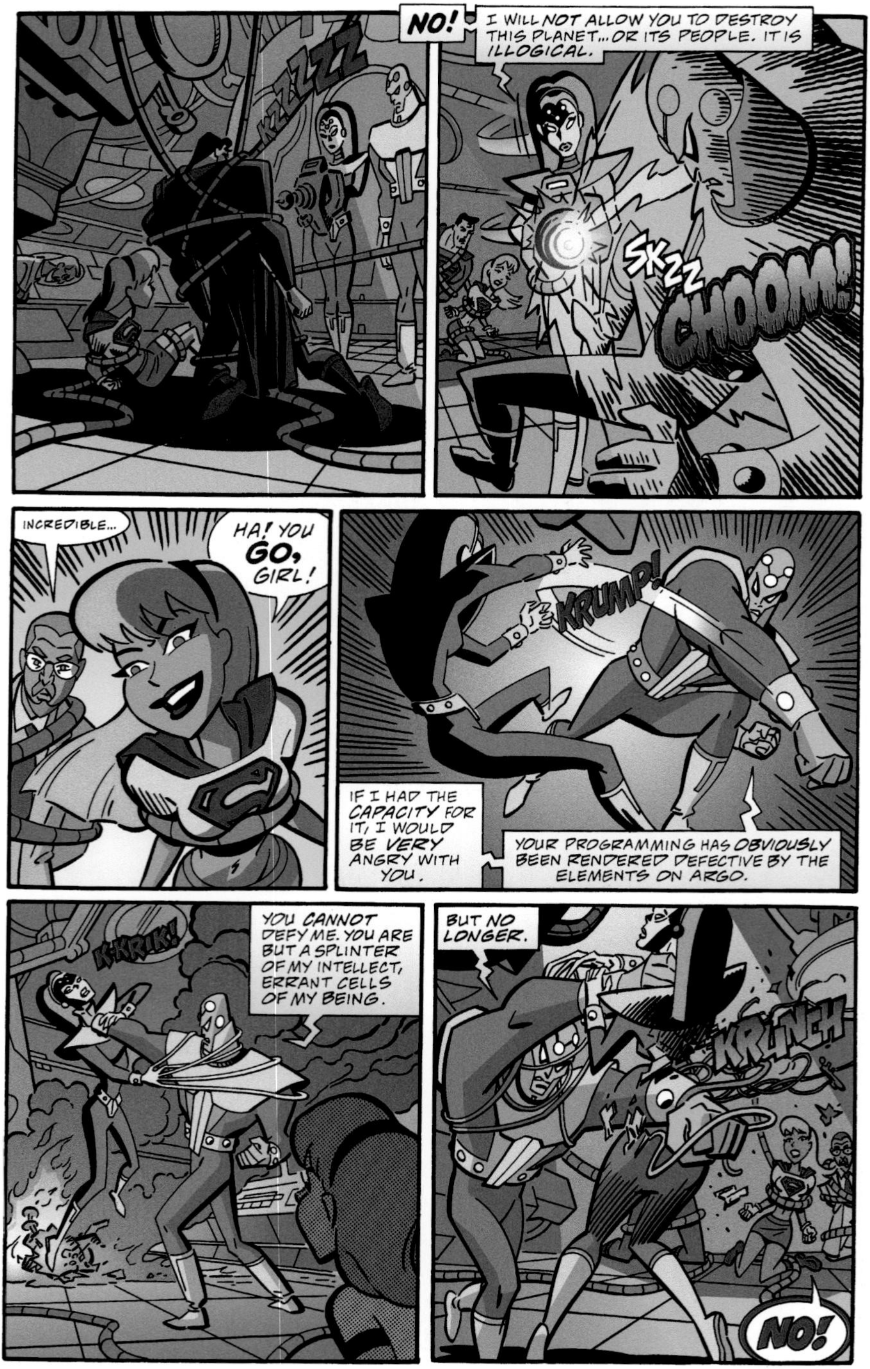
KZZZZZZ
NO!
I WILL NOT ALLOW YOU TO DESTROY THIS PLANET... OR ITS PEOPLE. IT IS ILLOGICAL.
SKZZ
CHOOM!
INCREDIBLE...
HA! YOU GO, GIRL!
KRUMP!
IF I HAD THE CAPACITY FOR IT, I WOULD BE VERY ANGRY WITH YOU.
YOUR PROGRAMMING HAS OBVIOUSLY BEEN RENDERED DEFECTIVE BY THE ELEMENTS ON ARGO.
K-KRIK!
YOU CANNOT DEFY ME. YOU ARE BUT A SPLINTER OF MY INTELLECT, ERRANT CELLS OF MY BEING.
BUT NO LONGER.
KRUNCH
NO!

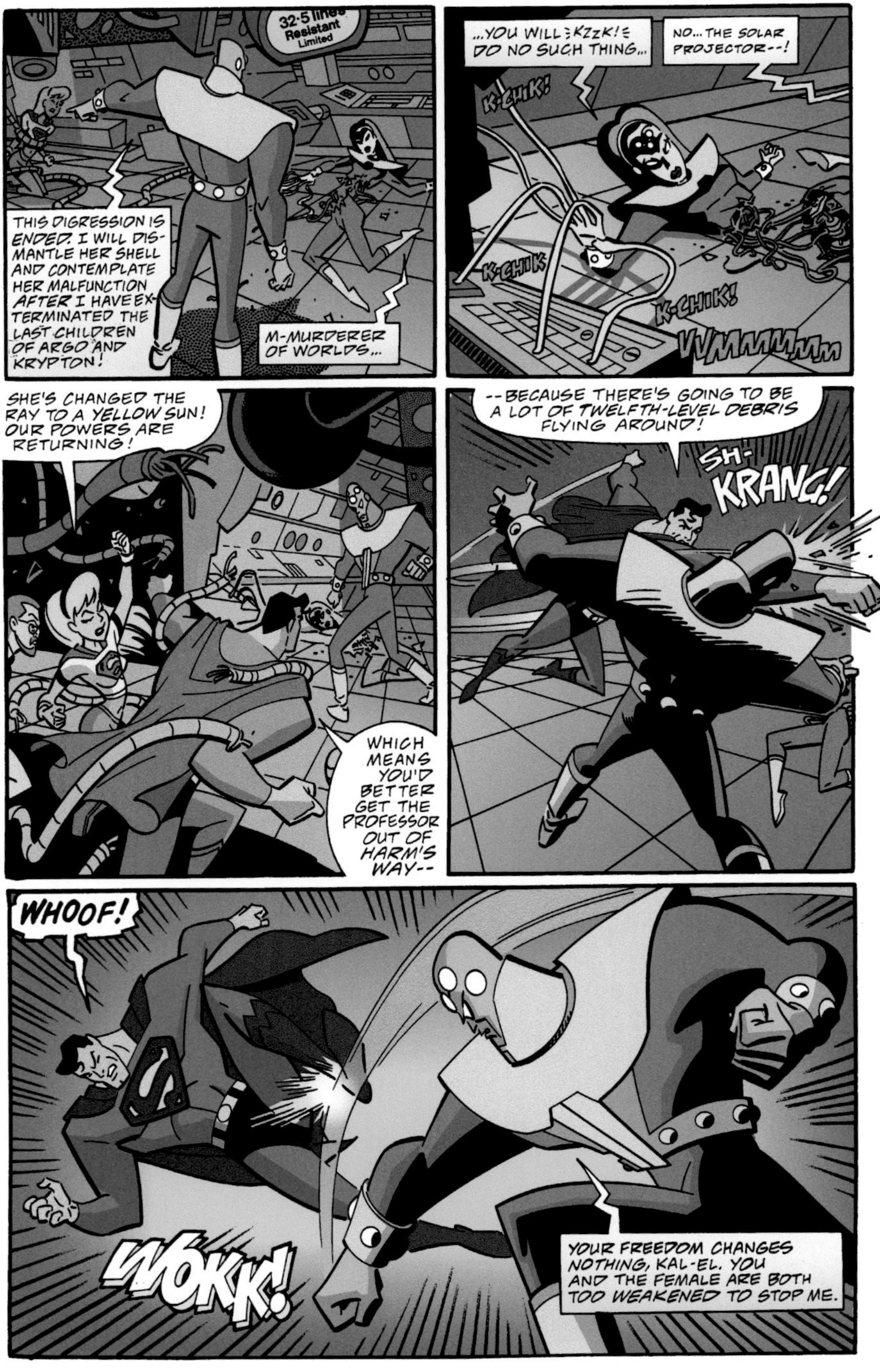
32·5 lines Resistant Limited
THIS DIGRESSION IS ENDED. I WILL DISMANTLE HER SHELL AND CONTEMPLATE HER MALFUNCTION AFTER I HAVE EXTERMINATED THE LAST CHILDREN OF ARGO AND KRYPTON!
M-MURDERER OF WORLDS...
...YOU WILL :KZZK!: DO NO SUCH THING...
NO... THE SOLAR PROJECTOR--!
K-CHIK!
K-CHIK!
K-CHIK!
VVMMMMMMM
SHE'S CHANGED THE RAY TO A YELLOW SUN! OUR POWERS ARE RETURNING!
WHICH MEANS YOU'D BETTER GET THE PROFESSOR OUT OF HARM'S WAY--
--BECAUSE THERE'S GOING TO BE A LOT OF TWELFTH-LEVEL DEBRIS FLYING AROUND!
SH-KRANG!
WHOOF!
WOKK!
YOUR FREEDOM CHANGES NOTHING, KAL-EL. YOU AND THE FEMALE ARE BOTH TOO WEAKENED TO STOP ME.

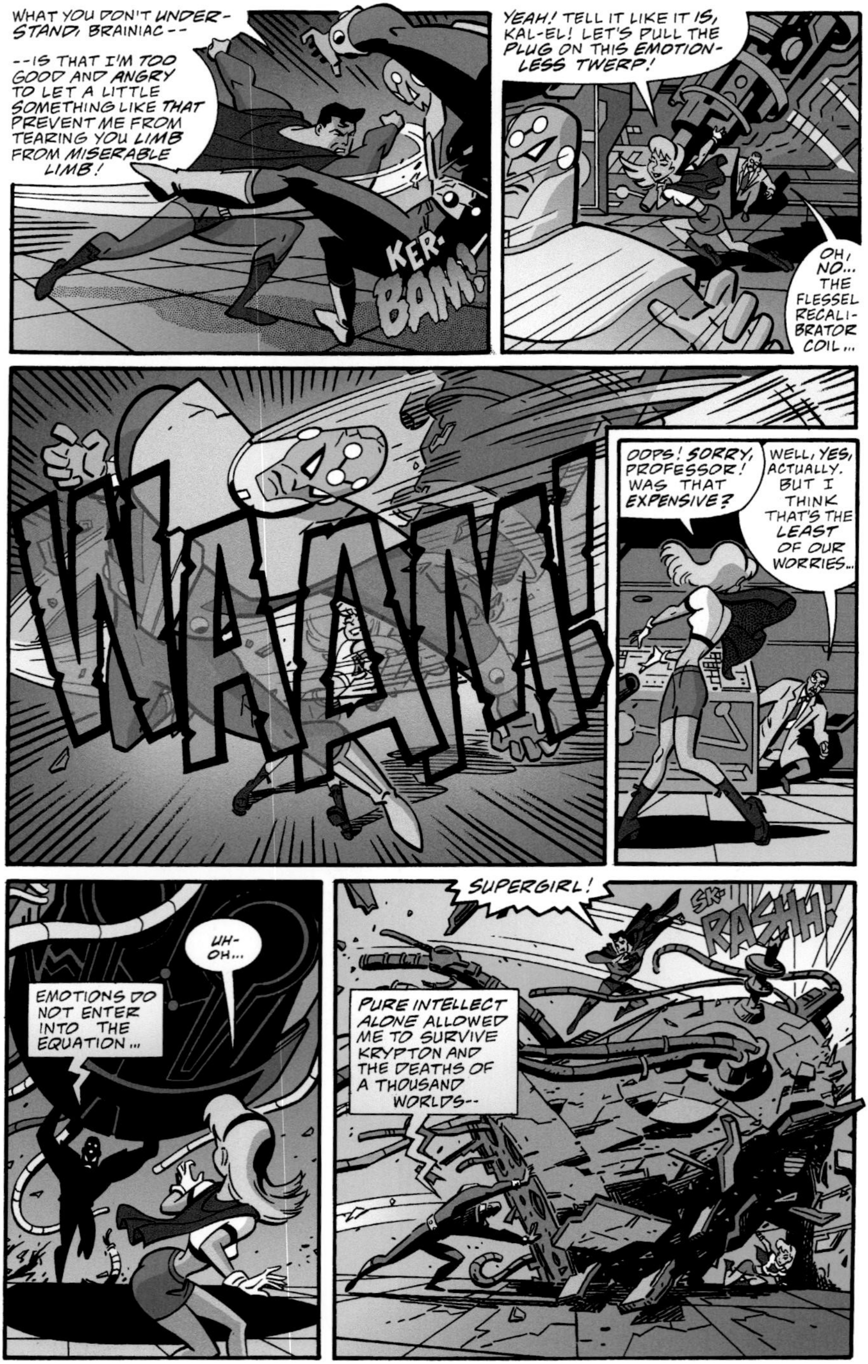
WHAT YOU DON'T UNDERSTAND, BRAINIAC --
--IS THAT I'M TOO GOOD AND ANGRY TO LET A LITTLE SOMETHING LIKE THAT PREVENT ME FROM TEARING YOU LIMB FROM MISERABLE LIMB!
KER-BAM!
YEAH! TELL IT LIKE IT IS, KAL-EL! LET'S PULL THE PLUG ON THIS EMOTIONLESS TWERP!
OH, NO... THE FLESSEL RECALIBRATOR COIL...
WAAM!
OOPS! SORRY, PROFESSOR! WAS THAT EXPENSIVE?
WELL, YES, ACTUALLY. BUT I THINK THAT'S THE LEAST OF OUR WORRIES...
EMOTIONS DO NOT ENTER INTO THE EQUATION...
UH-OH...
SUPERGIRL!
SK-RASHH!
PURE INTELLECT ALONE ALLOWED ME TO SURVIVE KRYPTON AND THE DEATHS OF A THOUSAND WORLDS--

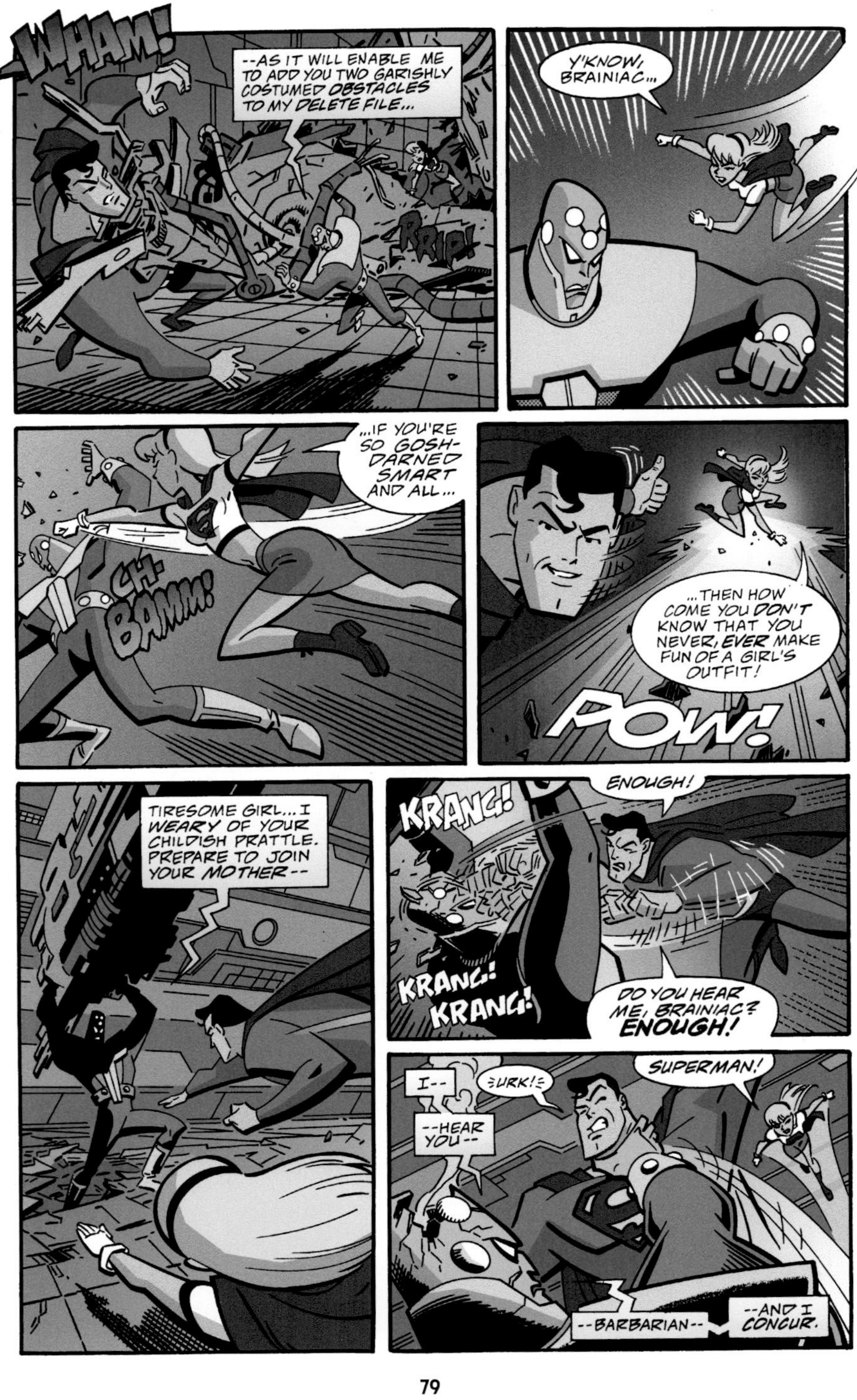
WHAM!
--AS IT WILL ENABLE ME TO ADD YOU TWO GARISHLY COSTUMED OBSTACLES TO MY DELETE FILE...
RRIP!
Y'KNOW, BRAINIAC...
...IF YOU'RE SO GOSH-DARNED SMART AND ALL...
CH-BAMM!
...THEN HOW COME YOU DON'T KNOW THAT YOU NEVER, EVER MAKE FUN OF A GIRL'S OUTFIT!
POW!
TIRESOME GIRL... I WEARY OF YOUR CHILDISH PRATTLE. PREPARE TO JOIN YOUR MOTHER--
ENOUGH!
KRANG!
KRANG! KRANG!
DO YOU HEAR ME, BRAINIAC? ENOUGH!
I--
URK!
SUPERMAN!
--HEAR YOU--
--BARBARIAN--
--AND I CONCUR.

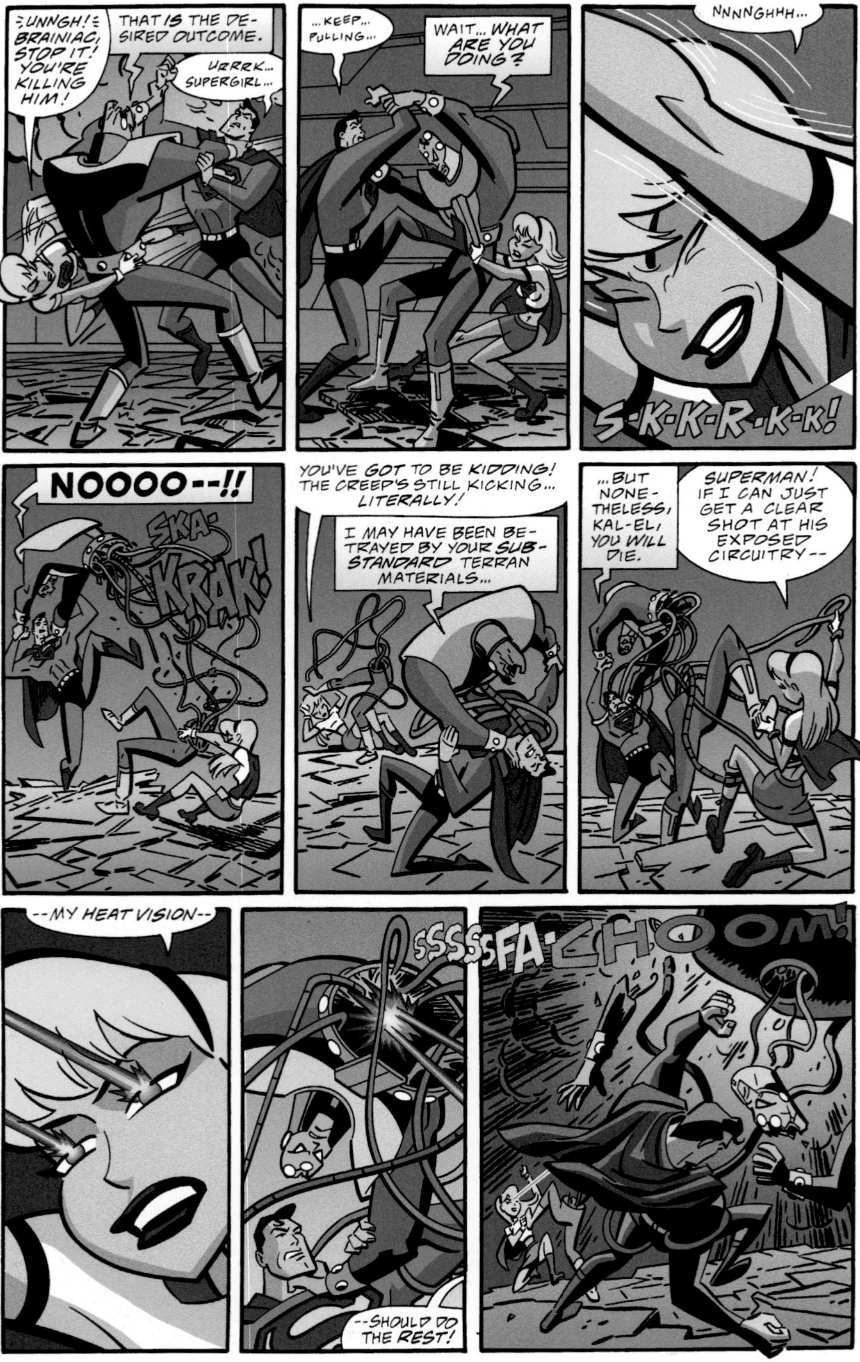
UNNGH! BRAINIAC, STOP IT! YOU'RE KILLING HIM!
THAT IS THE DESIRED OUTCOME.
URRRK... SUPERGIRL...
...KEEP... PULLING...
WAIT... WHAT ARE YOU DOING?
NNNNGHHH...
S-K-K-R-K-K!
NOOOO--!!
SKA-KRAK!
YOU'VE GOT TO BE KIDDING! THE CREEP'S STILL KICKING... LITERALLY!
I MAY HAVE BEEN BETRAYED BY YOUR SUBSTANDARD TERRAN MATERIALS...
...BUT NONETHELESS, KAL-EL, YOU WILL DIE.
SUPERMAN! IF I CAN JUST GET A CLEAR SHOT AT HIS EXPOSED CIRCUITRY--
--MY HEAT VISION--
--SHOULD DO THE REST!
SSSSSFA-CHOOOM!

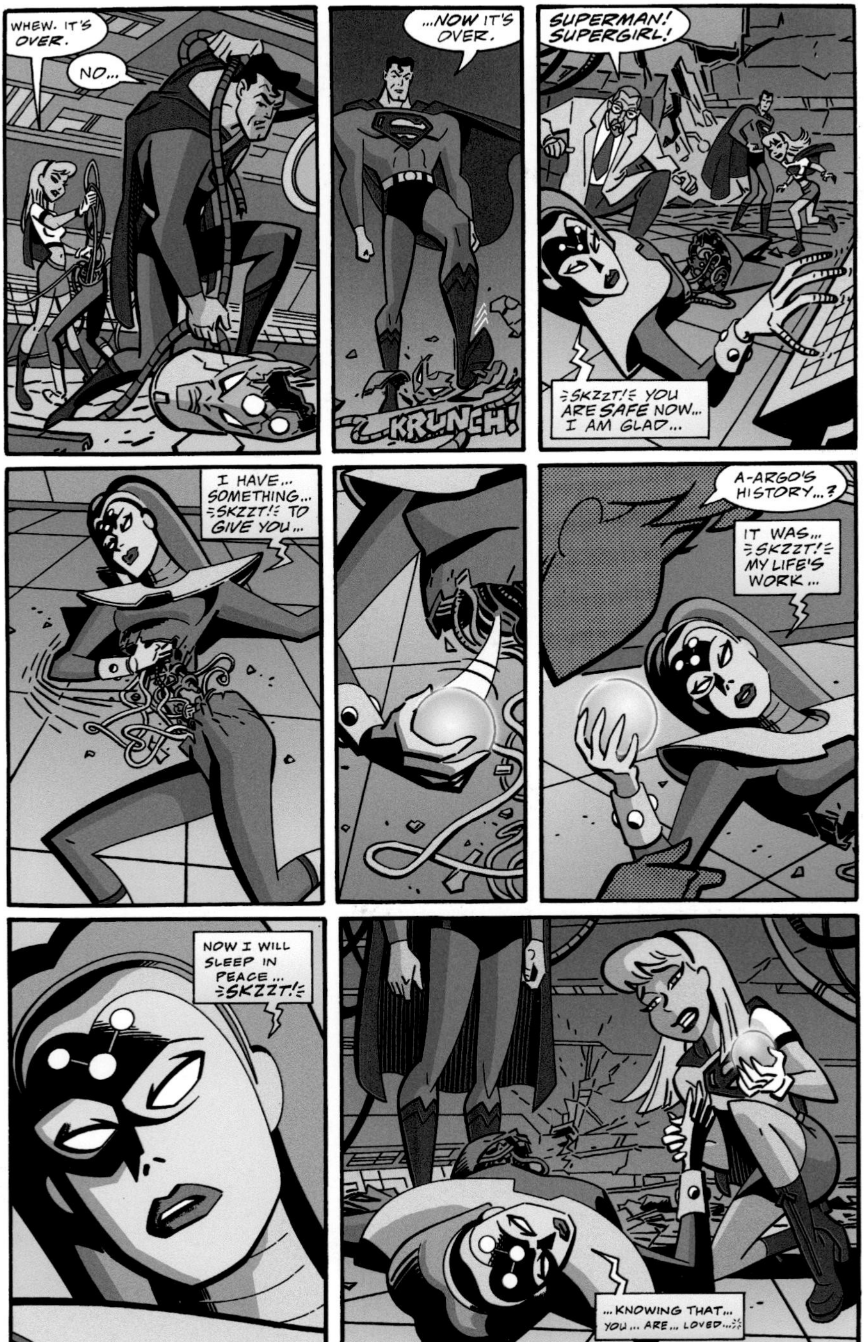

WHEW. IT'S OVER.
NO...
...NOW IT'S OVER.
KRUNCH!
SUPERMAN! SUPERGIRL!
SKZZT! YOU ARE SAFE NOW... I AM GLAD...
I HAVE... SOMETHING... SKZZT! TO GIVE YOU...
A-ARGO'S HISTORY...?
IT WAS... SKZZT! MY LIFE'S WORK...
NOW I WILL SLEEP IN PEACE... SKZZT!
...KNOWING THAT... YOU... ARE... LOVED...

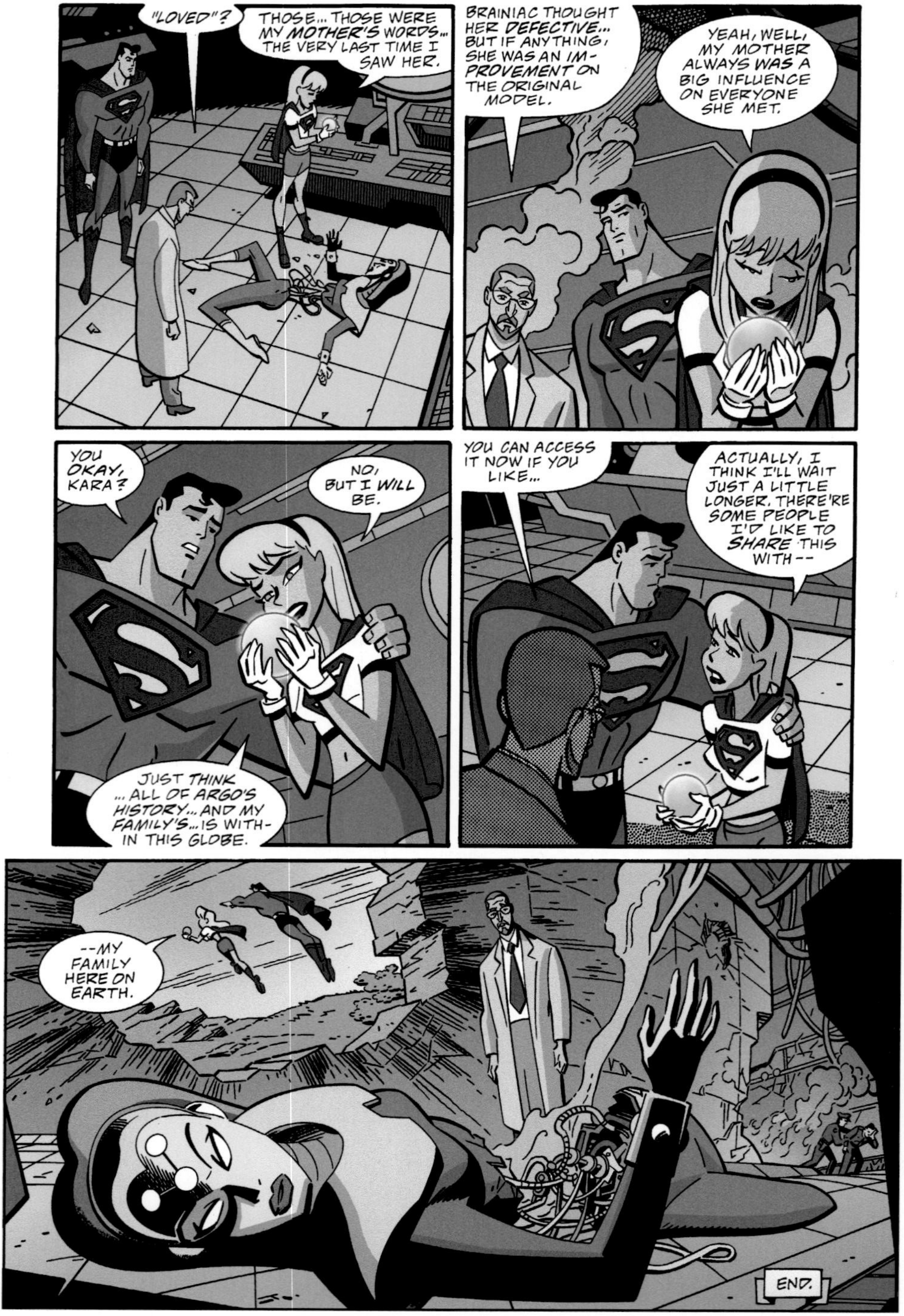
"LOVED"?
THOSE... THOSE WERE MY MOTHER'S WORDS... THE VERY LAST TIME I SAW HER.
BRAINIAC THOUGHT HER DEFECTIVE... BUT IF ANYTHING, SHE WAS AN IMPROVEMENT ON THE ORIGINAL MODEL.
YEAH, WELL, MY MOTHER ALWAYS WAS A BIG INFLUENCE ON EVERYONE SHE MET.
YOU OKAY, KARA?
NO, BUT I WILL BE.
JUST THINK ... ALL OF ARGO'S HISTORY... AND MY FAMILY'S... IS WITHIN THIS GLOBE.
YOU CAN ACCESS IT NOW IF YOU LIKE...
ACTUALLY, I THINK I'LL WAIT JUST A LITTLE LONGER. THERE'RE SOME PEOPLE I'D LIKE TO SHARE THIS WITH--
--MY FAMILY HERE ON EARTH.
END.

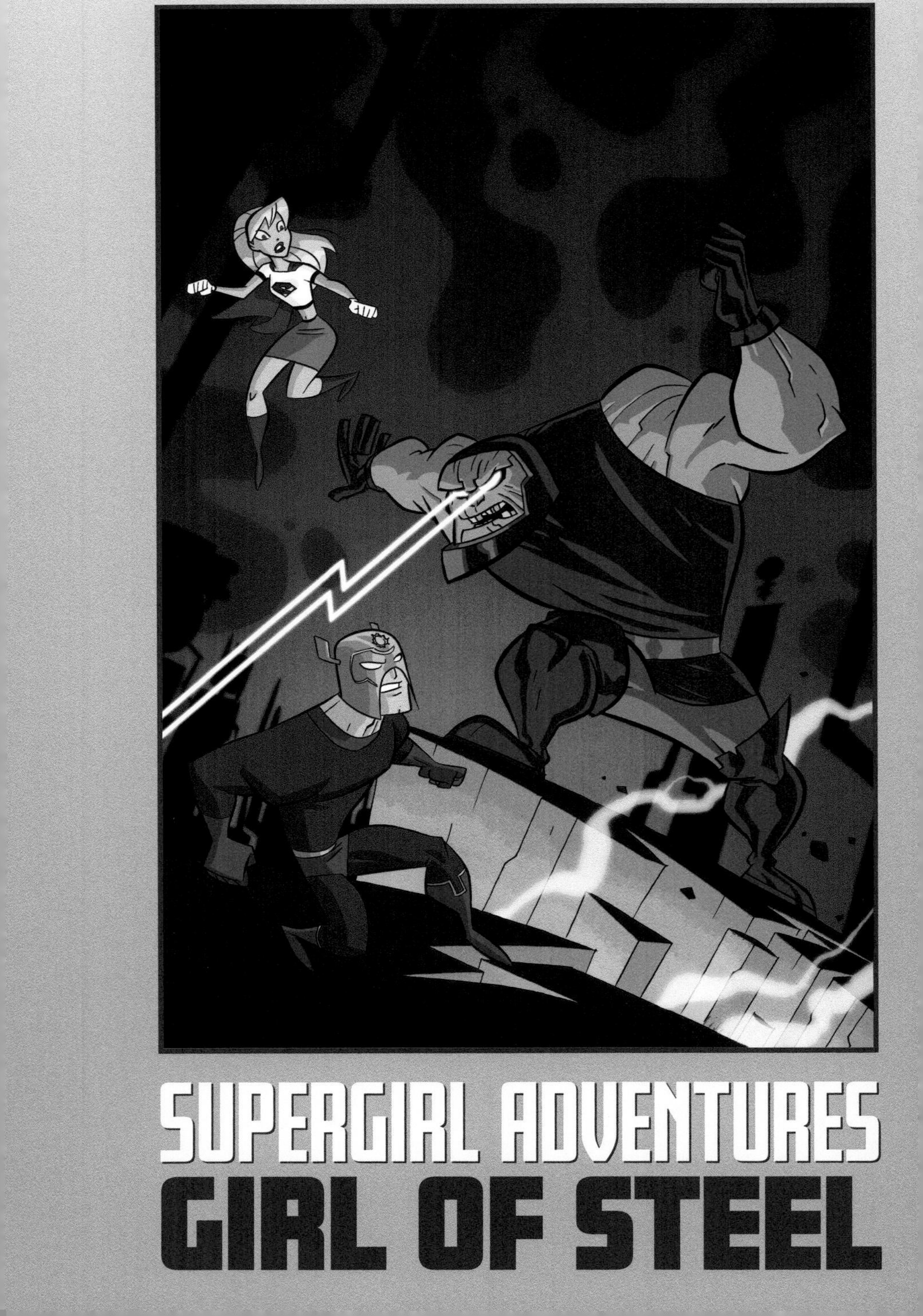

# SUPERGIRL ADVENTURES
# GIRL OF STEEL

SUPERGIRL

Cover by BEN CALDWELL

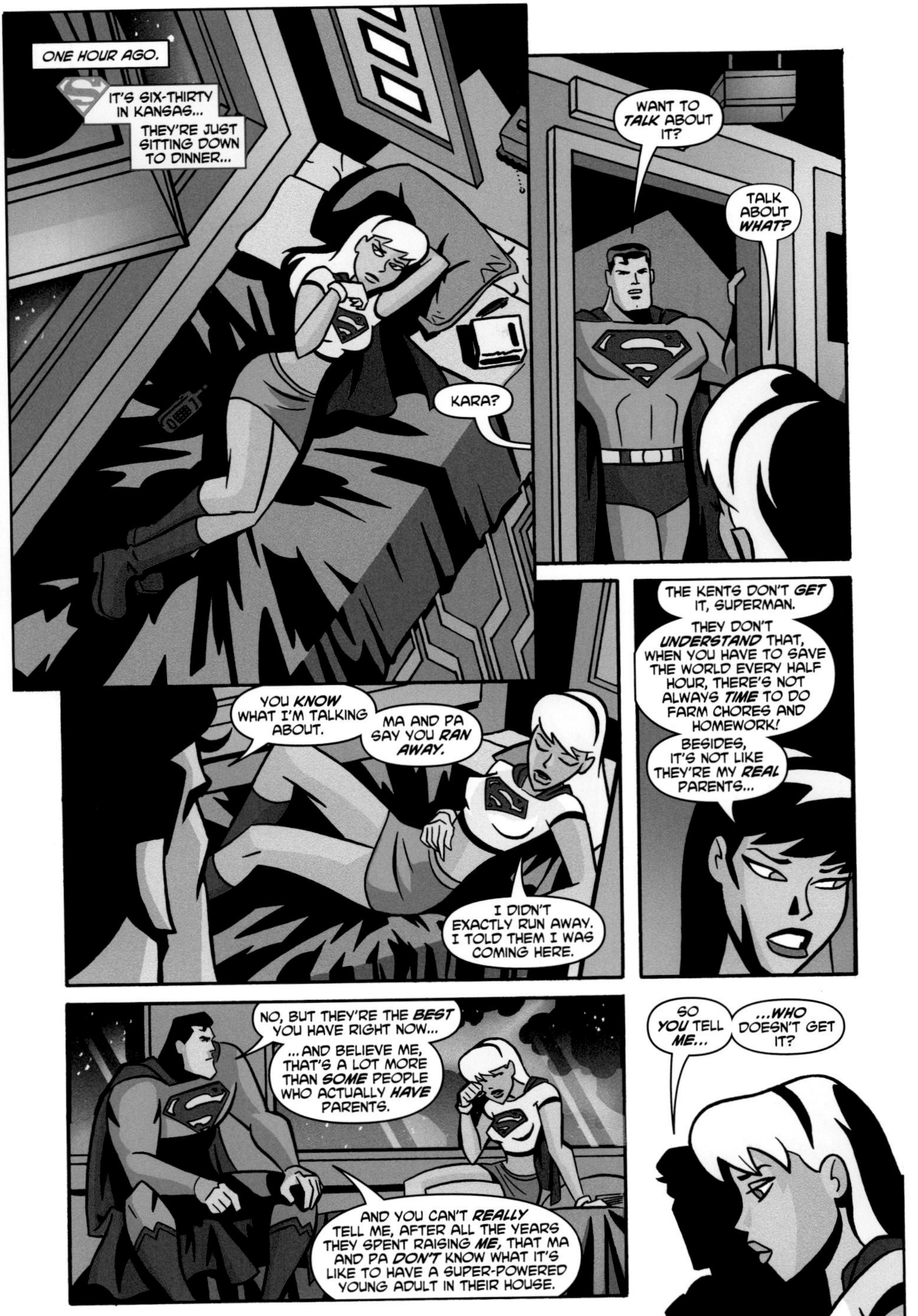
ONE HOUR AGO.
IT'S SIX-THIRTY IN KANSAS...
THEY'RE JUST SITTING DOWN TO DINNER...
KARA?
WANT TO TALK ABOUT IT?
TALK ABOUT WHAT?
YOU KNOW WHAT I'M TALKING ABOUT.
MA AND PA SAY YOU RAN AWAY.
I DIDN'T EXACTLY RUN AWAY. I TOLD THEM I WAS COMING HERE.
THE KENTS DON'T GET IT, SUPERMAN.
THEY DON'T UNDERSTAND THAT, WHEN YOU HAVE TO SAVE THE WORLD EVERY HALF HOUR, THERE'S NOT ALWAYS TIME TO DO FARM CHORES AND HOMEWORK!
BESIDES, IT'S NOT LIKE THEY'RE MY REAL PARENTS...
NO, BUT THEY'RE THE BEST YOU HAVE RIGHT NOW...
...AND BELIEVE ME, THAT'S A LOT MORE THAN SOME PEOPLE WHO ACTUALLY HAVE PARENTS.
AND YOU CAN'T REALLY TELL ME, AFTER ALL THE YEARS THEY SPENT RAISING ME, THAT MA AND PA DON'T KNOW WHAT IT'S LIKE TO HAVE A SUPER-POWERED YOUNG ADULT IN THEIR HOUSE.
SO YOU TELL ME...
...WHO DOESN'T GET IT?

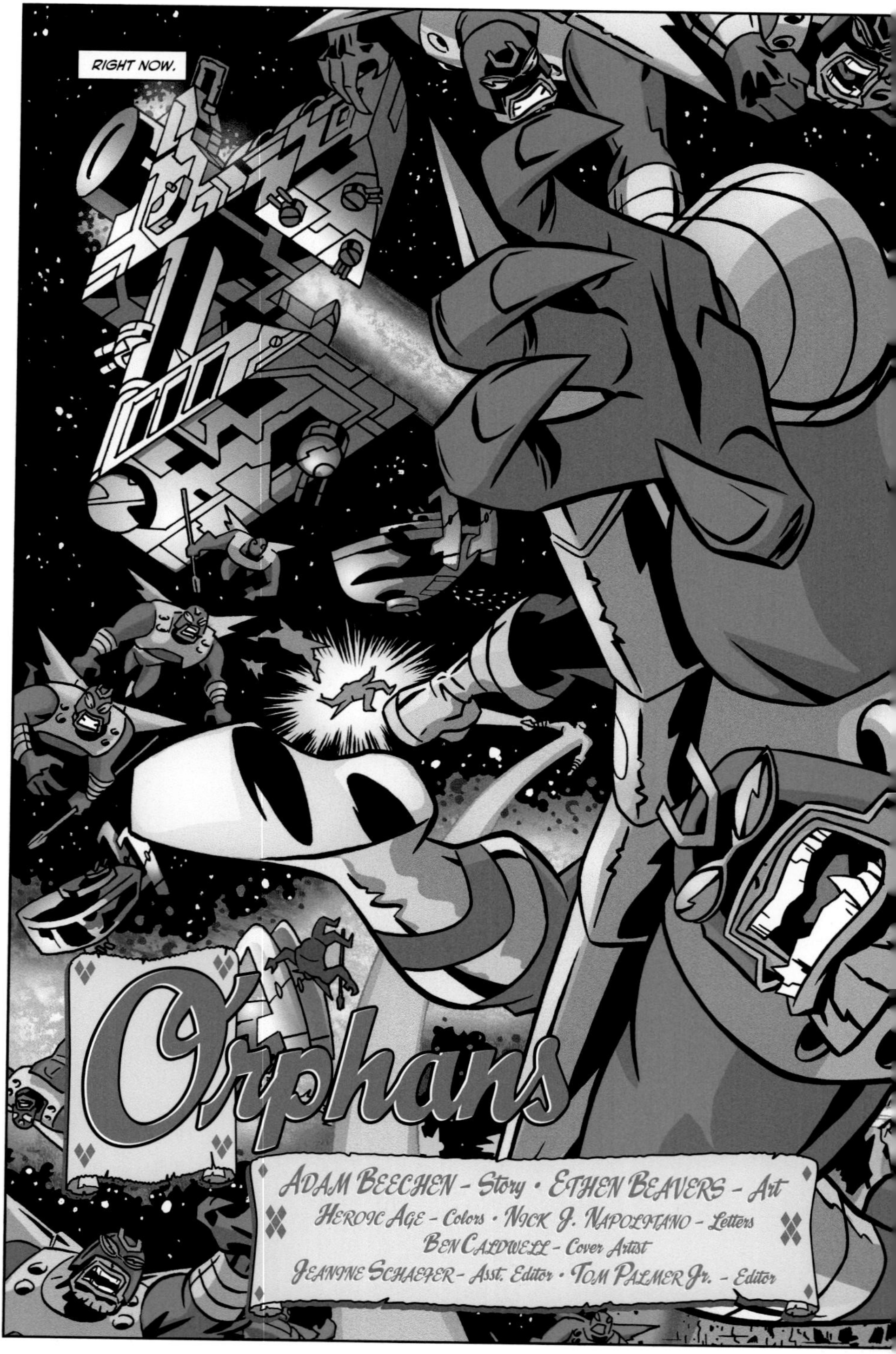
RIGHT NOW.
Orphans
ADAM BEECHEN - Story • ETHEN BEAVERS - Art
HEROIC AGE - Colors • NICK J. NAPOLITANO - Letters
BEN CALDWELL - Cover Artist
JEANINE SCHAEFER - Asst. Editor • TOM PALMER Jr. - Editor

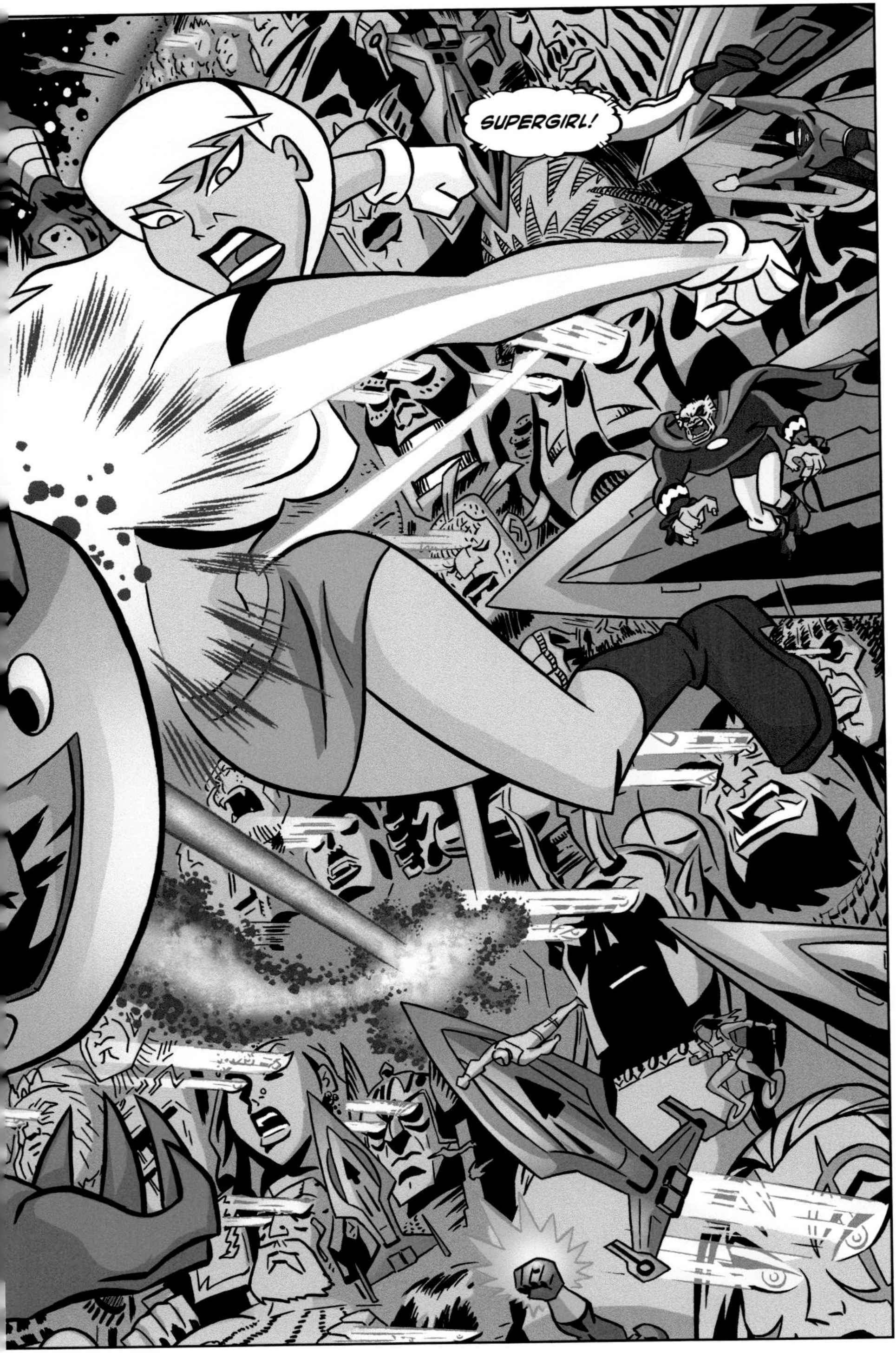
SUPERGIRL!

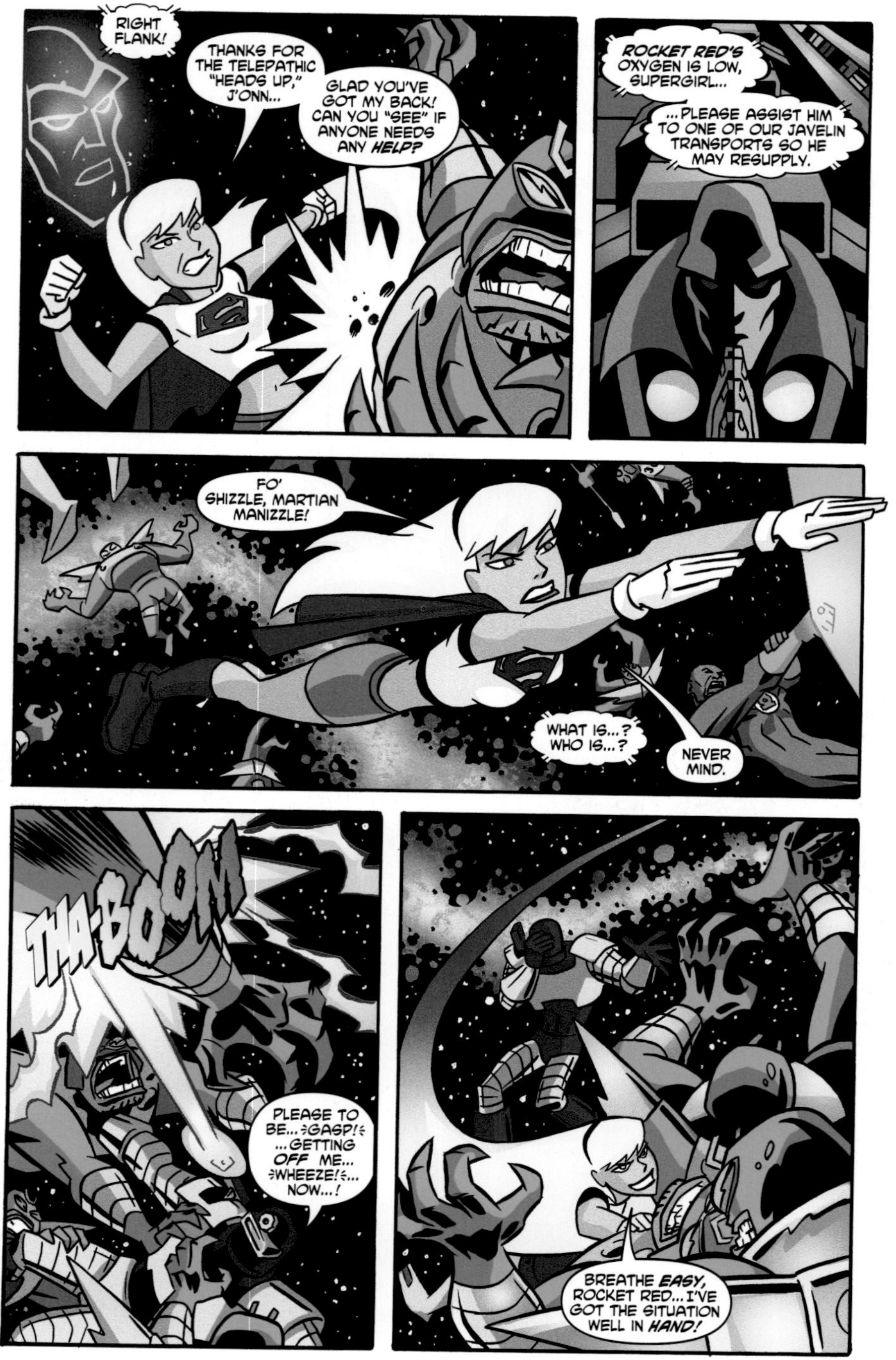
RIGHT FLANK!
THANKS FOR THE TELEPATHIC "HEADS UP," J'ONN...
GLAD YOU'VE GOT MY BACK! CAN YOU "SEE" IF ANYONE NEEDS ANY HELP?
ROCKET RED'S OXYGEN IS LOW, SUPERGIRL...
...PLEASE ASSIST HIM TO ONE OF OUR JAVELIN TRANSPORTS SO HE MAY RESUPPLY.
FO' SHIZZLE, MARTIAN MANIZZLE!
WHAT IS...? WHO IS...?
NEVER MIND.
THA-BOOM
PLEASE TO BE... GASP! ...GETTING OFF ME... WHEEZE!... NOW...!
BREATHE EASY, ROCKET RED... I'VE GOT THE SITUATION WELL IN HAND!

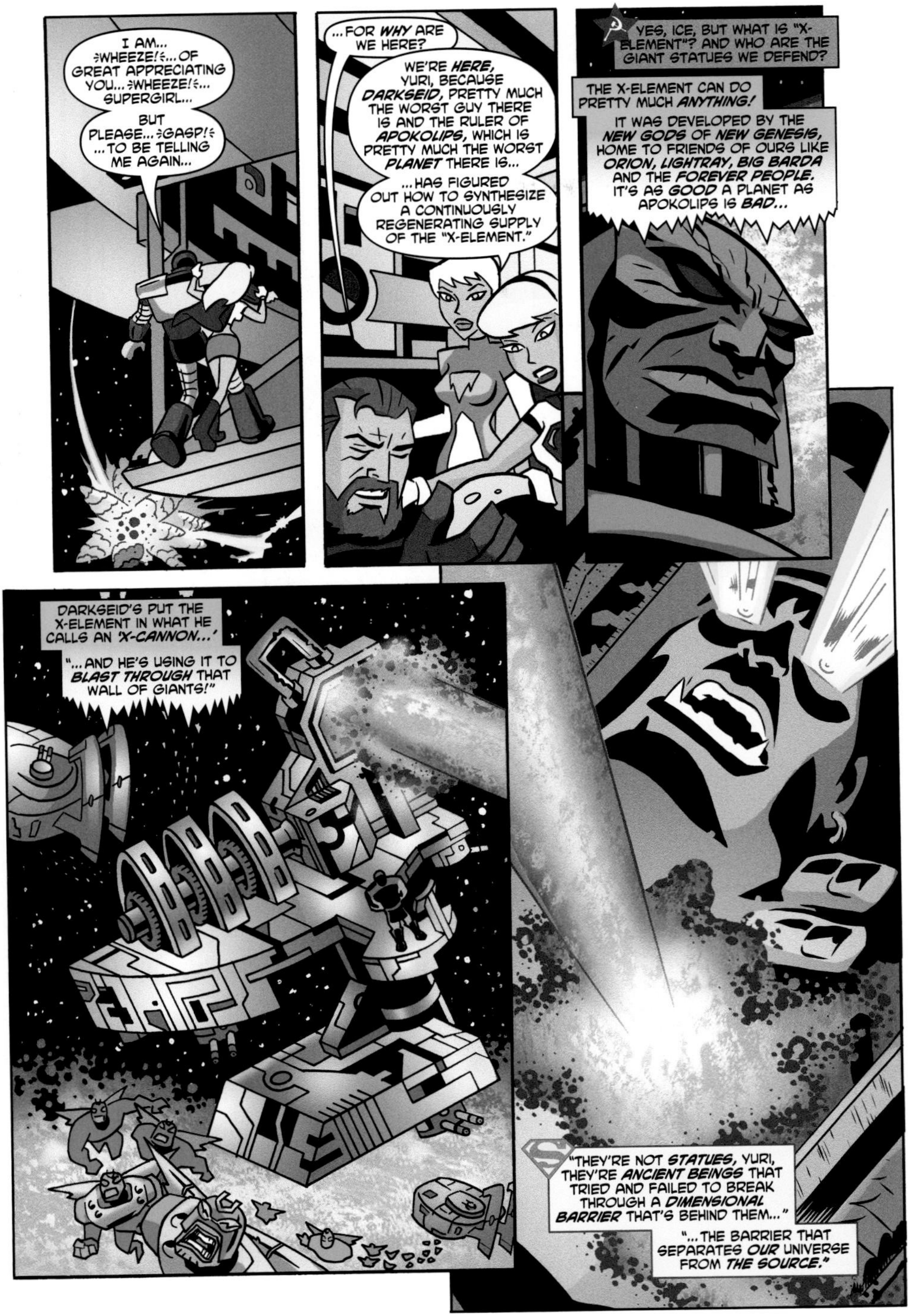
I AM... ⁑WHEEZE!⁑... OF GREAT APPRECIATING YOU... ⁑WHEEZE!⁑... SUPERGIRL...
BUT PLEASE... ⁑GASP!⁑ ...TO BE TELLING ME AGAIN...
...FOR WHY ARE WE HERE?
WE'RE HERE, YURI, BECAUSE DARKSEID, PRETTY MUCH THE WORST GUY THERE IS AND THE RULER OF APOKOLIPS, WHICH IS PRETTY MUCH THE WORST PLANET THERE IS...
...HAS FIGURED OUT HOW TO SYNTHESIZE A CONTINUOUSLY REGENERATING SUPPLY OF THE "X-ELEMENT."
YES, ICE, BUT WHAT IS "X-ELEMENT"? AND WHO ARE THE GIANT STATUES WE DEFEND?
THE X-ELEMENT CAN DO PRETTY MUCH ANYTHING!
IT WAS DEVELOPED BY THE NEW GODS OF NEW GENESIS, HOME TO FRIENDS OF OURS LIKE ORION, LIGHTRAY, BIG BARDA AND THE FOREVER PEOPLE. IT'S AS GOOD A PLANET AS APOKOLIPS IS BAD...
DARKSEID'S PUT THE X-ELEMENT IN WHAT HE CALLS AN 'X-CANNON...'
"...AND HE'S USING IT TO BLAST THROUGH THAT WALL OF GIANTS!"
"THEY'RE NOT STATUES, YURI, THEY'RE ANCIENT BEINGS THAT TRIED AND FAILED TO BREAK THROUGH A DIMENSIONAL BARRIER THAT'S BEHIND THEM..."
"...THE BARRIER THAT SEPARATES OUR UNIVERSE FROM THE SOURCE."

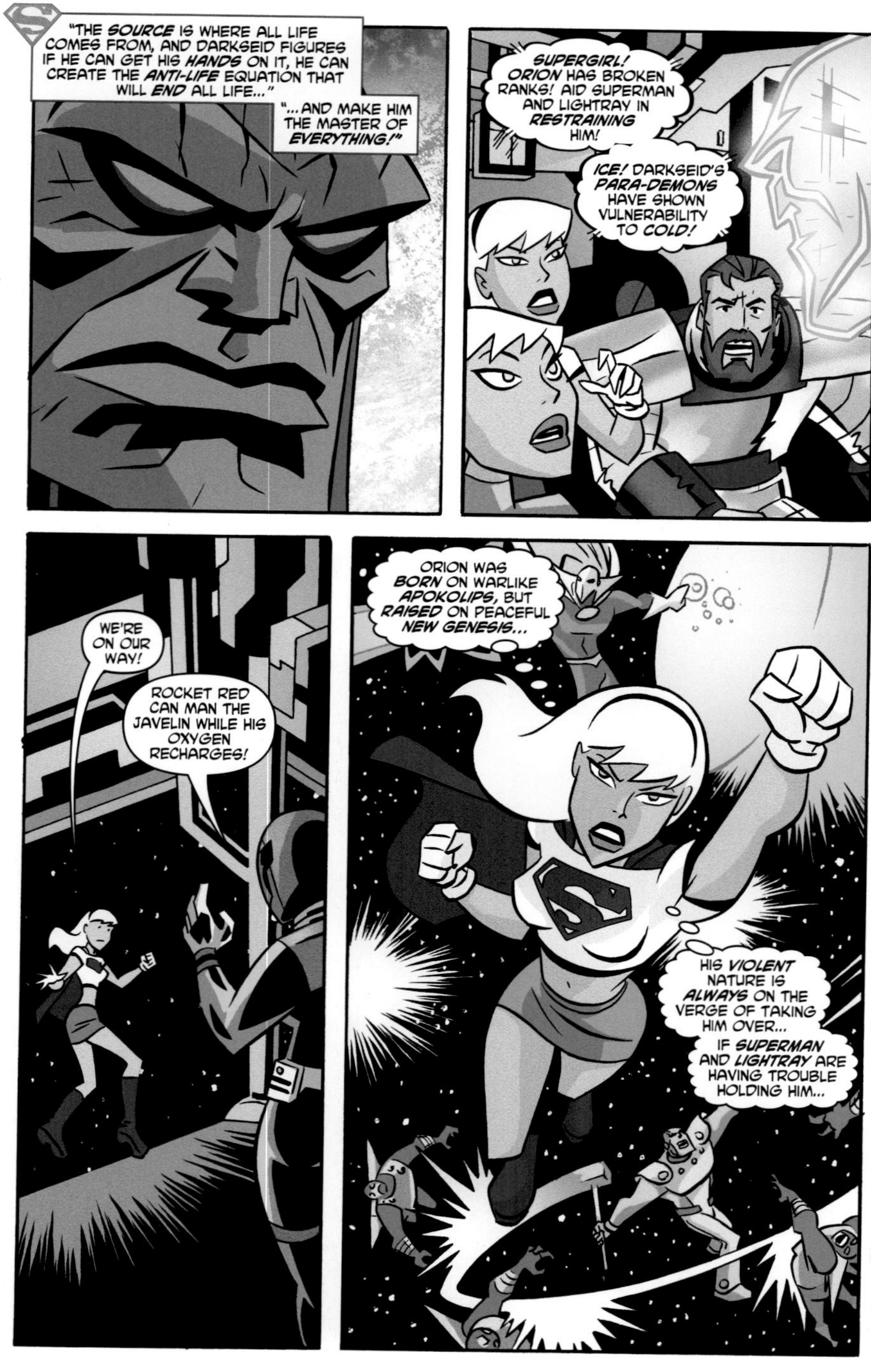
"THE SOURCE IS WHERE ALL LIFE COMES FROM, AND DARKSEID FIGURES IF HE CAN GET HIS HANDS ON IT, HE CAN CREATE THE ANTI-LIFE EQUATION THAT WILL END ALL LIFE..."
"...AND MAKE HIM THE MASTER OF EVERYTHING!"
SUPERGIRL! ORION HAS BROKEN RANKS! AID SUPERMAN AND LIGHTRAY IN RESTRAINING HIM!
ICE! DARKSEID'S PARA-DEMONS HAVE SHOWN VULNERABILITY TO COLD!
WE'RE ON OUR WAY!
ROCKET RED CAN MAN THE JAVELIN WHILE HIS OXYGEN RECHARGES!
ORION WAS BORN ON WARLIKE APOKOLIPS, BUT RAISED ON PEACEFUL NEW GENESIS...
HIS VIOLENT NATURE IS ALWAYS ON THE VERGE OF TAKING HIM OVER...
IF SUPERMAN AND LIGHTRAY ARE HAVING TROUBLE HOLDING HIM...

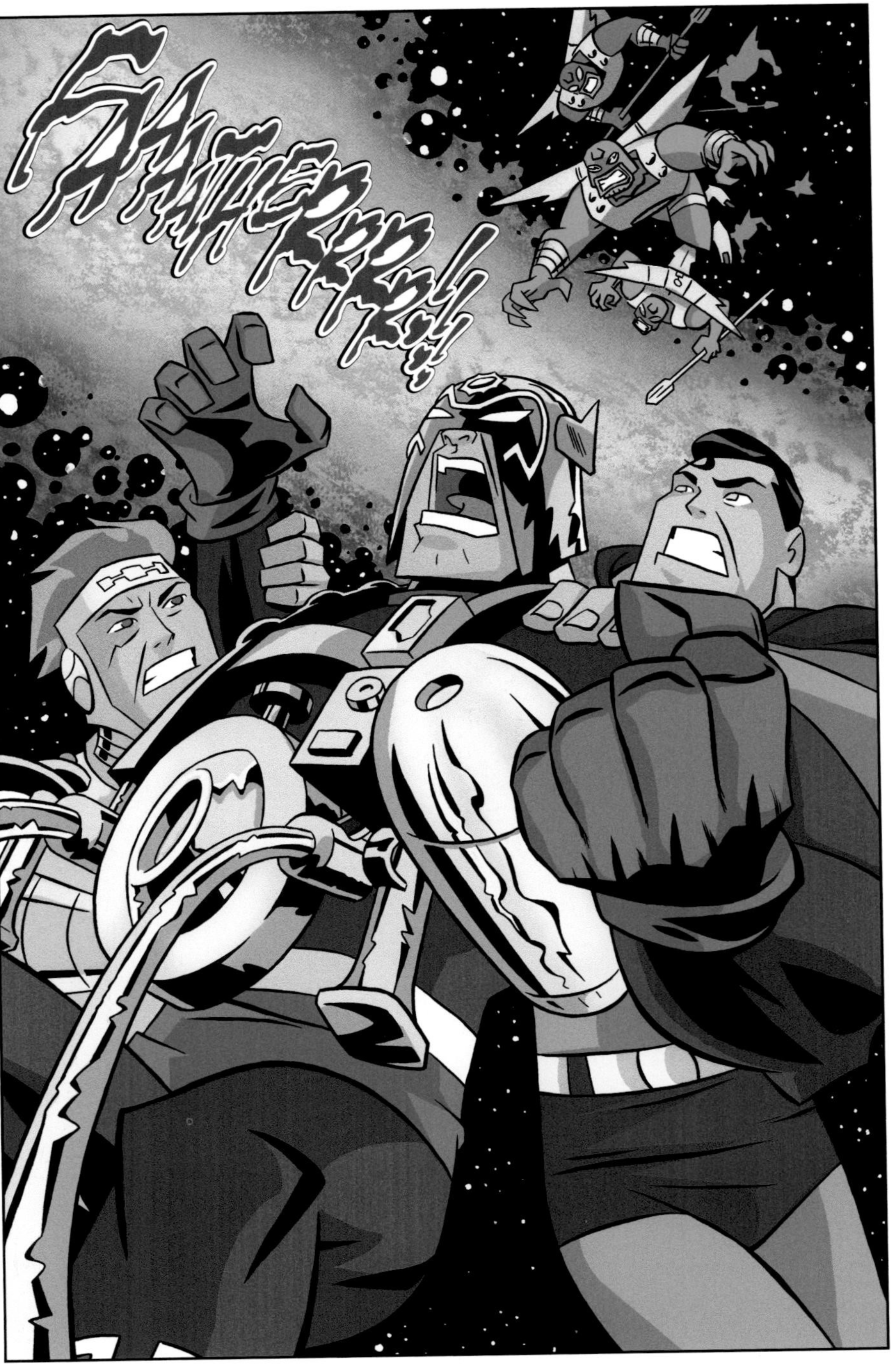

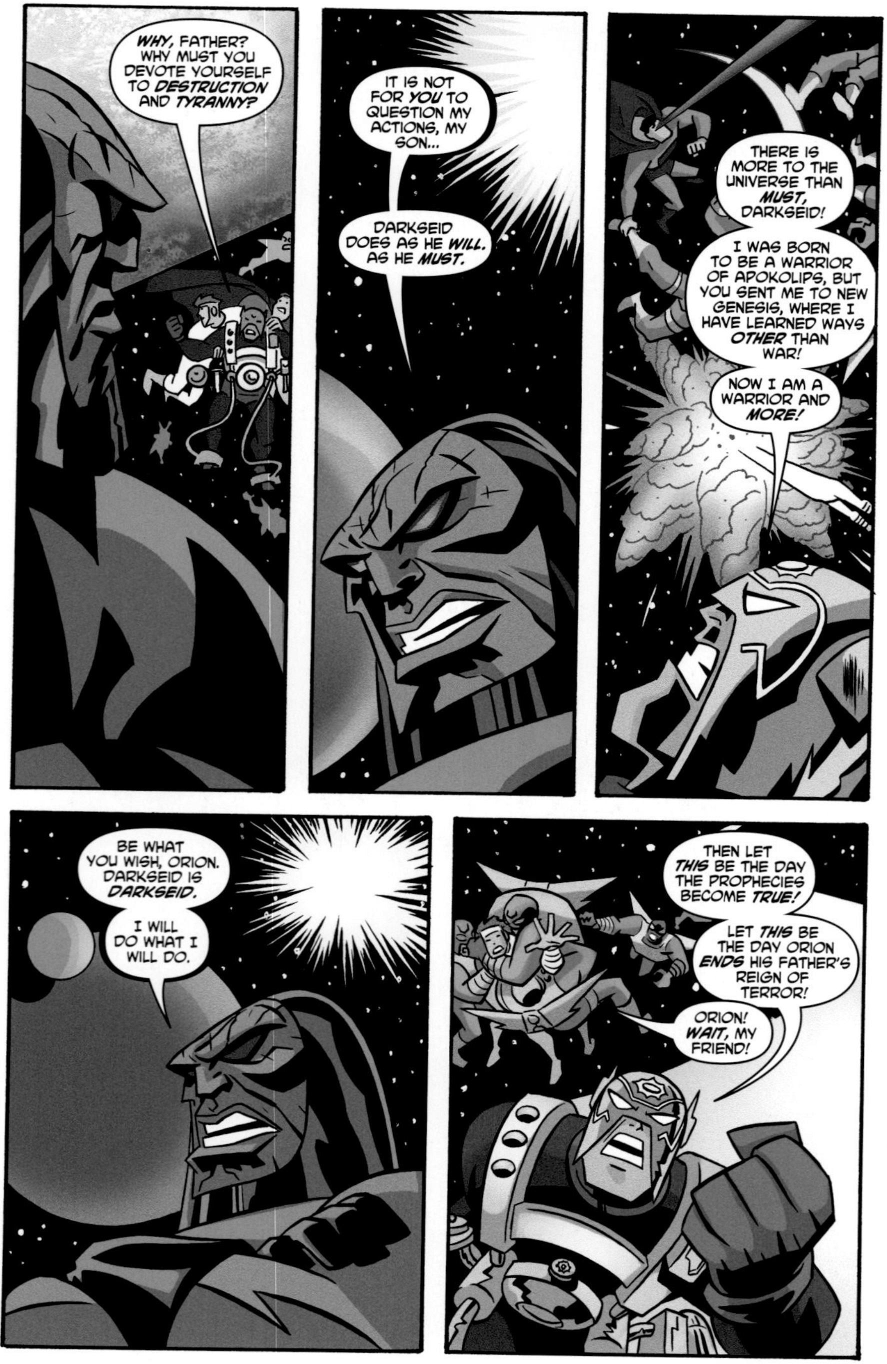
WHY, FATHER? WHY MUST YOU DEVOTE YOURSELF TO DESTRUCTION AND TYRANNY?
IT IS NOT FOR YOU TO QUESTION MY ACTIONS, MY SON...
DARKSEID DOES AS HE WILL. AS HE MUST.
THERE IS MORE TO THE UNIVERSE THAN MUST, DARKSEID!
I WAS BORN TO BE A WARRIOR OF APOKOLIPS, BUT YOU SENT ME TO NEW GENESIS, WHERE I HAVE LEARNED WAYS OTHER THAN WAR!
NOW I AM A WARRIOR AND MORE!
BE WHAT YOU WISH, ORION. DARKSEID IS DARKSEID.
I WILL DO WHAT I WILL DO.
THEN LET THIS BE THE DAY THE PROPHECIES BECOME TRUE!
LET THIS BE THE DAY ORION ENDS HIS FATHER'S REIGN OF TERROR!
ORION! WAIT, MY FRIEND!

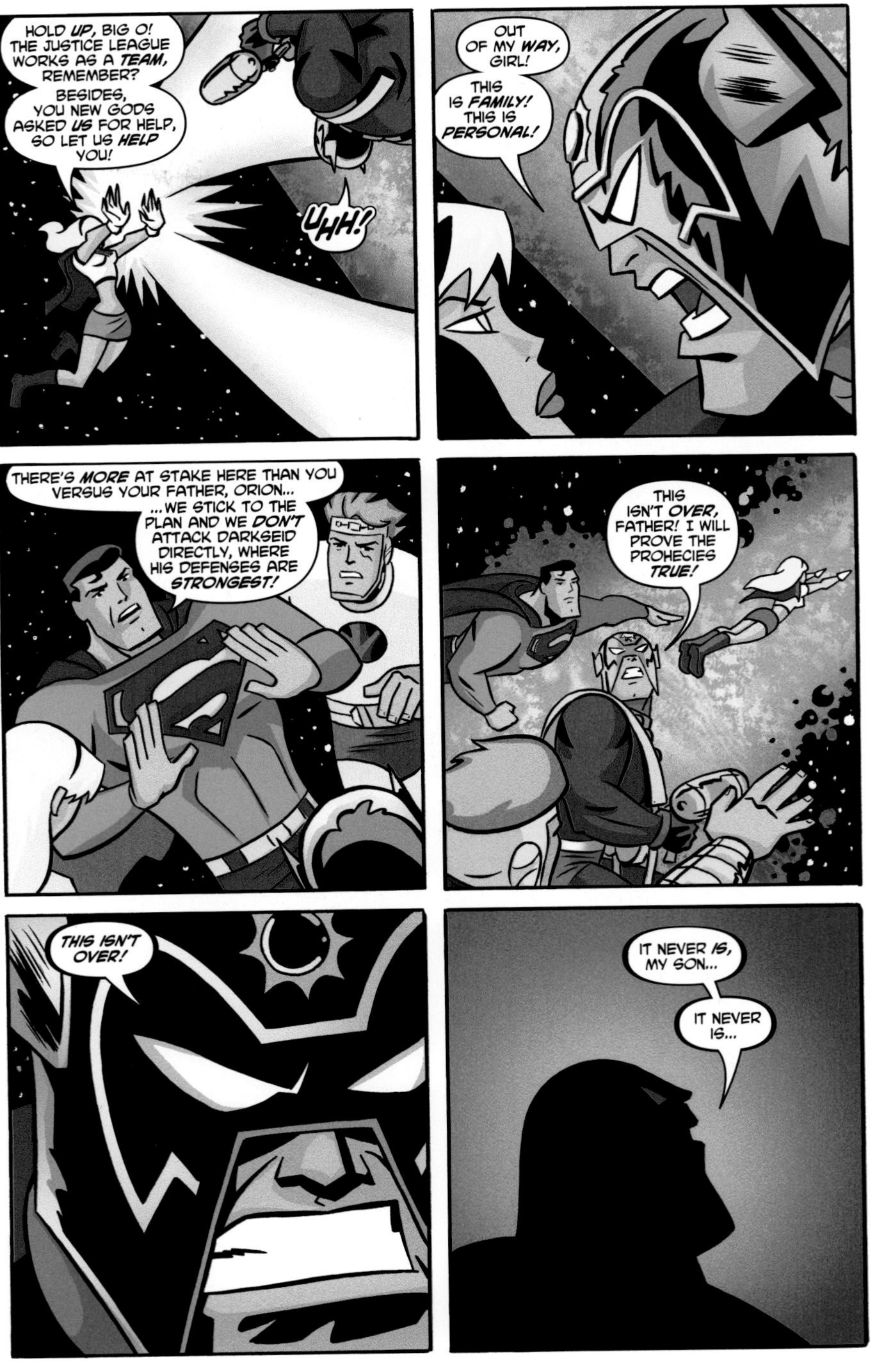
HOLD UP, BIG O! THE JUSTICE LEAGUE WORKS AS A TEAM, REMEMBER?
BESIDES, YOU NEW GODS ASKED US FOR HELP, SO LET US HELP YOU!
UHH!
OUT OF MY WAY, GIRL!
THIS IS FAMILY! THIS IS PERSONAL!
THERE'S MORE AT STAKE HERE THAN YOU VERSUS YOUR FATHER, ORION...
...WE STICK TO THE PLAN AND WE DON'T ATTACK DARKSEID DIRECTLY, WHERE HIS DEFENSES ARE STRONGEST!
THIS ISN'T OVER, FATHER! I WILL PROVE THE PROHECIES TRUE!
THIS ISN'T OVER!
IT NEVER IS, MY SON...
IT NEVER IS...

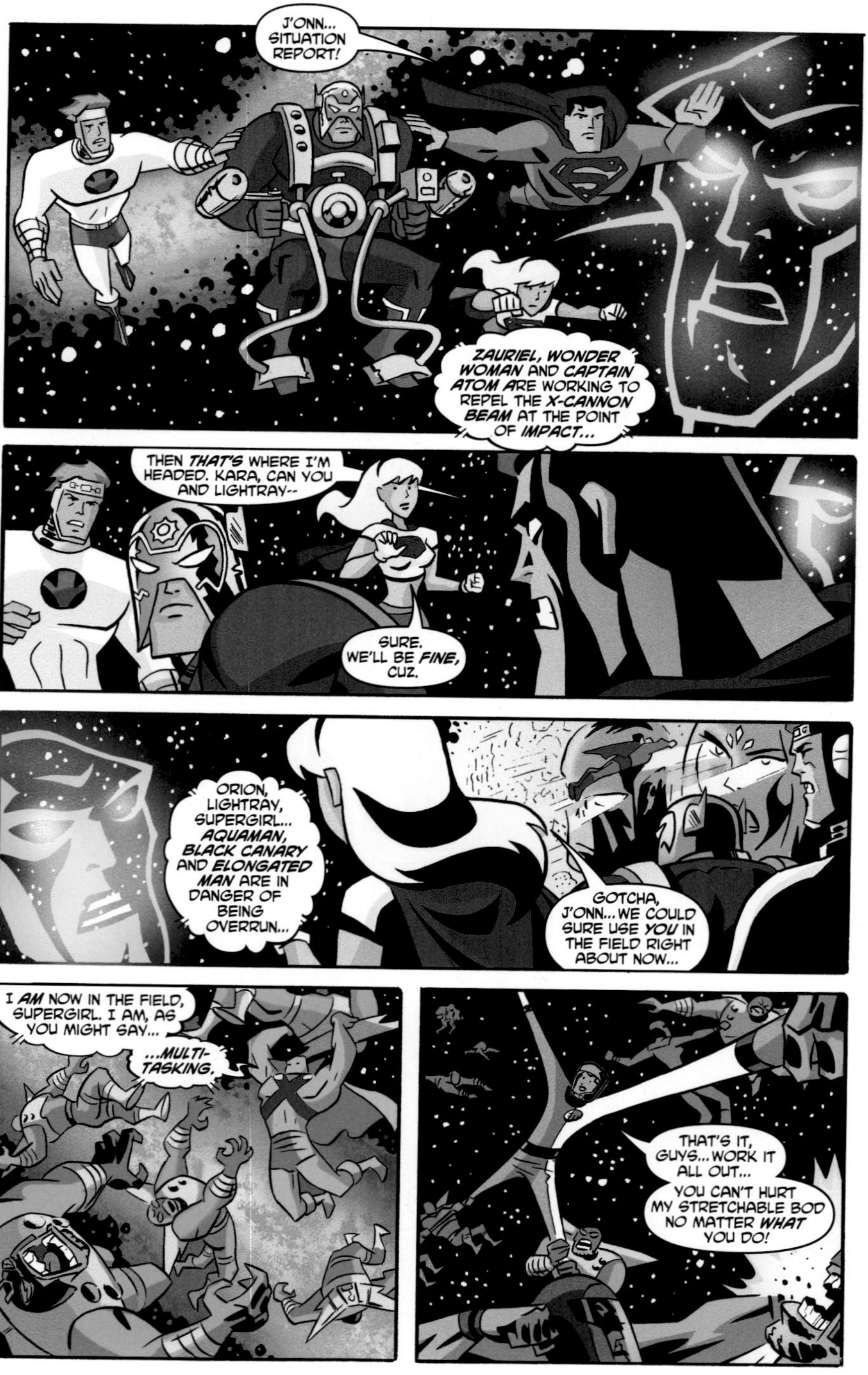
J'ONN... SITUATION REPORT!
ZAURIEL, WONDER WOMAN AND CAPTAIN ATOM ARE WORKING TO REPEL THE X-CANNON BEAM AT THE POINT OF IMPACT...
THEN THAT'S WHERE I'M HEADED. KARA, CAN YOU AND LIGHTRAY--
SURE. WE'LL BE FINE, CUZ.
ORION, LIGHTRAY, SUPERGIRL... AQUAMAN, BLACK CANARY AND ELONGATED MAN ARE IN DANGER OF BEING OVERRUN...
GOTCHA, J'ONN... WE COULD SURE USE YOU IN THE FIELD RIGHT ABOUT NOW...
I AM NOW IN THE FIELD, SUPERGIRL. I AM, AS YOU MIGHT SAY...
...MULTI-TASKING.
THAT'S IT, GUYS... WORK IT ALL OUT...
YOU CAN'T HURT MY STRETCHABLE BOD NO MATTER WHAT YOU DO!

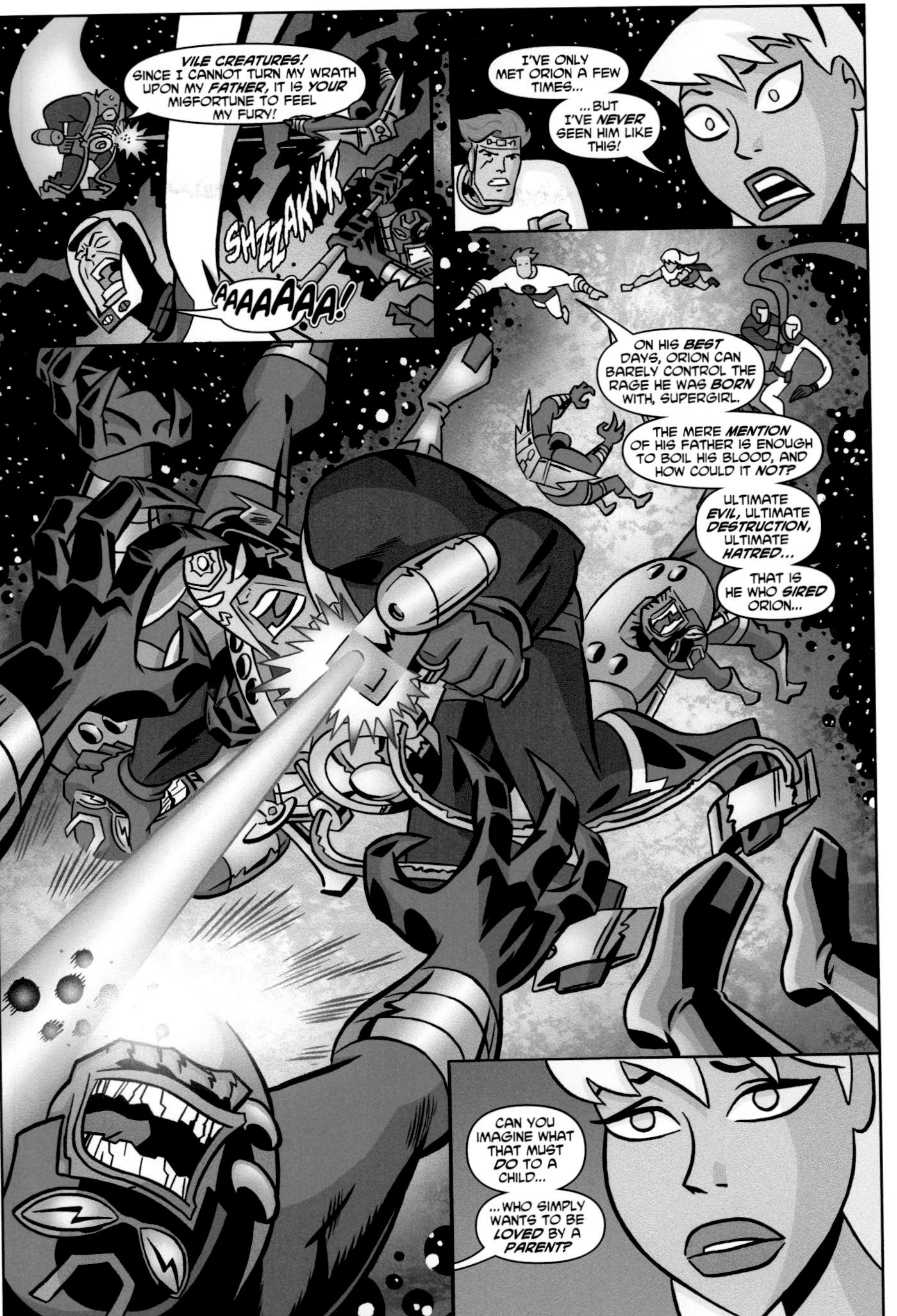
VILE CREATURES! SINCE I CANNOT TURN MY WRATH UPON MY FATHER, IT IS YOUR MISFORTUNE TO FEEL MY FURY!
SHZZZAKKK
AAAAAAA!
I'VE ONLY MET ORION A FEW TIMES...
...BUT I'VE NEVER SEEN HIM LIKE THIS!
ON HIS BEST DAYS, ORION CAN BARELY CONTROL THE RAGE HE WAS BORN WITH, SUPERGIRL.
THE MERE MENTION OF HIS FATHER IS ENOUGH TO BOIL HIS BLOOD, AND HOW COULD IT NOT?
ULTIMATE EVIL, ULTIMATE DESTRUCTION, ULTIMATE HATRED...
THAT IS HE WHO SIRED ORION...
CAN YOU IMAGINE WHAT THAT MUST DO TO A CHILD...
...WHO SIMPLY WANTS TO BE LOVED BY A PARENT?

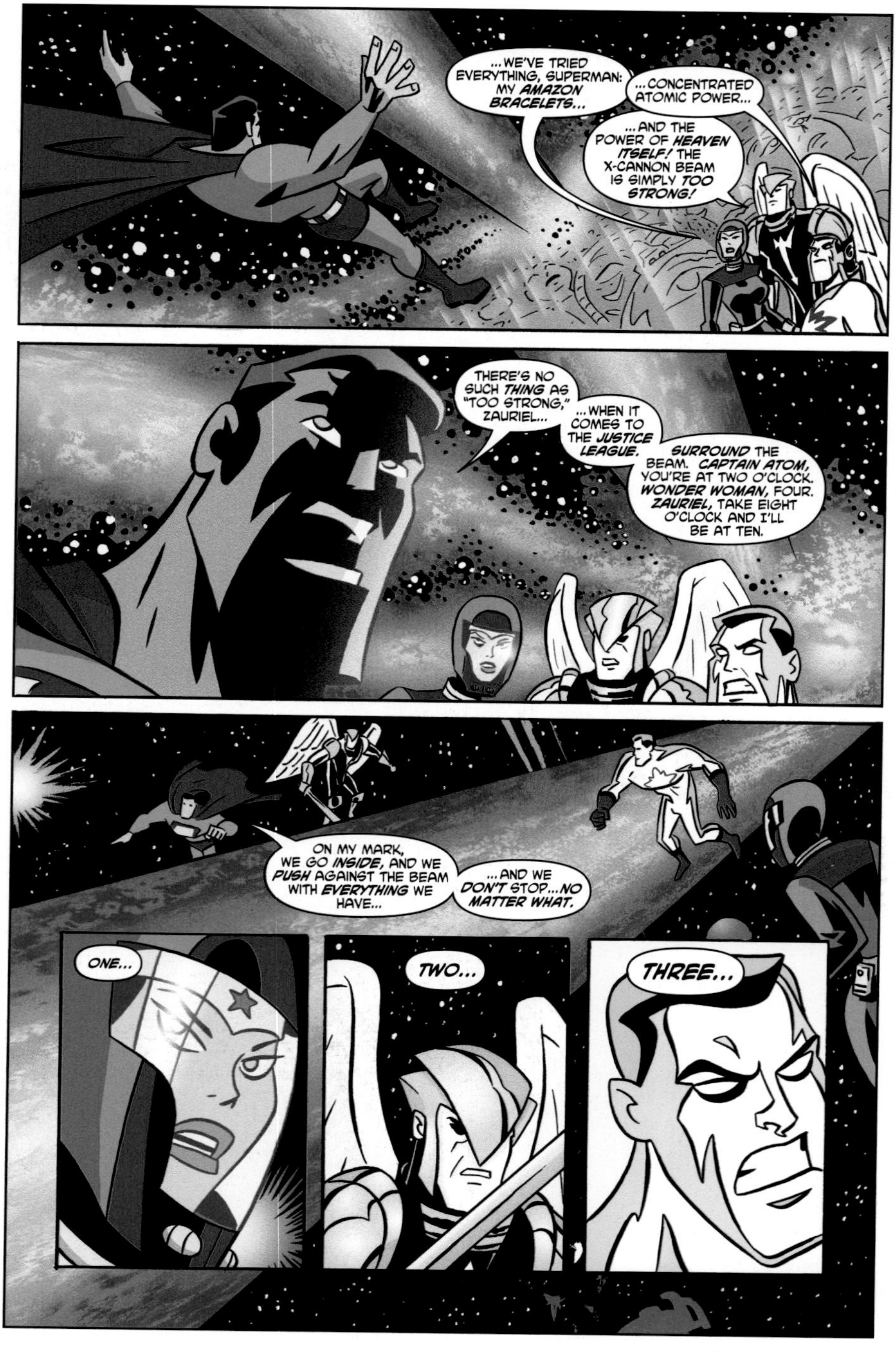
...WE'VE TRIED EVERYTHING, SUPERMAN: MY AMAZON BRACELETS...
...CONCENTRATED ATOMIC POWER...
...AND THE POWER OF HEAVEN ITSELF! THE X-CANNON BEAM IS SIMPLY TOO STRONG!
THERE'S NO SUCH THING AS "TOO STRONG," ZAURIEL...
...WHEN IT COMES TO THE JUSTICE LEAGUE.
SURROUND THE BEAM. CAPTAIN ATOM, YOU'RE AT TWO O'CLOCK. WONDER WOMAN, FOUR. ZAURIEL, TAKE EIGHT O'CLOCK AND I'LL BE AT TEN.
ON MY MARK, WE GO INSIDE, AND WE PUSH AGAINST THE BEAM WITH EVERYTHING WE HAVE...
...AND WE DON'T STOP...NO MATTER WHAT.
ONE...
TWO...
THREE...

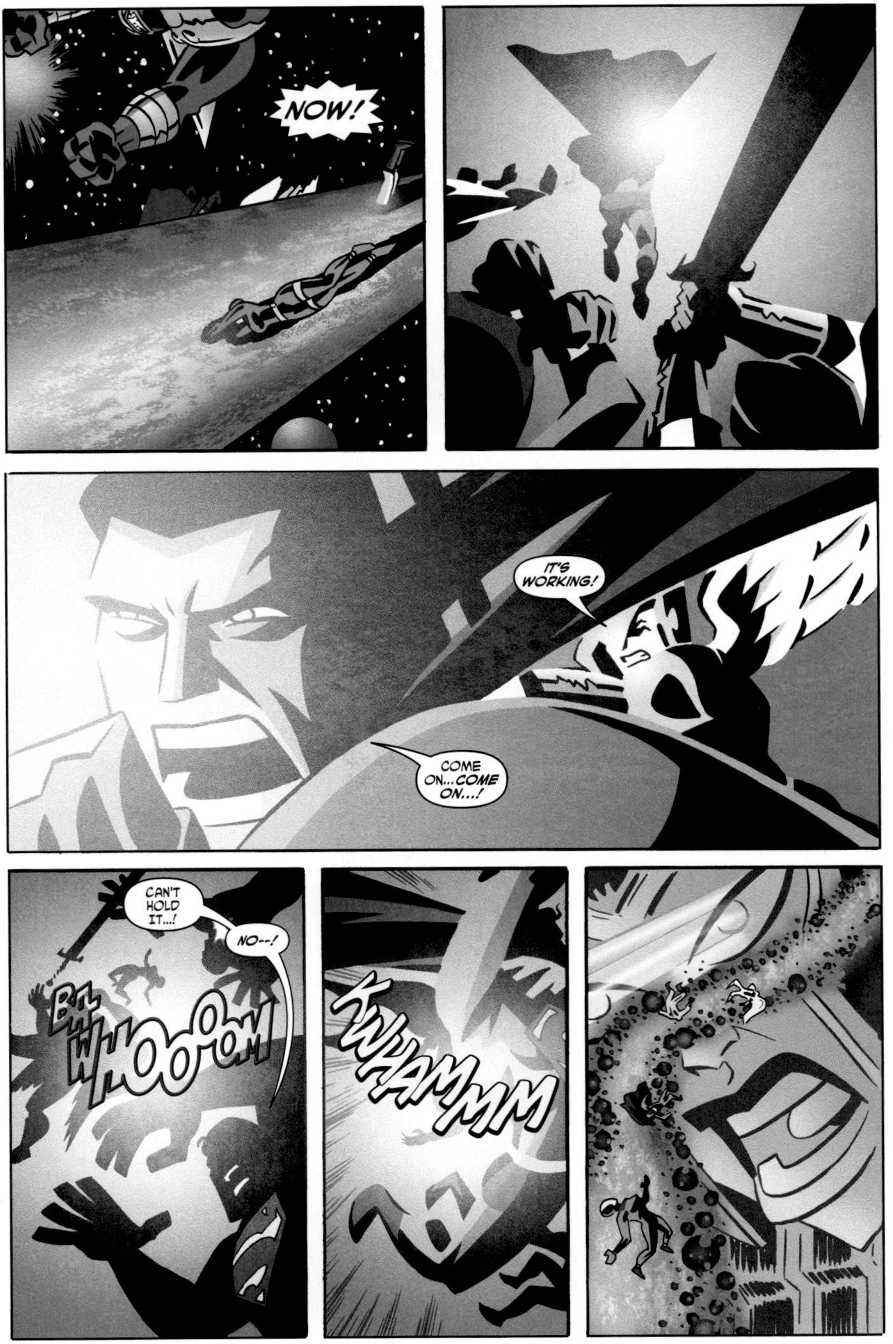
NOW!
IT'S WORKING!
COME ON...COME ON...!
CAN'T HOLD IT...!
NO--!
BA WHOOOOOM
KWHAMMMM

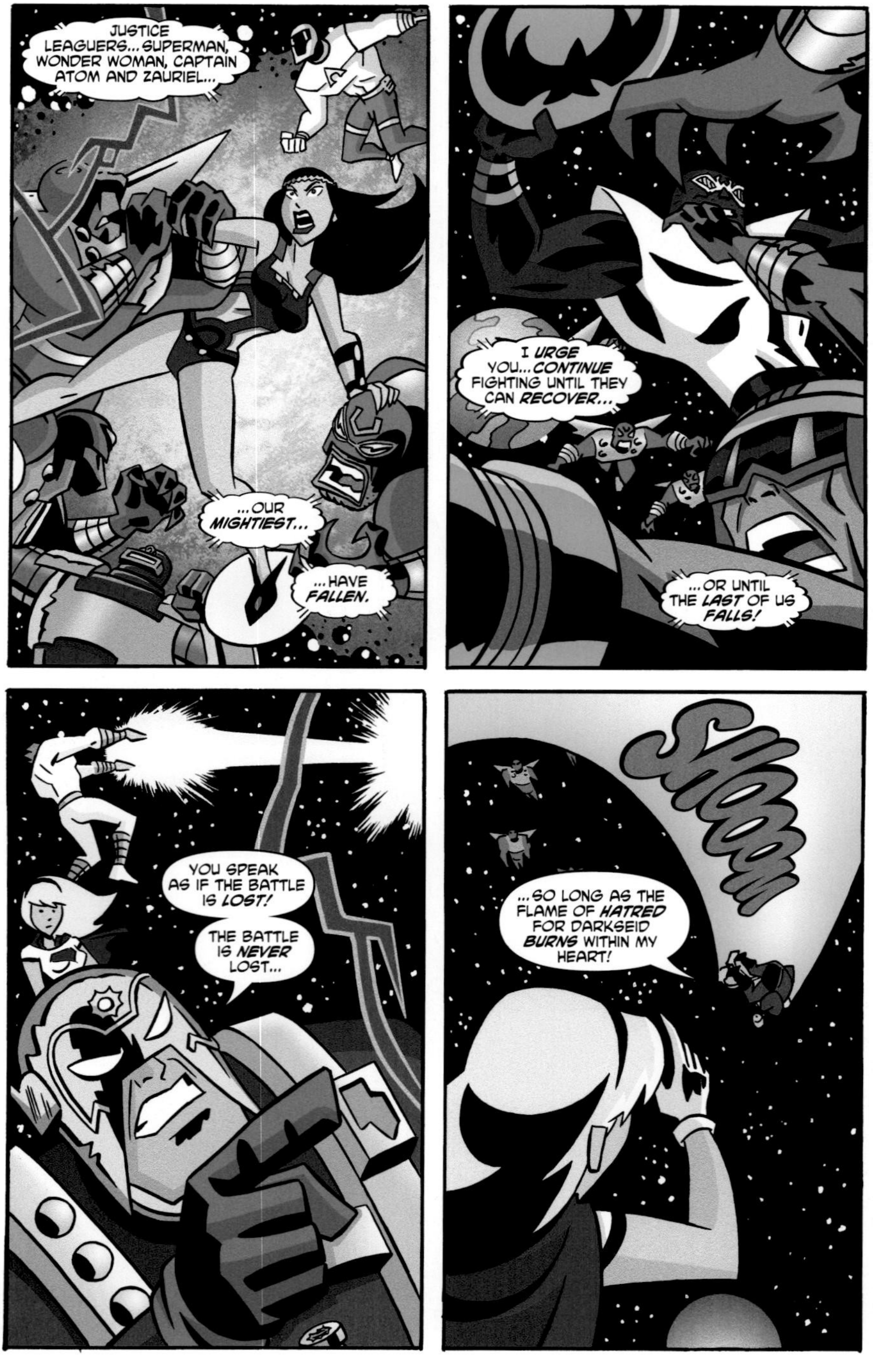
JUSTICE LEAGUERS... SUPERMAN, WONDER WOMAN, CAPTAIN ATOM AND ZAURIEL...
...OUR MIGHTIEST...
...HAVE FALLEN.
I URGE YOU... CONTINUE FIGHTING UNTIL THEY CAN RECOVER...
...OR UNTIL THE LAST OF US FALLS!
YOU SPEAK AS IF THE BATTLE IS LOST!
THE BATTLE IS NEVER LOST...
SHOOM
...SO LONG AS THE FLAME OF HATRED FOR DARKSEID BURNS WITHIN MY HEART!

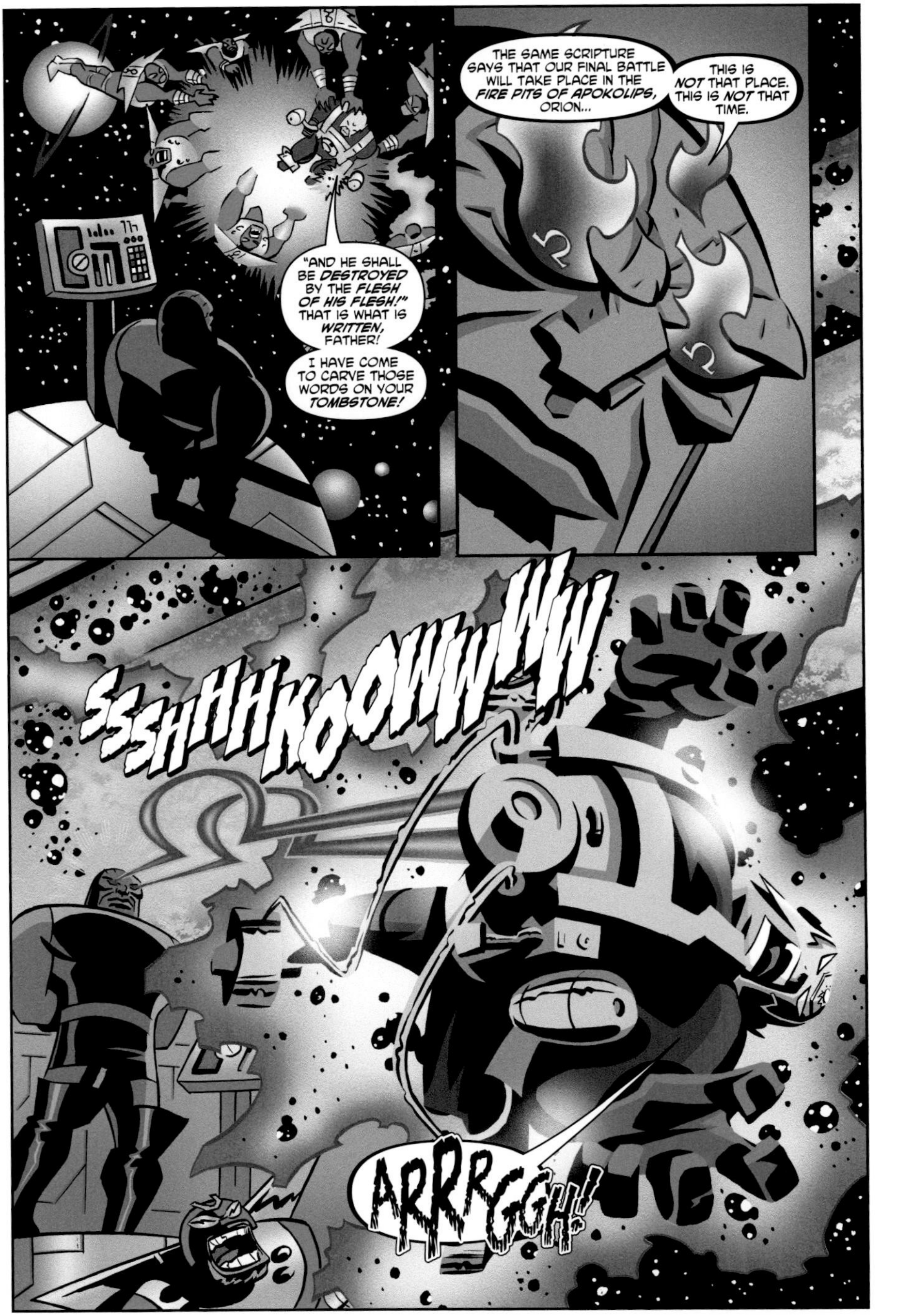
"AND HE SHALL BE DESTROYED BY THE FLESH OF HIS FLESH!" THAT IS WHAT IS WRITTEN, FATHER!
I HAVE COME TO CARVE THOSE WORDS ON YOUR TOMBSTONE!
THE SAME SCRIPTURE SAYS THAT OUR FINAL BATTLE WILL TAKE PLACE IN THE FIRE PITS OF APOKOLIPS, ORION...
THIS IS NOT THAT PLACE. THIS IS NOT THAT TIME.
SSSHHHKOOWWWWW
ARRRGGH!

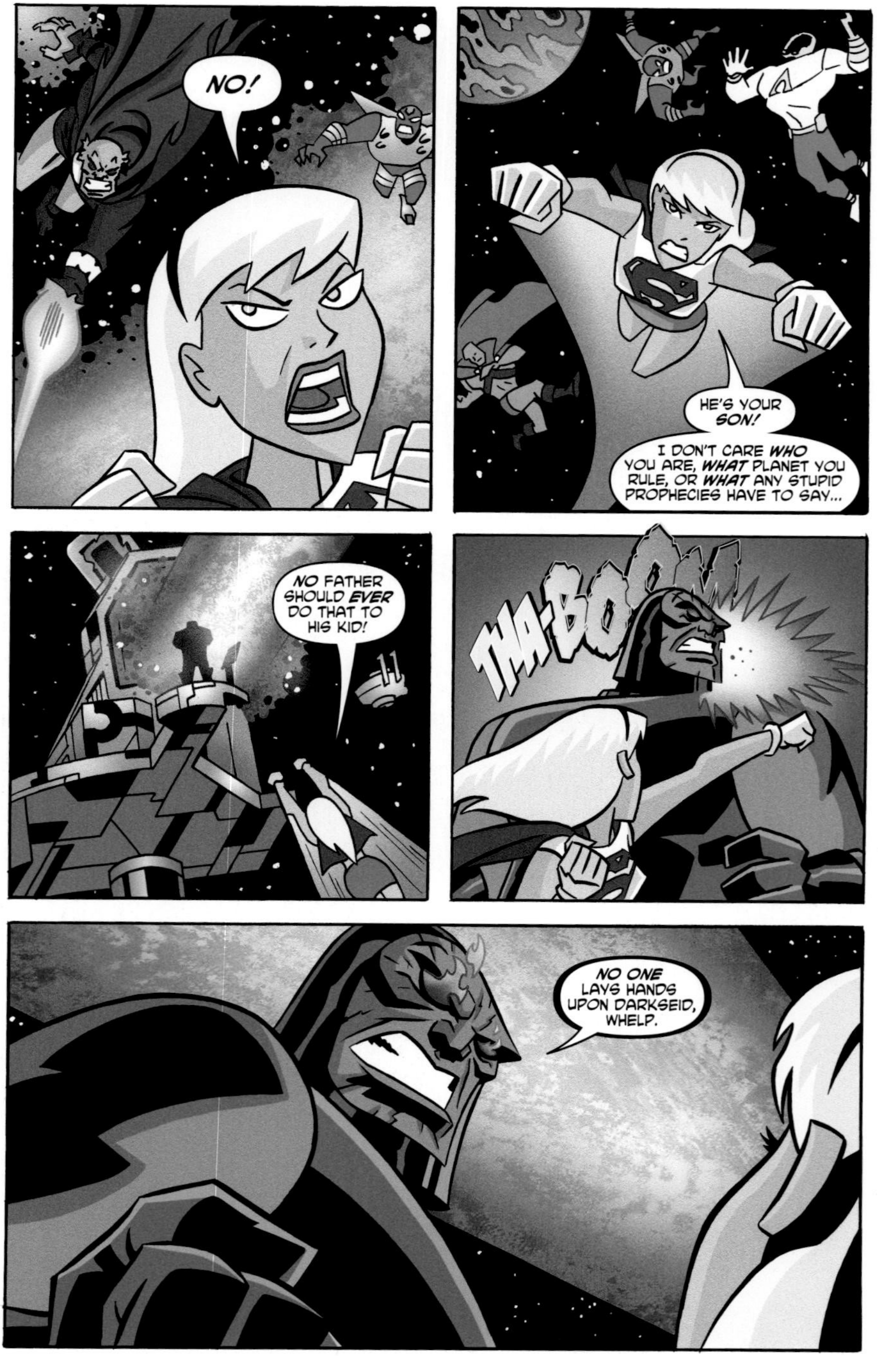
NO!
HE'S YOUR SON!
I DON'T CARE WHO YOU ARE, WHAT PLANET YOU RULE, OR WHAT ANY STUPID PROPHECIES HAVE TO SAY...
NO FATHER SHOULD EVER DO THAT TO HIS KID!
THA-BOOM
NO ONE LAYS HANDS UPON DARKSEID, WHELP.

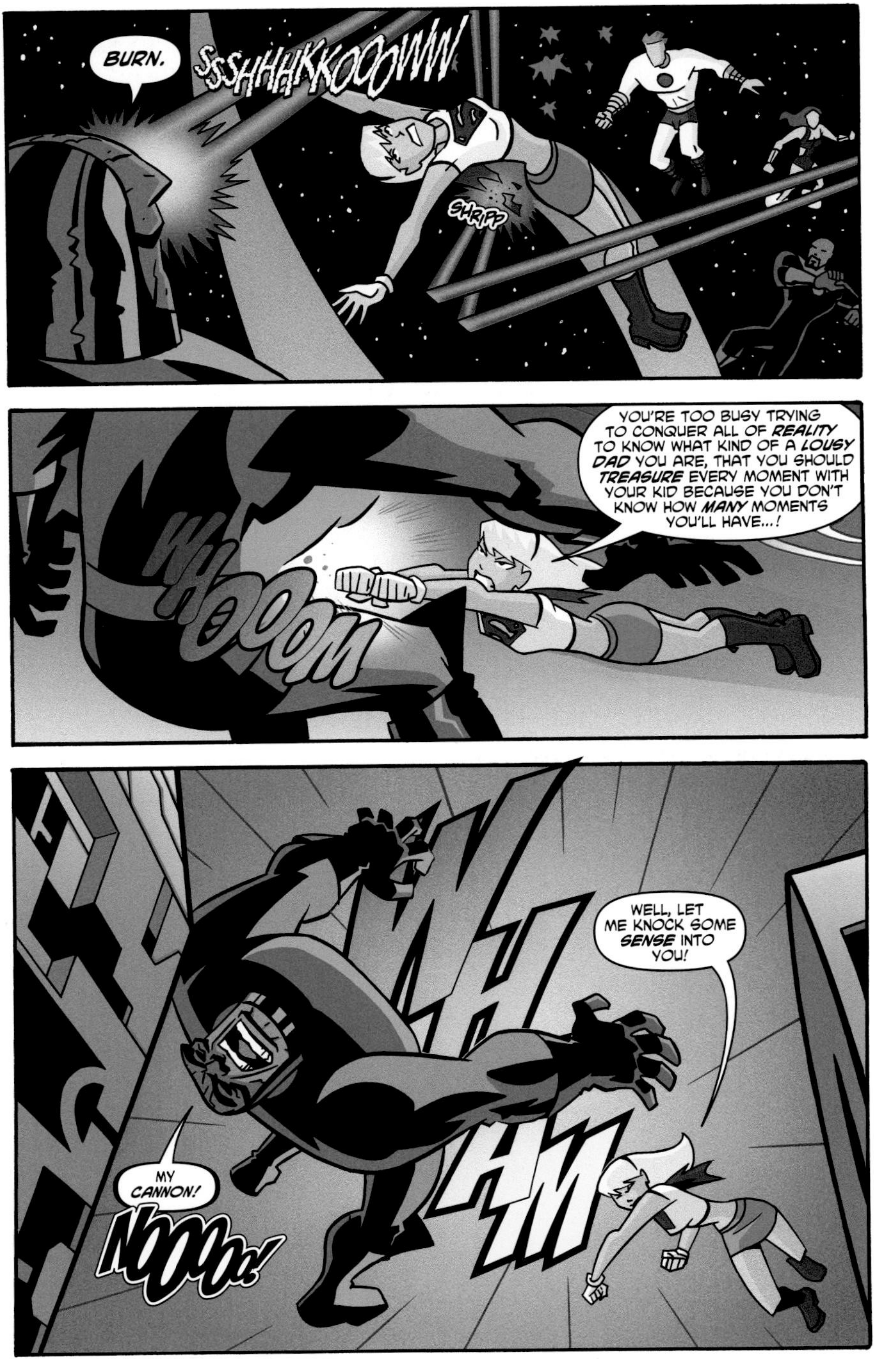

BURN.
SSSHHHKKOOOWW
SHRIPP
YOU'RE TOO BUSY TRYING TO CONQUER ALL OF REALITY TO KNOW WHAT KIND OF A LOUSY DAD YOU ARE, THAT YOU SHOULD TREASURE EVERY MOMENT WITH YOUR KID BECAUSE YOU DON'T KNOW HOW MANY MOMENTS YOU'LL HAVE...!
WHOOOOM
WELL, LET ME KNOCK SOME SENSE INTO YOU!
WHAM
MY CANNON!
NOOOOoo!

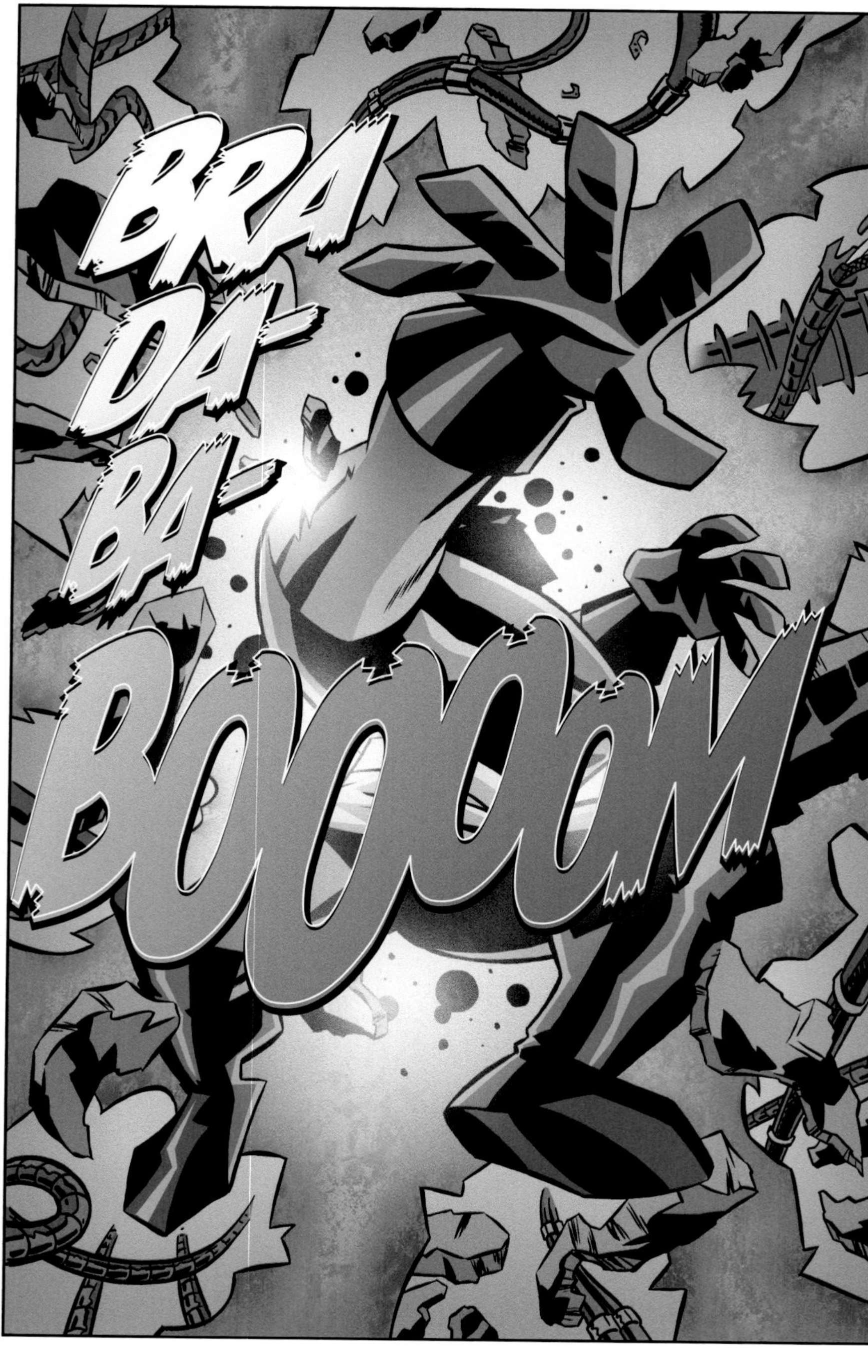
BRA
DA-
BA-
BOOOOM

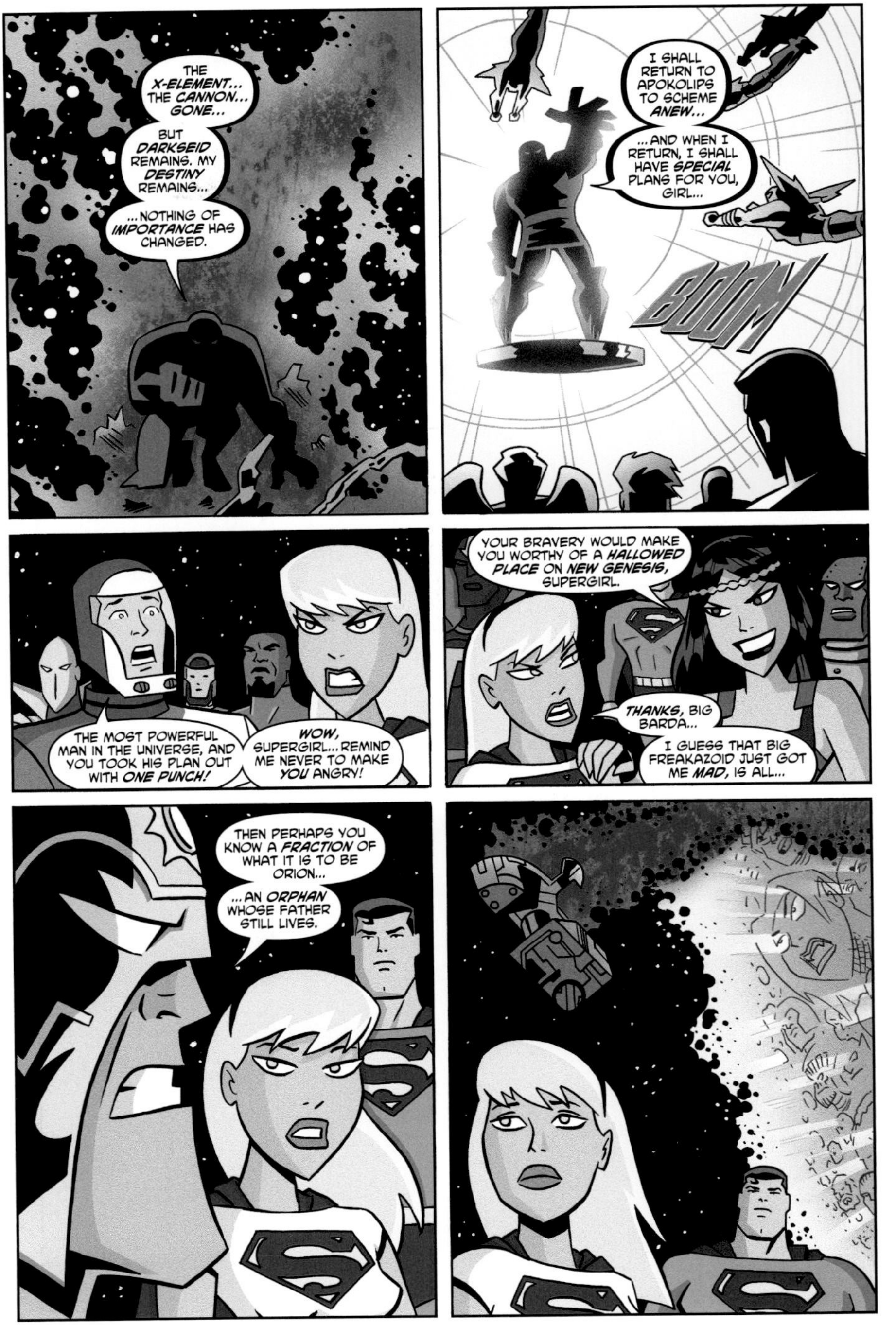
THE X-ELEMENT... THE CANNON... GONE...
BUT DARKSEID REMAINS. MY DESTINY REMAINS...
...NOTHING OF IMPORTANCE HAS CHANGED.
I SHALL RETURN TO APOKOLIPS TO SCHEME ANEW...
...AND WHEN I RETURN, I SHALL HAVE SPECIAL PLANS FOR YOU, GIRL...
BOOM
THE MOST POWERFUL MAN IN THE UNIVERSE, AND YOU TOOK HIS PLAN OUT WITH ONE PUNCH!
WOW, SUPERGIRL... REMIND ME NEVER TO MAKE YOU ANGRY!
YOUR BRAVERY WOULD MAKE YOU WORTHY OF A HALLOWED PLACE ON NEW GENESIS, SUPERGIRL.
THANKS, BIG BARDA...
I GUESS THAT BIG FREAKAZOID JUST GOT ME MAD, IS ALL...
THEN PERHAPS YOU KNOW A FRACTION OF WHAT IT IS TO BE ORION...
...AN ORPHAN WHOSE FATHER STILL LIVES.

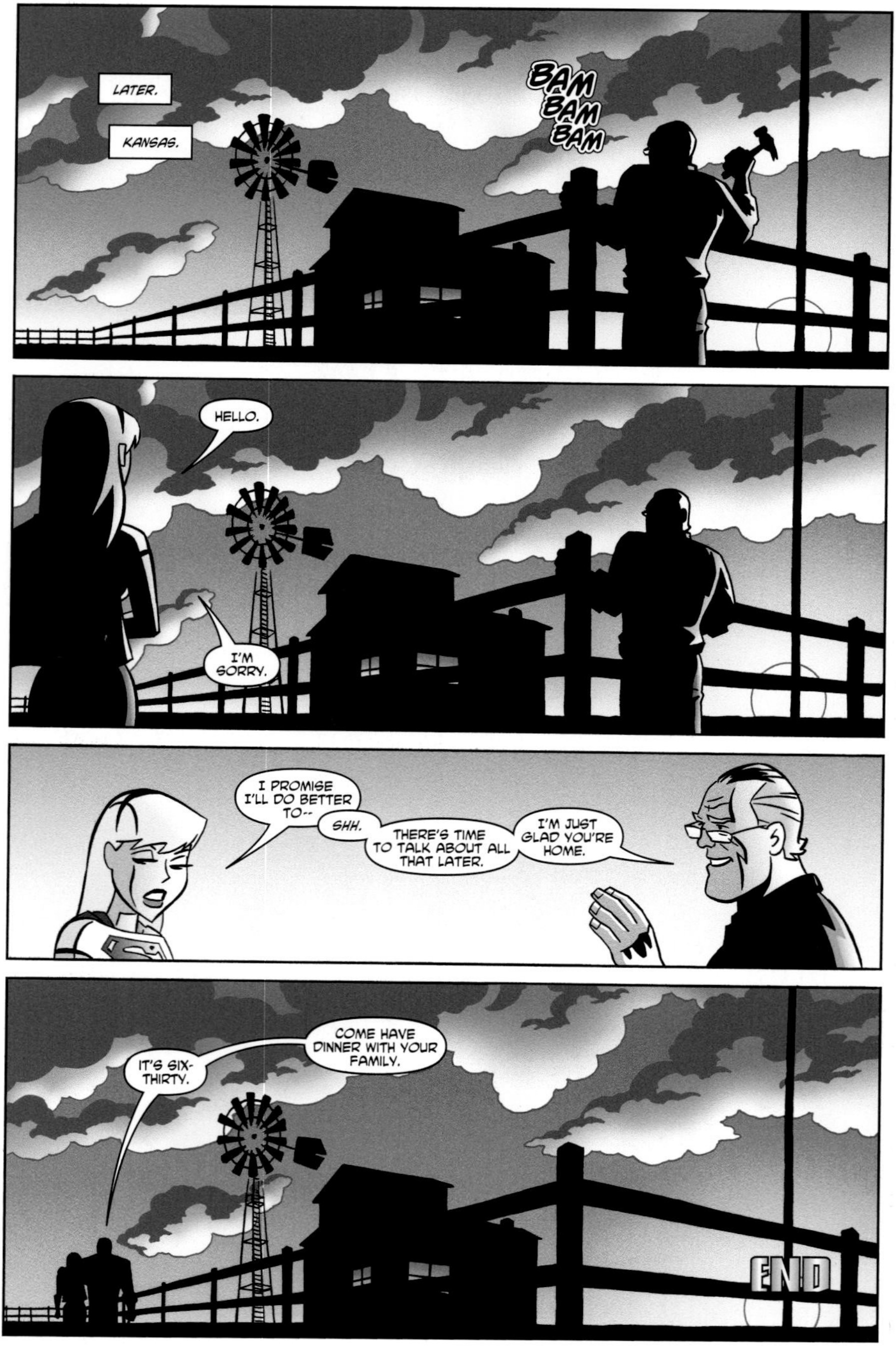
LATER.
KANSAS.
BAM BAM BAM
HELLO.
I'M SORRY.
I PROMISE I'LL DO BETTER TO--
SHH.
THERE'S TIME TO TALK ABOUT ALL THAT LATER.
I'M JUST GLAD YOU'RE HOME.
IT'S SIX-THIRTY.
COME HAVE DINNER WITH YOUR FAMILY.
END

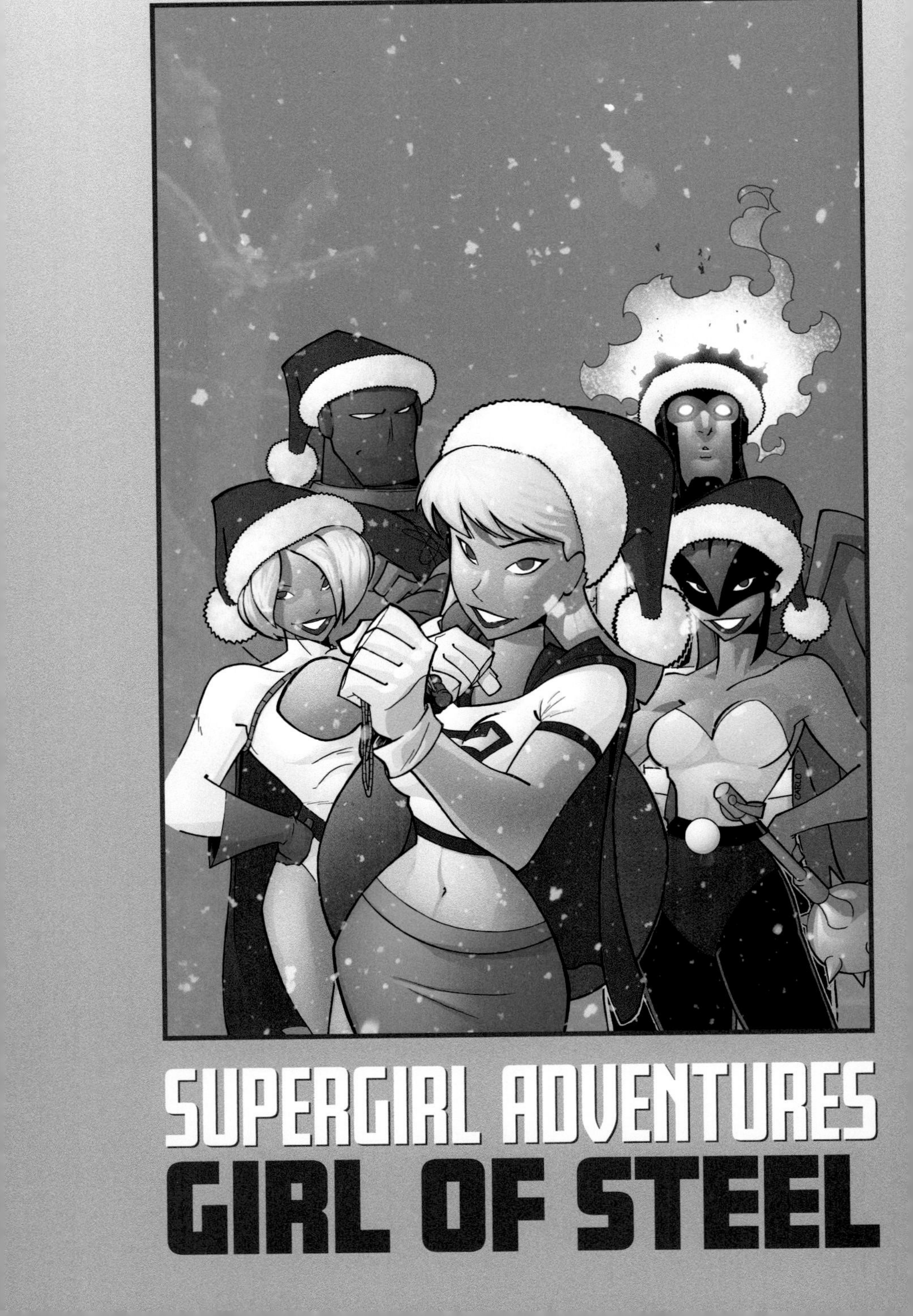
CARLO

# SUPERGIRL ADVENTURES
# GIRL OF STEEL

Cover by CARLO BARBERI

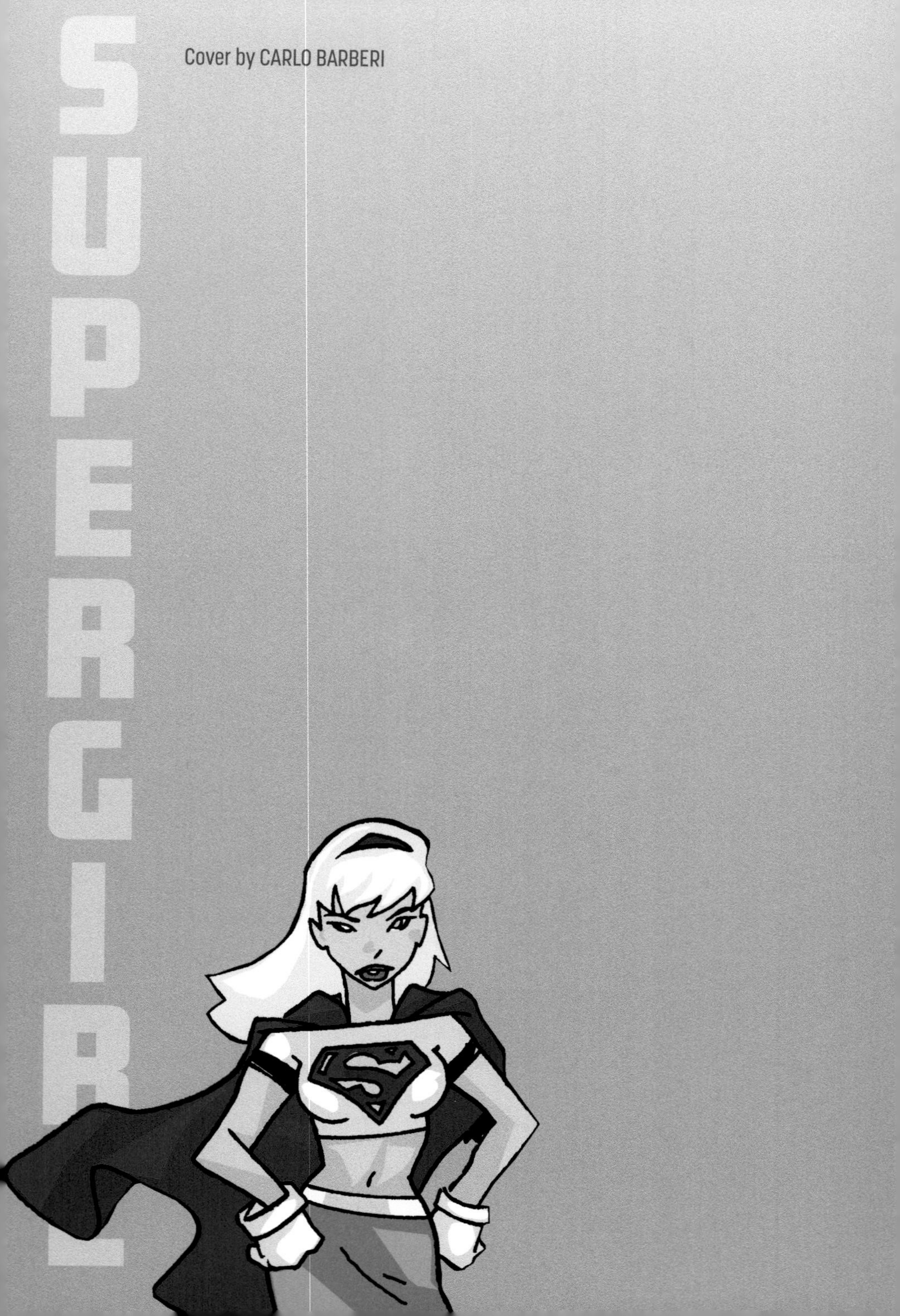
SUPERGIRL

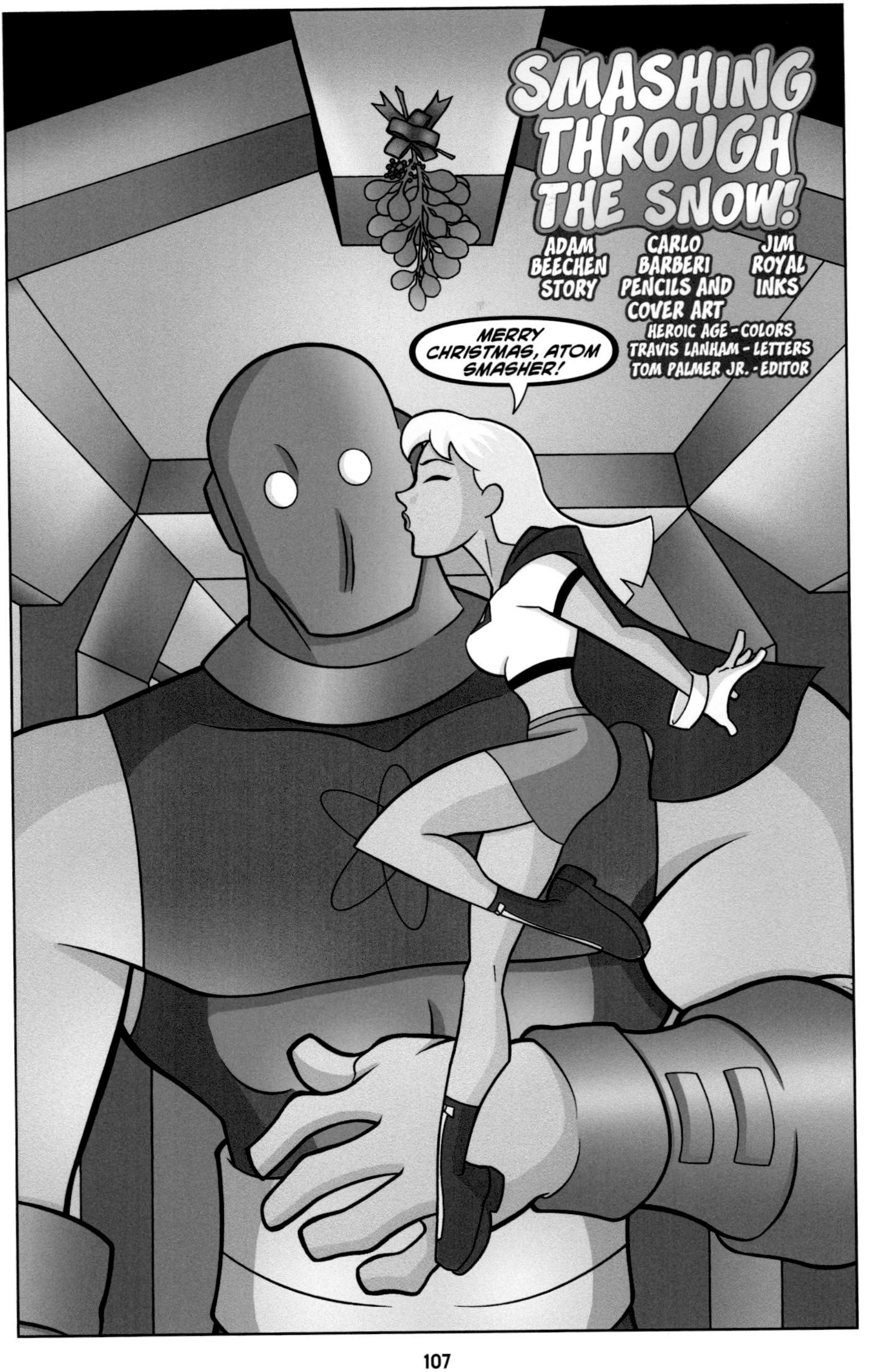
SMASHING THROUGH THE SNOW!
ADAM BEECHEN STORY
CARLO BARBERI PENCILS AND COVER ART
JIM ROYAL INKS
HEROIC AGE - COLORS
TRAVIS LANHAM - LETTERS
TOM PALMER JR. - EDITOR
MERRY CHRISTMAS, ATOM SMASHER!

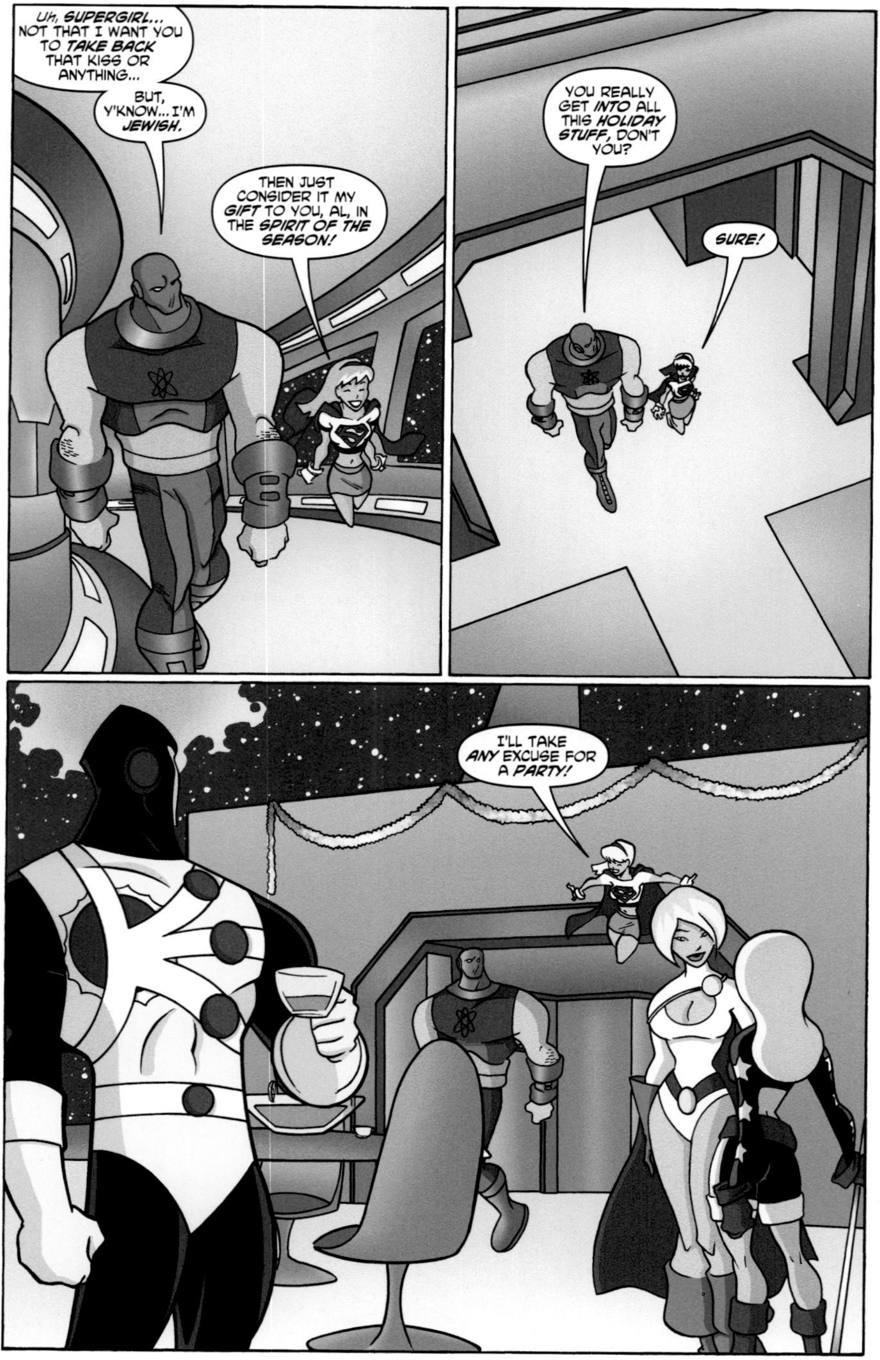
UH, SUPERGIRL... NOT THAT I WANT YOU TO TAKE BACK THAT KISS OR ANYTHING...
BUT, Y'KNOW... I'M JEWISH.
THEN JUST CONSIDER IT MY GIFT TO YOU, AL, IN THE SPIRIT OF THE SEASON!
YOU REALLY GET INTO ALL THIS HOLIDAY STUFF, DON'T YOU?
SURE!
I'LL TAKE ANY EXCUSE FOR A PARTY!

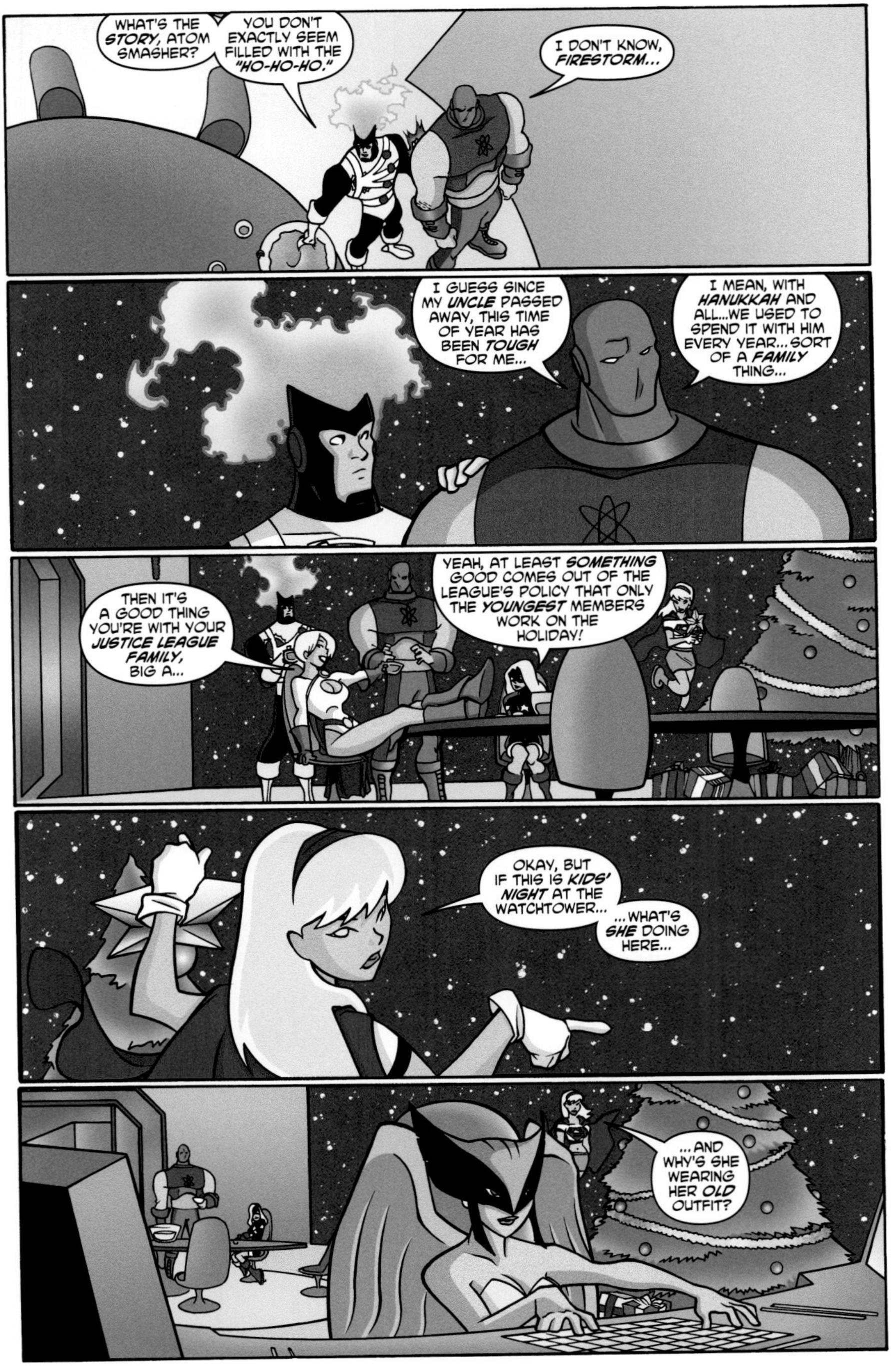
WHAT'S THE STORY, ATOM SMASHER?
YOU DON'T EXACTLY SEEM FILLED WITH THE "HO-HO-HO."
I DON'T KNOW, FIRESTORM...
I GUESS SINCE MY UNCLE PASSED AWAY, THIS TIME OF YEAR HAS BEEN TOUGH FOR ME...
I MEAN, WITH HANUKKAH AND ALL...WE USED TO SPEND IT WITH HIM EVERY YEAR... SORT OF A FAMILY THING...
THEN IT'S A GOOD THING YOU'RE WITH YOUR JUSTICE LEAGUE FAMILY, BIG A...
YEAH, AT LEAST SOMETHING GOOD COMES OUT OF THE LEAGUE'S POLICY THAT ONLY THE YOUNGEST MEMBERS WORK ON THE HOLIDAY!
OKAY, BUT IF THIS IS KIDS' NIGHT AT THE WATCHTOWER...
...WHAT'S SHE DOING HERE...
...AND WHY'S SHE WEARING HER OLD OUTFIT?

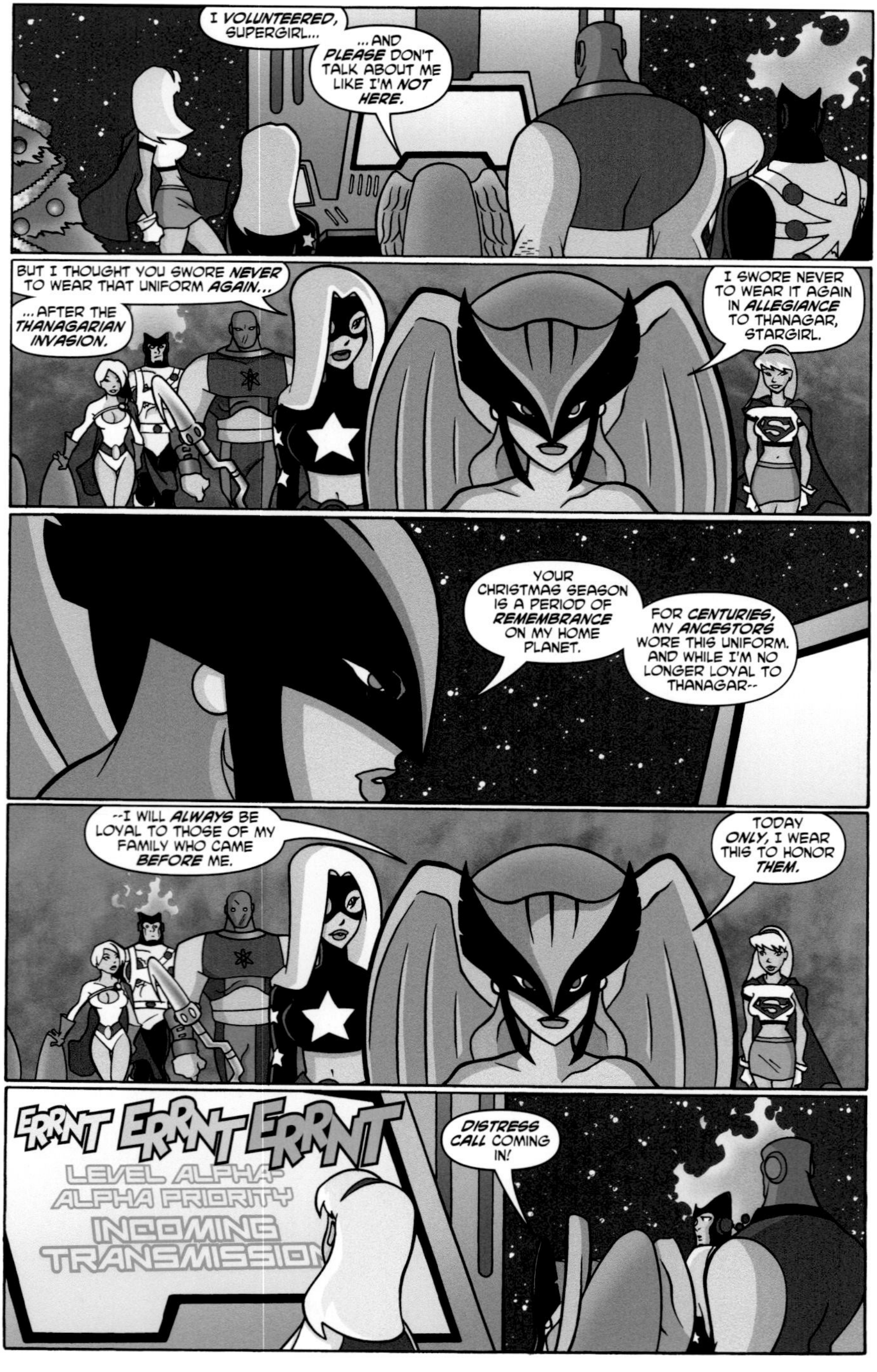

I VOLUNTEERED, SUPERGIRL...
...AND PLEASE DON'T TALK ABOUT ME LIKE I'M NOT HERE.
BUT I THOUGHT YOU SWORE NEVER TO WEAR THAT UNIFORM AGAIN...
...AFTER THE THANAGARIAN INVASION.
I SWORE NEVER TO WEAR IT AGAIN IN ALLEGIANCE TO THANAGAR, STARGIRL.
YOUR CHRISTMAS SEASON IS A PERIOD OF REMEMBRANCE ON MY HOME PLANET.
FOR CENTURIES, MY ANCESTORS WORE THIS UNIFORM. AND WHILE I'M NO LONGER LOYAL TO THANAGAR--
--I WILL ALWAYS BE LOYAL TO THOSE OF MY FAMILY WHO CAME BEFORE ME.
TODAY ONLY, I WEAR THIS TO HONOR THEM.
ERRNT ERRNT ERRNT
LEVEL ALPHA-ALPHA PRIORITY
INCOMING TRANSMISSION
DISTRESS CALL COMING IN!

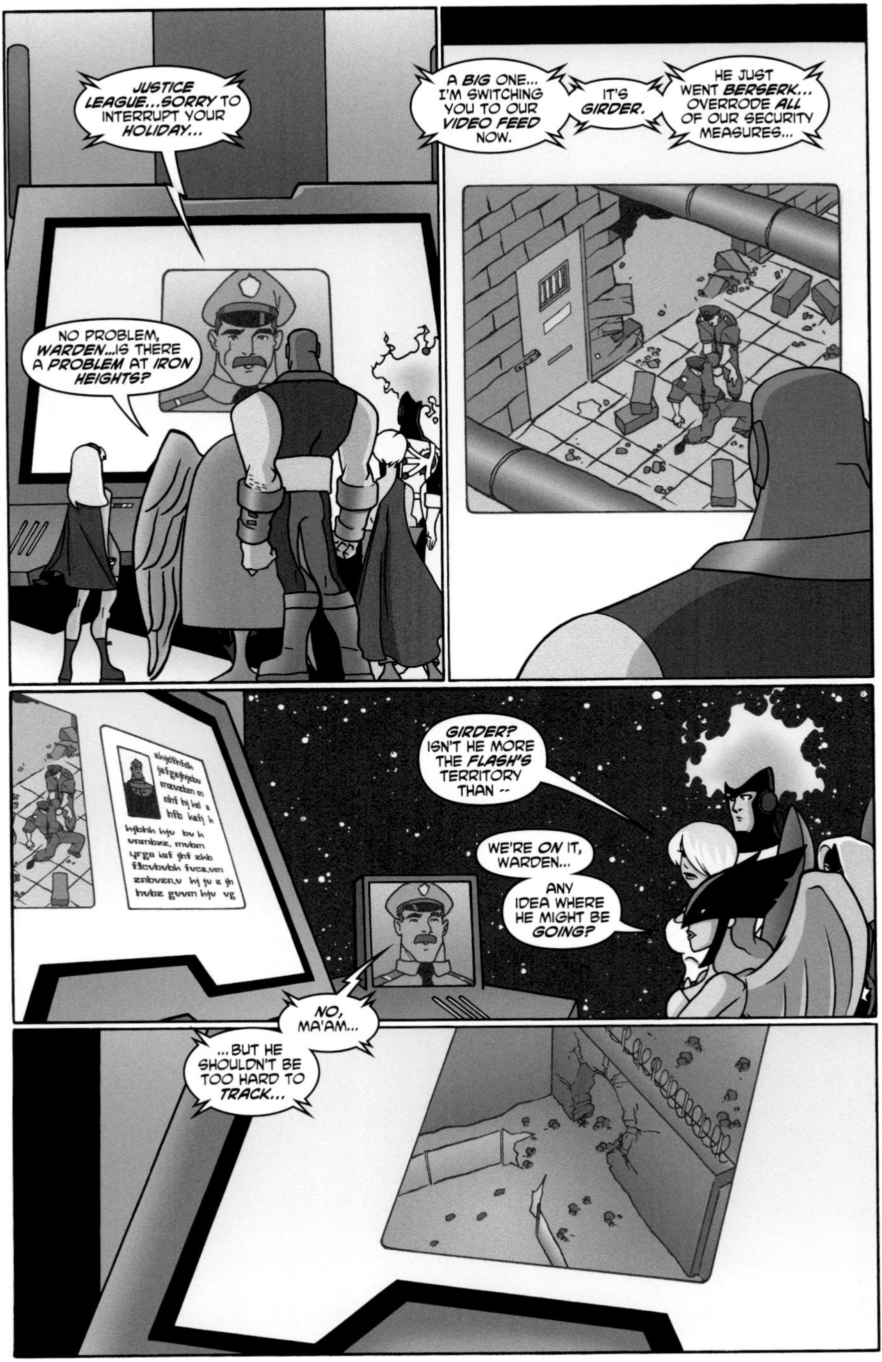
JUSTICE LEAGUE...SORRY TO INTERRUPT YOUR HOLIDAY...
NO PROBLEM, WARDEN...IS THERE A PROBLEM AT IRON HEIGHTS?
A BIG ONE... I'M SWITCHING YOU TO OUR VIDEO FEED NOW.
IT'S GIRDER.
HE JUST WENT BERSERK... OVERRODE ALL OF OUR SECURITY MEASURES...
GIRDER? ISN'T HE MORE THE FLASH'S TERRITORY THAN --
WE'RE ON IT, WARDEN...
ANY IDEA WHERE HE MIGHT BE GOING?
NO, MA'AM...
...BUT HE SHOULDN'T BE TOO HARD TO TRACK...

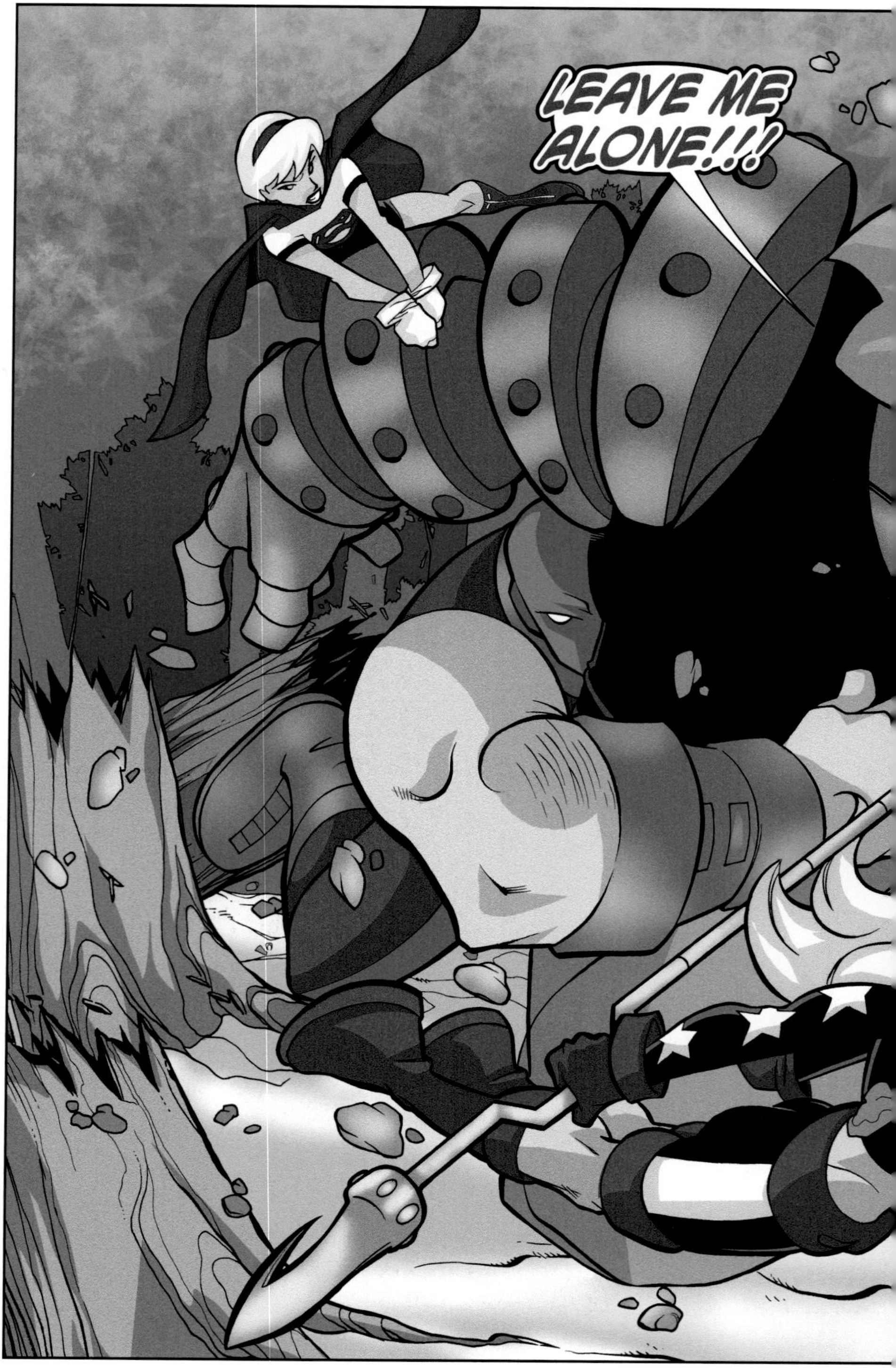
LEAVE ME ALONE!!!

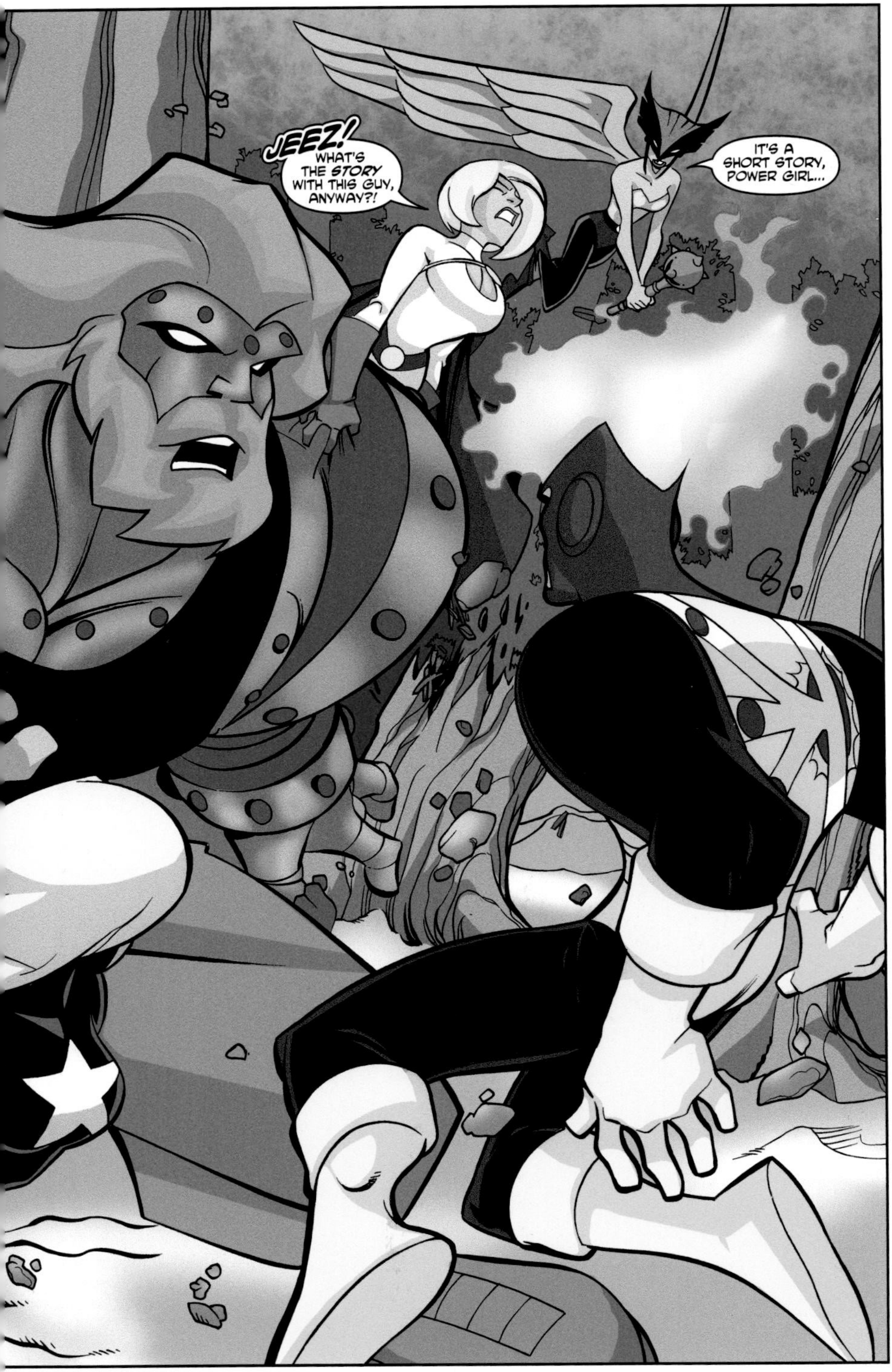
JEEZ! WHAT'S THE STORY WITH THIS GUY, ANYWAY?!
IT'S A SHORT STORY, POWER GIRL...

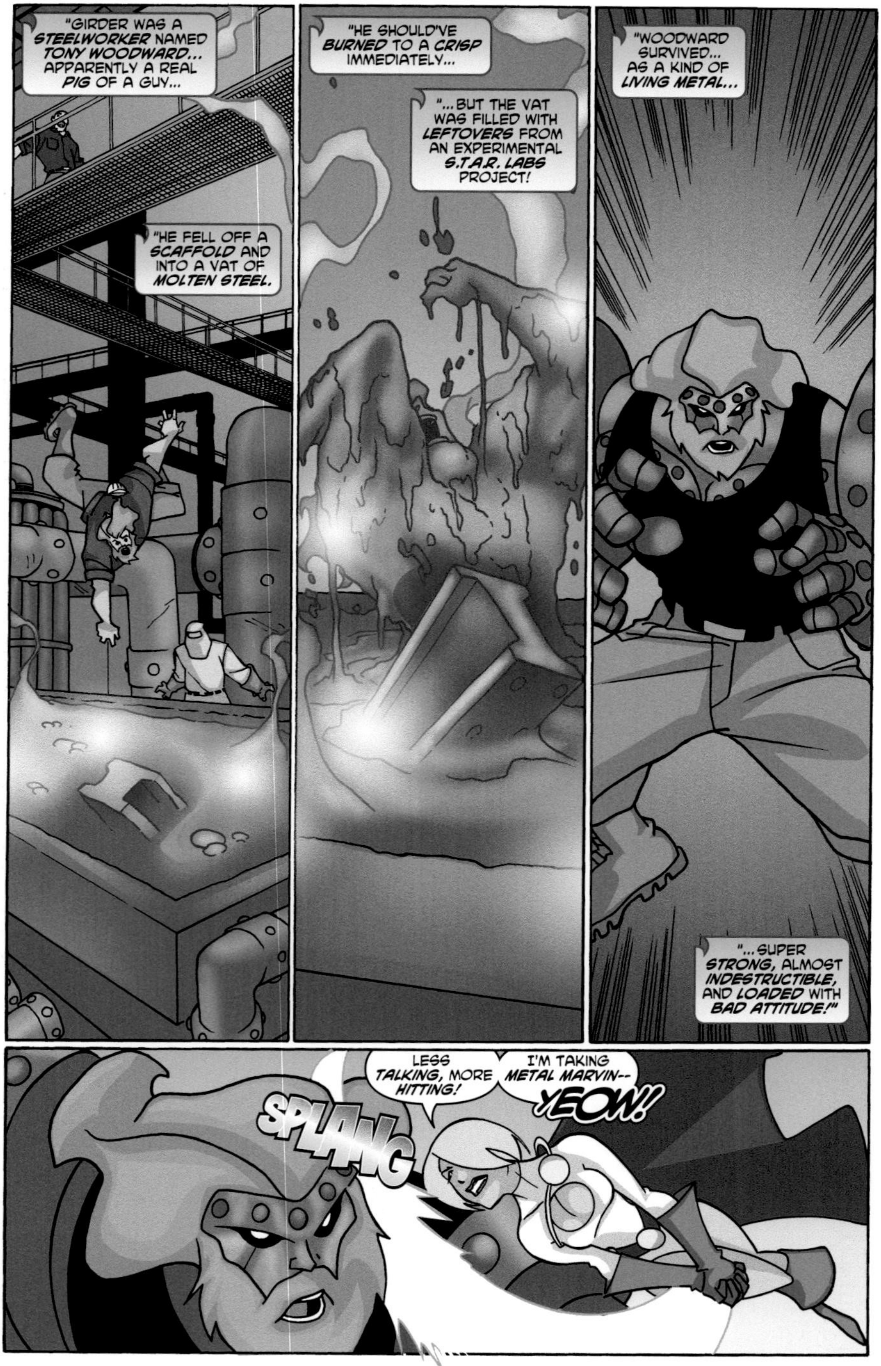
"GIRDER WAS A STEELWORKER NAMED TONY WOODWARD... APPARENTLY A REAL PIG OF A GUY...
"HE FELL OFF A SCAFFOLD AND INTO A VAT OF MOLTEN STEEL.
"HE SHOULD'VE BURNED TO A CRISP IMMEDIATELY...
"...BUT THE VAT WAS FILLED WITH LEFTOVERS FROM AN EXPERIMENTAL S.T.A.R. LABS PROJECT!
"WOODWARD SURVIVED... AS A KIND OF LIVING METAL...
"...SUPER STRONG, ALMOST INDESTRUCTIBLE, AND LOADED WITH BAD ATTITUDE!"
LESS TALKING, MORE HITTING!
I'M TAKING METAL MARVIN--
SPLANG
YEOW!

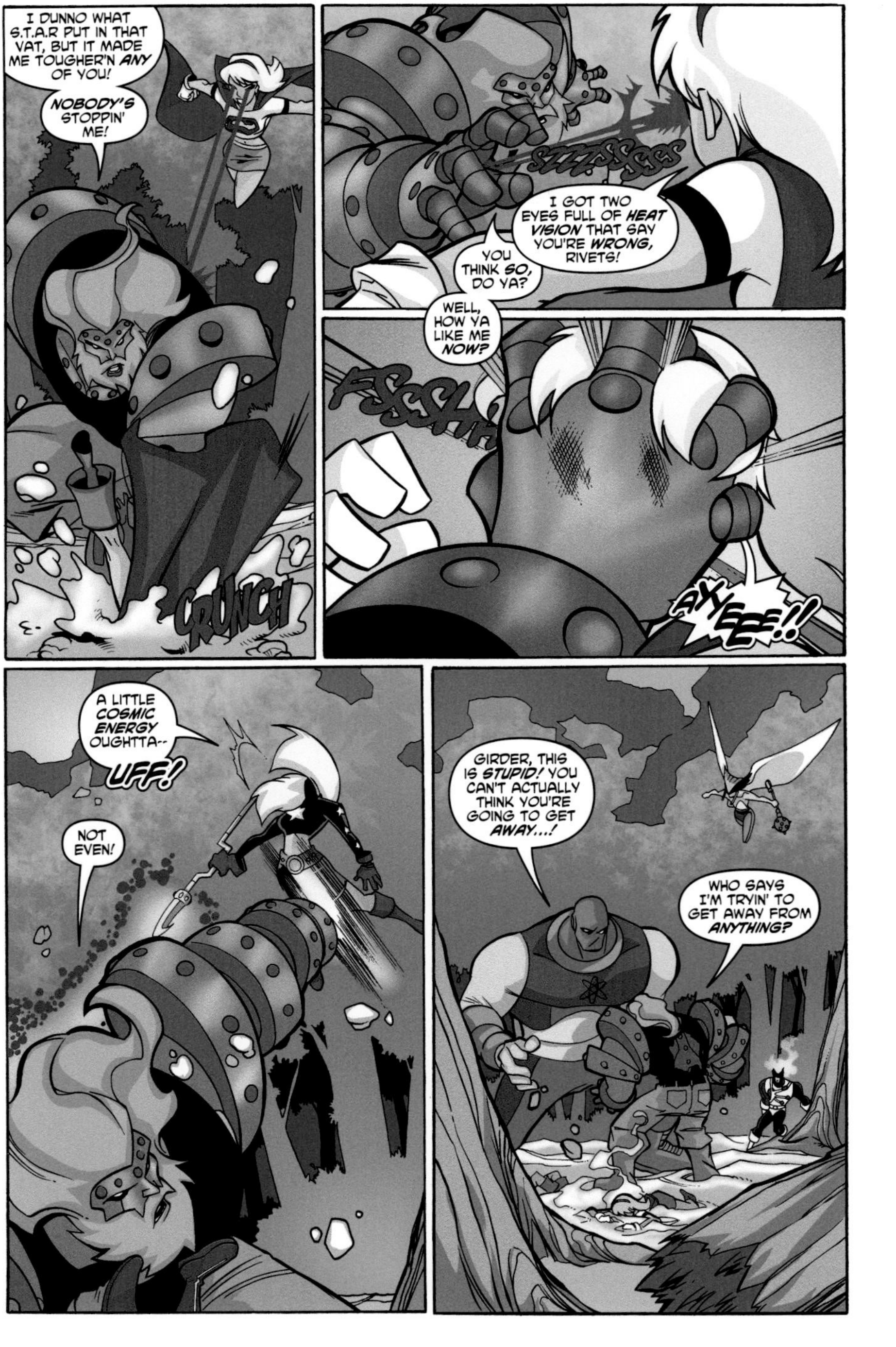
I DUNNO WHAT S.T.A.R PUT IN THAT VAT, BUT IT MADE ME TOUGHER'N ANY OF YOU!
NOBODY'S STOPPIN' ME!
CRUNCH
SSSSSSSS
I GOT TWO EYES FULL OF HEAT VISION THAT SAY YOU'RE WRONG, RIVETS!
YOU THINK SO, DO YA?
WELL, HOW YA LIKE ME NOW?
FSSSHH
AYYEEEE!!
A LITTLE COSMIC ENERGY OUGHTTA--
UFF!
NOT EVEN!
GIRDER, THIS IS STUPID! YOU CAN'T ACTUALLY THINK YOU'RE GOING TO GET AWAY...!
WHO SAYS I'M TRYIN' TO GET AWAY FROM ANYTHING?

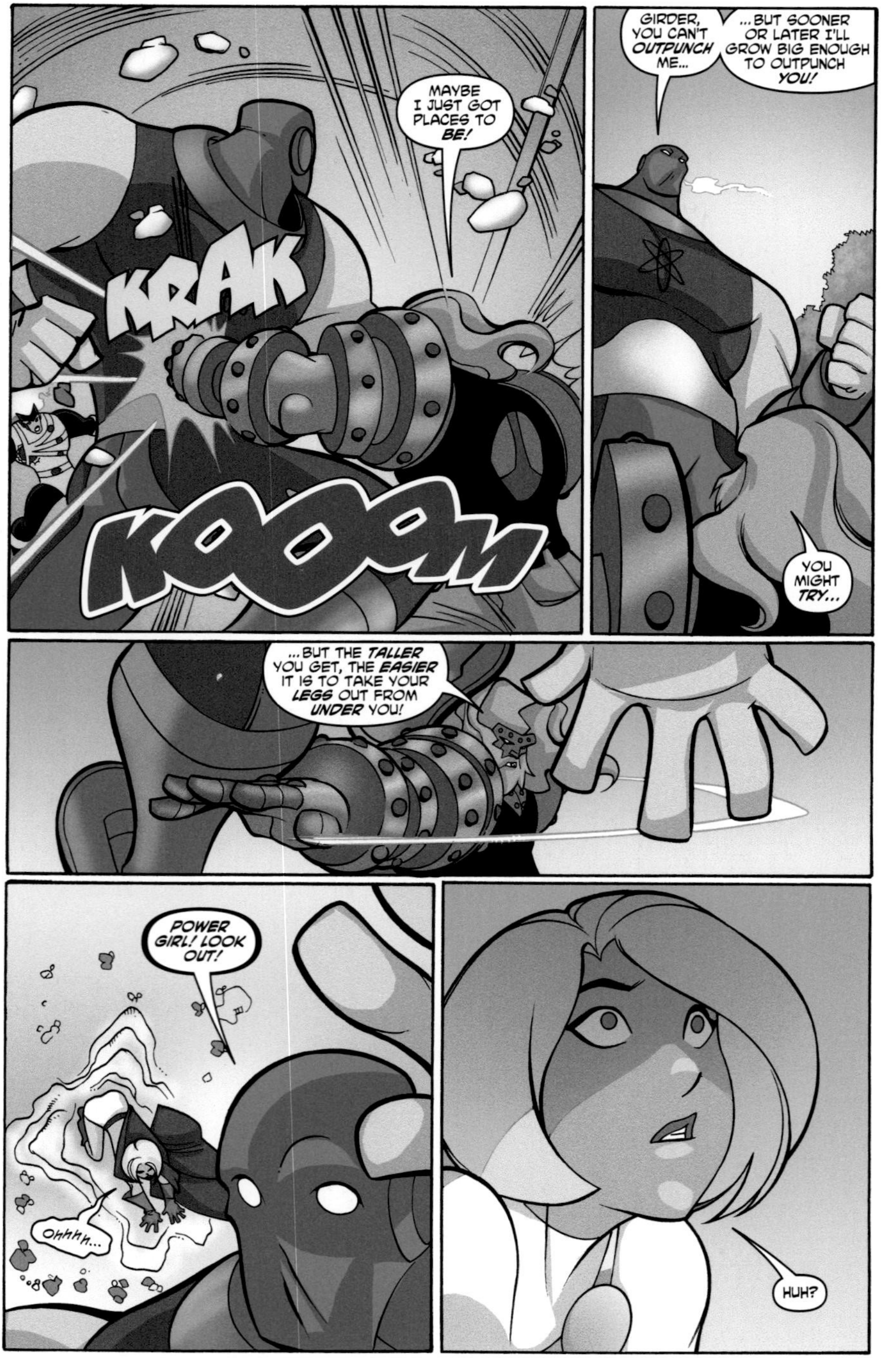
MAYBE I JUST GOT PLACES TO BE!
KRAK
KOOOM
GIRDER, YOU CAN'T OUTPUNCH ME...
...BUT SOONER OR LATER I'LL GROW BIG ENOUGH TO OUTPUNCH YOU!
YOU MIGHT TRY...
...BUT THE TALLER YOU GET, THE EASIER IT IS TO TAKE YOUR LEGS OUT FROM UNDER YOU!
POWER GIRL! LOOK OUT!
Ohhhh...
HUH?

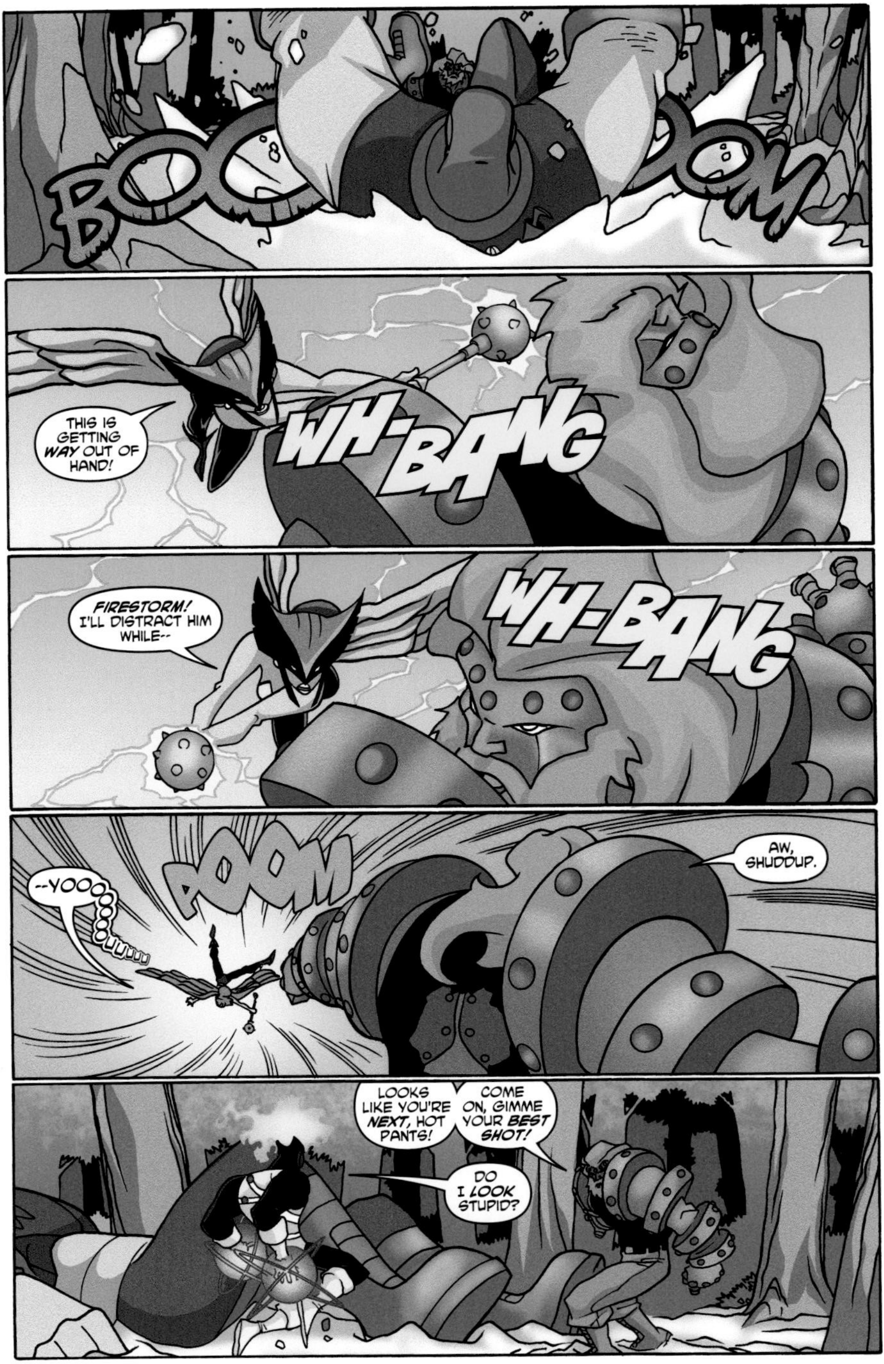
BOOOOM
THIS IS GETTING WAY OUT OF HAND!
WH-BANG
FIRESTORM! I'LL DISTRACT HIM WHILE--
WH-BANG
--YOOOOOOuuuuu
POOOM
AW, SHUDDUP.
LOOKS LIKE YOU'RE NEXT, HOT PANTS!
COME ON, GIMME YOUR BEST SHOT!
DO I LOOK STUPID?

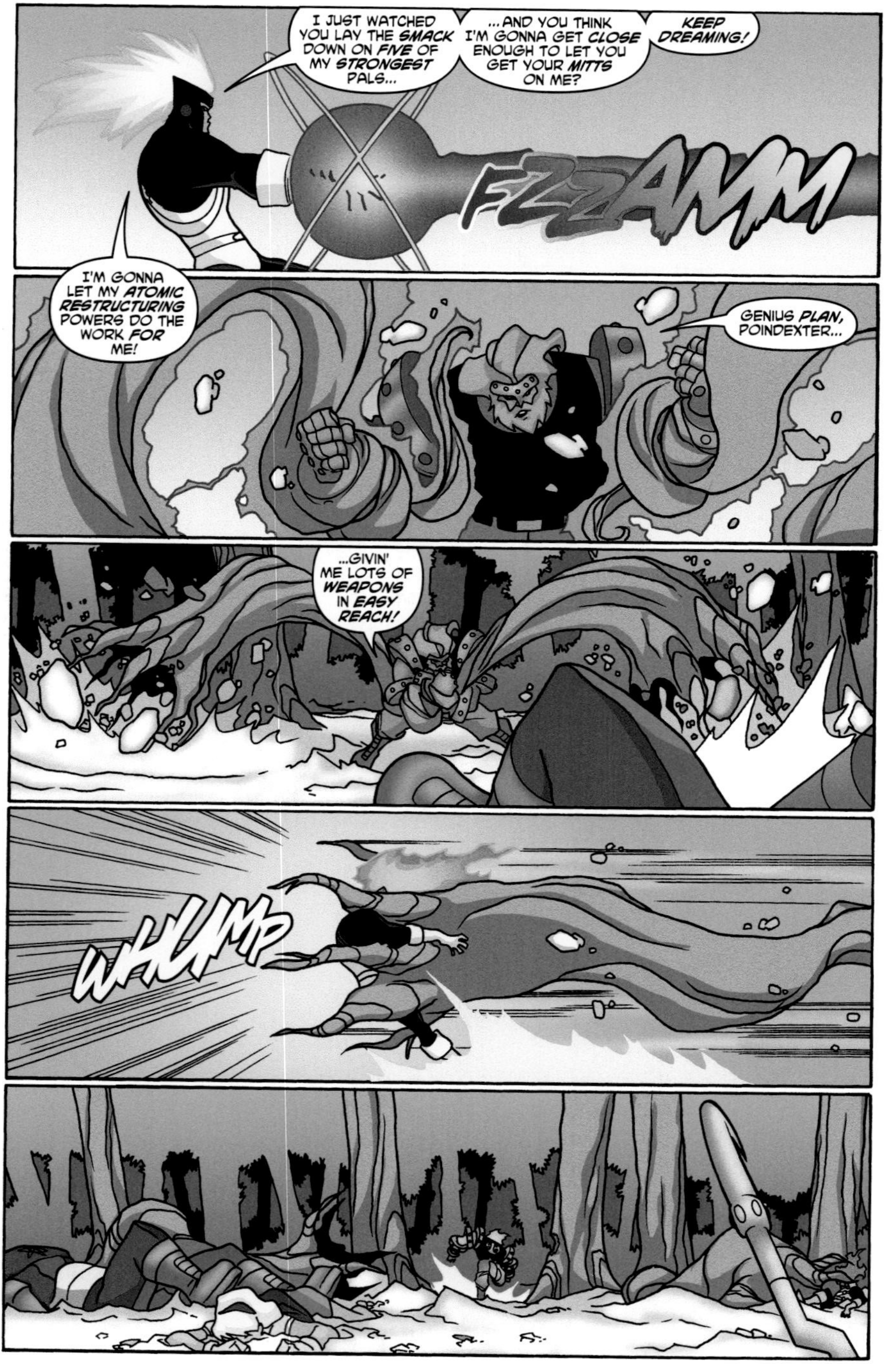
I JUST WATCHED YOU LAY THE SMACK DOWN ON FIVE OF MY STRONGEST PALS...
...AND YOU THINK I'M GONNA GET CLOSE ENOUGH TO LET YOU GET YOUR MITTS ON ME?
KEEP DREAMING!
FZZAMM
I'M GONNA LET MY ATOMIC RESTRUCTURING POWERS DO THE WORK FOR ME!
GENIUS PLAN, POINDEXTER...
...GIVIN' ME LOTS OF WEAPONS IN EASY REACH!
WHUMP

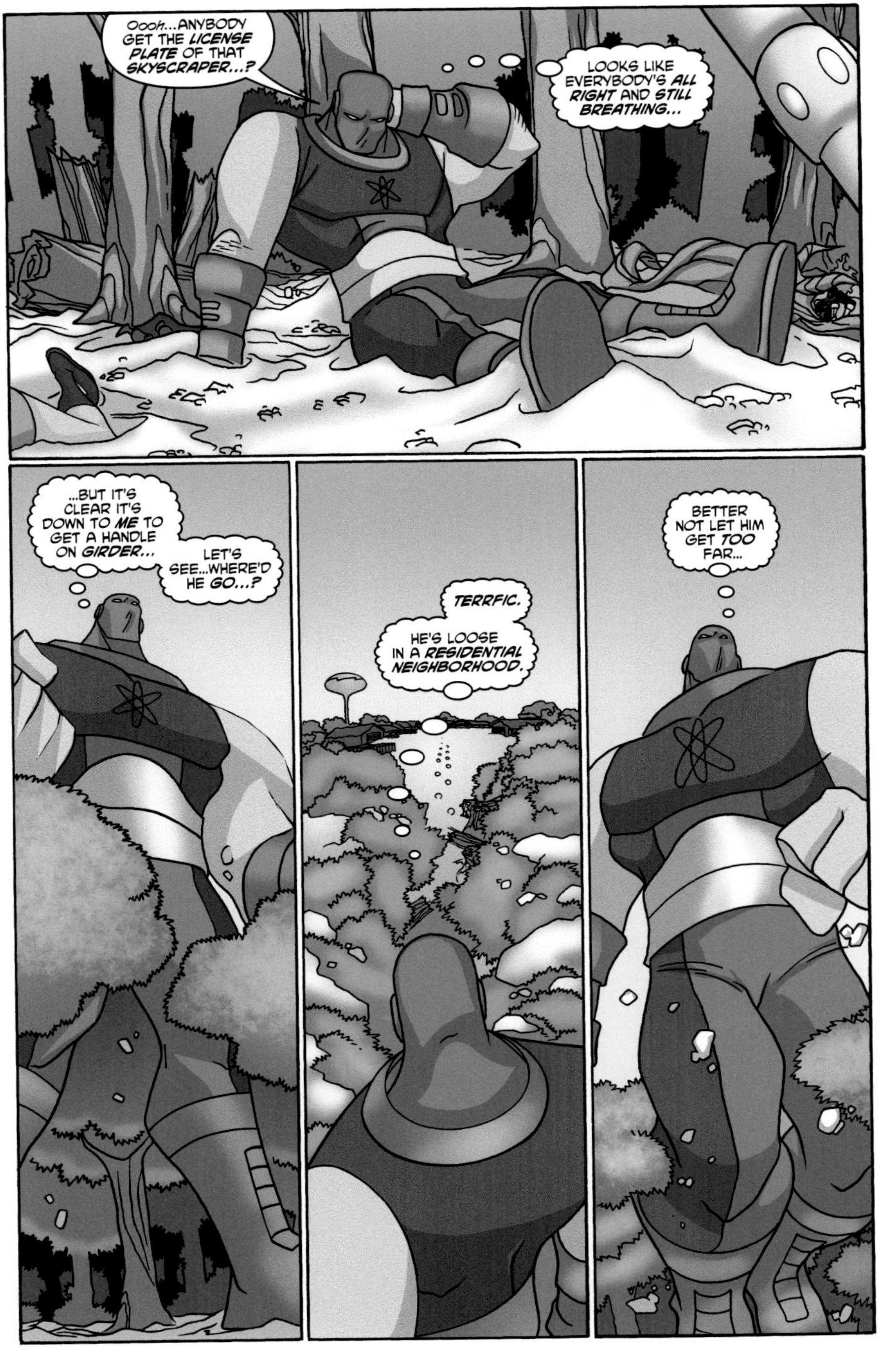

Oooh...ANYBODY GET THE LICENSE PLATE OF THAT SKYSCRAPER...?
LOOKS LIKE EVERYBODY'S ALL RIGHT AND STILL BREATHING...
...BUT IT'S CLEAR IT'S DOWN TO ME TO GET A HANDLE ON GIRDER...
LET'S SEE...WHERE'D HE GO...?
TERRFIC.
HE'S LOOSE IN A RESIDENTIAL NEIGHBORHOOD.
BETTER NOT LET HIM GET TOO FAR...

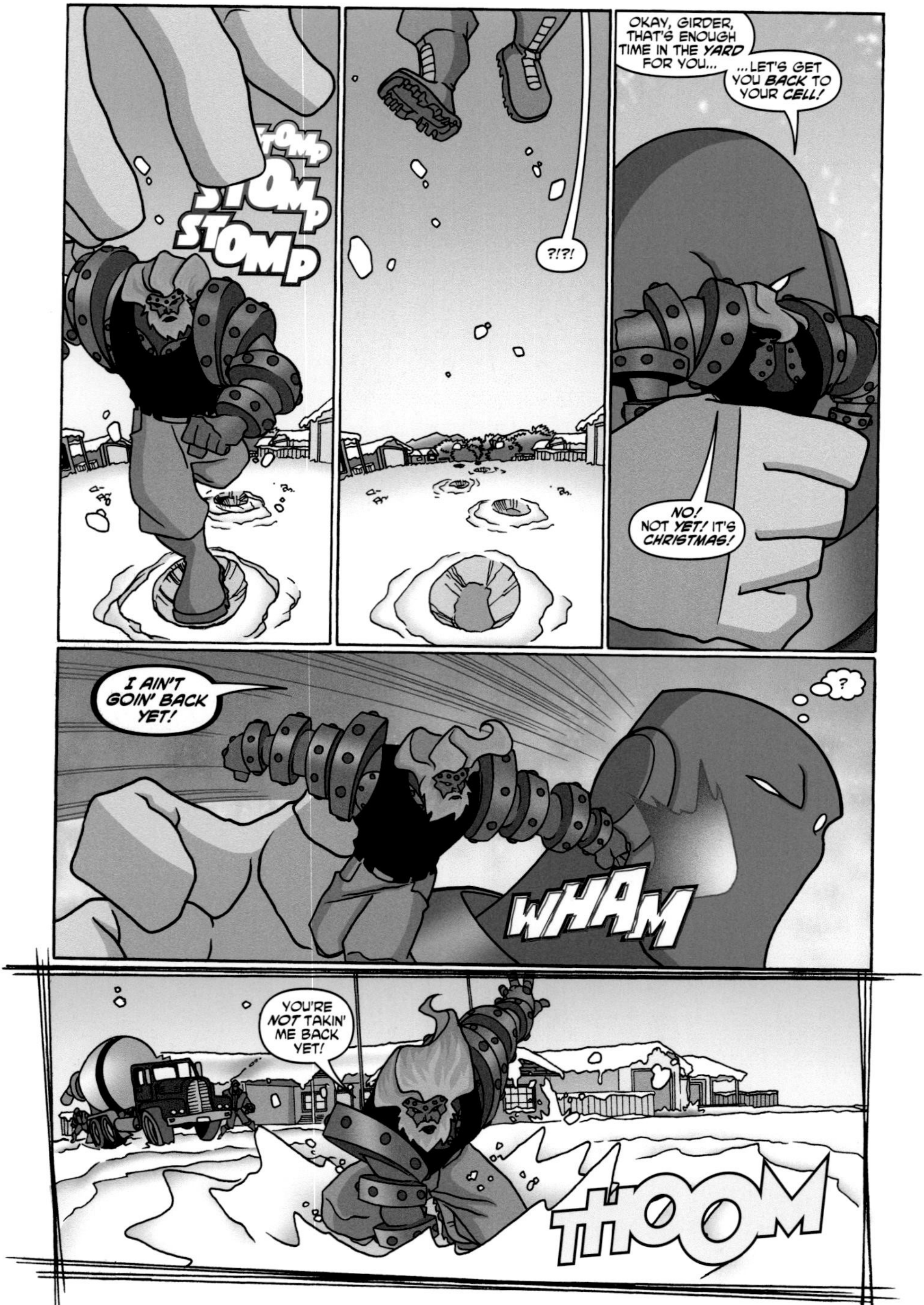
STOMP
STOMP
STOMP
?!?!
OKAY, GIRDER, THAT'S ENOUGH TIME IN THE YARD FOR YOU...
...LET'S GET YOU BACK TO YOUR CELL!
NO! NOT YET! IT'S CHRISTMAS!
I AIN'T GOIN' BACK YET!
?
WHAM
YOU'RE NOT TAKIN' ME BACK YET!
THOOM

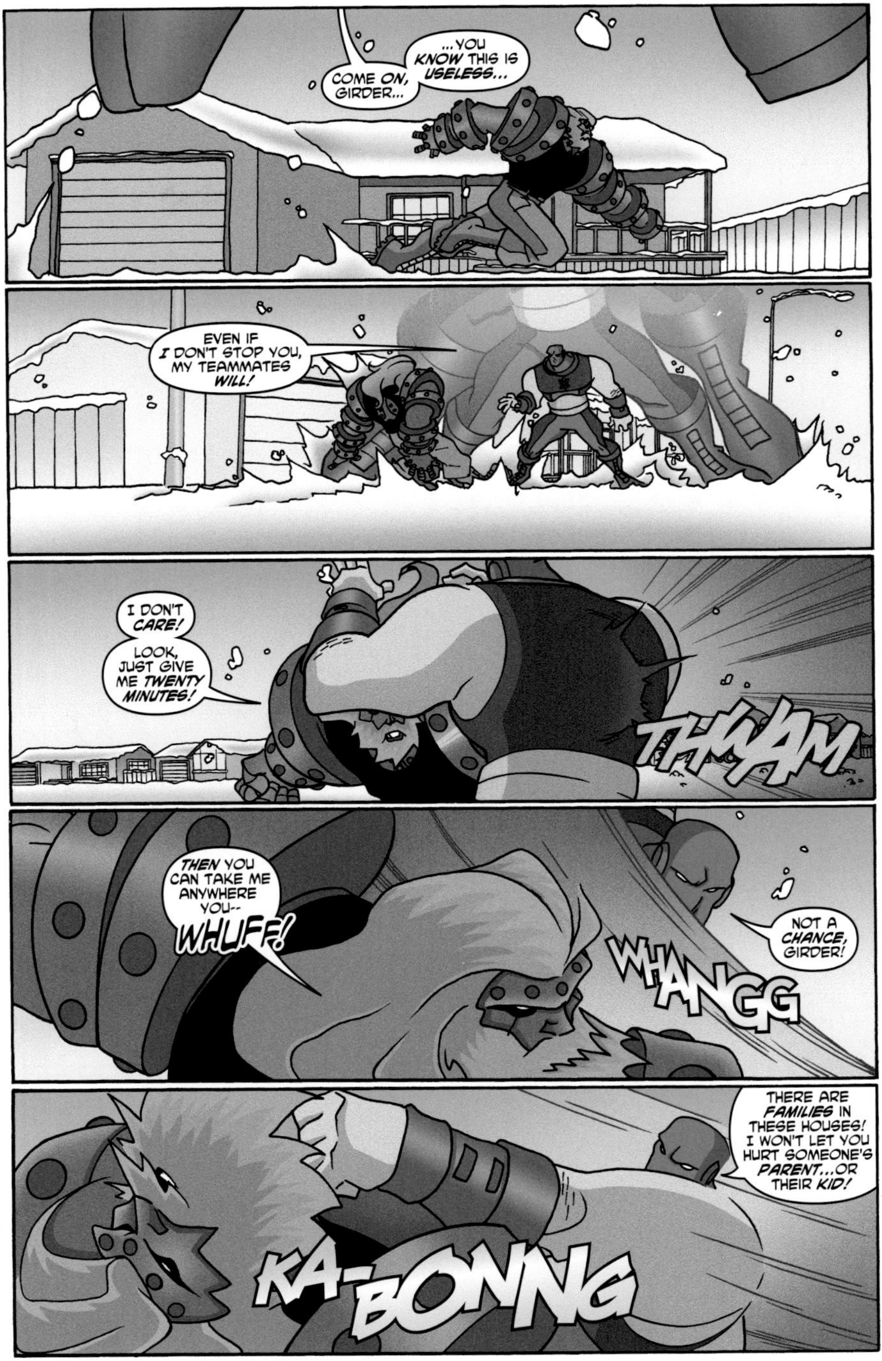
COME ON, GIRDER...
...YOU KNOW THIS IS USELESS...
EVEN IF I DON'T STOP YOU, MY TEAMMATES WILL!
I DON'T CARE!
LOOK, JUST GIVE ME TWENTY MINUTES!
THWAM
THEN YOU CAN TAKE ME ANYWHERE YOU--
WHUFF!
NOT A CHANCE, GIRDER!
WHANGG
THERE ARE FAMILIES IN THESE HOUSES! I WON'T LET YOU HURT SOMEONE'S PARENT...OR THEIR KID!
KA-BONNG

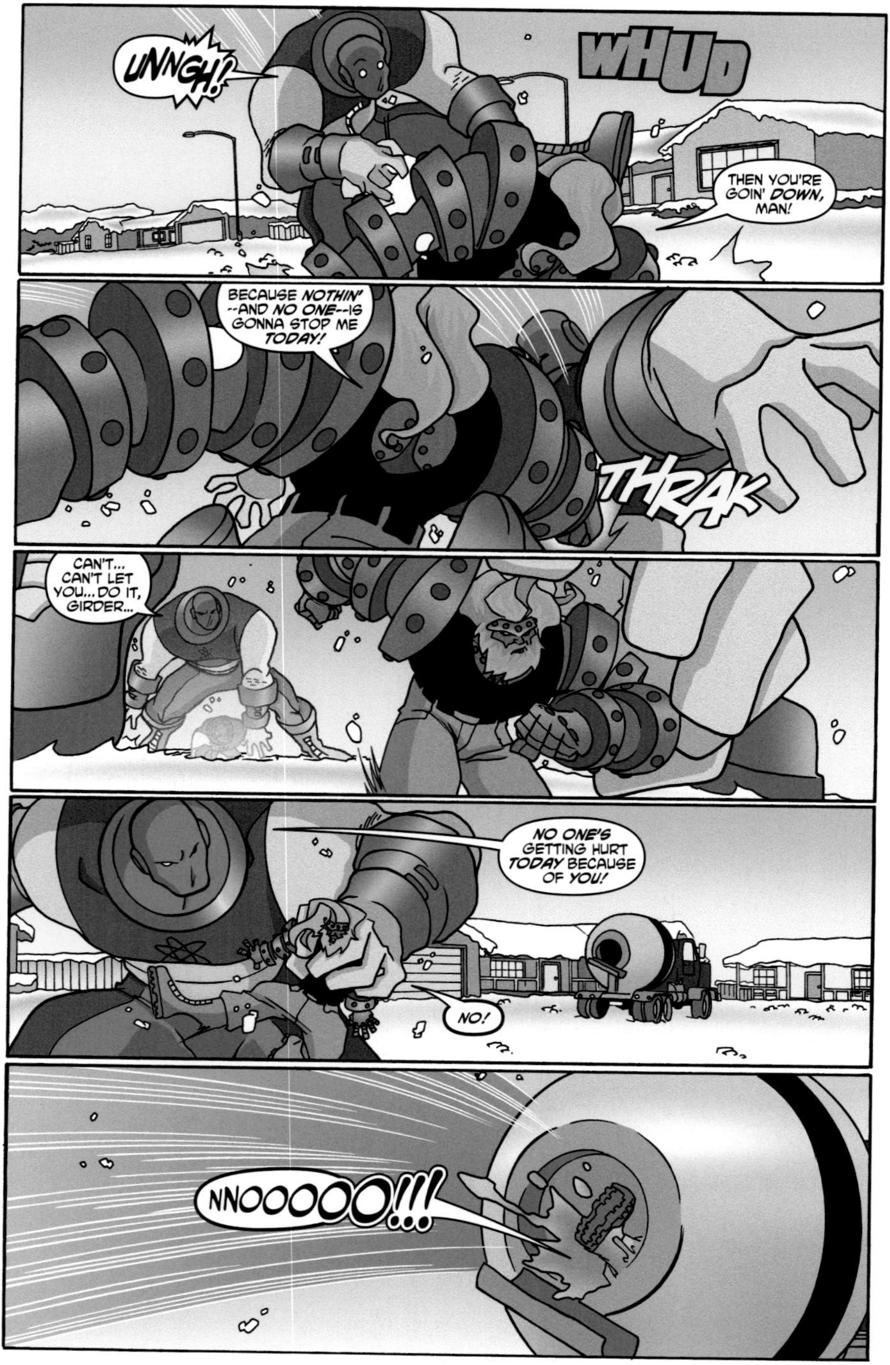
UNNGH!
wHUD
THEN YOU'RE GOIN' DOWN, MAN!
BECAUSE NOTHIN' --AND NO ONE--IS GONNA STOP ME TODAY!
THRAK
CAN'T... CAN'T LET YOU... DO IT, GIRDER...
NO ONE'S GETTING HURT TODAY BECAUSE OF YOU!
NO!
NNOOOOOO!!!

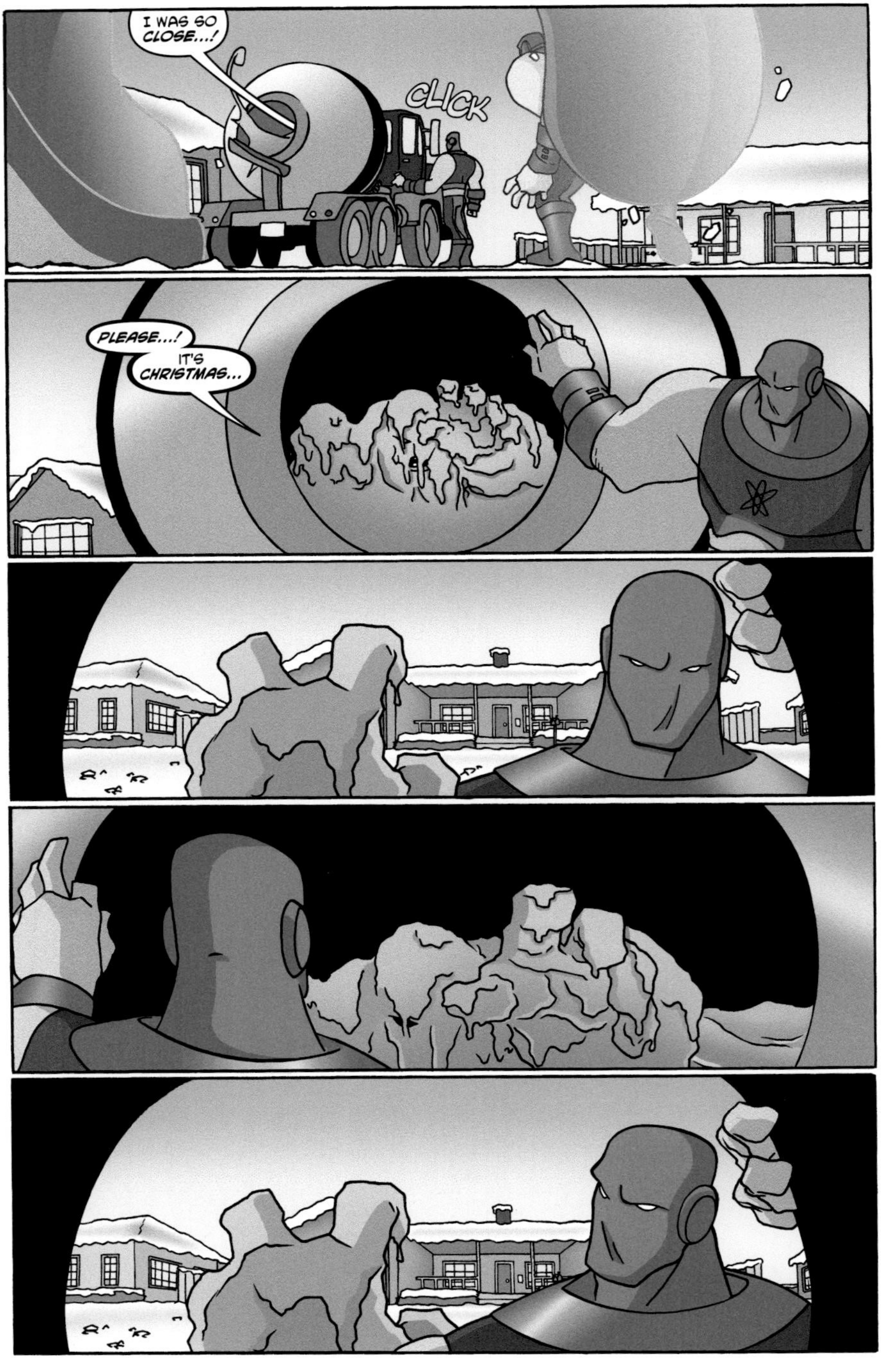
I WAS SO CLOSE...!
CLICK
PLEASE...!
IT'S CHRISTMAS...

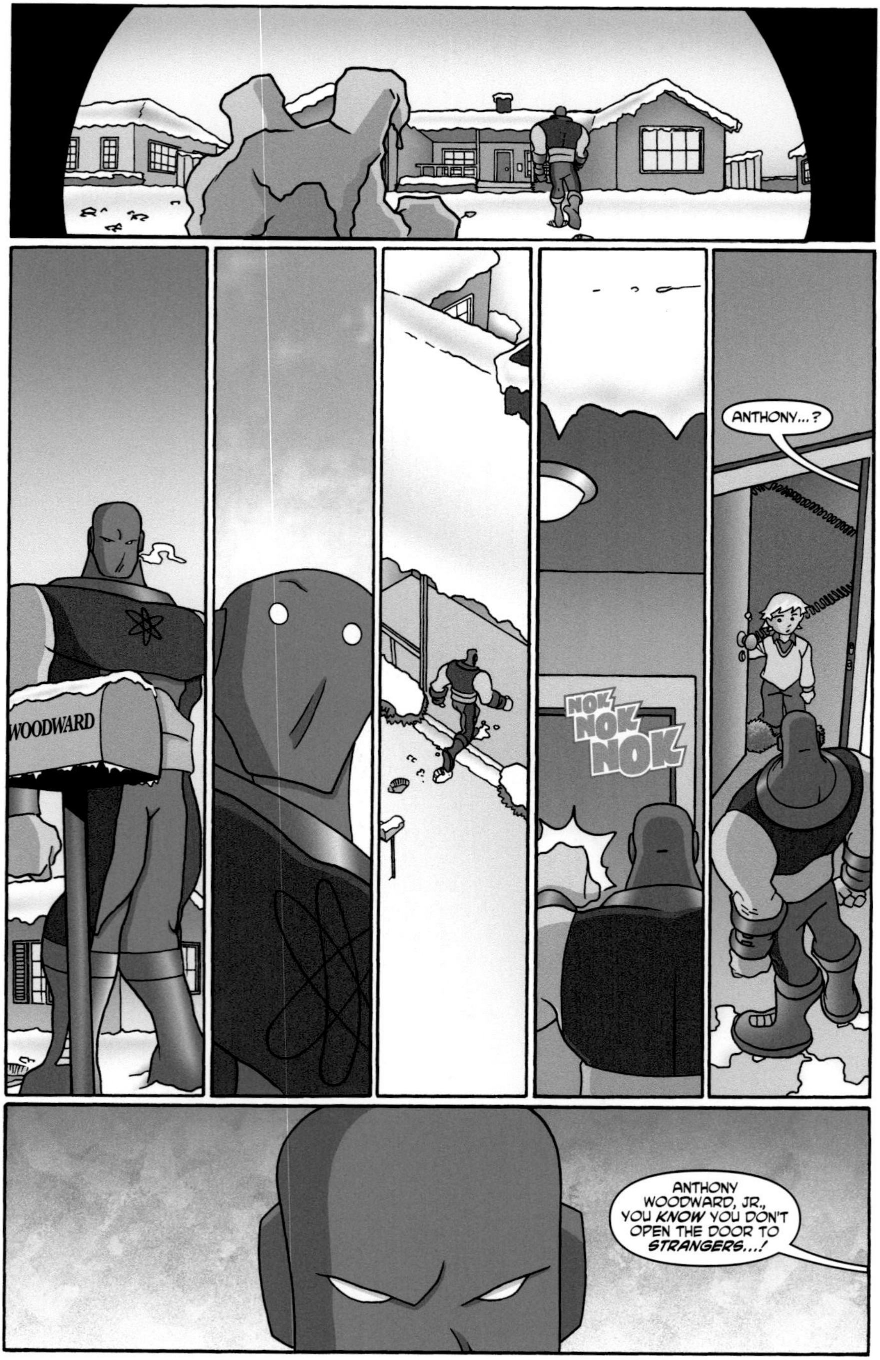
WOODWARD
NOK NOK NOK
ANTHONY...?
ANTHONY WOODWARD, JR., YOU KNOW YOU DON'T OPEN THE DOOR TO STRANGERS...!

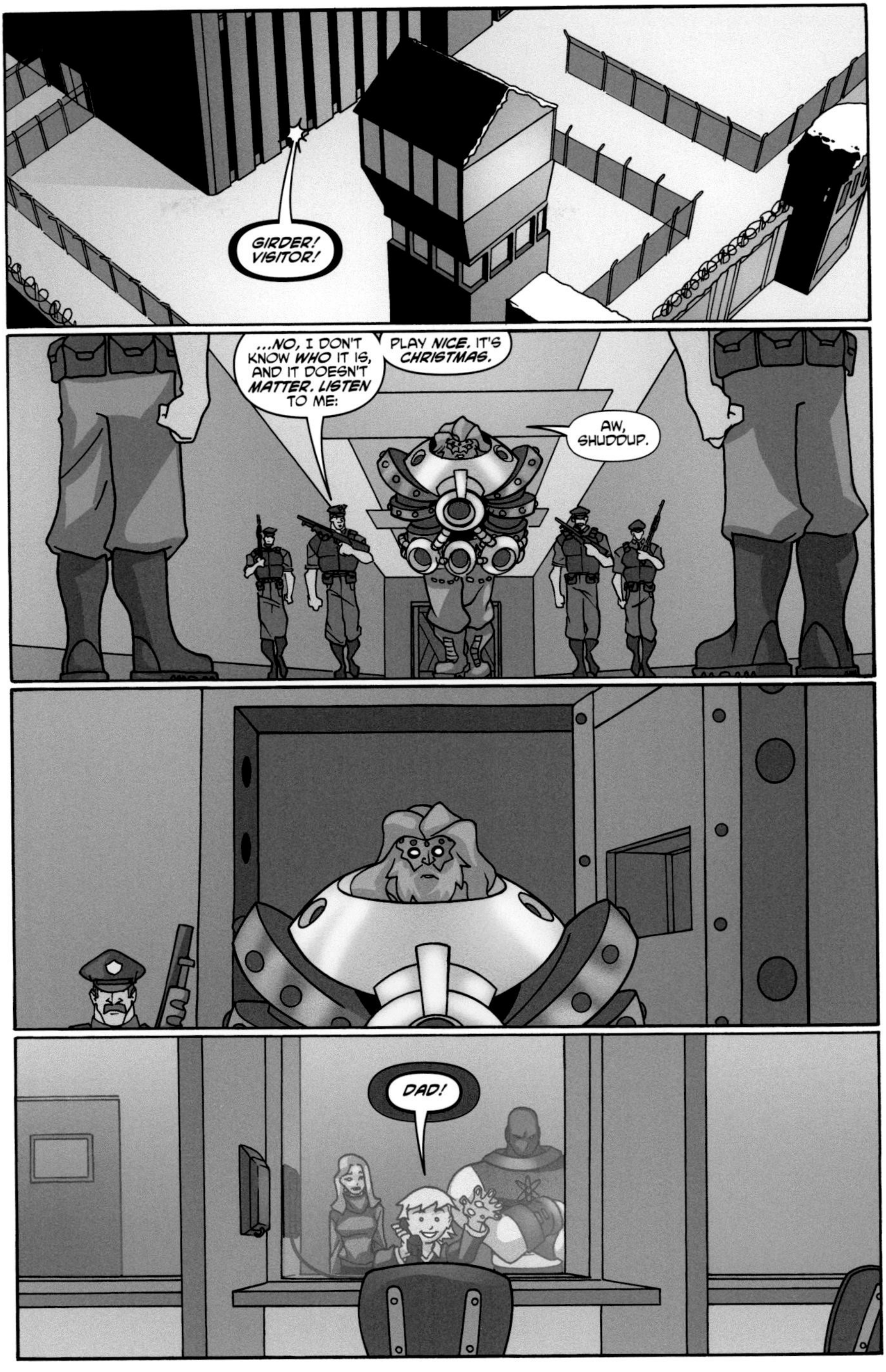
GIRDER! VISITOR!
...NO, I DON'T KNOW WHO IT IS, AND IT DOESN'T MATTER. LISTEN TO ME:
PLAY NICE. IT'S CHRISTMAS.
AW, SHUDDUP.
DAD!

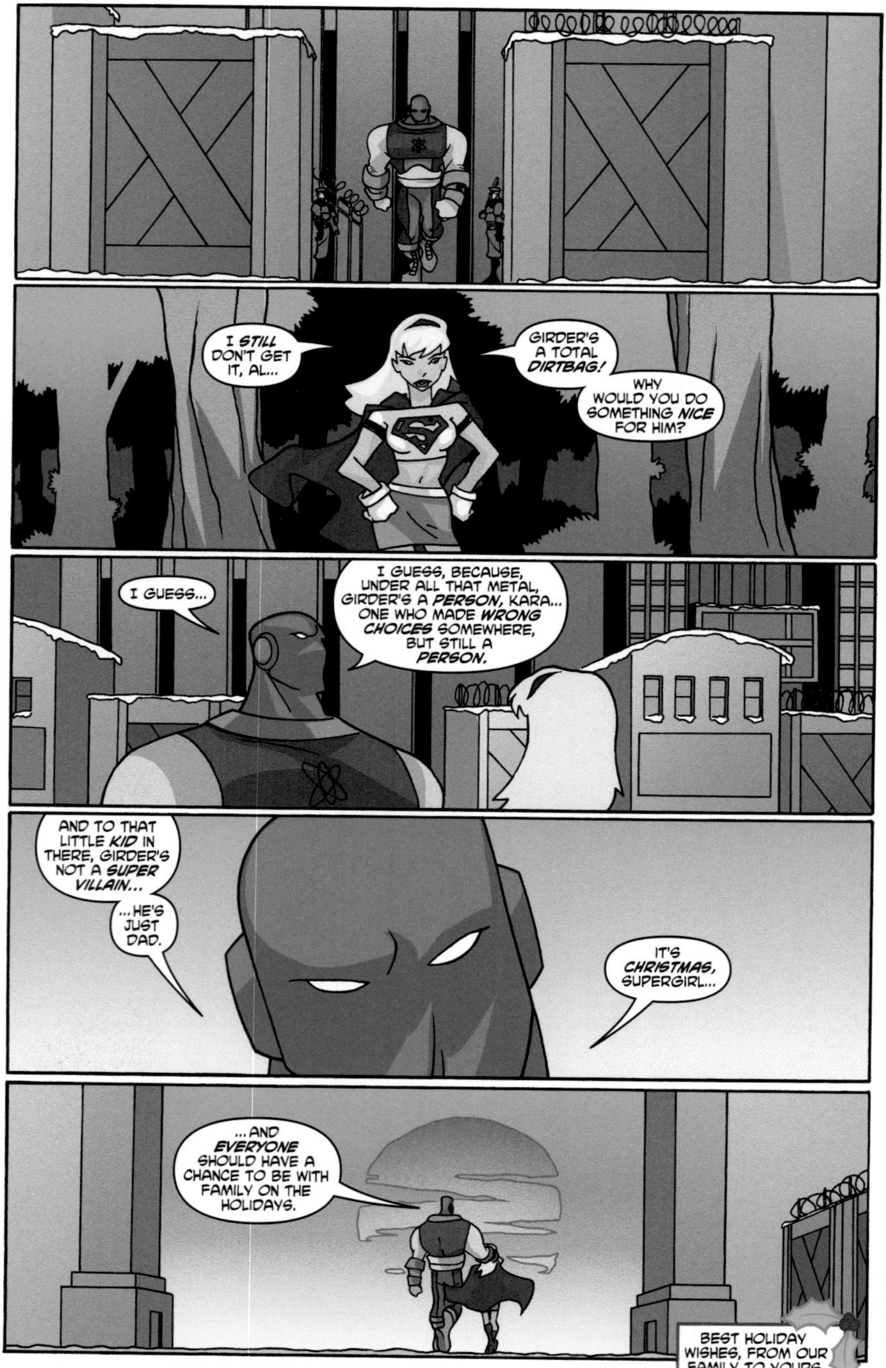
I STILL DON'T GET IT, AL...
GIRDER'S A TOTAL DIRTBAG!
WHY WOULD YOU DO SOMETHING NICE FOR HIM?
I GUESS...
I GUESS, BECAUSE, UNDER ALL THAT METAL, GIRDER'S A PERSON, KARA... ONE WHO MADE WRONG CHOICES SOMEWHERE, BUT STILL A PERSON.
AND TO THAT LITTLE KID IN THERE, GIRDER'S NOT A SUPER VILLAIN...
...HE'S JUST DAD.
IT'S CHRISTMAS, SUPERGIRL...
...AND EVERYONE SHOULD HAVE A CHANCE TO BE WITH FAMILY ON THE HOLIDAYS.
BEST HOLIDAY WISHES, FROM OUR FAMILY TO YOURS.